PRAISE FOR
The Secret Spice Café trilogy
BY PATRICIA V. DAVIS

"...a beautifully structured novel that builds layer upon layer of meaning, held together with gossamer threads and magic..."

—*The Huffington Post*

"I loved this book! It is a delicious, heady brew of magic, witchcraft, ghostly apparitions on an iconic vessel, the ever-intriguing *Queen Mary*. Patricia V. Davis writes with passion, presenting each scene with a dash of humor and an intimate connection with all characters, living and haunting."

— Kate Farrell, past president, Women's National
Book Association, SF Chapter

"…Ghosts aside, Davis does a beautiful job of melding factual history with fiction. And it's a story well told."

— J.H. Moncrieff, *Award-Winning Author of City of Ghosts*

"The story is so detailed, readers who visit the *Queen Mary* and search the decks for The Secret Spice Café will be disappointed to discover it doesn't exist. But that's okay, because it does exist in these pages."

— Tom Varney, *Queen Mary* modeler, Steamship
Historical Society of America

"So imaginative and so much fun, you won't want to put it down. I love a good ghost story, but a ghost story that has more than thrills within its pages makes a very rich ghost story, indeed."

— Ann Garvin, *USA Today* bestselling author

"Spicy, mercurial, edgy. The supernatural elements permeating the plot dish up a wicked blend of romance and a dash of humor that keeps the story line involving and fun, and readers on their toes and guessing. Highly-recommended."

— *Midwest Book Review*

"Smart and sassy — great for fans of Liane Moriarty."

— Marsha Toy Engstrom, *Book Club Cheerleader*

"Patricia V. Davis captures the essence of grand magic performance in this haunting novel."

— David Copperfield

*The Secret Spice Café Trilogy is an
Official Pulpwood Queens Book Club Selection*

SPELLS & OREGANO

BOOK TWO

THE SECRET SPICE CAFÉ

ISBN 13: 978-0-9899056-8-8

Published by HD Media Press Inc.

THIS IS A WORK OF FICTION. Names, characters, places, dates, and incidents are either the product of the author's imagination or are used fictitiously.

Names: Davis, Patricia V. (Patricia Volonakis), 1956- author. Title: Spells and oregano / Patricia V. Davis. Description: Albertson, NY: HD Media Press Inc., [2017] | Series: The Secret Spice Café trilogy; book II. Identifiers: ISBN: 978-0-9899056-6-4 (hardback) | 978-0-9899056-8-8 (paperback) | 978-0-9899056-9-5 (Kindle) | LCCN: 2017949226 Subjects: LCSH: Mothers--Fiction. | Women psychics--Fiction. | Veterans--Fiction. | Magicians--Fiction. | Queen Mary (Steamship)--Fiction. | Ghosts--Fiction. | Magic--Fiction. | Restaurants-- California--Long Beach--Fiction. | Family secrets--Fiction. | Man-woman relationships-- Fiction. | Self-realization in women--Fiction. | Redemption--Fiction. | LCGFT: Ghost stories. | Romance fiction. | Magic realist fiction. | BISAC: FICTION / Contemporary Women. | FICTION / Visionary & Metaphysical. | FICTION / Magical Realism. Classification: LCC: PS3604.A97269 S64 2017 | DDC: 813/.6--dc23

Cover design and typeset by Tanya Quinlan

Interior design inspired by the *RMS Queen Mary*

Printed in the United States of America

SPELLS & OREGANO

BOOK TWO

THE SECRET SPICE CAFÉ

PATRICIA V. DAVIS

HD Media Press Inc.

To David Copperfield,
who makes the whole world believe in magic,

« AND »

to Niko V., who makes me believe in myself,
almost as much as I believe in him.

ACKNOWLEDGEMENTS

For three works of fiction that are categorized as 'magical realism,' I certainly end up doing a lot of research. And it's through that research that I've met so many fascinating people. For *Spells and Oregano*, there is everyone to thank from two combat veterans, to a beautiful chef, to a top paranormal investigator, to the world's greatest magician. Some things I learned from expert consultants: why butter should not be microwaved, what styles of gowns were worn in the 1930s, where I might hide a body on the *Queen Mary*, poisonous spiders can be purchased online, a magic show is more work than you can possibly imagine, and war is even worse than you think.

To all of those who shared their expertise and their time with me, I truly appreciate you and want to thank you by name. If you've been omitted inadvertently please let me know. We still have one more book in the series, and I will make it up to you. My thanks to:

» **Consultants:** Sara Klotz de Aguilar, Art Deco Era Motor and Fashion Group, Art Deco Society of California, Art Deco Society of Los Angeles, Harry Batchelder, Jay Braiman, Captain Will Kane, Andrew Davis, Scott Davis, Stuart Davis, Bekki Fahrer, Porter Gilberg, Fran Hirsch, Alice Jurow, Bruce Laker, Long Beach Police Department, Beat Meienberg, Jo Murray, Robert Phillips, Nina Snyder, Nicole Strickland, Tom Varney, Bob Wubker, Louie Zarcone. Extra Special Thanks to Joe Bertoldo, James Brandmueller, and Michael Castain

» **Chefs and Cooks:** Amber Burke, Simona Carini, Todd Henderson, Lindsey Keesling Hoffart, Ann Casolaro Minard, Pat Riley. Extra Special Thanks and a warm hug to Carmen Shenk

» **Photographers and Filmmakers:** Shaun Barnette, Parker Chittenden, Amy Liam McCallum, Kenny Regan, Lydia Selk. Extra Special Thanks to Joe Bertoldo and Niko Volonakis

» **All Kinds of Help and Inspiration:** June Allen, Denise Boone, Michael Bottrell, Connie Breeze, Trish Clifford, Douglass Christensen, David Copperfield, Debbie Davis, Pete Davis, Stacy DeRosa, Steve Eberhard, Ann Garvin, Dian Hodge, Maria Karamitsos and WindyCity Greek, Georgia Kolias, Sally Kuhlman, Avi La, LGBTQ Center of Long Beach, Lake Las Vegas Village, Peg Lozier, Gilbert Mansergh, Doug McPhail, J.H. Moncrieff, Marietta Neihaus, Ralph Rushton, George Schneider, Lizzie Snyder, Seasons Market in Lake Las Vegas, Emily Seruga, Becky Spratford, StokerCon2017, Lisa Vella, Xaver Wilhelmy, Michelle and Abby Wolven, Vin Zappacosta. Extra Special Thanks to Cynthia and Sarita Taylor, the Secret Spice Crew, and to Kathy L. Murphy and her Pulpwood Queens

» **My Fabulous Publishing and Promotions Team:** Gordon Warnock, Jen Karsbaek, Laurie McLean, Fuse Literary, Jane Hunter, Kelly Preston, Arnold Knightly

» **And sincerest and deepest thanks to:** *The Royal Mail Steamer Queen Mary*

"Every saint has a past and every sinner has a future."

— *Oscar Wilde*

PROLOGUE

Bensonhurst, New York, Good Friday, March 29, 1991

The bad man was back and Mama was afraid.

She pushed Santi into the kitchen cupboard under the sink. Shoved next to the drain pipe, he could barely fit. When he opened his mouth to protest, she pressed her hand against his mouth.

"Statti tsitto! Be quiet!" Mama spoke Sicilian only when she wanted her sons to know she meant business. "Promise me you won't come out. Promise me you won't let him know you're here, no matter what happens. *Promise* me, Santino!"

She also used their full names.

Santi didn't want to promise. He wanted to stay with her, to protect her. He wasn't a baby. He was six. But Mama's eyes looked so, so scared when she whispered to him, that to make her feel better, he promised. Before he was left alone in the dark, before the cupboard door closed completely, Santi saw her hands shake.

Those shaking hands would be one of his last memories of his mother.

In the confined space, the sound of his blood rushing faster and faster through his veins was louder to him than the fist he could hear pummeling on their apartment door. He pressed his lips together so he wouldn't cry out when the bad man shouted his mother's name.

"Gina! I know you're in there. Open up, goddammit, or I'll break this door down!"

When the bad man kicked against the wood, Santi's whole body jumped. He wanted *Nannuzzu.* Oh, how he wished for his *Nannuzzu.* And he wanted his brother too.

But *Nannuzzu* and Luca were at the Brooklyn Bridge, for the Way of the Cross. Luca had laughed at him when Mama told Santi he had to stay home just because of his stupid cold. *Why* did Luca always get to do things he couldn't? Luca was always so lucky. And now look what'd happened — he had to hide in the dark, by himself. He had to hide, and he was just as scared as Mama was.

———●

Elliot Abramson lived with his wife in the one-bedroom apartment downstairs from Gina and her sons. He'd been deaf in one ear since he was seventeen, when, while in the infantry in WWII, a 37mm artillery shell had exploded closer to him than a shave with a straight-edge razor. As a result, he walked with a limp and kept the sound on his TV up way too high, whenever his wife wasn't around to tell him to lower it. "If Satan himself knocks on our front door we won't hear him, Eli," was her fondest saying.

She had the right of it. Today she was out playing mahjong, and Eli didn't put it together soon enough that the strange sounds he heard were coming from the outside hallway, not from the old John Wayne flick. He turned down the volume to listen with his good ear.

Oy, not again. It was Rocco Miceli making all the racket. For more than five years, he'd seen the hell the young woman was being put through by her estranged husband.

Eli empathized with Rocco's sickness. But the banging on his wife's door and the screaming threats? That was too much. Things were getting way out of hand. One of these days, Gina or one of those cute twin boys of hers was going to get hurt. Eli knew she'd never call the cops. Poor kid still held onto the hope that her 'real' husband would return someday. When he heard the flimsy door crack as Rocco slammed his body against it, Elliot didn't waste time. Regardless of what Gina would want, he hurried over to the phone as fast as his bum leg could get him to it.

———•

Gina was devastated to see Rocco stomp into her kitchen over the splinters of her demolished front door. It was unfathomable to her that he was capable of that kind of violence. Friends, family, had all warned her that one day he might completely snap. No matter what they'd told her about his condition, she still couldn't bring herself to believe that he'd ever truly harm her or their sons.

But here he was — the man who'd adored her, who'd treated her like a princess ever since they were teenagers — looking at her in a way she'd have never imagined he could or would. A look that had her quaking.

As he came toward her, she stood in front of the sink, her hands clenched together in an effort to steady herself, the backs of her trembling legs pressed firmly against the cabinet that held Santi. She knew why Rocco was here, and he wasn't getting anywhere near her baby.

"You changed the lock," was the first thing out of his mouth. "Why would you do that?" He was breathing so hard he could barely get the question out.

Gina heard the real confusion in his voice. "Oh, Rocco." Fresh compassion washed over the terror. She'd never stop hurting for him. Ever. "Have you forgotten? I had that lock changed months ago. The *last* time you tried to break in."

"What are you talking about? I never did that. Who's making you say these lies about me?"

She stayed silent as she stared back into his long-lashed, southern Italian eyes. First thing about him she'd fallen for back in school. Even the nuns hadn't been able to resist the flirtatious fun in them, she remembered. Now she saw nothing in them but madness.

"Answer me, dammit! Who's telling you to say these things?"

When he gripped her shoulders, she willed herself not to call out for help, not to glance down at the cupboard behind her. "Nobody's telling me anything, Rocco. Please. Please listen." She pressed her palm against his chest. "You need help."

"Don't say that to me!" In what Gina hoped might be a glimmer of lucidity, he responded, "I *can't*. Don't you see? I can't go back to that hospital, Gina. The things they do to me there … I can't function with what they give me."

"There might be other drugs, other things to try —"

"No. You don't get it. They make me … I … I can't think. I can't feel anything." His hands, still at her shoulders, squeezed. "I can't make love to you."

She closed her eyes against the pain of those words. How could she explain that they hadn't lived together, haven't been lovers for more than five years? She knew she shouldn't, and yet she couldn't help but stroke his face. "Why, Rocco, why? How could this happen to you after so many years out? I just don't understand. I'll never understand."

Seeing her soften toward him, he took his chance. "Let me have the boy, Gina. He's dangerous."

She went rigid at once and pulled back from him. "No, he *isn't*, Rocco. He's just a kid. We've been over this and over this." She heard the shrill desperation in her voice, and knew that Santi was hearing it too. Please God, let him stay put.

Willing herself to speak calmly, she reasoned, "Rocco, this idea you have about him — it's just another strange thing that's come into your head. Don't you see that?"

His grip on her shoulders tightened. "If he stays with you, he'll hurt somebody, I'm telling you. He needs to come with me. I need to take him underground."

She saw it, then. His countenance altered just enough, in just such a way, for her to see that she'd misjudged how ill he was. It dawned on her then what he might be capable of, what he might do. Quick as lightning, she reached out behind her, blindly, to the countertop next to the sink, and fumbled for the wooden knife holder. Grasping one of the knives, she held it toward him.

"Get out," she whispered. "Get out *now*. You're not getting near either one of my kids!"

Her body went cold when amusement flickered in his eyes. In a flash, his manner changed again, and with no effort at all, he twisted the knife out of her hand. She heard it clatter when he threw it behind her into the sink. She tried shoving him next, but it was like pushing a pile of boulders. She kicked him in the shin, ducked away from him, and ran. He yanked her back by her hair before she could get to the phone.

"Get off me! Get off!" She pummeled and scratched at his hands.

Without letting go, he swung her around to face him, and bellowed, "Where's Luciano? Where's Santino? Where are my sons, goddammit?"

"They're not here!" She flicked a glance at the sink, and was horrified to see that the cupboard door was now slightly ajar. Trying to stall — to *think* — she told Rocco part of the truth. "They're with my father. At the bridge."

He released her at once, stumbling back from her like a drunk. "The bridge?" The change in him from rage to frenzied fear flummoxed her. "They're at the *bridge*?"

Standing there in the bright, homey kitchen, where his little boy was hidden from him and the wife he cherished shrank from him, he saw only one bridge — a smoldering one that had been blasted to pieces. He saw human body parts flung across torn and twisted rails. He saw the corpses of his men scattered on the sandy, weeded bank. He saw mothers and babies with straight black hair and sun-browned skin floating lifeless among the dead fish in a river that had turned scarlet with blood. He saw a jeep in flames on its side, two Marines still trapped within, screaming as their flesh burned. He'd gotten there too late that time.

This time he wouldn't.

Gina went ashen when he pulled a P226 out of his jacket. "Oh, my God, Rocco — where did you get that? You're not allowed to have that!"

He made for the ruined door. "I have to save them."

"No! You can't go out with that." As frightened as she was, as light-weight and delicate, it was a tribute to how much they'd once loved and trusted each other that she stepped in front of him, a powerful-ly-built, trained Navy Seal.

But in his delusion, she wasn't his little Gina. She was an enemy intent on sabotage.

"Get out of my way!" He picked her up and flung her behind him as easily as his sons flung their toys, and kept on. And like those toys, it was just that easy for Gina to break. Rocco didn't know what he'd done until he heard the sickening crack of her head hit against the cor-ner of the kitchen countertop. Turning from the steps, he saw her, on her back on the linoleum tile, her shoulder bent, her neck twisted at a terrifying angle.

That's when he remembered who she was.

"Gina!" He ran to her and knelt by her side. "Oh, no, no." Lifting her hand, he touched her wrist. "Not my baby, not my Gina. Oh, God, please no." He placed his ear against her chest, willing her heart to beat. "Please, God. No!"

It was a warm spring day for New York, and Gina had left the apartment windows open. Rocco's wails of torment nearly drowned out the sirens, the slamming of car doors outside the building, the sound of feet drumming on the pavement.

He was very clear now, on where he was and what he'd done. He could hear them as they came into the building, their voices and questions to the old man who lived downstairs distinct and commanding through the door he'd split apart. When they started up the stairs, cautiously, guns drawn, he leaned down over his wife, and, like the prince who'd kissed Snow White, he touched his lips to hers.

"Gina," he whispered, "I love you. I'm sorry, my baby, my beautiful girl. I didn't mean to hurt you. You know I would never have hurt you." He put his gun to his temple. "I'm coming with you now."

Huddled under the sink, Santi eyes and mouth were clenched shut. He couldn't feel his legs. They hadn't gone numb the way they sometimes did when he stayed in one position for too long while watching TV. It was as if there were a nothingness where they should have been. But he could feel his stomach. It felt like it did when he had to go to the bathroom and didn't know if he could hold it. He could hear his heart pounding in his ears as though it were separate from his chest, in the cupboard with him somehow, there in the dark. Only that couldn't happen. None of this could be for real.

Wake up. *Wake up*, Santi, wake up. The words spun round and round in his head.

Any minute he'd open his eyes and he'd be in his bed, for sure. Then he could get up and fall asleep again on the soft, fluffy throw rug in Mama's room. She never chased him away, always pretended she didn't notice he was lying there, so he wouldn't feel ashamed that he was scared.

That's all this was — a terrible nightmare.

Except, when he peeked out, he saw the bad man drop to his knees next to Mama, and cry and cry. He knew who the man was now.

When he heard the police, his hysteria pitched. They'd find him. They'd know it was his fault Mama was hurt so bad, because he'd stayed hidden, because he hadn't jumped out to help her, like Batman would.

As he pulled back behind the cupboard door again, he heard two gunshots — one right after the other — *Kapoom! Kapoom!* The sounds were so loud and so close, scarier than when he heard them in the movies. That's when he knew that this wasn't a nightmare, that they'd shot him, and he would die now because he hadn't helped his mother. That's when he screamed.

He screamed for his brother, "Luca! Luca!" His brother was magic. His brother was the only one who could make it all stop.

He was still screaming Luca's name when they pulled him out of the cupboard.

Luca was having fun even though he kind of wasn't supposed to since it was Jesus's Dead Day. Luca always found a way to have fun, no matter what. It was fun being outside, looking out at the water and the skyline. The Verrazano was his favorite bridge, even though it was hard to pronounce. It was fun holding a lit candle. No way would Mama have let him if she were here, but *Nannuzzo* said he was big enough. Besides, Luca knew a secret trick to keep the candle steady so he wouldn't accidentally set fire to any of the ladies' hair, like happened sometimes when people weren't careful.

Nobody knew about all the tricks he could do except Santi. Sometimes, even Santi thought he was making them up. Like when they were both here last Easter, all of a sudden he could understand what the priests were saying while they prayed. He'd asked Mama what language they were speaking, and she told him it was Latin. He'd whispered to Santi, "I can speak Latin," and Santi said, "Shut up. No, you can't, you liar."

But Luca wasn't lying. He could speak Latin. He didn't know how he'd learned it, just as he didn't know how come he could do the magic tricks that he saw David Copperfield do on television. David Copperfield was his favorite magician, and Luca could do almost all the magic he could do, except make the tigers or the pretty girls disappear. Luca didn't have any tigers, and he didn't know any pretty girls except his mother, and if he made her disappear, he thought she might scold him. He did make Leonardo, their turtle, disappear once, but Santi said if he didn't bring him back he would tell.

He wished his brother were here now. He knew Santi was probably still mad at him for teasing him that morning. He felt bad about that, except that Santi was so much fun to tease, sometimes Luca couldn't help himself. Everything was so serious to Santi. If Santi were here, he'd probably tell Luca that he shouldn't call it "Jesus's Dead Day." But he still might smile about it a little. If Luca managed to make Santi laugh, that was his best magic trick of all.

Nannuzzo gave him a nudge. "Uh oh. Get ready. *Signora* Zarcone's coming over."

Signora Zarcone knew Luca's mother's family, the Castellettis, way back from when both families had still lived in Sicily. She'd once told Luca that she remembered when *Nannuzzo* was born. That seemed impossible. He wondered how old Signora Zarcone was compared to Jesus.

"*Figgiu beddu*. Beautiful little boy!" Mrs. Zarcone zeroed in on Luca, engulfing him in the overpowering scents of fried meatballs and Jean Nate After Bath Splash. His grandfather managed to snatch the candle he was so proud of just before he dropped it.

Mrs. Zarcone was too intent on pinching Luca's cheek to notice. "*Beddu!*" she declared again. "You're so handsome." She inclined her head to his grandfather. "*Ciao*, Paolo. *Comu si*? Your grandson's getting so big, God bless him." When Luca rubbed his cheek, she cackled. "Where's your brother today, eh?"

"He had to stay home, *Signora*. He's sick." Luca smiled at her even though his cheek was throbbing. *Signora* Zarcone reminded him of the witch who made the poisoned apple. Her back was so hunched that she wasn't all that much taller than he was. And she smelled kind of funny. But she was okay. Any minute now she'd open her handbag and pull out something for him — a piece of gum or chocolate, maybe even a quarter.

Mrs. Zarcone made *tsk*-ing sounds. She peered at him. "You got the eyes of your father, that *povero pazzu*. Which one are you — Luciano or Santino?"

Paolo Castelletti stiffened at the comment about his son-in-law being a 'poor crazy one.' People saying things like that was disrespectful to his daughter. She was the one to feel sorry for, raising two boys by herself and putting up with that *cafone's* antics. Like hell Rocco was crazy. Nobody got shell shock ten years after the fact, no matter what the doctors said. It had to be drugs. Not only that, the whole neighborhood knew better than to mention him in front of the twins. They'd been told nothing about their father, and now, from the look on Luca's face, he knew he'd have questions to field. To distract the boy, Paolo answered the old bat himself.

"It's Luciano, *Signora*. You can tell them apart because Santino doesn't have a birthmark, and Luciano does. See?" He pointed to just above the neckline of the boy's t-shirt. Mrs. Zarcone leaned in closer and gasped. Luca's birthmark was bright red, and in the perfect shape of a star.

"*Madonna mia!*" She crossed herself. "He's got the devil's mark."

Paolo went from insulted to furious. Old lady or not, he wanted to slap her. Putting his arm around his grandson, he pulled him away. "*Buon giorno, Signora,*" he said, his voice tight. "Have a good Easter."

Luca tugged the hem of his grandfather's suit jacket as they followed the rest of the procession. "*Nannuzzo,* why did *Signora* Zarcone say those things?"

"Eh." Paolo dismissed her with feigned casualness. "Pay no attention. She's old. She's probably senile."

Luca didn't know what 'senile' meant. "But do I? Have my father's eyes, I mean?" That had caught his attention more than her denouncement of his birthmark.

Paolo hesitated before answering. "You have beautiful eyes. And yes, they are like your father's. But your smile — now *that* is just like your mother's."

The answer pleased Luca. He took his grandfather's hand as they walked along together and he thought about his mother's smile. It was beautiful. Like his father's eyes, he supposed. He wished he'd seen them, just once.

Although, now he could see them. Just like that — a picture of his father's eyes, his father's entire face — appeared inside his head, clear as crystal. Why he was so sure it was his father he didn't know. It should have been a good feeling to be able to see him, if only in his mind, but there was something ... something that didn't feel right.

He stopped short, as inexplicable dread filled him. He could see his mother now also, lying on what he recognized were the worn, yellow squares of their kitchen floor. Her eyes were closed. Her face looked too white against her black hair. She was lying too still.

Luca's breathing went harsh and rapid as he saw Santi next.

Santi was screaming.

Mama! Mama! Luca! Help me! Help me, Luca!

Paolo looked down at his grandson's bowed head. The little boy had started shivering as though with fever. He was squeezing Paolo's fingers so tightly that the arthritis in his joints ached. "*Chi ce?* What is it, Luca?"

Luca looked up. "I want to go home. I want Mama. I want Santi. Santi … *Santi!*"

The next thing Paolo knew, he was running back across the bridge, his knees nearly buckling from the weight of a shrieking, terror-stricken Luca in his arms. He had no idea what the hell was happening.

Mrs. Zarcone crossed herself again as they ran by.

CHAPTER ONE

Saturday, September 28, 2013, 8:30 p.m.
Restaurant Guy Savoy, Las Vegas, Nevada

The sleek gray, contemporary dining table was illuminated by a chandelier made with Krug champagne bottles, its tabletop graced with three Bernardaud china place settings that were rimmed in gold and custom embellished with the Krug crest. Flanking those were three sets of Le Joseph glasses by Riedel that were shaped precisely to amplify the aromas, tastes and bubbles of the Krug Grande Cuvée champagnes. And, on the wine red wall across from the table, the same prestigious name was painted in gilded lettering.

The Krug Room is the only one of its kind, housed within an already uber-posh restaurant, the Guy Savoy. The private alcove holds one sole Chef's Table, reserved for only two to six guests. Those diners willing to pay for this pricey epicurean experience with the acclaimed chef, get an up close look at the impeccable kitchen as they're served unforgettable French delicacies, complimented by some of the finest champagnes in the world.

The fortunate three dining there that particular evening were Sarita Taylor, her mother, Cynthia, and her stepfather, Raul Ferreira.

Nine years into their relationship, two years of which they'd been married, Raul was still besotted with Cynthia. He loved Sarita as though she were his own, and in honor of her birthday, this dining experience was only one highlight of a four-day weekend with which he'd surprised the two women who were most important to him.

The lavish celebration was a far cry from how Sarita and her mother had last experienced Sin City, but it wasn't only due to Cynthia and Raul's marriage that those days of financial adversity were behind them. Their own restaurant was doing wonderfully well, and Raul was proud of them both for all they'd achieved on their own.

Cynthia and Sarita did their utmost to show him how much they appreciated his generosity by raving over the parade of dishes brought out to them — dazzling dishes that had started with a refreshing Concassé of Oysters with Seaweed and Lemon Granité, and would complete with a velvety Terrine de Pamplemousse for dessert.

Little did Raul know that his stepdaughter was trying like hell not to let on that she was getting sick to her stomach. However, Cynthia, with her finely-honed Miss Clavel instincts, suspected that something was not right.

"So — how's your birthday so far, *filha?*" Her sharp gaze made Sarita feel like a teenager again.

"Everything is fabulous. Perfect." It was all she could do to keep from fidgeting. "Um, would you both just excuse me for a minute, please?"

"If you're going to the toilet, let me go with you —"

"No, no — I've just remembered I've got to make a call. Work," Sarita improvised, smiling brightly, too brightly. "I'll just be a minute, *Mãe.*" She managed to make her escape before embarrassing herself.

Alone in the elegant ladies' lounge, Sarita still felt unsteady as she washed her hands and splashed cool water on her face.

Good God. Poor Raul would be mightily disappointed if he learned where her five hundred dollar meal had ended up. It was a shame, because she hadn't been lying when she'd said it was delicious. There was nothing wrong with the food or the company. She loved seeing how happy her mother and stepfather were together.

She just didn't want to be here. She'd been feeling jumpy all day. Her panic attacks were becoming more frequent lately and her ...

'condition,' as she referred to it, was acting up again. After it had been mostly dormant for so long, she'd built up hopes that perhaps it was becoming less powerful as the years went by.

No such luck. The visions she'd been having the last few weeks had gotten even more intense since they'd arrived in Vegas two nights before. Worse, these had nothing to do with Naag. Nine years after his death, he still haunted her sleep now and then, and she'd wake up with her breath hitching, her body soaked with perspiration, the image of his lifeless, staring eyes as clear in her mind and heart as they'd been the day he died. She accepted those nightmares, welcomed them even, as her penance. This particular nightmare, however, had nothing to do with him. It was a vision from her childhood, one she'd thought was gone for good.

She'd been ... three? Or maybe four, when she first shot out of a sound sleep, shrieking, frightening her poor mother witless. At the time, neither one of them knew about her condition. That first night, Cynthia had been able to soothe her little daughter back to sleep. But she'd been at a loss when for a week afterward Sarita couldn't close her eyes without being tormented by those same images.

Just as Cynthia was feeling frantic enough to spend what little money they had on a doctor who specialized in night terrors, an unexpected package came from New Orleans. Inside was a slim red candle and a small, brown leather pouch tied closed with a white silk cord. The pouch held a curious collection of items. There was also a note, scripted in purple ink, addressed to them both with a flourished hand. The note had been written by *Manman* Taylor, Sarita's Haitian grandmother, whom she'd never met.

"What does it say?" Sarita had asked, as Cynthia tore it open and examined it.

Her reply had been both pensive and oblique. "They're instructions."

With the leather pouch under her pillow, Sarita had slept dreamlessly that night, and every night for seven years thereafter. She was twelve when the pouch went missing. She searched in and around her bed and everywhere else she could think of, but it wasn't to be found. To Sarita, it was one of the most distressing losses of her childhood. That worn-out pouch — known as a '*gris-gris*'— was her one connection to a grandmother she'd never met. A grandmother whom she hadn't known was a Vodou priestess.

The day she lost *Granmè* Taylor's charm was the same day Cynthia brought Raul Sr. home. Sarita didn't put it together until years later that she'd known he was coming because she no longer had the powerful *gris-gris* to block her ability of sight. Four years later, in their restaurant aboard the *Queen Mary*, what she was able to see that no one else could, forever changed her life and the lives of the five people closest to her.

Even so, for nearly a decade now, the transmissions in her head had simmered down, relatively speaking. The anti-anxiety medications helped. The therapy didn't. She had to see a psychiatrist once a month in order to get the pills, but it was a waste of his time and hers, since she couldn't very well tell the doctor the truth, now could she? She wasn't willing to take the chance that doctor-patient confidentiality would extend to a confession of murder.

Now, with no forewarning, the vision she'd had as a child, the one her grandmother's charm had blocked, was back. She'd nearly forgotten it, but now that she was seeing again, it was no wonder she'd been so affected by it as a child. She could barely stand it twenty years later, as a grown woman. Not only did she not know why it had returned, she was as clueless to what it meant as she had been when she'd first seen it. It was a jumble of people and places all unknown to her, doing things she didn't understand.

What made this particular nightmare even more unnerving was that it was virtually soundless: a little boy whose terror she could feel, hiding someplace dark and cramped. He'd open his mouth and scream, but it was like someone had pressed the 'mute' button on a TV remote control. An abrupt change and he was somewhere else — a big, beautiful bridge, with hundreds of people. There he was smiling and holding a candle, but then he was screaming again, and an old man was holding onto him tightly, and running with him, running, running. There was another man, younger than the first, whose face she couldn't see, and a fire on — was it that same bridge that was burning? She just couldn't tell. But the fire grew, huge and unstoppable. She could feel the scorch of it in her throat and lungs as a constant companion these days, as though she were right there, wherever it had happened, breathing in the smoke and fumes, overtaken by the crushing heat.

Dammit, *why* would this come back to her after all this time? Even though it was reasonable to assume that whatever horrific incident it revealed had occurred long ago, there was something portentous about its return.

Taking deep breaths to steady herself, she inspected her face in the mirror. Nothing like vomiting over a toilet to enhance one's appearance. They'd notice right away if she didn't reapply her lipstick and fix the mascara smears under her eyes. Her hair was a wreck too.

As she rummaged in her handbag for makeup, she caught a movement to her left and swung around, hoping that her mother hadn't decided to follow her in after all.

A woman stood about three feet away, looking back at her. In her early thirties or thereabouts, she was chicly dressed, although more casually than most of the other diners, in black stretch pants, black ballet flats, and a white cashmere cardigan with tiny pearl buttons. Around her neck a delicate gold cross twinkled on a thin gold chain. She had shiny black hair that swung loose to her shoulders, dark winged brows and smoky eyes that looked solemn as she stared at Sarita. It wasn't unexpected that someone else would walk into the lounge, but when the woman began to pixelate like a low resolution image on a screen, and the pattern of the wall tiles behind her became visible through her body, Sarita dropped her handbag, its contents skittering across the floor.

"Crap!" She lunged for the change that was rolling everywhere, then thought again and stayed where she was to keep her eyes on the ghost.

"I'm sorry — I didn't mean to scare you." The woman's voice had a muffled quality, as though it were coming through a waterlogged speaker. "I'm not supposed to be here, but I had to meet you in person."

"What? Why? Who are you?"

"Sarita, are you in there?"

With a small popping sound, the woman vanished just as Cynthia walked in and found Sarita kneeling on the floor.

"What happened? Are you all right?'

"Yes, yes. I ... just dropped my handbag." Sarita risked a glance to where the woman had been. Gone, thank God. No way in hell did she want her mother to know about her latest Danny Torrance moment. It had taken Cynthia seven years after Naag's death to stop worrying about her daughter and allow herself a life of her own. Now that she and Raul were living together at last, Sarita was determined that nothing would impinge on their happiness.

"Are you sure?" As Sarita dumped everything back into her bag, Cynthia scrutinized her sharply, and noticed that her mascara was smeared. "You don't look well. Have you been crying? Was it the work call that upset you? I was afraid managing the restaurant alone might be too much for you. I *told* Raul we should wait until we had someone to take Jane's place. I said —" She stopped herself when she caught her daughter's expression. "I'm fussing, aren't I?"

Sarita stood, her things gathered back up, her agitation temporarily lessened. There was something to be said for having someone you could count on to love and support you always. Cynthia's mothering style had been claustrophobic to Sarita when she was a teenager, but now that they were no longer snuggled in each other's pockets, she appreciated how lucky she was to have her mother's unconditional love.

What was the old saying? 'Good friends keep your secrets, great friends help you bury the body.' Well, her mother had done exactly that, hadn't she? And as hard as that aftermath was to live with, Sarita loved Cynthia all the more for it.

"Yes, you're fussing." With a smile, she touched her mother's face. "But not too much." Turning to the sink, she spoke with more firmness. "*Mãe*, I've been managing the Spice for two years now, and I love it. You know I'm handling it just fine. It's not like you don't call once a week to make sure of it. Even Jane calls from whatever darn port she and Antoni are in."

Running her brush through her hair, she glanced at Cynthia and noticed that her assurances weren't having the desired effect. Maybe telling her mother part of the truth might divert her attention. "Okay, look — this wasn't about work," she admitted. "I had to say something to get out of there, because I didn't want Raul's feelings to be hurt. I'm fine now, but —" she tilted her head toward the toilets, mentally crossing her fingers as she uttered the lie — "the meal was … a bit rich for me. I guess I've been spoiled by Cristiano's cooking."

"Oh." Cynthia's tension drained. "Is that all? Well, that's a relief." Hastily, she corrected herself. "I mean, I'm not relieved that you got sick."

Sarita smiled at her. "I know what you meant." Thankful her mother was off the scent, she dampened a tissue and used it to clean up the mascara.

"Don't worry, I won't tell Raul." Cynthia patted her arm. "And we'll use our waistlines as an excuse to get out of eating dessert. That should help. Besides, we're running late anyway. We don't want to miss the beginning of the show."

Sarita paused, her lipstick tube halfway to her mouth. "What show?"

"Another present for you." Cynthia's eyes lit up as she freshened her own makeup. "Angela gave Raul the tickets when she found out about his plans. Her cousin's boys are performers right here at Caesar's. Magicians. I read about them in *Las Vegas Weekly*. They've got great reviews. And they're very good-looking. Identical twins, no less." She gave Sarita a saucy wink. "One for me and one for you, eh?"

It was an effort for Sarita to hide her dismay. For the past two days her mother and stepfather had been enjoying their holiday, and believed she was enjoying hers. Concealing the fact that ominous visions had been in her head the whole time had been a monumental task, making her feel ill even before she'd booted up dinner. The ghostly visitation had been the last straw. Maybe she was a coward, but she didn't want to see any more, didn't want to know what any of it meant. She wished she could make it all stop, as her grandmother had been able to do. What she wanted now more than anything was to go back to her room, switch off the lights and crawl into bed.

But for a few hours longer, she somehow had to manage to calm nerves that were already stretched thread-thin, and sit through what promised to be a loud and kitschy Las Vegas act. She'd do it, because she could see that her mother was pleased with the prospect of the show. With Raul's hectic schedule, they'd never been able to do anything like this together before. She wouldn't allow herself to ruin it for them.

Resigned, she glanced around casually one more time to be sure that her visitor hadn't returned. Turning back to Cynthia, she forced up another perky smile. "Magic, huh? That sounds like fun."

Backstage at the Colosseum Theatre at Caesar's Palace, Santino Miceli surveyed his domain.

Strategy. Practice. Timing. And a code of silence. One without any of the others would spell disaster. As a master illusionist, it was Santi's job to be sure that his audience let go of their sense of doubt and became mystified and exhilarated by what reviewers had declared, "The World's Greatest Magic Show." Tonight those elements were more crucial than ever, when he would perform his newest, most ambitious sleight of hand yet.

He stopped a stagehand who was carrying a familiar-looking costume. "Hold it. Where you going with that?"

The stagehand looked apprehensive as he answered, "One of the Minervas got sick, Mr. Miceli. Stacey told me to bring this to the dressing room for her replacement."

Santi's voice was sharp as he spoke to their production manager through his headset mike. "Stacey — the Minervas — who's out and who's in?" As Stacey murmured reassurances to him through his earpiece, Santi's jaw clenched. "Is the new girl the same height?" He listened with growing frustration. "That's not good enough, Stacey. The platform still has to be adjusted. Tell Gordon and get back to me as soon as he takes care of it."

When she clicked off, he swore under his breath, and his eyes never stopped as he scanned the area behind the stage. Ten minutes until curtain. Everything should have been ready to go. Even something such as a girl having to be replaced could cause a major problem this close to show time.

After talking to Stacey, Santi clipped out orders to another crewman. "I want that screen moved forward." He jabbed a finger toward a painted scenery panel. "It's at least twelve inches off. I can see it from here. *Measure* it. I don't want to have to check it again."

Santi relied on thirty people. Thirty people doing the right thing at the right time was vital to his success. It was not only his talent as a performer, it was his organizational genius, his knack for hiring only the best and most trustworthy technicians that made him what he was. Like a game of Tetris, each illusion was a puzzle to be constructed against the clock. Every piece had to interlock seamlessly as part of the whole. Not a one was inconsequential. All it took was a small slip up by anyone with even the most seemingly minor role to play – a props handler, an onstage assistant, a gaffer on the lighting crew – and he could be left disgraced in front of his audience, unless he was able to shift gears right there on the spot.

Tonight far more than a dent to his pride was at stake. The final illusion, if not executed to perfection, could cost him all.

While he checked every detail, barked out orders for last-minute adjustments to scenery and props, he conferred through his mike with his main players — the theater manager, the lighting director, Joanie — his female onstage assistant — and even the conductor of the orchestra. As his eyes zeroed in on his brother, who was standing in the wings, casually flirting with a pretty, clearly star-struck extra, Santi ground his jaw.

Luca looked so naturally at ease, so sure of himself. There would never be any mistakes, never any fear of humiliation or real danger for Luca. It was only his — Santi's — toil and tears that had earned them their magic act, their reputation, their fame and their enormous fortune.

He'd always be the better magician. That he knew for sure, and he was about to prove it again this evening. But as for Luca, one look, one flick of his wrist, and he was able to recreate the feats that Santi practiced over and over, for endless hours, to get just right.

Although identical twins, some quirk of fate, some random mutation of their monozygotic DNA, had given Luca something extra — something that Santi would always desire and always lack.

Yeah, his brother was one lucky bastard.

And did he appreciate his gift? No. It was just one more diversion for him. Everything was a game to Luca, especially their act, which he went along with simply for the ride, adding nothing to it at all but his glibness and good looks.

Seething, Santi walked over, his one glare at the extra had her scurrying off, but Luca didn't pick up on his twin's mood. "Hey, bro." He smiled easily. "We all set?"

"Yeah, we're all set. No thanks to you."

There was no way for Luca to mistake Santi's mood after that. "What do you mean? I did everything you asked me to do." He dug into his tuxedo pocket and pulled out a wrinkled sheet of paper. "Here — look," he said earnestly "— it's all done, Santi, I swear."

Santi didn't have to glance at the list. He knew every item by heart, and he'd already made sure it had all been seen to. He just hated his twin's blasé attitude. Santi's passion — the unique and spectacular world of illusion — meant little to Luca.

But that would all change with their new finale, when Santi would show Luca what real talent was.

Thirty seconds. At the signal that came through their earpieces, there was no more time to nitpick. The brothers hurried to their places offstage to wait for their cue. Standing on Santi's left, Luca squinted across to the wing opposite where Joanie was positioned. He'd noticed that she hadn't been herself all throughout rehearsal, and still looked agitated and preoccupied. First Santi, now Joanie. All this tension was not a good thing right before curtain. Where was it coming from? It was enough to make even Luca grow concerned. He smiled and gave her a thumbs up to reassure her, then leaned toward his brother and muttered in Sicilian, "What's up with Joanie? She's fidgety."

From one side of the stage to the other, Santi and Joanie exchanged a look. Something about that look felt off to Luca. But when Santi only grunted, Luca relaxed again. He knew what the problem was.

"Uh oh," he teased. "You two have a fight? You know, Santi, some-times I wonder what's harder work for her — this shit, or putting up with your grumpy ass."

When Santi still didn't respond, Luca's good-natured smile faded. "You're not nervous over the new part, are you?"

"No, I'm not," he lied, as he put his headset aside and adjusted his lavalier mike and earpiece. "Not at all. So don't even think about jumping in. I want your word on it. I don't need you hovering over me, waiting for me to fuck up, so you can be the hero."

Luca could have kicked himself. It was the wrong thing to ask at the wrong time. He was used to Santi's resentment by now, but this time his remarks were uttered with so much more than his usual vitriol that Luca rushed in to reassure him. That was his second mistake.

"C'mon, Santi — what're you talking about? You've never fucked up. Look at this set-up. I wish I had an eye like yours. I can't even keep my bedroom organized." He gave Santi a playful jab on his arm. "Hell, bro — we're rich because of you."

Similar thoughts had just been going through Santi's own mind, and Luca had said them out loud sincerely. Yet all Santi wanted to do was punch him in the face. He'd had enough of feeling like the 'lesser' twin. He'd had enough of his brother coming to his rescue, or smiling at him with saccharine reassurance like some doting nanny when a new illusion he was working on didn't come out right the first time.

He sure as hell was not going to allow that tonight.

As the lights went down, Stacey's voice came through their earpieces, *"House is full, gentlemen. Get ready for your cue."*

"Stop it. Stop being so goddamn patronizing, for once, will you?"

"I'm not being patronizing. I meant it."

Why Luca's words should hit a nerve now, Santi didn't stop to think. The bitterness burst out of him, almost without his consent. Leaning toward Luca so that none of the nearby stagehands would hear, his whisper was sneering, "You know what, *bro?* I'm sick to death of your idiot savant privilege and your phony encouragement and your … your naïve, upbeat attitude. Why don't you, for once, just shut the fuck up?"

Luca's head snapped back as though he'd been slapped. He clasped his brother's arm. "What the hell, Santi? Why are you so mad at me? I'm your brother. I love you."

The musicians struck up the opening music, and the announcer's introduction boomed through the audio system — "Ladies and gentlemen, Caesar's Palace Las Vegas is proud to present —"

Fists clenched, face hard, Santi yanked his arm away. In the dimmed lighting, the brothers stared at each other in their matching black tuxedos, their profiles impossible to tell apart but for their expressions: one of baffled hurt, one of jealous fury.

"On in … three … two… one … Go!"

"The Miceli Brothers!"

Slapping on the beaming smile he reserved solely for performances, Santi swept passed Luca, while Luca only just managed to don his own professional mask as he followed out onto center stage. Though reeling from the unprecedented outrage, now was not the time to fixate on what might be going on in his brother's head. He'd deal with it after their act.

After so many performances together their switch to entertainer mode was reflexive and flawless, no matter what had taken place between them offstage. Even before the applause died down, the brothers were looking out into their audience in a way that made every man and woman sitting there feel as though their attention was fixed on them alone. They made quite the picture: Tall, slim, and broad shouldered in their elegant attire, thick black hair with threads of burnished copper that gleamed under the overhead lights, alluring smiles so white against their dark Italian skin, and eyes as shiny and dark as the olives hanging ripe in the groves of their ancestors' native Sicily. This masculine splendor was made all the more enticing because it was times two. Ever since their first appearance as young up-and-comers on the Las Vegas scene eight years before, they'd been the media's darlings, featured on every local television channel, on taxis and billboards all throughout the city, and on the covers of everything from *Vanity Fair* to the newest women's periodical, *Cougar Dash*.

The stage behind them was presented just as impeccably as they were. No expense was spared for the fantastical set which, in keeping with the Caesar's Palace theme, featured a Roman forum ten stories high. In front of the forum was a remarkably authentic looking portico of six Ionic columns upon which were bronze-colored statues of the goddess Minerva in various poses and stages of dress and undress. The dark-haired Minervas were a perfect contrast to the twins' lovely assistant, the golden-haired, green-eyed Joanie, who looked smoking hot and Roman-ish in a one-shouldered, flowing white mini dress. Their celebrated costume designer had earned her pay with this clever piece. No one could tell it was fashioned from material durable enough to hold up against wear and tear as Joanie was sawed in half, suspended in midair, and squeezed into spaces small enough to crush a mouse.

To dazzle the ears as well as the eyes, drums throbbed, then ebbed seductively into the background when Santi began their patter:

"Good evening and welcome, everyone!" His voice through the mike was as smooth and rich as the music. "My name is Santino Miceli and —" he bowed dramatically — "I am a magician." With a flourish, he extended his arm toward Luca. "And this is my brother, Luciano. He doesn't work for a living, either."

Luca smiled and stepped forward as the audience chuckled. "Hello, everyone. Thank you for being here tonight. I trust you'll keep our secret and not tell our family what my brother and I do. They'd be so embarrassed. They think we're still in prison." Laughter floated through the theater again. Luca went straight into their first simple illusion — an appetizer of sorts — holding up his hand which held two glittering coins, manipulating them in and out between each finger as deftly as he and Santi were manipulating their spectators.

"These silver pieces I'm holding are very, very old …"

And so it began. The four thousand spectators got their money's worth, soon to see why these particular magicians had earned their reputation for excellence. The settings, costumes and sound production were just window dressing for the superbly presented illusions. In a blink, Santi turned a dozen snow-colored doves into blood red roses. He handed them to Luca who jumped down from the stage, and with a bow and a silly leer, presented them to a lucky young woman sitting in the second row. As he hopped back up, the statues of Minerva that had seemed for sure to be made of plaster, sprang to life and changed places by leaping nimbly from column to column. A graceful white horse appeared from nowhere and disappeared again as soon as Joanie leapt on its back. Much to their audience's delight, every illusion, which started with the modest and became increasingly more complex, was interspersed with the banter, laughter, and charm of the Miceli brothers.

The twins made their work look easy, when it was anything but. Even so, only once did Luca have to intervene to rectify an error made by Joanie. Usually as adept on stage as they were, she was even more distracted now than she had been before the show. She backed into a Roman urn that concealed one of the stage lights, nearly knocking it over. Discreetly, Luca waved a hand to halt the tottering vessel. Luca saw Santi's jaw tighten, but couldn't tell if his brother's disapproval was aimed at him and his magicks, or at poor Joanie.

The rest of the illusions went smoothly — every one unique and just as masterful as anything Luca's sorcery could conjure up. He and Santi performed for a solid hour and a half under the hot lights, not for one second giving away any physical discomfort, the nerve-wracking aspects of pacing, or the discord that still hummed between them. Discord that had apparently transmitted itself to their assistant.

But the closer they drew to the finale, their new grand illusion, the more apprehensive Luca became. Not only could the tension they were all feeling trigger clumsiness as it had in Joanie earlier, but it could make this illusion even more dangerous than it already was. Though they'd practiced to exhaustion, Luca was still worried. He knew that it *should* work, and that Santi was more than capable of pulling it off. Santi had insisted that he be the one to debut it. As demonstrated by his conniption earlier, Luca knew that his brother needed to prove he could accomplish this without Luca's sorcery. These were all good reasons he should step back and let Santi have his moment. Yet all he could think was how devastated he'd be if anything happened. While visually stupendous, 'The Fires of Pompeii' was a feat that could be deadly for the magician who performed it.

The change in the music began with the pulsing tempo of a single kick drum, and everyone in the arena knew that something special was about to happen. A bongo came in, then another and another, their beats both elemental and ominous.

The Minervas moved again. Surging down from the columns on silken red cords, they flexed, reeled and undulated until they reached the ground. To the sound of the drums they moved in time, sensuously, sashaying offstage in twos. The drums boomed faster, louder, continuing to tantalize, as the electronic portico and forum moved soundlessly upstage right and back, out of the way. From stage right and stage left, the six Minervas glided back in, each acrobat now balancing a seven-foot high, unlit gas torch which they placed in holders already affixed to center stage. Out the women twirled a second time, and back in again with six more torches, and then out once more, until eighteen torches were positioned, three by six in a square, at center stage. With a crash of cymbals, the torches lit. Flames from their tips shot up three feet high, and Luca felt the sweat trail down his back.

Though he promised he wouldn't, he couldn't help himself. Covering his mike, he whispered, "Santi, are you sure? Please let me go first."

It never occurred to him that he was being controlling. Since their parents' deaths, when he spent months afterward waking up to screams coming from the next bed, he'd sworn he'd never leave his brother alone and unprotected again. For more than twenty years, he'd retained that vigilant concern.

It was no real wonder that Santi had had enough of it. Mouth set firm, he didn't even spare Luca a glance.

A violin and an electric guitar came in with spellbinding chords, as a long cloth harness that looked like an elongated straight jacket was slowly lowered by pulleys from the ceiling, to dangle downstage center. Joanie was already in place beside it, looking just as overstrung as Luca felt. Santi positioned himself in front of her, facing the audience. Joanie faltered before she held up a pair of handcuffs so the crowd could see them. Her eyes caressed her lover as he, appearing stoic and calm, put his arms behind his back. With a perceptible shudder, she locked his wrists together. It all came across to the audience as theatrical. No one apart from the three main players could know that the emotions were genuine.

The music continued to thrum. Now it was Luca's turn. With one last look at his brother, he walked forward onto the apron of the stage and addressed the crowd:

"Imagine. Imagine hanging upside down above these torches, your face and body completely covered, your arms locked together behind your back. Imagine dangling ten stories above this stage."

The words he'd memorized made knots of his guts as he said them out loud. The lights, the heat from the fires burning behind him, and his own nerves had more moisture running down his spine and glistening on the sides of his face.

"Imagine that you have less than three minutes to escape before the flames reach you, burn through your ropes and plummet you, on fire, to the ground."

Willing himself to trust in his brother's skill, he kept his gaze fixed on the audience as they, not he, could see behind him to where Joanie covered Santi's face and head with a dark hood, positioned his arms and ankles into the hanging harness, checked that his bonds were secure, and then stepped back to exit the stage. Somehow Luca's eyes locked onto the girl in the second row who still held the flowers he'd given her earlier in the show. She stared back at him. In her lap, the red roses shook, and a few petals fell, like drops of blood, to the floor. When he realized that the poor girl was looking truly petrified, he broke off eye contact.

Turning slightly, his face like waxed marble now, he extended his hand to where Santi was suspended, covered and tied. Though his throat felt parched, he willed his voice to come through, clear and unwavering, over his lapel mike. "Ladies and gentlemen, I present to you — Santino Miceli and 'The Fires of Pompeii!'"

Drums pounded. Guitars wailed. The audience clapped and cheered their encouragement as Santi was raised feet first on the pulleys, to hang high above the stage floor. The music reached a crescendo as he was swung into position over the torches, and Luca hurried off stage to watch from the wings.

Joanie was waiting for him there, in tears. She grabbed his arm and pulled at him, dragging his focused attention away from Santi. "You have to come with me. I need to talk to you, Luca. It's very important."

"*Now?*" Luca asked. "Are you for real?"

"Yes, now. I need to talk to you," she insisted before he could complete his protest, "in my dressing room. Please."

Cynthia and Raul watched the stage, enraptured, unaware that Sarita was shivering. Thorns pricked her fingers as she clutched the roses in an effort to stop her tremors. When they lit the torches, she understood. The sights and sounds of the auditorium receded as her old vision replayed itself in her mind.

Two little boys. Not one, as she'd always assumed. Twins. Luciano and Santino Miceli.

Though her gaze remained pinned to the action in front of her, the flames she saw were not from the torches burning precariously close to the grown Santino now hanging from the rafters. No, the only fire she could see in front of her was the fire from her old nightmare.

This time the nightmare had sound. This time she could hear gunshots. This time she could hear those little boys as they screamed for each other: *Luca! Luca! Santi! Santi!*

"Santi! No, Santi, *No!*"

The fire roared and flamed, hotter and higher. Someone patted her shoulder briskly, repeatedly. "Sarita, get up! Get up!"

It was Raul. Still in a daze, she looked up at him. His face showed his horror, but he kept his voice calm. "Quickly, dear, quickly — they are evacuating the auditorium. We must leave."

She dropped the roses as he gently pulled her up out of their row and into the aisle. Stumbling to her feet, she looked around and saw ushers and security guards guiding people toward the exit doors. The quiet was uncanny. Just up ahead, she saw her mother looking back at them. Having been propelled into the crowd, Cynthia waited, white-faced, for them to catch up. And right next to Cynthia was the woman Sarita had seen in the ladies' lounge. The woman stood frozen in the aisle, tears running down her face, her eyes focused on something behind Sarita and Raul, as people staggered past her, or right through her.

Swiveling her head to look back at the stage as Raul kept his arm firmly about her waist, Sarita then saw what the woman saw, what everyone else had seen as she'd sat in a trance: sprinklers still going like mad, torches and scenery blackened and wet, paramedics and firefighters crawling all over the stage, and Luciano Miceli on his knees, being held back by stagehands, his hair and tuxedo drenched, as for not the first time in his life, he sobbed out his brother's name.

CHAPTER TWO

Nine months later...

Monday, June 30, 2014, The Secret Spice Café on the RMS Queen Mary, Long Beach

Rohini went hunting for her husband and found him holed up in the scullery.

"Why are you hiding back here?"

"I am not hiding, Rohini. I am cutting up chickens." But he kept his face down, focused on the cutting board with deliberate precision. She knew something was amiss.

"Why not the kitchen?" Since the day of Naag's death, the scullery had become their least favorite place to work. He looked stern as he continued to chop. "Hey." Coming up next to him, she poked him in the side. "What's going on with you, my love?"

Cristiano said nothing as he separated the chicken parts into piles — wings, legs, breasts — and then deftly began filleting the breasts. When he could stall no longer, he tilted his head back toward the kitchen. "Angela is in there with Vincenzo and Douglas."

Ah. Now she knew what the problem was. "Oh, for heaven's sake, Cristiano. How long do you intend to avoid her?"

"No, no, no, I am not avoiding her. I just wanted to be alone so I could ... think, Rohini. That's all."

She crossed her arms against her chest. "You're thinking?"

"Yes, dammit." His face was flaming and he still wouldn't look at her. "I am thinking."

Her smile was mischievous. "About what, exactly?"

He slapped the carving knife down and turned to her. "If you must know, I am thinking about retiring."

Now her eyebrows winged up in disbelief. "Oh, my. That's something I never expected to hear from you." She studied his face. "Are you feeling all right?"

"I'm fine. I'm fine," he assured her as she stared up at him. He thought about how to propose what was on his mind. "It's just that … I'm sixty years old, Rohini. In my family, we don't live very long."

"Stop that." She wrapped her arms around him and held on fiercely. "Don't *say* that."

"You know it's the truth." Tenderly, he kissed the tip of her nose, not wanting to touch her with hands that he'd been using to cut chicken. "Just listen to me, please? You've never been anywhere but here and India —"

"I love it here," she put in quickly. "I love our work here."

"Yes, and so do I. But we've been doing it day in, day out — the same kitchen, the same routine. Are there no other places in the world you'd like to see?" His eyes were soft. "You mentioned Italy to me once. You said that Angela had described Rome, and you thought it sounded romantic. I was wondering …" He stopped, annoyed with himself for feeling foolish. When he spoke again, it struck Rohini that he sounded endearingly shy. "I mean, I know at our age this is probably silly, but we never had a honeymoon. I thought that maybe we could go."

The look on her face told him everything. Italy. Oh, how she would love it. And going with him would be divine.

Even so, she felt compelled to make a case for staying put. She would hate for him to have any more regrets after all he'd lost and all he'd been through. "Cristiano, all you've ever wanted was to be a chef, and you lost it for so long." She gestured around them. "We've put so much of ourselves into this. We work hard, true, but ten years of doing something you love — we both love — is that enough time for you? Are you sure you're ready to give it up?"

He suspected that would be her argument, so he presented a counterpoint. "It doesn't have to be all or nothing, *mi amor*. We can still be here part time if we wish. We can afford to hire an additional chef to help, like Angela did —"

"Hah. *You* work with another chef? I'll believe that when I see it."

"I can work with another chef. I can," he insisted, as she eyed him dubiously. "Besides, it's not just for the time off. It's important that we do this. We should get away from here for a while. For Sarita's sake."

"Oh." Gravely, she looked at him. "So you've noticed. She thinks she's hiding it. She does that for Cynthia. For all of us."

"Certainly I've noticed." He turned back to his cutting board. "What do you take me for?" With indignation, he began carving again.

Facing his back, Rohini sat in one of the metal chairs with a long sigh.

Cristiano shook his head. "Not even twenty-six years old, dammit." He waved his knife in the air. "It's worse than it was, not better. I'd hoped that when she came back from her birthday trip, she'd be more relaxed, venture out more."

He didn't see his wife nod sadly in accord from behind him. "Well, in all fairness, that trip turned out to be a terrible experience." Her eyes closed on the thought and she shuddered. "To have seen that, to have to stand by, and not be able to stop it. And the other twin. Good heavens. I feel most sorry for him. His whole family — gone."

Cristiano gave her an eloquent look. Words of shared loss passed between them without a sound. Rohini got up and put her arms around him again.

"All the more reason to live a little." Hands still not free, he kissed her cheek this time. "I've got to finish this now. We'll talk more about this tonight."

From the kitchen they heard Angela's raised voice. Cristiano colored up again.

Rohini's smirk was gleeful as she read his expression. "I can't believe you're reacting like this. You — the first male feminist in my life. I thought for sure you'd say that she should be able to do whatever she wishes."

"I suppose she should." But he was unable to fathom why she would wish to do this particular thing. And what was he to say to her when he saw her, when she knew that *he* knew why she'd been gone for two weeks? The reason was evident to everyone. He'd heard some of the cleaning crew gossiping about it earlier until Inez scolded them.

Looking down at his wife, he admitted to himself that he'd hate it if she changed one thing about her body. It was perfect just as it was. She was still the most beautiful woman in the world to him and always would be, although she'd probably never truly believe that. *Dios.* What advertisers did to the female self-esteem was criminal.

Seeing his frown, Rohini poked him again. "You're going to have to face her sooner or later. And when you do, try to be supportive, please. We all hoped that one day she'd spread her wings, and she's doing so, at long last."

He sent her a sardonic look. "Rohini, I'm a chef. I know what wings are." Picking up two chicken breasts from his work station, he held them up to her. "These are not wings."

———•

Sarita looked forward to Mondays when The Secret Spice Café was closed. Although there was still work to do on a Monday to ensure that their award-winning restaurant ran smoothly, after all these years, it was second nature to them all. Rohini and Cristiano had been their head chefs, with Angela in charge of their scrumptious desserts, since they'd opened. All three chefs shared the trips to the market and the ordering of foodstuffs. Sarita handled the office work and was also dinner hostess, assuming both roles ever since Jane and Cynthia had moved on. An early riser and timely with her chores ever since she was a child, it usually took her only until mid-morning to settle accounts and make sure that all the bookkeeping was in order.

Once her responsibilities had been seen to, she could spend the rest of her day doing what she loved most: reading. Reading stimulated her intelligent mind, just as her online college courses had. Reading kept boredom at bay, and brought faraway realms to her, in the safe haven of her cabin aboard a ship that traveled no longer. Above all, reading did a better job than her medications could of quieting her devils for a time.

Jane had sent her an e-reader for her last birthday, and it was convenient and practical to have so many books at her fingertips with just the press of a button. Still, she loved the tactile feel, and even the smell, of a book's pages. She'd preferred using an actual pencil to underline salient bits of prose or thought-provoking facts. She loved to flip through again when she'd finished, and savor those parts a second time. Though she read whatever struck her fancy, history still remained her favorite.

She was a sophomore in high school when her mother bought a percentage of The Secret Spice and she'd become bewitched by the *Queen Mary*'s background story almost before they'd unpacked. Especially when she'd ascertained that there were nearly as many dead people aboard as there were alive. Though her eagerness to recite particulars about the ship at the merest excuse had exasperated those closest to her, they'd been proud of her when her knowledge had helped solve not one, but two tragic murders that had taken place on the *Mary* years before.

A decade later, her interest still hadn't waned. Today, while the warm weather beckoned so many to the outdoors, and the sea breeze coming in from the open portholes in her stateroom teased at her nose, she was rereading the biography of the English queen for whom the ship had been named. This time, she was searching for clues as to whether the spirit who haunted the galley of their restaurant was just one of the anonymous many who'd remained behind after their deaths, or was, as Rohini alleged, Mary of Teck herself.

Victoria Mary Augusta Louise Olga Pauline Claudine Agnes, informally known as 'May' after her birth month, was successively the Duchess of York, the Duchess of Cornwall, and the Princess of Wales before she became Queen consort of the United Kingdom and the British Dominions, Empress of India, and the wife of King-Emperor George V. Although a princess of Teck from the Kingdom of Württemberg in Germany, she was born and raised in England.

As Sarita read on, thoroughly engrossed in the queen's life story once again, it struck her that for someone who'd been born into so much, who'd had power and wealth, May's existence seemed somewhat pitiable.

She'd lost three sons to an early death, and one to estrangement. Edward had ascended to the throne as King of England, only to abdicate the same year so that he could marry the woman he loved, the twice-divorced American socialite, Wallis Simpson. It was a choice his mother didn't support, one for which she swore she'd never forgive him, and their rift lasted until her death.

To Sarita, it was poignant how, in his memoirs, Edward had written so affectionately of his early years with his mother. "Her soft voice, her cultivated mind … were all inseparable ingredients of the happiness associated with a child's day …"

But then later, after she'd died, he condemned her vehemently in a private letter to his wife — the woman she'd abhorred. "My sadness is mixed with incredulity that any mother could have been so hard and cruel towards her eldest son for so many years, without relenting a scrap. I'm afraid the fluids in her veins have always been as icy cold as they are now in death."

Had Mary ever lamented her hardheartedness? Sarita wondered. If so, was that the reason her spirit had stayed behind — if indeed it had — to become part of the ship that was her namesake?

And all the ghosts that tread the ship, tread the planet — had they all remained earthbound because of a crushing regret?

Would she be one of them someday?

That thought made her restless. She closed the book. Maybe she'd go for walk instead.

Carrying herself like a queen aboard the *Queen*, Sarita walked along the teakwood decks that were once smooth as her own skin, but had now grown weathered. The day was as marvelous as any summer day by the ocean in southern California will be, and she raised her head toward the sun, basking in its warmth. More than a few tourists turned to watch her, some with envy, some with admiration, and some with an almost suspicious curiosity at the 'otherness' of her looks, lovely as they were.

Sarita's beauty had been bequeathed to her by her Brazilian mother and her Creole grandmother. She was uncommonly tall, her breasts and hips full, her legs long and shapely. Mocha brown hair, shot through with gold, spilled thick and naturally curly over her shoulders and was a perfect foil for the doe-like eyes framed by thick, dark brows and long lashes. The rest of her face was nothing short of a miracle. Plump, un-painted lips, sculpted nose and cheekbones, and velvety skin the shade of which told a story of ancient races coming together over centuries.

Sarita knew the reason strangers stared, and she hated it. None whose eyes followed her would have ever guessed the terrible estrangement she felt. While they saw her shell, she saw their lives. They were couples sightseeing with children, best friends on an outing, lovers away for a long, romantic weekend. So many people with human connections she'd never permit herself to have.

Gentle wind wafted along the Sun Deck, ruffling the waves of the ocean, the waves of her hair, as she stopped against the rail to watch the gulls flying over the water. A detail she'd once heard about them came back to her, and she smiled wistfully at the thought: Seagulls are monogamous creatures that mate for life.

But it wasn't just the tourists who watched Sarita. The spirit of the ship watched her as well, with a heart anchored by the writing on the wall:

I've been captive here, in this one spot, for so long. Look at me, Sarita — take a closer look. I'm fading away, bit by stealthy bit. And you? How much longer can you bear to stay before you start to fade away too?

The ship knew that no matter what the girl's answer to her question might be, nor how many years she'd managed to keep herself sequestered thus far, she couldn't hide from what was coming aboard to find her.

———●

"Oh, my God. What have you done to yourself?"

Just back from a visit to the east coast, Douglas and Vincenzo sat in the kitchen. Angela had invited them aboard to hear about their trip, and to have them taste-test her latest confection, Brandied Sour Cherry

Tartlets. But Vincenzo had left his plate untouched as he stared at his mother in disbelief.

In an attempt to keep the mood light, Angela straightened her back. "I'll give you two guesses, son."

Douglas dug into his treat, doing his best to be as unobtrusive as possible, but at his future mother-in-law's retort, he couldn't help but snort out a laugh.

Vincenzo turned his displeasure onto him. "You think this is funny?"

"I hadn't thought anything. Not a breast man myself."

Angela laughed at the one-liner. Vincenzo did not. Seeing that, Douglas sighed and put down his fork. "Come on, Vin. This is none of our business."

Angela slapped her thigh. "There you go! Thank you, Douglas. I appreciate that. Now tell me — is it too sour?"

"Not at all. The brandy gives it just enough sweetness. The crust is nice and light. It's a perfect summer dessert, Angela."

She smiled at him, ignoring her son. "And how was Florida? I bet your parents were happy to see you."

"They were. They miss us since we moved out here. They —"

"Excuse me." Vincenzo cut him off irritably, and turned back to Angela. "Ma, what came into your head? What made you do this? Can you tell me that, at least?"

Angela shrugged. "What can I say, Vincenzo? When I was a teenager, I asked God to make them grow. It was just one of many prayers that went unanswered. So I took matters into my own hands. 'God helps those who help themselves'."

"That's ridiculous." Vincenzo's current frame of mind was too censorious to be humored. "You're not a teenager anymore. You're *fifty-five*."

He didn't see Douglas roll his eyes, but Angela did. His commiseration was the one thing that prevented her from smashing a cherry tartlet over her only child's head. As an alternative to that, she tried another joke. "You're thirty-four, and you're wearing purple high tops. If you can do that, I can do this."

"That's an entirely different thing."

"Why?" she asked him. "Why are you the only one who's allowed to have any fun?"

"*Fun?* You had surgery, dammit. And you waited until we were away so I wouldn't find out about it until it was too late!"

"You don't have to shout, Vin," Douglas tried, although he knew he was wasting his breath. Not if their hair were on fire would anyone in *his* family even think of shouting. But people yelling at each other was just one of the things he'd learned to get used to being in a relationship with an Italian. Particularly if that Italian had a mother who'd finally found her own feet after years of being trod upon.

Mouth compressed, Angela whisked away Vincenzo's plate and dumped it into one of the sinks with a crash, untouched pasty and all. "Boy, oh, boy — if this isn't ironic, I don't know what is. You're turning into your father, do you know that?"

Vincenzo stood up, his fists clenched at his sides. "Don't say that to me. That's not nice."

"You're not kidding it isn't." Hands on her hips, she spun around to face him, trying to sound more resolute than she felt. "You know, kiddo, I love you like crazy, but I don't need your approval to do the things I want to do."

"What — things like *this?*" he shot back. "You're like a different person."

Angela thought if he could only get a glimpse of the look on his face, see the way he was standing over her — so rigid and disapproving — he'd know she was right. He was Marco all over again.

But Vincenzo went on, ticking items off his fingers, "First, you hook up with somebody who was only five years older than I am. Then, without saying a word about it ahead of time, you decide to hire someone to take your place here so you can take off on a one-month trip overseas."

"I don't get why that bothers you. Was I on a trip with a dozen men I met on Swinger Chat? I was with my brother and sister-in-law on their boat. What's the problem?"

"The problem is I don't even know you anymore. Look at —" he waved his arm at her bosom — "this!"

Though by now her cheeks had reddened, she threw up her hands in her own defense. "So, what? What's it to you? Why are you acting like this?"

"That's what I want to know, too."

Douglas's intervention startled both mother and son.

Vincenzo waited a beat. "You're kidding me. You agree with this? You'd want your mother to do something like this?"

Douglas's voice was calm, but he was taking note of Vincenzo's antagonistic body language, and didn't find it at all appealing. "If it made her happy, I guess I would, Vin. Either way, we don't get a vote."

"Oh. My. God. I don't believe this. I'm getting the hell out of here." He marched to the kitchen doors and pushed through them with force. They swung back and forth behind him.

Douglas and Angela exchanged a look. "I'd better go after him." He set his empty dish in the sink and kissed Angela on the forehead. "Stick to your guns. Don't worry. He'll get over it."

After he left, Angela took a few deep breaths. Oh, well. She supposed she deserved it. Vincenzo had forgiven her for taking so long to get used to his orientation when he first came out, so she'd give him the time he needed to get used to her new boobs. That was fair, wasn't it?

Bending to catch her reflection in the stainless steel top of her work table, she ran her hands over her new silhouette. She liked the way she looked. She felt desirable and pretty, and those feelings had been on short order throughout most of her adult life. It was her body, dammit. She'd given up the younger boyfriend because the relationship had made her son uncomfortable, but she had to draw the line somewhere. Douglas was right. If she wanted to have plastic surgery, it wasn't Vincenzo's call. And she saw no reason why he would get upset that she'd taken a trip. What was wrong with living a little? She squeezed her eyes shut and leaned back against her work station. She'd wasted too many years. The thought made her feel abruptly cold ...

Behind her, the cookware hanging from the ceiling hooks over Cristiano and Rohini's work station began to swing and clink together.

"Oh, don't you start too," she murmured.

The clinking elevated to a loud — a very loud — clanging and banging of pots.

"Geez, what's got you all worked up?" When she looked behind her to see, her breath caught in shock.

Standing in front of the cook station was a woman in black stretch pants, black ballet flats, and a white cashmere cardigan with tiny pearl buttons. Her smoky eyes were solemn as she looked back at Angela.

"Oh, my God. *Gina?*"

Angela was staring at — staring *through* — her long-dead cousin.

By the time Cristiano had gathered the courage to walk back into his own galley, Gina's ghost was gone, and Angela sat in a daze at her work station, drinking cooking brandy straight from the bottle.

"She's been dead for more than twenty years. She's buried in Holy Cross Cemetery in Brooklyn. That's like three thousand miles from here, for petessakes. What did she do — hitchhike?"

Angela was pacing so rapidly, Rohini and Cristiano felt like they had front row seats at Wimbledon.

"Even when it finally dawned on me that this place is haunted, I never for one minute imagined that my dead relatives would start showing up." She slapped her palms to her mouth. "Oh, my God — I just had a horrible thought: What if it's my husband next? Or, even worse, my mother?"

"But, Angela, when you came back from her son's funeral, you told us how much you loved Gina."

She looked at Rohini with distress. "Oh, I didn't mean to imply that I wasn't happy to see her." She grimaced. "Well, sort of. I mean … if she'd just dropped by to say hello, it might have been nice. But she was … distraught. I could barely make out what she was saying, she was talking so fast. Her voice sounded kind of distorted, and she kept repeating that she wasn't supposed to be here."

"Perhaps the reason she appeared to you is because she knows how you feel about her. You also said you could see right through her." Rohini was already formulating a theory. "But when you first saw Lee, you had no idea he was a spirit because he looked and sounded so —" she searched for the word — "corporal. Am I right?"

Angela resumed her pacing. "Yeah. He looked as alive as any of us."

"Just as Jackie looked when she appeared to Jane."

"What are you getting at, Ro?"

"Angela, will you sit down, please? You're making me dizzy. No, no, no — don't drink any more brandy. You'll give yourself a headache." Cristiano moved the bottle out of her reach. "Let me make you some peppermint tea."

Rohini shifted over so that he could reach behind her into the cupboard where she kept her spices and herbs. "I'm wondering if perhaps Lee and Jackie were able to appear as they did because they died here, on the ship. Their spirits were fully *here*. But as you say, your cousin died in New York. Perhaps that makes it more difficult for her to show herself in this location. You told us that she said she wasn't supposed to be here, and that the pots started banging together right before she appeared. That makes me wonder if —" she lowered her voice as she pointed above her head — "she didn't want her in the kitchen."

"You think if you whisper 'she' can't hear you?" Cristiano put in wryly as he handed Angela a cup of steaming tea. "She hears everything." He glared at the walls.

Angela breathed in the soothing scent of mint. "So what are you saying — the deceased have protocols they have to follow? They get a handbook, maybe, like in *Beetlejuice?*"

Rohini looked at her blankly. "I beg your pardon?"

"It's a reference to an eighties film," Cristiano clarified. "It probably wasn't very popular in India." He turned back to Angela. "What exactly did your cousin say?"

She cradled the warm cup between her hands. "She said it's urgent that I contact her son. Her surviving son, I mean." Under the circumstances, that clarification was necessary. Her shoulders slumped. "Neither of you is going to like this part. She ... wants him to work with us."

"With us?" Cristiano frowned. "What do you mean?" Interpreting Angela's silent entreaty, his eyes narrowed. "You mean here, in the restaurant? How is that possible? No, no, no. You couldn't have heard her correctly."

"I know what I heard, Cris." Inwardly, she braced herself. Even before she opened her mouth she knew he was going to fight her on this.

Who could blame him? What she was proposing was ridiculous, and they all knew it.

"I think it's a wonderful idea." Rohini didn't know what made her say that, but as soon as Angela put forth the proposal, something about it sounded … right. Then she noticed her husband gawking at her.

"How is this a wonderful idea, Rohini? It's preposterous, is what it is. He's a magician, not a cook."

She smiled slyly. "Oh, is that so? Well, dear husband, the last review you insisted I read about you said your cooking was 'sorcery.' So what's the difference?"

Before he could respond to that little jibe, Angela held her palm up. "Hold it a minute, you two. Let's not get off track."

She moved her mug of tea aside, and leaned in. "Cris, it's not as nuts as it sounds. First of all, the men in my family cook. We're Italian. That's what we do. But even if you're not comfortable with having him work as a line chef, he can work with me. I can teach him my dessert recipes, and if he wants to learn, he will, believe me. Ever since he was a kid, when he put his mind to something, no matter what it was, he excelled at it. He was always so laid back, we could never understand how he managed it. But he did."

She thought back to her days in New York, the twins at their grandparents', after Gina and Rocco were gone. "It used to make his brother crazy," she added, her tone forlorn.

"What possible reason could he have to want to work here?" Cristiano demanded, doing his best to ignore that both women's eyes had gone misty at the thought of Santino. Tears always made him lose his balance, especially his wife's tears, and it was clear that for this argument he'd need to stay on his toes. "He's a performer. A successful, wealthy, famous performer." He emphasized each word. "*Not* a cook. It makes no sense," he reiterated, glowering at both of them.

"I don't know why he'd want to, or even if he will." Though it was hard for her, Angela stood firm. "But I have one very solid argument in favor of asking him, at least, Cris. His dead mother found a way to appear to me here, from her grave all the way across the country, and begged me to do so."

Rohini sent Cristiano a contrite look. "That's understandable." Her voice sounded small when she added, "At least, to me, it is."

He was sure they were joking. The idea was farcical. "Have neither of you thought about how Sarita is going to feel?"

Angela lowered her gaze. "I don't believe it's any of her concern." When she looked up again, both Rohini and Cristiano could see her determination. "When Jane and Cynthia were running the office, you were the one who told me they had no business interfering with my decisions as pastry chef, Cris. And that the three of us —" she motioned to encompass them and tapped her finger on the work table — "should maintain the kitchen separately from the dining room. I think that still holds true now that Sarita is in charge, don't you?"

Hastily, Cristiano waved that issue aside. "That's not what I'm referring to, Angela. Have you forgotten that Sarita was there? Raul said she was so overcome, he had to pull her out of her seat. What if seeing Luca here upsets her?"

The entire time Angela had been debating with Cristiano, Rohini's intuition was humming. There was … something. Something Angela didn't want him to know.

With one eye still on Angela, Rohini lightly touched her husband's arm. "But Cristiano, maybe this would be a good thing for her. Weren't we saying this morning that we have to stop protecting Sarita so much? That she needs to stop hiding?"

He felt trapped. And surprised that his wife would use his own words against him. "I did say that, yes. But that doesn't mean we should forget her traumas. This one, or … the previous."

"I'm sorry, Cris, but Luca was traumatized too." Angela was not backing down. Now that she'd recovered from her cousin's unexpected visit, she understood how desperate Gina must have been to attempt it. Firmly, she voiced that thought out loud. "For his mother to appear to me, he's in some kind of trouble. I love Sarita just as much as you and Rohini do. But this is my family."

Cristiano found it hard to digest that his wishes were being superseded. When he'd first signed on as head chef, Jane and Cynthia were still here, and together they'd been as obstinate as two donkeys facing off on a narrow mountain road. He became used to being bossed about and having his opinions on any number of matters concerning the running of the restaurant marginalized. But in the kitchen, things had always been different. Apart from the occasional casserole pot sent flying in his direction by an invisible She-devil, he reigned supreme as galley king. Angela and Rohini never questioned his opinions on anything to do with food or its preparation. This was a first.

Though his wife was looking at him with sympathy, her body language told him everything. She was leaning toward Angela in solidarity. He observed the latter's set jaw, and it occurred to him that she'd changed more about herself than just her physique.

"Fine." His hands went up in surrender. "I'm outvoted." He pulled out his car keys. He had a long list of errands that he should have started on an hour ago. "No one understands the obligations of family better than I. Even so, my stomach is telling me this is going to be trouble." Face stiff, his black eyes encompassed them both as he stood up and pointed to them each. "You and you. If anything happens, this was your idea. You will be the ones responsible." And with that admonition, he strode out.

Rohini watched until he was out of sight and then turned to eyeball Angela. "All right — what's going on? I've never seen you hold your ground against him like that. There's more to what your cousin said that you didn't want to say in front of him, isn't there?"

Angela rubbed her left temple. It had been years since she'd had one of her tension migraines, but between the argument with Vincenzo and now this, she needed to get out of this kitchen and go lie down in her cabin for a while, or she'd have a whopper before the day was out. But the avid look in Rohini's eye was a definite indication that she would not be put off.

Angela didn't want to worry anyone, so she'd planned on keeping Gina's warning to herself. But all Gina had managed to get out before she started to disappear was that there was a danger coming, and Luca needed to be here. It was cryptic. As for Luca, Angela wasn't sure how much he knew, either. Maybe it wasn't a bad idea to tell Rohini. She'd always had an 'in' with the spirit world. And she could be trusted to keep a secret, even from her own husband. Of that, Angela was sure.

"Yep." Her tone was grim. "You guessed it, Ro."

CHAPTER THREE

That same day, Nando Hotel, Las Vegas

The temperature outdoors was rising to what would be a ghastly hundred and ten degrees Fahrenheit. Inside the sumptuously-appointed penthouse, the air conditioning circulated cold air rank with the mingled odors of spoiled food, pricey booze, designer perfume and stale pot. The glass-walled living room was strewn with empty bottles. Any liquid left in them had leaked out hours before onto the expansive travertine tile flooring, or soaked into the fibers of the Persian carpets. Cut crystal glasses stained with lipstick and filled with wet cigarette butts, delicate china plates sticky with leftover chocolate mousse or dried-out caviar, made rings of crust on the marble dining table. More dishes were stacked high and unwashed in the kitchen sink, along with grimy piles of sterling silverware.

He lay sprawled on his back on one of the Italian leather sofas, his six-foot frame stretched from end to end. He was still wearing socks and trousers, but sometime during the night he'd taken off his shirt, exposing the muscled, yet too thin arms and chest. The party had started on Saturday night, and he'd collapsed onto the couch early Sunday morning, so hungover that he didn't even stir when the chambermaid opened the door to the suite, took one look, swore loudly, and then stomped back out again, slamming the door behind her.

A cloud shifted, and the light coming in from the panoramic windows above the Strip beamed straight at his closed eyes. He could sense it even in his stupor, and all at once he was dreaming again. Neither the pills nor the alcohol had thwarted that. His arms and legs twitched fitfully, and his breathing became uneven.

It was always about the fire. He would always feel it on his face. He would always smell his brother's cooked flesh —

"Wake up, Luca, dammit."

He jerked in his sleep, pulled himself out of the dream. Someone was leaning over him. Blearily, he opened his eyes.

Long, flaxen hair tumbled around a woman's face, a face that swam in and out of focus. Her perfumed cleavage was inches away from his nose. He recognized the scent as one he usually found pleasant, but right now, between his hangover and the remnants of the nightmare, it was making him want to hurl. Luckily for them both there was nothing whatsoever left in his stomach.

He cleared his parched throat, smacked his dry lips, and shifted to his less numb side.

She pushed on his arm. "Luca!"

He squinted up at her. "Desiree."

In spite of her name, her bottle-blonde hair, and her D-cup chest, Desiree was not a showgirl, but when he'd arrived in Vegas, he wondered if the look was a municipal ordinance. Whether they were cocktail waitresses, real estate flippers, or kindergarten teachers, women who lived in Vegas tended to look like Desiree. He'd even signed autographs for eighty-year-olds who were bleached blonde and stacked.

Desiree was Luca's accountant, and she was an excellent one. She was also the woman he was sleeping with, but if her look of revulsion was any indication, that arrangement was about to come to an end.

As he struggled to pull himself up, she moved to sit in one of the wingback chairs opposite. Staying horizontal for that long had kept the dizzy spell and the crushing, tumbling sensation at bay for hours. Sitting up had brought it on tenfold, and the blood rush made him feel as though he were falling into his own skin from the top of his head down. He sat, hands holding his head, elbows on his knees. She crossed her legs, made a "*tch*" sound of impatience. He looked up, fidgeting just a tad, as she stared at him stonily, tapped her fingers on the arm of her chair, swung one of those long legs back and forth, back and forth. The message was unambiguous. And the pendulum motion wasn't helping his nausea.

When she spoke, it was less climactic than she might have thought it would be. "I don't want to be with you anymore, Luca."

Bingo. He knew it was coming, and wished he could care. But there wasn't much he cared about these days. Still, he was a gentleman, and the protocols of a relationship required that he stand by for her postmortem. Reasonably alert now, he replied as was expected of him. "I'm very sorry to hear that, Desiree. May I ask why?"

Desiree didn't want to have this conversation. She'd seen Luca when his temper was riled, and though it had never been directed at her, she knew it would be when she said what had to be said. But she had a soft spot for him, and felt she had to try to save him from himself. Even so, she stalled, waving her arm at the chaos. "I think your cleaning lady might have quit. I caught her just as she was storming toward the elevator."

His breath tasted rancid after the long, drunken sleep and the two days without food. He rubbed his hand across his face, longing for his fatigue and apathy to be wiped away with the gesture. "I have a feeling this is going to take a while. I need coffee. Want some?"

He felt her eyes on him as he walked over to the sink, lifted out some of the soiled plates so he could fill the glass carafe with tap water. When he started spooning ground beans into the coffee maker, she said softly, "Luca. You need help."

Without looking at her, he laughed humorlessly. "Don't be ridiculous."

"It was fun for a while, going out with you, getting a buzz on now and then, but it stopped being fun when drinking was all you wanted to do. You're an alcoholic, you know." She leaned across the coffee table, picked out a nearly empty bottle of Valium she'd spotted amongst the soiled dishware. "And possibly an addict."

"Oh, for chrissakes." He flung the metal coffee scoop at the sink, hitting one of the plates. The fragile porcelain cracked. "Why should you give a shit?"

"Don't talk to me like that." Her tone was firm, but there was compassion in her eyes. He'd lost so much weight, but his handsome face looked bloated. He was so unhealthy, so unhappy. And there was not a damn thing she could do about it.

Catching her look, Luca swore again. The last thing he wanted was her pity. "Look, if you want to stop sleeping together, we'll stop sleeping together. But I don't need any lectures. It's not like we meant that much to each other, anyway."

"I loved you." That wasn't true, but she said it to make a point.

He called her on it, in as despicable a way as she'd ever heard from him. "C'mon, Dez, let's be honest here. You loved the photos of us in *People*. You loved the money I spent on you." His leer was offensive to them both. "I'm pretty sure you loved the sex. But me, in particular? Nah. Don't think so."

She stood up, the movement composed, but inside, she was trembling. "You're an arrogant, self-absorbed dick."

"Why, Dez," he scoffed, "Does that mean you don't 'love' me anymore?"

He could see how much his sarcasm hurt her, in spite of her effort to hide it. He knew she didn't deserve this, but what she'd said about him being an alcoholic had blindsided him. He didn't think of himself that way and it was reflex to strike back. Disgusted with himself, he put the carafe down and held up his hands. "I'm sorry. For everything I said — okay? You're right. I'm a dick."

Watching him root around for a clean cup in the filth he'd made of the beautiful kitchen, her face revealed her disenchantment. Less than a year before, he'd been so different. He'd always had a dark and brooding side, but mostly he'd been charismatic, appreciative of life. Now he was just another depressing example of Las Vegas overindulgence and prodigality. She did care about him, but sticking around to watch him slowly kill himself just wasn't her thing.

"I do hope you clean yourself up. It would be such a shame if you didn't. Good bye, Luca." She hitched her handbag over her shoulder and started toward the door.

"Wait a minute, Dez."

She turned.

"Uh ... I know it's tacky for me to ask, under the circumstances, but ... are you still doing the books for me?" He didn't care about the money — never had — but he wouldn't know where to start with the boatload of paperwork she handled for them.

Though Desiree should have been offended, being a practical woman, she was not. Even though Luca was no longer performing, what with all the other investments and holdings the twins had made together, Miceli Enterprises Inc. was one of her most lucrative accounts. And Luca also had her doing his personal taxes. All in all, a nice chunk of change.

She lifted her shoulder. "I have no problem with that, if you don't. But there's something you need to know." She hesitated. "I know you don't like hearing about Santi's estate."

His face went grim again, immediately. "You're right. I don't give a damn about it."

"I understand that." This time her attitude was more patient, more sympathetic, especially since they'd switched over to business. "But like it or not, apart from some charities and what he bequeathed to Joanie, he left the bulk to you. And you made me the executor. I would think that, considering how often you told me how hard he worked for it, you wouldn't want anybody stealing it from him." When all she got was a blank stare, she spelled it out. "There's money missing. That's what I came by to tell you."

"How much money?"

"Nearly two million that I've found so far."

His bloodshot eyes widened. "Of Santi's? That's a hell of a lot. How's that possible?"

"My suspicions are that a few vendors, knowing that Santi's ... gone, might have done something shady." Her chin hardened in resolve. "If so, I'll find out."

When he smiled at her, he meant it. "I'm sure you will." That was one thing he knew he could count on from her.

She said good bye again, and this time he didn't stop her. As much as he didn't want to admit it, he knew she was right to leave him. She had self-respect, for sure. He smirked bitterly. What was the meme he'd seen recently? 'A girlfriend would be nice, but right now, I'm in a serious relationship with alcohol and bad decisions.'

Speaking of, he stared at the coffee pot he'd just picked up again. Caffeine alone wouldn't do the trick if he intended to function at all for the day. With the dregs of the nightmare still eating at him and Desiree's declaration of his shortcomings, his head had started to throb. He needed a drink.

The carafe shattered with force in his hand, the water hitting his face and bare chest, drenching him with cold. He sucked in a breath, blinking rapidly as water streamed down into his eyes.

"Holy shit!" He looked down at the plastic handle, the only thing that remained in his grasp. "How in the hell …?"

Wiping his face on his forearm, he took a dustpan out from under the sink, and bent down to sweep up the wet pieces of glass.

He yelped when the door to the fancy subzero crashed open next. The fridge was stocked with nothing but limes, lemons, and beer. He watched, slack-jawed, as the beer bottles popped in syncopated rhythm, and a torrent of expensive, imported ale washed down from the refrigerator shelves to flood across the kitchen tile. He had to crouch low to the ground as a blur of yellow and green citrus shot toward him like cannon balls.

The refrigerator uprising ceased when there were no longer any rebels left. With caution, Luca bent forward to examine the fridge interior, his heart going like a jack hammer. One last, unbroken bottle exploded. He fell back, barely missed being gouged by flying glass.

"What the fucking *fuck?*"

Was this another nightmare? Was he having them while he was awake now? As few and far between as they were, he'd always embraced his visions, even when they heralded something dire. They were a part of who he was. But now, after months of sodden drunk, pills, despair, and lack of sleep, he could no longer make sense of anything. He couldn't distinguish visions from dreams, dreams from nightmares. He was flat on his ass on his kitchen floor, surrounded by lemons, limes, spilled beer and broken glass, and covered from head to chest with cold water.

Maybe he'd done this himself? In addition to his other symptoms, his powers were also out of whack.

While he was still trying to come to grips with what he'd just experienced, a magazine from the rack near the sofa came sailing across the room to slap him in the face and fall open next to him, down onto the wet tile. Face up, its front and back covers were soon soaked with beer.

He stared down at it, the headache that had been stalking him since he woke up building behind his eyes. Even in his befuddled state, he was getting a sense — no — he *knew* that whatever was in that magazine was going to shake up his life. And as pathetic as that life was at present, he didn't think he could survive another upheaval.

Warily, he picked it up. It was last month's *Via* travel magazine, a subscription that came automatically with the Triple A membership Santi had signed them up for. Luca never looked through any of the issues, and they'd just piled up for the past year with the rest of Santi's junk mail that Luca couldn't bear to discard.

Now, he squinted at the article on the open page, and saw that it featured photos of several recommended restaurants in Southern California. And one of them was ... Cousin Angela's restaurant?

Air conditioning and damp made him shiver as he read:

The Queen's Spicy Secret:
A Favorite Dining Spot On Board a Historic Ship

He studied the four people in the photo. It was captioned: *Owners Angela Perotta, Cristiano and Rohini de la Cueva, and Sarita Taylor stand outside The Secret Spice Café, housed aboard the Queen Mary in Long Beach, California.*

The last time he'd seen Angela was at Santi's funeral, where she'd been wan and weepy-eyed. She looked happy in the photo. He was glad. First cousin to his father, '*Cugina* Angela' was a very nice woman. She was older than he and Santi, so they'd been taught to call her 'Cousin Angela' as a show of respect.

He knew of but hadn't met the de la Cueva couple. But Sarita Taylor looked familiar.

As he peered at her image, he unconsciously touched the birthmark on his collarbone. The room began to tilt and swirl. He felt like he'd been shoved onto a roller coaster against his will. With a groan, he flopped back on the wet tile and closed his eyes.

A film reel started to roll behind his lids, one he vaguely remembered seeing before. Sarita Taylor, younger than she was in the magazine photo, was alone and crying, in some sort of a curved, wooden room that was lit dimly by candlelight. He hadn't seen her before then, hadn't known her name then, but he'd been there, with her. Not physically, but in his mind. It had been years ago, when dreams of beautiful damsels in distress had been pathetically common.

In the vision, he'd spoken to her, tried to reassure her. She'd been afraid of something … something important she needed to do. What was it that he'd said to her, while she stood there in the faint light, so tangled up and frightened? He couldn't recall. It was such a long time ago. It had just been a dream he'd forgotten. Until now.

When the reel changed, his heart wrenched. Now he saw her with her head being held back, her hair twisted painfully in a man's grip, a man who held a knife to her neck. Blood trickled down the skin of her throat, as she tried valiantly not to show her terror.

Luciano! She's in trouble. You have to go to her, Luca mia — you have to help her!

With an agonized shout, he jumped up, clutching his head. It crushed with pain. He thought it would explode from the pressure.

He knew that voice. He hadn't heard it since he was six years old, but he knew that voice. He could barely get her name out.

"Mama?" he whispered. "*Mama?*"

God help him. He couldn't this handle now. This couldn't be real. Desiree was right. He couldn't deny it anymore.

Straightening up, he held his arms out in front of him. They shook like he was palsy-stricken. Even so, he forced himself to concentrate on one of the broken bottles, imagined the pieces pulling back together, the bottle mended. For him, ordinarily, that's all it took — the desire to repair.

A few of the brown shards of glass wiggled, then went still.

There was his proof. His drinking was no longer recreational. But if this was another malicious gift sent to him by Johnny Walker Blue, maybe he should be thankful. Maybe that meant that all he'd just experienced wasn't an authentic vision. He'd so much prefer that. He'd take whatever neurological damage he might have caused himself over the possibility that his mother was calling to him from her grave.

No. He wouldn't believe it. Why would she come to him after all this time, about a girl who was a stranger to her, a girl he'd forgotten he'd had a vision about years ago?

Though his head was still fuzzy, he tried to reason it through. In the twenty-nine years of his life, he'd never been this messed up. He wasn't the average person. Who knew what kind of effect the crap he'd been putting into his system might have on someone like him? If that were the case, then all of what he'd just experienced was explainable.

He missed his brother so much, and his brother had died traumatically. Naturally, that would remind him of his mother. As for the girl, people had nightmares, saw weird things in their heads, all the time. Tomorrow, he'd go to a doctor … or somewhere … and start getting himself back on track. Plenty of drunks in Vegas. There had to be an AA meeting held somewhere nearby. He'd stop taking the Valium too. He'd stop everything, cold turkey. He'd be like Santi was — focused, determined. He'd beat this. Santi wouldn't have wanted him to fall apart like this, anyway. No matter that he'd felt cheated of the powers Luca had, Santi had loved him.

The image of Sarita with a knife to her neck was not as easily dismissed. Not even for — as Desiree had pointed out — an arrogant, self-absorbed dick like him.

He stood in silence a while longer. One more time, he whispered, "Mama?"

Nothing. No sounds other than the hum of the air conditioning.

His mother wasn't here. No one was here. He was alone. That was a relief to him, as cowardly as the feeling was.

At least the room had stopped spinning. But he still heard a buzzing. It was several seconds before he grasped that the sound was coming from his phone. He found it there on the coffee table, next to his bottle of pills. He picked it up and looked at the incoming number. Drained, shattered, he sank down on the carpet.

God help him.

Somehow, he managed to compose himself enough to tap the screen and speak.

"*Cugina* Angela. *Comu si?*"

CHAPTER FOUR

One month later ...
Monday, July 28, 2014, back at The Secret Spice

"A chocolate dessert is the ultimate indulgence. So it has to be worth the sin, you know? It has to smell rich. It has to taste decadent. It has to look luscious. It has to shout out: 'I am a celebration! You *must* have me.'"

Angela dumped a hill of sifted flour onto the work table and used her bare hands to circle a hole the size of her palm into the middle of the white. "So, for my Raspberry Chocolate Truffle Tarts, first off is the sweet pastry. If the pastry's not light and delicate, it doesn't matter how good the filling is." She held up her fingers and waggled them. "The trick to the perfect texture is how you use these."

Dumping butter, sugar, a single egg yolk, and a pinch of salt into the empty center of flour, she cautioned her rapt pupil, "The butter has to be softened, but never in a microwave. God forbid. The temperature of the fat won't be even if you cheat like that. Uneven temperatures make for a doughy crust, not a crust that melts in your mouth. Remember that, sweetie. You just let the butter sit outside the fridge until it becomes room temperature."

"But I did, just like you showed me, Angela, and the crust still didn't taste like yours."

Angela planted her flour-dusted hands on her hips. "And did you think that you'd be able to do in two tries what it took me years to get right? You have to be willing to practice over and over again if you want to be a great pastry chef."

"That's all I've wanted to be since the first time you let me bake cupcakes with you."

Angela chuckled at the heartfelt answer. "So, try it again, Marisol."

Marisol held her breath as, for the third time that afternoon, she put her fingertips into the flour and, as Angela had instructed, used 'a delicate touch' to pull it to the center and mix it with the other ingredients. Her look of intense concentration was so reminiscent of Cristiano's when he worked, that Angela had to smile. The kid could be great at this if she kept at it, but she was only fourteen. It was possible that this was just a passing fancy for her. Still, she never missed a chance to be in the kitchen on any Monday that Angela had the time to work with her, and her cheesecake was already pretty darn good. But cheesecake was easy-peasy in comparison to this. It was a good pastry crust that separated the men from the boys, which was why Angela had chosen the task — as a test to see if Marisol would persevere.

And the teen passed with flying colors. Putting her own fingers into the dough, Angela checked the consistency and nodded. "Much better. Next, we have to —"

"Marisol Luisa McKenna! What are you doing in this kitchen?"

At the angry exclamation, Angela looked up in surprise and Marisol with guilt. Inez had come in, holding a mop in one hand and pulling a wheeled bucket with the other. "How dare you disobey me? Did I or did I not tell you that you were punished?"

Marisol's look went from guilty to sullen. "Dad said I could."

"Oh, *Dad* said, did he? And did you tell Dad that I said that you had to stay in your room this afternoon?"

"No." Marisol lowered her eyes as she uttered the lie. She wasn't about to throw her beloved adoptive father under the bus.

But Inez was no fool. She knew her daughter's Machiavellian tactics by now. With saccharine sweetness, she asked, "No? Are you sure? Let's go ask him, why don't we?"

When Marisol just glared at her in mutinous silence, Inez slammed her mop back into the bucket, sloshing water onto the kitchen floor. She jabbed her gloved finger in her daughter's direction. "I knew it. *Malcriada!* Get back to your father's shop, and don't you dare move from there until I am finished here. We are going to have a family discussion about *this*."

After Marisol trudged out, Angela expelled the breath she'd been holding. "Oh, Inez. I'm sorry. I had no idea she wasn't supposed to be in here today."

"No, Angela, please — we both know this is not your fault. I appreciate that you take the time with her. At least, when she is with you, I know she is learning not only the baking, but some … some … self-discipline. Certainly she is not getting that lesson at home."

Angela winced as Inez bent down and, with erratic movements, used a rag to sop up the spilled water. She hated getting involved in friends' personal squabbles. But she'd become close to the McKenna family. When Marisol was four, she and Michael had saved Angela's life. She felt she had to say *something*. "You know he doesn't mean it. You know he loves you both —"

"*Si*, that's what everybody tells me." The wet rag was dropped back into the bucket with a splat. "My mother tells me. My friends tell me. Even Michael himself tells me." She looked up at Angela, her exasperation plain. "And in the meantime, he doesn't see that he's turning our daughter into a spoiled brat." She straightened up, and pulled off the wet cleaning gloves. "I thought it was sweet how he doted on her when she was little, because she never had that from a father. But it's enough now. He's overdoing it. I don't know my own child anymore. It's like a devil has got inside her and I don't know how to get it out."

"Oh, now. She's not that bad." Angela wiped her hands on her apron and put her arm around Inez's shoulder. "It's basically her job right now to break the rules. Boy, do I remember Vincenzo at that age." Her eyes were kind as she offered the only guidance she could. "If it were me, I'd talk to him. Tell him you feel undermined. He loves you. You can make him understand."

The doors from the dining room swung open, and Inez forgot her problems at the sight of the strikingly handsome young man who walked through. *¡Órale!* she thought. Who is this?

"Luca." Angela was relieved at his timing. A soggy crust, a crumbly crust, she knew how to fix. But family problems? Hardly.

Luca stopped short. He was picking up nuance. "Am I interrupting?"

"Not at all." Angela made the introductions proudly. "Luca, this is my good friend, Inez. She's in charge of the cleaning crew for the *Mary*."

"Nice to meet you, Inez." Luca dazzled her a second time with his smile. He ticked his index finger in the air. "You're Marisol's mother, right? I met her when I got in earlier."

As displeased as Inez was with her daughter at present, she had to chuckle, imagining Marisol's reaction when confronted with Luca. "You, as well. Angela told me that you were coming to help her for a while." She couldn't resist the postscript, "But she didn't mention how handsome you are."

Santi would have known how to respond to the remark in a way that would charm Inez. But not Luca. Offstage he was more introverted than people assumed. He never thought about his looks until a stranger mentioned them, something that happened too often for his comfort. As usual, he just gave a weak smile and clammed up.

Angela came to his rescue. "Have you finished unpacking?"

"I have. It's a beautiful stateroom. Are you sure cousins Tony and Jane won't mind?"

"Don't be silly, sweetie. You're family. Besides, they have no plans to come back for the foreseeable future. Our cabins were included in our leasing agreement, and that one's just been sitting empty."

Inez decided this was her cue to leave them to their business. "Well, I'm sure you both have a lot to discuss." She pushed the bucket and mop against the wall. "Angela, I'll send Alan over later to finish up in here." She frowned as her thoughts flew back to Marisol. "I have some things to deal with at home."

Angela was offering Inez a commiserating look, when the rest of what she'd said registered. "Alan? Is that the new guy?"

"*Si.*" Inez studied her friend. "Why? Is something wrong?"

"Uh ... no. Not really." Angela dithered. "He's just kind of ... off-putting." And wasn't that an understatement? she thought to herself.

Inez locked her fingers together in old nervous habit. When she'd first met the four owners of The Secret Spice, she was a chambermaid for the ship. Though the women had encouraged her friendship, it had taken some time to get used to thinking of them as peers. But she'd been head of Housekeeping for the past seven years, and was damn good at it. Even so, her old insecurities surfaced every once in a while, and this was one of those times.

"I'd hate to let him go just because of that. He's one of my best workers." Her tone was more defensive than she'd intended and Angela picked up on it.

"I wasn't questioning your choice in hiring him, Inez." She did her best to sound reassuring. "I was just pointing out that his ways are ... shall we say ... odd."

Inez knew that what was going on with Marisol was affecting her attitude. She told herself not to take Angela's comments personally. "He is unusual, there is no doubt. But he is a veteran. Maybe he has some stress issue?"

Luca shifted uncomfortably. He'd agreed to work with Angela, so he supposed he'd have to get used to being privy to conversations like these. He slanted her a glance, wondering if Inez's disclosure about whoever this employee was had brought his father to mind.

From her glance back at him, he saw that it had. "PTSD, huh? Yep. That certainly could be his problem."

After Inez left, there was an awkward silence between them as they each speculated over how much the other knew about the true reason he was here, and whether or not the topic should be brought up. Finally, Angela relied on the Italian standby. "You must be starving."

"I had something on the flight." That wasn't true. He hadn't taken a plane to get there, but he wasn't about to tell her that.

"You ate airplane food?" He might as well have confessed to eating live slugs. "Oh, my God. Don't tell that to Cris when you meet him. It could give him a heart attack."

It was as if she'd conjured up their chef with the mention. She and Luca turned when they heard the back door slam and Cristiano's voice come booming through from the scullery. "I don't care, *senor!* That is not an excuse!"

Rohini trailed into the kitchen, carrying grocery bags and looking worn out. She dumped everything on the cook station. "Oh, my. What a morning."

"Who's he hollering at in there?" Angela asked by way of greeting.

Rohini heaved a sigh. "We had an oil change on the delivery truck, and as we were driving back from the market, suddenly there was a burning smell." She raised her eyes to the heavens as they heard Cristiano switch from infuriated English to even more incensed Spanish. "Apparently they forgot to tighten something and the oil was leaking out."

"Oh, my God, Ro. Is the engine damaged?"

"We'll know soon enough, I suppose." Wearily, she smiled at Luca. "What an introduction to your new colleagues, yes?" She went to him and took his hand. "I'm Rohini." Tilting her head in the direction of the scullery, she added with some discomfort, "The man screaming his head off in the other room is my husband, Cristiano, as I'm sure you've surmised."

Luca smiled down at her and covered her hand with his own. She seemed pleased to meet him.

Cristiano was not going to be nearly as welcoming as his wife. He strode into the kitchen emanating outrage, with barely a glance Luca's way. "*Ay Dios mío.* If we ran this place the way that *imbécil* runs his repair shop, we would be out of business in a week." He pulled open the fridge and poured himself some cold water.

"Cristiano," Rohini chided gently, "You didn't say hello to Luca."

Eyeing Luca over his glass, Cristiano nodded curtly. "Hello." To the room at large he announced, "I still have to bring in the rest of the groceries. Let's hope nothing got spoiled between this damn heat and all the delay."

"Want a hand?" If Luca was taken aback by the brusqueness, he didn't let it show, putting it down to agitation over what might be a seized engine.

Cristiano would have refused the offer of help, but he caught his wife's pointed look, and with a terse shrug, he said instead, "Why not? Follow me."

After the men went out the back, Angela sent Rohini a worried glance. "Hoo, boy. This is going to be tougher than I thought."

"Tell me about it. That oil leak was the topping on the cake. He's been unbearable all morning, knowing today was the day his 'nemesis' would arrive. I love him dearly, but honestly, when it comes to his work, he can be so persnickety."

Angela snorted. "Persnickety. That's one way to describe him, I guess."

Rohini began unpacking bags. "Have you mentioned anything to Luca yet about Gina?"

"No. Ghosts are business as usual around here, but I have no idea what his beliefs are, or if she contacted him." Angela went over to her own station to clean up what was left after Marisol's expulsion. "Call me a worrywart, but I'm concerned that if I tell the kid I saw his dead mother in my kitchen, he might go to Vincenzo and convince him that I need to be put in a home. With the way my son's been acting lately, he might jump at the chance."

She dumped the old flour and used non-toxic cleaner on the work surface. "I thought I'd feel Luca out first, see how much he knows, if anything. It's entirely possible he accepted my job offer solely because he's at loose ends since —" she lowered her voice as if Luca could hear her from outside where the truck was parked — "his brother's accident."

"Hmm. Perhaps. Perhaps he's here solely to take his mind off painful memories." But Rohini was not convinced of that. She'd sensed something about Luca just as she had when she'd first met Sarita.

They could hear Sarita in the dining room, talking with the woman who delivered their linens.

"Thanks again, Kristine. The soiled ones are in the bag behind the bar. Just stack the fresh ones on one of the tables. We'll see you next week."

It sounded like she was right outside the kitchen doors. Rohini shot a look at Angela, who put a finger to her lips. They hurried back to their tasks, conspicuously industrious when Sarita came in.

"Well, there you are! And where've you been all morning?" Angela's cheeriness was so over the top, Sarita literally took a step back.

"Uh, it's Monday, remember? I was in my office doing paperwork. Where else?"

"Well, ready to take a break? How about some lunch, huh?"

"Angela, why are you talking like that? You sound like you're about to sell me a used car."

With a delicate sound of impatience, Rohini turned to Sarita. "This is her way of telling you that Luca has arrived."

"I see. Well, don't worry, I assumed that, since you said he'd be flying in this morning." Sarita picked up a fresh tart from the cooling rack and bit into it. "Mmm. God, these are sinful. They taste amazing even without the raspberries on them. Don't tell me Marisol made them?"

"Not yet, but we're getting there. If her mother doesn't ship her off to boarding school in Siberia first. I'm a little worried about that kid, to be honest. She and Inez had another one of their arguments, and Inez banished her from the kitchen."

As Angela filled them in, both she and Rohini kept their attention on Sarita, wondering whether she was feeling as calm about Luca's arrival as she appeared.

Far from it. Knowing she'd be face to face with the boy and the man whose tragedies she'd witnessed in both nightmare and reality, it had taken all the courage Sarita could muster to wander casually into the kitchen as she normally would at lunchtime. Now that she'd managed that, she wanted to get this first meeting over with as quickly as possible.

So, where was he?

As though she'd pulled the question from Sarita's mind, Rohini motioned toward the back. "Luca's out at the truck with Cristiano, helping him bring in supplies. We had some car trouble this morning and got back late."

Still eating, Sarita nodded. Doing her best to sound relaxed, she changed the subject. "He's not our only new person, is he? I met Alan today. At sixty-thirty, he was already in my office, cleaning. I wasn't expecting anybody in there so early. I opened the door and actually yelped." She looked pained. "I hate to say this, but does anyone else find him, um, disconcerting?"

"Yep." Angela nodded. "I thought it was just me."

"No. He makes me nervous as well." Rohini rubbed her hands up and down her arms. "The way he just stares for the longest time, like —" she struggled to explain —

"A fox stares at a hen he can't reach?" Sarita put in drolly.

Angela slapped her hand down on the table. "That's it. And if you ask him something, it takes him forever to answer." She made a face. "Although, to be fair, Inez told me he's a veteran."

"Is that so?" Rohini's brow knit. "I suppose I'm getting old, but it's unusual for a vet to have dreadlocks, isn't it?" It occurred to her that she was being unkind, so she hastened to add, "I do quite like them, however."

"Thinking of getting Cris to change his look?" Angela teased. Her thoughts went back to Alan. "Well, God only knows what he went through over there." She shifted her attention to Sarita. "When you met him, did you …you know —" she circled her hand in the air — "get any vibes or whatever?"

"For heaven's sake, Angela," Rohini put in before Sarita could reply. "We've said time and again, Sarita's gift doesn't work that way. It comes and goes."

Sarita grimaced as she licked chocolate off her finger. "Yeah. Like a bad case of acne."

"Oh, darling. I wish you wouldn't see it like that." Rohini looked so crestfallen that for the first time Sarita felt her back go up.

"Rohini, I'm sorry, but I wish *you* would stop insisting that it's a gift, because it doesn't feel like one to me."

Enough was enough. As much as Sarita regarded her as an honorary aunt, Rohini wasn't the one who had to deal with the consequences of her so-called 'gift.' If it was so damn rewarding, why did she feel such angst over the prospect of having to meet Luca — a stranger who had no idea that she knew intimate details about his past?

As was her habit, Angela stepped in to smooth things over. "Well, I think —"

Whatever conciliatory remark she had in mind remained unsaid, as they heard the back door open and the men return. All three women stiffened when, for the second time that day, Cristiano's voice came through as aberrantly loud and condescending.

"No, no, no — do not put any cardboard boxes *there*. That table is for food preparation only. Who knows where these boxes were stored? Do we want their filth on our raw meats and fish? No, we do not. Put them on the far table, and put what's in them in that pantry over there. The rest go in the kitchen."

"Oh!" Listening to him, Rohini felt her skin heat. "How could he?" Her whisper sounded scandalized. "I've never heard him speak that way to anyone."

There was no time for the other two to reply as Cristiano trounced in, a heavy plastic carton filled with two dozen glass containers of milk and cream balanced against his thighs. Without a word to any of them, he plopped down the carton, turned his back, and began storing the containers in a refrigerator. He didn't have to look behind him to know that three pairs of eyes were boring holes of reproach into his back.

They were right to condemn him, he knew. His behavior was disgraceful. Yet, he couldn't stop himself.

The instant he set eyes on Luca, the skin between his shoulder blades began to itch. It was a sensation that served as his personal alarm system — a portent of peril that had developed while he was in prison. It would come over him just when a fight was about to break out, or right before someone pulled out a shiv. He hadn't felt it in years, but he'd felt it today. He wasn't a seer like Sarita or even an empath like his wife, but even so, he was certain that Luciano Miceli spelled danger. Until he found out more about him, he was not about to welcome the boy with open arms.

The 'boy' in question was stacking bags and jars of foodstuffs into the back pantry as commanded, while doing some fuming of his own.

What an arrogant asshole, he thought. How in hell had Angela managed to work with the guy for ten years? He'd been with him for only ten minutes and already wanted to smack him.

He hefted a giant jar of marinated artichoke hearts and then paused with it in his hands as something occurred to him: When Angela contacted him, he could no longer doubt that his mother had sent him a message. What if he'd misunderstood her purpose in sending him here? The chef had been in prison for manslaughter, hadn't he? Maybe it was Angela he was supposed to help, not Sarita. He remembered *Nannuzzo* telling him, years ago, that even though it was Luca's father who was related to Angela by blood, it was Gina with whom she'd been close. Maybe Angela felt intimidated by Cristiano.

Well, they'd see about that, wouldn't they?

He shoved the jar of artichokes into the pantry. The thing had to weigh at least ten pounds. He looked over the rest of the contents still left in the cartons: Twenty-pound bags of various kinds of rice, cans of tomato paste half as big as his torso — everything was super-sized and damn heavy. With a quick glance at the doorway to be sure he couldn't be seen, he held his breath and hovered his hands over the boxes. At first the contents wobbled and lurched like old men trying to lift themselves out of deck chairs, but ultimately they floated up and glided gracefully into the pantry. Luca grunted with satisfaction. After a month of sobriety, fresh air, and exercise, his powers were kicking back in. It felt good.

The oversize freezer across the room startled him when it jolted on. He swung around. Damn, the thing was noisy, and by the looks of it, old. He squinted at it. Something was … unique about it. Just what he didn't know.

For the first time since his arrival, he took careful note of his surroundings. "Huh," he muttered.

He went back to work. The two remaining boxes he'd been told to bring to the kitchen were not nearly as heavy as the ones he'd just finished unpacking. He checked them for breakables and saw one held fresh vegetables, the other several dozen eggs. Stacking them carefully, he carried them through to the galley, his thoughts focused back to the obnoxious chef, to Angela's puzzling close-lipped invitation, and to what his mother's true purpose might be for sending him to a ship that he could already tell was more than it had appeared to be at first glance.

Focused on all that, he was wholly unprepared for the sight of Sarita standing in the kitchen, right there, next to his cousin. He knew what she looked like. And yet, he just froze.

Where his life had taken him, beautiful women were abundant. While he appreciated them, his balanced sense of ego understood that it was his money and fame, not necessarily him personally, that appealed to them. For that reason, he'd never lost his head over a female face and form. At least, not since he was very young.

Until now. He could do nothing but stand helplessly and stare.

Angela and Rohini, still embarrassed by the exchange they'd heard between the two men, didn't pick up on the instantaneous effect Sarita had on Luca. But Cristiano did. Even in the face of his misgivings about the boy, he had to hide a smirk, remembering full well his own response to his first sight of Rohini, and the subsequent results. He glanced up at the pots hanging from the hooks on the ceiling. They remained motionless, so far.

Angela made the introductions. "Luca, this is Sarita."

"Hello," was all Sarita managed. It was the best she could do, as blindsided by him as he was by her. She'd been a wreck, thinking that she'd have a psychic episode as soon as they were in the same room. It never occurred to her he would affect her in another way altogether.

He was, in a word, gorgeous. Trapped as she'd been in her visions the night of the fire, she hadn't registered that particular attribute. She was noting it now, and her reaction to his physical presence made her feel gauche. Suddenly, she was Marisol — a high school girl with a teen magazine, fawning over a hunky star. An impish thought came from nowhere to pester her — was that a smidgeon of chocolate tart she felt stuck to her upper lip? She rolled her tongue over it, just to be sure.

The sight of that tongue darting out was sensory overload to Luca. Blood rushed to pivotal points of his body. Like rusty hinges, his elbows gave out, releasing the boxes he'd been clutching like a life preserver. The next thing he knew, everyone was jumping back. Free-range eggs cracked on the floor, organic lettuce and onions rolled like severed heads, and local-grown tomatoes plopped and split, spattering their juice and seeds across Luca's boots and the hems of his trousers.

He assessed the damage, sure that his face was the color of those ruined tomatoes. When he looked up, Angela and Rohini were eyeing him with sympathy, Cristiano with contempt, and the goddess was doing her best to hold back laughter.

Way to make a good first impression, moron, he thought to himself.

Oddly enough, Luca's graceless mishap went a long way toward calming Sarita's nerves. She stepped around the Cobb salad he'd made of the floor to pull over the wheeled bucket left by Inez. With wicked amusement, she handed him the mop. "Welcome to The Secret Spice Café, Luca."

Late that night, the summer air was balmy and still. Yet, the ocean water surrounding the ship rippled restlessly. Those out on her decks who knew of such things whispered that the spirits were disquieted.

But it wasn't the spirits. The churning water foreshadowed the sea change coming for certain living denizens who lived and worked aboard the *Queen*, a change that would be brought about now that there was a sorcerer in their midst.

It started subtly, in the de la Cuevas' bedroom. For the first time in their marriage, disturbed by his ill-treatment of a young man who'd lost everything, Rohini turned away from her husband. As she lay on her side, Cristiano stared at her back with hurt, confusion, and even a trace of indignation. Neither of them got any real rest.

Angela was up late too, indulging in her old habit of self-doubt. Had she handled things well with her son, or was she in danger of losing him again? And Luca — did he know that Gina had sent him here? Was she wrong to ask Rohini to keep the details from Cris? There was one person she could trust to tell it to her straight. Midnight in Long Beach was seven a.m. in Rome. Jane was having breakfast when she heard the Skype tone.

Down the corridor, Sarita shifted under her summer-damp sheets, willing her mind to shut off. After a while, she gave up, switched on the bedside lamp, and picked up the book she'd been reading. It wasn't the first time she couldn't sleep for thinking about Luca. But her thoughts about him had taken a wildly different turn.

Luca was having similar thoughts about her. He wasn't sure that was wise, considering the circumstances behind his arrival. The ship was impressive, yet it still seemed surreal to him that he was here, and why. Leaning against the open porthole in the borrowed stateroom, he blew out smoke from the cigarette he knew he shouldn't have lit, using his skills to direct the vapor outside in a straight, steady stream. He wasn't up to heading out at this late hour to smoke on the Sun Deck. One cigarette, he reasoned, was better than having the drink he craved.

Eleven minutes away by car, in an elegant, Spanish-style townhouse in the gated community of Bixby Hills, Marisol was also up late, flipping through a *Saturn Girl* comic book with morose defiance. Her parents' bickering voices filtered through to her from their bedroom. In their same complex, in another townhouse, a restless Vincenzo lay awake, vexed that Douglas slept on beside him, peacefully unaware of his partner's sulks.

And in a different area of Long Beach entirely, not far from the Los Angeles River and the Seventh Street Bridge, in a squalid, one-room rental above a Cambodian restaurant, the man calling himself 'Alan' examined his face in the chipped bathroom mirror.

His tactics were working. The women were leery of him. That meant they'd stay the hell out of his way. As long as he continued to be a model employee, the sympathetic little Mexican who'd hired him would have no excuse to let him go. He'd scrub toilets on that ship every day. He'd sleep in this hellhole every night, ignoring the drug dealers, whores, and homeless who lived outside, the roaches and permeating stench of fried fish that lived within, and the rats that were everywhere. He'd tolerate it all, for as long as it took.

As the saying went, this was a dish best served cold.

CHAPTER FIVE

Saturday of Labor Day Weekend, August 30, 2014, just over one month since Luca's arrival

Standing in front of the floor mirror in her stateroom, Angela smoothed her hands down the sides of her gown. The sapphire blue was a good color for her. The bias cut, flared hem and deep back line was a celebration of old Hollywood glamour. She'd ordered the gown before she'd decided to have the surgery, but the seamstress had done an excellent job of letting out the high bodice so that the satin no longer pulled too tightly across the new proportions of her chest.

Turning so that her back faced the mirror, she adjusted the bow accent by her lumbar. She stepped back and lifted the hem to inspect her silver t-strap evening shoes. She wasn't as happy with them as she was with the dress. She'd bought them earlier from one of the festival vendors, along with an embroidered evening bag, opera-length black gloves, and a hand-held fan. Being true vintage, not a copy like her gown, the shoes didn't exactly fit, but for this one special night, she'd make do. They put the finishing touch on the 30s look, and she loved the Spanish heel.

Overall, she was pleased. But when she lifted her hem even higher and bent to adjust the seams at the backs of her stockings, a familiar pain over her left temple made her wince.

Darn it. She was so looking forward to this event. She hoped there wasn't a headache coming on.

Until just a few months before, Angela had thought her stress migraines were gone for good. They'd decreased in frequency after she was reunited with Vincenzo, and then, with the exception of an occasional twinge that was easily treatable with an aspirin or a session of yoga, they'd all but disappeared. Now she had to accept that not only were her headaches back, they hurt a heck of a lot more than she remembered. She also had to accept that, like it or not, they were directly related to what the people she loved were feeling or doing. That correlation was particularly troublesome as of late, since everyone she cared about was doing their best, currently, to mess up their lives. And the one making the biggest mess was the one she loved the most — her surprisingly narrow-minded son.

Moving over to the dresser, she pulled open the drawer where she kept a bottle of aspirin. He'd been happy, at first. Happy that, even though it had taken her two long years, she'd acknowledged his sexuality and welcomed Douglas with an open heart and mind.

She went to the mini-fridge and got out a bottle of water. He'd been happy with the long-distance relationship she'd had with Jack.

And why wouldn't he be? she reflected, as she popped two aspirin and sipped water. Jack had treated her very well. When he came out for weekends, he'd charmed them all, always listening patiently to Sarita's chatters about the *Mary*, always complementing Rohini on how pretty she looked, always raving about Cris's food and Angela's sweets. His lovemaking had also been ... charming, compared to what she'd grown accustomed to with Marco. Although, after years of disappointment in that arena, she'd secretly hoped there'd be a little more to it. Even so, Jack was a guy with whom the old Angela would have been quite content.

Then Jack mentioned that she should consider selling her share of The Secret Spice and moving to Texas with him. And when he also mentioned that he hoped she wouldn't be offended, but he "didn't approve of gays getting married," that had put paid to her relationship with Jack.

Angela never told Vincenzo nor anyone else that last thing, and maybe she should have. Instead, one night after the breakup, she'd allowed Cynthia to get her drunk, and in her inebriated state, she blurted out to her business partner — a woman who was as different to herself as chalk was to cheese — that all she really wanted was to — just once — experience what it was like to have the kind of sex she read about in Nora Roberts novels.

That's when she discovered how delicious it was to have a free-spirited friend who was not only open-minded, but close-lipped. Cynthia, knee-deep into her romance with Raul by that time, had grinned like the Cheshire Cat and said, "Just when I thought I might never use Harry's number again. You two should meet, Angela."

So Angela was introduced to Harry Clark — Harry, who was "not into marriage," who "liked dating smart, sexy, older women," and who was "perfectly fine with the idea of switching one out for the other, if the other were willing."

Angela decided that she was. As a result of that bold choice, while Cynthia experienced for the first time what it was like to be with a man who truly loved and respected her, Angela was introduced to a world she'd barely glimpsed, a world where crying out in pleasure while a man held her, naked in his arms, became as natural and commonplace to her as rolling out the perfect puff pastry.

And Vincenzo hadn't been at all happy about that. It surprised Angela to learn that her son was a traditionalist. That didn't fit in with the image she'd had of gays at all. When she learned that Vincenzo was embarrassed by his mother's liaison with a younger man, she broke things off with Harry, albeit much less enthusiastically than she had with Jack. It was flattering that Harry was more disappointed than Angela had expected him to be, but he understood, and they remained friends — another thing that displeased Vincenzo.

Now, there were her new breasts. Okay, she got it that no son wanted to think about his mother's sexual side. But c'mon — he was an adult, wasn't he? Yet he was behaving as childishly as Cris. Was it necessary for both men to avert their eyes every time she took off her chef's jacket?

Speaking of Cris … there was another migraine-inducing quandary.

She sighed and sipped more water. Jane had always cautioned her to be aware of the difference between 'feeling guilty' and actual guilt. Though it had taken her more than half a century, she was finally getting the hang of that. Even so, she still felt awful about the situation, since it had started when Luca came to work with them. Everything that was going wrong had started when Luca came to work with them, come to think about it.

But she was *not* going to think about it, or she'd get that headache, for sure. Instead, she sat down at her vanity with determination, and pulled out the new makeup she'd bought, along with the special hairbrush and bobby pins. Opening her laptop, she clicked on the video tutorial she'd saved that demonstrated how to twist her hair into 'victory rolls,' how to use the makeup to recreate 'screen siren lips,' and how to trace her eyeliner into an upturned triangle effect that had been popular in the day. When she was done, she'd take a photo of herself to send to Jane.

She was determined to enjoy herself. She was going to dance to Cab Calloway and — if she could keep the headache at bay — drink a Singapore Sling. She was going to greet people she knew from town and the customers of the Spice who'd come aboard, dressed in period clothing, for the Tenth Annual Art Deco Ball.

For this one special night, she was going to take Jane's advice to "ignore the lot of them." With the exception of Vincenzo and Douglas — the only two men she knew who owned bespoke tuxedos and wouldn't miss an opportunity to wear them, whether they were on good terms with one another or not — the rest of their livelihoods depended on the *Mary*. This was a charity event that raised thousands for her preservation, and yet every one of them had tried to wriggle out of it.

Inez and Michael's excuse was that they didn't want to leave Marisol home by herself. Angela wasn't buying it, but she'd had a look at the festival program, and the couple had donated generously in the name of their onboard business establishment, The Queen Mary Memorabilia and Postcard Shop. So, they were off the hook. As for the two chefs, last she'd heard from Rohini, she and Cris would put in an appearance, but they weren't staying long, since they were barely speaking either so, "what was the point?"

With a sound of vexation, she picked up the tube of 'Savage Red' lipstick and angled her laptop so she could see the screen and into her mirror simultaneously. At least Luca had agreed to attend graciously enough, God bless him. Of course, that was because Sarita was going to be there.

Reluctantly, that is. Angela risked a shake of her head. That kid acted like any activity which didn't involve books was like getting a root canal. Before she'd taken over for her mother, all the partners had warned her in advance that networking would be part of the deal. Sarita socialized when she absolutely had to, but she "hated being on display," as she put it. Hah. With a face like that, it was high time she got used to it, unless she planned on wearing a bag over her head for the rest of her life.

But … there was something between her and Luca. The air around them practically steamed whenever they looked at each other. Not that either one of them had worked up the nerve to do more than look, so far.

She smirked as she uncapped the tube. After her nights with Harry, she knew exactly what the problem was with every last one of them.

Why didn't they stop their nonsense and just get on with it? Watching them be angry and hurt with the other, avoid the other, pretend that the other didn't exist, and in general, act like idiots, she was glad she was single.

And if she got lonely, well … lucky for her she was a pastry chef. At least she had plenty of chocolate.

———●

Although the *RMS Queen Mary*'s glory days were long behind her, many still remembered those inimitable decades when she sailed the seas as one of the fastest and most luxurious ocean liners constructed by Cunard. Among the facilities available on board, she had two indoor swimming pools, one of which, the first-class swimming pool, spanned over two decks in height. She had beauty salons, libraries, children's nurseries, a music studio, a lecture hall, outdoor paddle tennis courts, and dog kennels. Her passengers had the convenience of telephone connectivity to anywhere in the world. The *Mary* was the first ocean liner to be equipped with her own Jewish prayer room – part of a policy to show that British shipping lines avoided the racism of Nazi Germany. Hollywood celebrities such as Fred Astaire, Greta Garbo, Betty Davis, Audrey Hepburn and many others stayed aboard, as well as dignitaries who included Queen Elizabeth, The Duke and Duchess of Windsor, and General Dwight Eisenhower.

Like those luminaries of yesterday, the ship in present day retained a patina of grandeur. It remained the world's most glorious floating embodiment of Art Deco design, offering a superlative setting for the Tenth Anniversary Festival. During her golden age, the art form, like the ship herself, represented opulence, exuberance, and progress. Apart from the aforementioned conveniences which were extraordinary for the time, the *Mary* brimmed with murals, woodcarvings, sculptures, and fixtures of exceptional craftsmanship. Many were made of such rare raw materials that they were now virtually matchless, and this voyage through time that was the annual ball was held as a way to raise funds for their upkeep.

It was a black-tie event that culminated five days of festivities and it was held in the Grand Salon. The largest room ever built aboard a vessel, the Grand Salon ran the entire length of the hull and spanned three decks in height. Back when the ship was still seafaring, it was used as the first class dining room, able to accommodate over eight hundred passengers. And like the rest of the ship, the salon was stunning.

Peroba wood from the Brazilian rainforest gleamed a rosy red and covered the walls and pillars, while intricate bas-reliefs, illustrating the history of ship building, were carved from pine and stained chocolatey brown. On the forward bulkhead was an ornate map of the transatlantic crossing, with twin tracks symbolizing the seasonal routes. During each crossing, a motorized model of the ship would indicate the vessel's progress en route. The crisp shades of chestnut, cream, and blue, all embellished with touches of gold, appeared fresh, although they'd been painted nearly eight decades before.

The aft bulkhead exhibited the largest piece of artwork on the *Mary*. At first glance, its intricate line work gave the illusion that it was a woven tapestry, but on closer examination one could see that it was mural art. It depicted trees and flora, birds and other wildlife — all rendered in minute detail on a frieze that traversed ceiling to floor. The painting framed a set of bronze grill doors that were polished to a gleam and boasted sculptures of mythological sea creatures. It was through these doors that the ship's captain entered every evening while the ship was at sea, and proceeded to the table reserved for him at the center of the salon to dine with his invited guests.

Now in front of those doors, a bandstand had been set up facing the dance floor. The rest of the salon was dotted with red brocade chairs and circular tables, each covered with a silky black cloth and elaborate dinnerware. The exclusive centerpieces for the event resembled chandeliers — palm-sized, oval-shaped crystals cascading in graduated tiers set high atop narrow, silver stems tall enough that those seated could get a clear view of the performers and dancers.

The ball was scheduled to begin at seven p.m., with music provided by Dean Mora and the *Queen Mary* Orchestra. Although it was only six forty-five, in anticipation of their first number, the room was already flowing with guests. Some milled about, perusing the artwork, greeting new arrivals, admiring each other's vintage regalia, while others gathered at their tables, sampling vodka gimlets, sidecars, and other drinks reminiscent of the era.

And hovering along the edges of the crowd, ethereal, unseen by most, were all the spirits aboard who'd been drawn to the ball by the achingly familiar sights and sounds of a time when they'd walked among the living.

Luca was beginning to see the ghosts. He took the whole 'I see dead people' thing in stride, same as he did his powers. It was the living with whom he'd worked for the past four weeks who troubled him.

There was no sign yet of the danger to Sarita his mother had hinted at, and he was growing impatient. The longer he stayed aboard the ship, the more he became ensnared by the part-daytime-soap, part-Gordon-Ramsay-reality-show that was life at The Secret Spice Café. A textbook example of that sort of ridiculous drama was this event. He'd allowed himself to be roped into attending in the hopes of spending some time away from the restaurant with Sarita. He hadn't been at the ball for five minutes and he already regretted that decision.

The mood was as buoyant and bubbly as the champagne cocktails. Except for at the table where he sat with Vincenzo, Douglas, and Cristiano, as they waited for the women to arrive. They were all in black tails and tie, excluding Douglas, who'd opted to contrast his tuxedo with a white tie and cummerbund. Being the only one with light eyes and hair, it was a deliberate and inspired choice. The quartet of handsome, elegantly-dressed men cut quite the dashing picture, until one perceived that the expressions they wore clashed with their evening finery. They looked less like they were attending an upscale bash and more like they'd been arrested on an erroneous charge of indecent exposure, and were waiting for their lawyers to come bail them out.

Douglas's face was pinched and drawn, and Vincenzo's jaw was clenched, tight enough to crack his teeth. They both sat stiffly upright, occasionally tapping a foot or staring off into space. Douglas, usually so affable, spoke only when spoken to, and looked as though he might start to cry at any moment. Vincenzo avoided looking at Douglas except to ask what he'd like to drink.

Cristiano was too preoccupied with his own concerns to notice the friction between the couple. He was slumped back in his chair, knees spread wide, hands balled into fists, inadvertently scowling out at the crowd as he brooded over an incident — a singularly, unfathomable incident — that had taken place in the kitchen that morning. Every now and again, he'd glance at Luca with narrowed eyes.

Naturally, all of this was unpleasant for Luca. He struggled to pretend he didn't notice that Vin and Douglas had quarreled before their arrival. And Cristiano — Luca didn't know what he was pouting about this time, but it had something to do with him. Nothing new there. The guy just couldn't stomach him, and Luca had no idea why.

Unless he'd picked up on Luca's infatuation with Sarita. Luca thought he'd been hiding it well. But if the great chef had glommed on to it … oh, hell, yeah. That would definitely stick in his craw.

'Infatuation?' Who was he kidding? Enchantment was more like it. He'd been poleaxed by her at their first, proper, up-close encounter, but in the weeks that had followed since, he'd become beguiled by the paradox of who she was, or who she might be. She pulled at him. He was drawn to the warmth of her spirit, and by the fact that she worked so hard to keep that part of herself hidden.

To start, he was certain — reasonably so, at least — that she was attracted to him. The five of them dined together at the restaurant almost every evening. Luca had come to appreciate the *en famille* routine. It helped him stick to his resolve to stay away from the booze. And when he joined the conversation, he'd catch Sarita stealing glances at him, even smiling at something he said. But when he tried to engage her, specifically, she found a way to cut it short, or to include the rest of the table. When she did speak, it was with lively intelligence, compassion, wit, and an understanding of the world that was unusual for someone who hadn't traveled much. Nightly, he wracked his brain to come up with a question about the ship, or any other topic he'd learned piqued her interest, just so he could get her to talk. She was always gracious, yet her behavior signaled that she wanted nothing more personal to do with him.

Although, somehow, he didn't think that was it, exactly. It was more like she was interested, but didn't want to *want* to be interested. And that didn't jibe, because she wasn't coy. He'd seen her dealing with all kinds of issues at the restaurant — inebriated guests, disgruntled crew members, incompetent service people — in a firm, but generous manner. Yet when it came to speaking with him, she closed up.

He'd also noted that she rarely left the ship. Several times since he'd arrived, he, Vincenzo, and Douglas had gone downtown for a night out, and Sarita always had an excuse for why she needed to stay behind. If she spent any of her limited leisure time with anyone who was under the age of fifty, it was with Marisol. It was then that he got a glimpse of the playful side of Sarita. She let her guard down with the teen, treating her like a younger sister rather than just a family friend. She and Marisol shared commonalities that Luca couldn't define. She was a woman capable of great depths of thought, deep wells of feeling, and yet he knew she was even lonelier than he was.

Lastly, it was the unconscious stop-and-go sexiness of her that got his blood up. At the restaurant, she deliberately downplayed her looks with conservative clothing, practical hairstyles and minimal makeup. Having spent so many years in Vegas, this was something he noticed right off. In Vegas, if a woman had Sarita's beauty, she found a way to optimize and capitalize on it. Luca didn't see anything wrong with that, or with the fact that Sarita chose to do the opposite. But it intrigued him, nonetheless, especially when she revealed hints of a hidden sensuality.

Like the time she spotted the freshly-made éclairs at Angela's work station and gave a little moan of delight. Leaning over to snatch one up, the edges of her modest, navy-blue suit jacket gapped open, and he got a glimpse of a lacy, black bra. Or the time when, after the restaurant had closed for the evening, she'd removed her sensible shoes to rub her feet, and he noticed that her toenails were painted vivid red.

She aroused him with no effort on her part at all, and that was one of the things that made her so appealing. But something was troubling her, he knew, and he needed to tread carefully.

His smitten musings screeched to a halt when he noticed that Cristiano was giving him that unnerving stare again. Yeah. Maybe he wasn't hiding his feelings as well as he thought.

Luca patted his trouser pocket. It was empty. He'd left his smokes on the dresser in the stateroom when he'd changed into the tux. Dammit. He'd worn enough of these monkey suits to last a lifetime. He shifted and twitched, fiddling with his bow tie, his cufflinks, the studs in his shirt. His silent debate with himself over whether he could risk a glass of wine only served to prove that he still lacked the self-discipline he was trying so hard to make habitual. He wouldn't start anything up with Sarita unless he was reasonably sure he had himself under control.

But as much as he now wanted to stay aboard the ship just so he could be near her, he was getting restless with the waiting for ... what, he didn't know. An entire month, and not even one more sign from his mother, nor one hint from Angela that she'd had any other reason to ask him here apart from helping her make pastries. What bull. They both knew it was absurd that she'd asked, and absurd that he'd agreed. He wasn't a pastry chef, and Angela had been here for ten years. She'd have to be blind not to notice that this whole ship was ... enigmatic. No, she'd asked him to come because she knew something. She had to.

He swore silently, and tugged at his tie again. Where was she, anyway? The restaurant was closed today in deference to the ball, so what was taking the women so damn long to get here?

In actuality, the women weren't late. It was only Luca's agitation that made it seem so. Just as the musicians took their places, Rohini entered the salon, wearing an ensemble she'd bought only that afternoon, in the hopes of impressing her husband. As she'd told Angela, she hadn't intended to stay at the ball any longer than business protocols dictated, but after seeing what had transpired in the kitchen that morning, she'd changed her plans. Cristiano had reached out to Luca in an attempt to make amends. For that reason, she was going to do the same for Cristiano — offer to make amends. Knowing him as she did, she thought her new gown might assist her in that endeavor, in a way they'd both appreciate.

The gown under consideration was inspired by Billie Holiday — white silk chiffon, body-clinging and strapless. To complete the look, she wore white suede heels with rhinestone ankle straps, and carried a matching white clutch. On her head, over one ear, she'd pinned a cluster of silk gardenias. Though not strictly the fashion of the time period, she'd left her long hair loose and flowing. Cristiano loved it that way. Her natural dark coloring against the light fabric of the dress was striking. She caught more than one look of appreciation aimed at her, and that was a nice little bonus. It felt good to know she could still turn a head. The question remained, however, what sort of effect she'd have on the man she'd smartened herself up for in the first place.

She needn't have worried. Her husband shot up out of his chair as soon as he spotted her from across the room. Luca didn't even have to glance behind him to know that Cristiano's better half had finally arrived. He choked back his mirth at the rapid change in the great chef's demeanor.

He looked like … a puppy. That was it — a puppy who was hoping the human he adored was going to take him outside to play.

All four men watched Rohini zigzag through the crowd. What a beautiful older woman she was, Luca thought. Did she have any idea how vital she was to her husband's happiness? If she did, she certainly wasn't using that knowledge to take advantage. Which probably meant, he surmised with a touch of envy, that her husband was just as important to her. They were the most unlikely couple he'd ever met, but observing them for the past weeks, as they cooked side by side, he noticed a synchronicity to their movements that reminded him of the way he and Santi had worked together when they were on stage: as though there was a symmetry to their separate thoughts, as though they knew what the other was going to do.

Nonetheless, there'd also been subtle signs — a small sound of impatience, a roll of an eye, a signal of irritation from Rohini that extended across the kitchen to her pal Angela — that indicated they were going through a rough patch.

Luca smiled and stood up along with the other men as she reached them. But, he knew women. The dress was like a press release that she intended to smooth things over in her marriage that very evening. And judging by the look on Cris's face, he was more than ready for that to happen.

"Hello, gentlemen. Oh, my. Don't you all look so debonair?" Rohini sounded blithesome as she circled around to greet them with a kiss on the cheek each, starting with Cristiano, who still looked stunned by her, and ending with Douglas. "Ah. White tie. A nice touch," she complimented him, as she raised her face to his.

"Look at you, Lady Day," Douglas responded as he leaned down for a kiss, but his voice lacked its usual warmth, a detail Rohini caught.

"Good evening, all." Angela had come up on them while Rohini was making her way around the table. Angela had a kiss for everyone too, but Vincenzo also got a pinch on the cheek — "My handsome son!"

"Ow," he responded with a weak smile, and rubbed his face.

"Angela, wasn't Sarita coming down with you?" Rohini asked, as Luca signaled for a waiter to take their drinks order.

"That was the plan, but she got a call from Security that there were lights left on at the Spice. She went down to make sure everything was okay."

"Not by herself, I hope. What if it was a break-in? People know the place is empty tonight," Cristiano fretted, as he pulled out two chairs across from him for his wife and Angela.

"Of course not, worry wart." Angela sat and scooted in closer to the table. "Two of the guards went with her. Believe me, the way she looks tonight, the whole team would have gladly escorted her down."

"'Security?' Are they the guys dressed like London bobbies I saw earlier?" Now that he'd gotten the waiter's attention, Luca focused on the update regarding Sarita.

"Yep, that's them. They always dress like that for special events. Clever, don't you think? Just a ginger ale for now, please. Thank you."

The waiter had come up to Angela as she responded to Luca. He jotted down Rohini's request for champagne next, and when he moved on to get the men's orders, Angela leaned in to Rohini and spoke in a low voice. "My God. You look gorgeous. And so did Sarita when I saw her earlier. I thought you two were going low-key. What did I miss?"

"We went shopping together this afternoon," Rohini whispered back. "I don't know why Sarita changed her mind, but as for me, something wonderful happened with Luca and Cristiano. I'll tell you all about it tomorrow. Tonight —" her voice filled with cheery naughtiness — "I'm trying to seduce my husband."

That news was a relief to Angela. Gleefully, she responded to Rohini, "Trying? There is no 'try,' young Skywalker. Not in that outfit. He'd have to be dead. And judging by how he's been staring at you, I'm going with alive."

The sound of clapping drew their attention. The musicians were cueing up.

"Good evening, and welcome to the Tenth Annual Art Deco Ball, here at the beautiful *Queen Mary*." The band leader addressed the crowd over the din of voices. "This evening, in honor of the occasion, we'll be presenting classic melodies made famous during the Big Band era. But to start, we'd like to play you a special song that was written by Henry Hall, exclusively for the maiden voyage of this glorious ship. Ladies and gentlemen, 'Somewhere at Sea.'"

"Oh." Rohini put her palms to her heart. "I love this song."

Angela was right. Cristiano could not take his eyes off his wife. But what she didn't know was that as spellbound as he was, he was also thoroughly perplexed. Only that morning, Rohini had been as withdrawn as she'd been every day for the past month. And at night ... well, the nights had been unbearable. He'd come to bed, and she'd either be reading, or pretending to be asleep. But now, here she was, dressed like this. And it was for him, he knew. The clothes, the hair, the warm looks — what had earned him this reprieve from the hell his life had been for weeks now?

A quick, sharp pain to his ankle jolted him out of his thoughts. Someone had kicked him. Deliberately. He looked around. Across from him, Angela was making faces. Her eyes looked like they were about to pop out of their sockets, and she was bobbing her head toward Rohini. What was happening?

Then, he got it — 'I love this song.' He wasn't usually so obtuse, but considering how things had been between him and his wife lately, he could forgive himself for finding the communiqué obscure. Which was why he felt caution was in order.

It took a second kick from Angela before he decided to risk public rejection. He turned to his wife. "Would you ... perhaps ... like to dance?"

The smile Rohini gave him should have melted the display of ice sculptures. "I would love to." She got up eagerly, set her handbag on the table, and put her hand in his.

Angela chuckled to herself. She'd be able to have that Singapore Sling after all. She felt the threat of headache lift away as Cris, still looking bemused, led Rohini to the dance floor.

She fixed an eye on Luca that was sharp enough to pinch. "So, what about you? Will I have to kick you under the table too, or do you have enough common sense to ask Sarita to dance? If she ever gets here."

Before Luca could respond to that, a man came up behind Angela and tapped her on the shoulder. She twisted around, and Luca saw her face light up.

"Harry! What a nice surprise."

"Hello, Angela. Yes, it was a spur-of-the-moment decision." He gave a quick nod to Vincenzo and Douglas and then focused his attention on Luca.

Angela took her cue. "Harry, this is Luciano Miceli, my cousin's son. He's here ... uh, visiting us for a while."

"Nice to meet you." Harry thought he recognized Luciano from somewhere, but then again, there was a family resemblance to Angela and Vincenzo, so perhaps that was it. Looking back at Angela, he said, "Well, I came over to ask you to dance. Are you going to turn me down?"

Luca noted that the request had been presented as a challenge. And the guy had been pretty terse in his greeting to Vin and Douglas. He also didn't miss that, while he had been introduced to Harry as a cousin, Angela hadn't told him who Harry was. In the Miceli family, an omission like that was considered rude. Like the rest of their clan, she was brought up on the social principle that there was nothing worse than bad manners. That could only mean she had an overriding reason.

Angela blushed pink at Harry's invitation, and then glanced over at Vincenzo as though she were seeking his permission. And Vincenzo, Luca saw, looked even more unhappy than he had when he'd first walked in.

Whereas Douglas's reaction was different. "Go ahead, kitten. Dance with Harry," he coaxed. "We'll keep an eye out for Sarita."

"Oh, are you sure?" Angela sounded hesitant as Harry took hold of her gloved hand and drew out her chair.

"Go," Douglas insisted. "Have fun."

After Harry led her away, Vincenzo turned to Douglas, a bite in his every word. "Did you have to do that?"

"Yes," Douglas snapped, and drained his drink.

———●

While Luca was absorbing new data about his two cousins' lives, Sarita was still in her office, battling an attack of nerves that had come upon her after Security left. They discovered nothing amiss, although she was sure she hadn't left any lights switched on. But the interval had given her time to second-guess her impulsive decision to spend the entire evening at the Grand Ball in the company of her friends ... and Luca.

Rohini's elation had been infectious when she'd commandeered Sarita for an impromptu shopping trip that afternoon. Sarita got swept up in helping her choose a gown, and before she knew it, she'd been persuaded by both Rohini and the proprietor of the vintage clothing shop to try one on too.

And what a gown it was.

Unlike those Rohini and Angela had chosen, Sarita's gown was a style that had been popular in the mid-1920s. Not floor-length, but dance-length, in a chemise style known as a '*garçonne* silhouette.' The fabric was shell-pink silk with an intricate pattern of seed pearls, crystal and silver bugle beads, and leaf-shaped sequins. The zig-zag hemline was trimmed with crystal-beaded fringe. The heels that went with it were ecru silk with instep straps and closed toes — the 'Mary Jane' variety dictated by the fashion of the day. There was also a matching pink bandeau, tastefully embellished with a jeweled clip. She could choose to wear it with her long hair down, as Rohini had. With such a dress and headband, she needed no jewelry, but again, the shopkeeper had enticed her with a darling rhinestone bracelet that added the perfect final touch.

Gazing at her reflection in the dressing room as the gown dazzled her with its shimmers and winks, she was tempted for the first time in years to let go of her anxieties and be reckless, just this once. She wanted the beautiful dress. And more, she admitted to herself, she wanted Luca to see her in it. She might even find the nerve to dance with him.

She didn't know why he'd decided to come to Long Beach, but she supposed that he needed a respite from the locale where his brother had been lost to him. His presence on the *Mary* was temporary, most certainly.

That being the case, she'd thought, Why not? Why shouldn't she buy the dress? Why shouldn't she allow herself to savor — just a teeny bit — the attraction she felt for him and that he, she could tell, felt for her?

The plan had seemed feasible enough that afternoon. But now that the hour had arrived to put it into action, she was losing her courage. Alone in her office in the dark, she berated herself out loud.

"You're spineless. It's just a party. What's the big deal? Just go in there and —"

A noise coming from the dining room stopped her mid-sentence. Angela had probably decided to come back for her.

Great, just *great*. Her raring-to-go business partner walking in on her while she was trying to calm her jitters would only make them worse.

"Angela, is that you?" she called out, gulping back the tremor in her voice. "Everything's okay in here. You go on ahead. There's no need to wait for me."

No response came. Not Angela, then, but she could definitely hear someone moving about in there. "Rohini?"

Honestly, sometimes those two were worse than her mother. She just needed five minutes to pull herself together. Why wouldn't they answer her?

She gasped when she made the connection between the sounds she was hearing and the lights left on. As she pounced for her phone, a shadow fell across the office floor, and a figure appeared in the open doorway.

Cristiano had allowed himself to relax marginally and take pleasure from Rohini being back in his arms. The spicy scent she wore, one that had intoxicated him since they first met, floated around them as she snuggled against his shoulder and hummed along to the words the tenor crooned:

"When shall I see ... my lover come home from the sea ...?"

At the same time, he didn't know what had brought about her change of heart, and he wasn't sure how he felt about it. Weeks of strain between them over a young man he knew was hiding something had chipped away at the foundation of trust they'd built together. Why had she dismissed his concerns so readily?

Fact: Together with his brother, Luca Miceli was worth millions. Fact: Said brother — renowned as an extraordinarily gifted magician — dies in a fire during a performance. How convenient for Luca, the sole remaining partner of their enterprise. And then, the dead man's twin, who knows nothing about any ghostly visitations, shows up at the *Mary*, just because Angela asked him to help her bake?

Bullshit.

The morning's incident had only served to confirm his misgivings. Rohini was in the kitchen at the time. Perhaps she'd seen what had happened and now shared his doubts about the boy?

"... *Hurry to me, great liner... for you can make my dream come true ...*"

On the other hand, as they followed the steps to the waltz, another thought occurred to Cristiano: His wife was ... how old now? Fifty-three? Fifty-four? Perhaps he'd overlooked the obvious.

Whatever the case, he thought it wise to wait until she brought it up.

He didn't have to wait long. She giggled as he twirled her — once, twice — and then smiled up at him. "I'm very proud of you for what you did this morning."

He kept his face blank. "And what, precisely, was that?"

"You asked Luca to cook with you."

His tone was careful. "You heard that?"

"Yes." She beamed at him.

His steps slowed as he searched his wife's face. "And you know that he made a perfect Salmon en Croûte? The crust, the succulence of the fish, the asparagus — all cooked to perfection?"

She gave him a look. "Mmm. I hope they start dinner service soon. You're making me hungry."

"Am I?" Her offhand attitude stumped him. "That's all you have to say about this, Rohini? Salmon en Croûte — one of the most challenging dishes to create. His was indistinguishable from mine. Me — a *cordon bleu*," he emphasized. "He told us himself that his only experience in front of a stove was when he was a child and watched his grandmother make tomato sauce. And yet, he turns out a flawless dish. This doesn't strike you as the least bit curious?"

Rohini's smile faltered as she looked up at her husband with dawning comprehension. "So, he has a gift. So what?"

"No, *mi amor*, that is not it. When I tell you it was indistinguishable, I don't exaggerate. I could not tell the difference. Not even by a nuance."

Her feet stilled in the middle of the dance floor. "What are you trying to say, Cristiano?"

Cristiano slid his hands from her waist to her upper arms. "Rohini, *think*, I beg you. Every dessert he makes for Angela is impeccable. I thought perhaps he'd inherited a family skill. So I challenged him with one of the most complicated recipes. And he *duplicated* it. That's just not possible." His voice mirrored his frustration over the crying violins behind them. "Can you not see that? Can you not see that he's hiding something?"

The first song ended. While the band dove right into their second — Benny Goodman's jazzy 'Sing, Sing, Sing' — and couples pivoted joyously from a waltz into a swing, Rohini pushed away from her husband. Amid the colorful whirl of movement, they were the only two who were still.

When she spoke, her voice was frostier than he'd ever heard it. "I'm tired. I'm going to bed."

Cristiano reached out and grasped her hands. "Wait. Please. I don't understand. Help me to understand."

As the cheery refrain went on — *"Now you're singin' with a swing, sing, sing, sing, sing, everybody start to sing —"* desperate for clues, he wrestled with how to present his question.

"Is this … are you … perhaps … starting your change of life?"

As soon as the words were out of his mouth, he wished he could swallow his tongue.

"What did you just say to me?"

"Rohini —"

With a look that sliced through him like a cold blade to the belly, she wrenched her hands free and barged off, leaving several surprised dancers in her wake.

—●—

"Omigosh, Alan, you scared me. Why do you sneak up on people like that?"

Everyone's least favorite cleaning crew member was standing in the doorway of Sarita's office, a large industrial key ring in one hand, a flashlight in the other. The dozens of keys dangled and clattered like a strange, broken wind chime as he took an awkward step back, and seemed even more jumpy than she was.

"My lapse in judgment, Ms. Taylor. Apologies."

"What are you doing here? Does Inez have you on a night shift?"

"No, ma'am. Well, yes, ma'am, in a sense. But not for her — as a guardsman of sorts. They got me doing that, because of the festivities and all."

A 'guardsman?' Who talked that way? She admonished herself for the thought instantly, embarrassed by her own insensitivity to what was clearly a regional dialect. Although for the life of her, she couldn't place it.

"So, you're on Security?" she confirmed.

"Yes ma'am. Silly of me. It says the very same right on this … this here decal." He stuttered through that, pointed at the emblem on his jacket, and then looked at her, rather shyly for someone usually so intimidating. Although, there was something behind the shy looks, something that Sarita couldn't identify, any more than she could his accent. "Boss told me a lamp here was on … uh … uh … or something, so they send me over."

This was the longest conversation she'd ever had with him, and it was enlightening. The poor fellow had social communication issues, as well as difficulty speaking.

"Well, that clears that up." Trying to be friendlier, to cut the tension, she smiled. "So ... why no bobby look for you?"

He stared back blankly. "Ma'am?"

Was the word 'bobby' beyond him? She tried again. "I meant, how come you're not dressed like a London policeman, like the rest of the Security team?"

"Oh, you mean them with the funny hats that cover their eyes? Nah, they needed me in this here. Blend in with the crowd, in case I got to step in. You know — stop folk from doing what they might regret. Them's terrible creatures sometimes. After a drink. Even just a little one. ... Dangerous creatures."

What appeared to be a smile slowly crawled across his face, but it didn't affect Sarita as a smile normally would. Quite the opposite. And he'd emphasized the word 'dangerous' in a way that made her question whether she was safe in here with him alone. Intentional or not, the dude was disturbing. She'd deal with whatever prejudices she might objectively have later, but for now, she wanted to be out of that office and away from him. If there was ever an excuse to go to the ball, this was it. She supposed she had to thank him for that.

"Hmm. Well, I know what you mean, but people are okay, for the most part, I've learned." That was decent, she told herself. That was as neutral an exit line as she was going to muster. She inched away from her desk and prepared to depart. Thankfully, he stepped aside. For a split second, she wasn't sure he would. The thought made her feel bad, and she resolved to be nicer to him henceforth. But in the light of day, in front of other people, not just now. He was still leering, his eyes fixed on the front of her dress. She really wanted to be gone.

"Well, I have to ... head off. Thanks so much for checking in on us." Her smile felt so forced she was sure he noticed. You'll lock up, I guess?"

"Yes, ma'am."

"Okay, good night, then. And ... uh ... thanks."

"You learned wrong."

It was muttered as she was already halfway out.

"I'm sorry?"

"You said you learned most of them are okay. You learned wrong. Most of them ain't."

There was silence for a moment as she looked back at him.

"Have ... have a nice evening, Alan."

———●

While Rohini and Cristiano waltzed, another significant exchange was also taking place on the dance floor at the same time.

"I have to say, you had me worried, Angela. I thought Luciano was my replacement."

Angela goggled at Harry as he spun her into the steps. "Are you kidding? We're cousins. Besides, I'm not a cougar by trade, Harry." She winked at him. "You were my one-off exception."

"Oh, please," he scoffed. "I'm thirty-nine, if you remember. Not exactly fresh out of kindergarten." Pulling her closer as they moved in tempo, he thought about how he could expound on the subject without making things uncomfortable. He missed being with her. With a warm smile, his eyes moved over her. "You look beautiful, by the way. The style of the day becomes you."

"Thank you." She'd learned to accept male admiration without too much embarrassment, but couldn't resist adding, "My toes hurt in these heels."

He chuckled, expertly turning her left and right. "Suffering for fashion, are we?"

"You tell me. You're in the same boat I am. No pun intended. I bet what you're wearing isn't much more comfortable. Although I have to return the compliment — you look very handsome. I've never seen a midnight blue tuxedo before."

"It's my tribute to the Duke of Windsor. Midnight blue was his color preference over black formalwear, and he made it all the rage back then."

She tucked her tongue in her cheek. "The Duke of Windsor. You don't say?" Harry had always been a popinjay when it came to his wardrobe. God bless him, he had a back story for every jacket and pair of pants he wore.

Then it came to her. "Wait — you mean Edward, right? Queen Mary's son. The guy who abdicated to marry that divorcée. Somebody Simpson." She paused as the music swelled. "Was it 'Wallet'?"

"'Wallis,' actually. But they probably would have given you that one on *Jeopardy*." He teased her right back, making her laugh.

"I'd better get points. Living here, living with Sarita, I've had ten years of lessons, like it or not. Sarita told me all about poor Edward. It's a sad story. But I bet she doesn't know about his trendsetting blue tuxedo. I'll get to turn the tables on her — tell her something she doesn't know, for a change."

And here, unexpectedly, was the lead-in Harry needed. Ignoring the rest, he was suddenly serious as he ventured, "It's always a sad story to feel emotionally blackmailed into living a life we don't want to live."

Angela's glance in Vincenzo's direction was automatic. Even as the tenor belted out the solo, her son's granite-faced countenance rang volumes louder as he watched her and Harry dance. She shuffled her aching feet, wishing she hadn't been so fixated on wearing shoes that didn't fit.

"My son and I made our peace long ago. He's forgiven me for being so close-minded."

It exasperated him that she'd deliberately misunderstood. "You know that's not what I meant." He leaned in closer to her, and it struck her that what she glimpsed in his eyes was hurt.

Her face fell. "Oh, Harry, I'm sorry. I didn't think our breakup would matter that much to you. Honestly, I didn't." The big, dark eyes she'd emphasized with such special care pleaded for his tolerance. "It's just ... I don't want to lose him again."

For several seconds, he said nothing. Then, with a succinct nod, he stepped back. "Got it. Just be careful, Angela, that you don't lose yourself. *Again.*"

With that admonition, he steered her back to her seat long before their dance would have ended, gave a terse salute to the table at large, and took himself off.

No one spoke after he left. Vincenzo looked across at Angela, and she fidgeted like a disobedient child. Tapping her foot, she pretended that the music had her attention. Luca, unwilling bystander, strained for something innocuous to say to cut the tension and came up with nothing.

Douglas was on his third vodka gimlet. Slightly tipsy, he leaned across his plate to address Angela. "I don't think I heard anyone else say it, Angela, so let me be the first. You look amazing." He raised his glass to her.

"Aw. Thank you, sweetie." The smile Angela sent his way wobbled.

Douglas continued. "I mean, the hair, the makeup — you nailed the whole look." He waved his glass to emphasize his words, and some vodka dashed onto his cuff. The music seemed to recede as he turned to his partner. "Right? Right, Vin? Doesn't she look beautiful? Tell her." He nudged Vincenzo with his elbow. "Tell your mother she looks beautiful."

Luca had a bad feeling about where this was going. The very air felt suddenly altered. If Sarita were present, she'd have seen that the ghosts lingering in the ballroom had all at once fixed their attention on Angela, who wasn't smiling anymore. She looked pale. She glanced back and forth between Vincenzo and Douglas.

When Vincenzo countered, it was with unmistakable spite. "She sure got into the spirit of the thing. Didn't you, Ma? You got lipstick all over the rim of your glass. When did you get that dress? Bet you had to get the top altered, right?"

The remark was vile, and Luca's first instinct was to say something scathing to Vin, but he checked himself. Here was not the place to unleash Sicilian tempers. He kept his mouth shut as he observed the montage: Angela, hurt but trying not to show it. Vincenzo, furious with Angela. And Douglas, disgusted with Vincenzo.

As the latecomer, he'd walked in on the second act and had no clue what parts of the play he'd missed. But, man — what the hell?

The waltz was coming to an end. Angela hoped Ro and Cris had enjoyed their dance. She had a sip of ginger ale. It had gone flat and warm. Although her insides were quaking, she managed to answer her son with an outward semblance of calm. "Yep. That is correct."

There was a blast of horns and a racy drum roll as the band gave the audience their all. With a half-smile to Luca, Angela ticked her finger in the air. "Benny Goodman. One of the greats. Your grandparents had all his albums. Your mother and I used to dance to this in their living room when we were kids."

She got up. If she didn't leave right now, she'd lose her composure, for sure. "I'm going to call it a night, boys. These shoes hurt. Let everyone else know, will you?"

As soon as she was out of sight, Douglas focused on Vincenzo. "You outdid yourself tonight. You are one piece of work." The statements hit their mark with all the more force due to how quietly they were uttered. Downing the rest of his drink, Douglas pushed back his chair. "I'm out of here too."

Vincenzo caught his wrist. "Wait." He floundered for something to say. "You've had too much to drink, Doug. Let me drive you home."

Douglas shook loose of his hand, much like, unbeknownst to him, Rohini had pulled away from Cristiano only moments before. "Don't bother." His tone was acerbic, but he still kept his voice low. Public arguments were not his style. "I'll take a cab." His final comments were for Luca, and they were sincere. "I apologize for shitting all over your evening. Vin is right. I'm not myself. I hope we see each other under better circumstances someday." And with that, he was gone.

Feeling about two inches tall, Vincenzo met Luca's eyes.

"*Dee, dee, dee, bah, bah, bah, dah,*" the vocalist intoned. Luca tipped his head toward the exit, motioning to his cousin that he should go after Douglas, but Vincenzo wasn't convinced that he was the bad guy in the scenario. As the trombones blew, he sat and seethed.

In the end, he made his choice, brash as it was. "I've lost my appetite. If Sarita doesn't show, I'll be at the Observation Bar, if you want to meet me there."

Luca gave him a tactful nod, but thought that pulling out his own fingernails would be preferable to sitting at a bar with his cousin just then. He barely had time to exhale after Vincenzo left before he spotted Rohini barreling in his direction, indignation on her face. A saxophone came in, and she looked like she was marching in time to it, with her husband following close behind.

"Listen to me, please listen to me —" Even with the music playing, Luca could hear Cristiano implore.

"Don't touch me. Don't even talk to me," Rohini muttered back at him. She reached her chair, grabbed her handbag, and stamped away again, with nary a glance at Luca.

Hell — what now?

Whatever it was, Cristiano blamed him for it. He rounded on Luca, his dissatisfaction with the current state of his marriage, his suspicion and ire, all bubbling over like a pot of overcooked, frothing linguini.

"This is *your* fault!" Though he was in a rage, he kept his voice at a whisper, glancing left and right to be sure no one on either side could overhear. But the people near them continued to laugh and talk, as the music did its part to distract them from his wrath.

The chef hovered over Luca. He was so wild-eyed, Luca thought he might be drunk. And the only way to handle drunks, he'd learned in Vegas, was not to engage. Even though his heart knocked against his chest, he sat motionless while Cristiano hissed, "You're up to something, and I want to know — right now, *dammit* — why in hell you are here."

Luca's brow lifted. The guy evidently saw himself as the alpha rooster whose job it was to protect all the chicks in his hen house. Even so, until he had a chance to talk to Angela, Luca was staying mum.

"Look, dude," he countered, keeping his manner composed, "I appreciate that this is an unusual situation. But I'm not here to cause any trouble."

Cristiano was not appeased. Moreover, being called 'dude' had only served to aggravate him further. "There's something peculiar going on." He jabbed his finger at him. "There's something peculiar about *you*. And I'm going to find out what it is."

The band concluded "Sing, Sing, Sing" just as he stalked off, making himself the fifth person to have left in umbrage, at — Luca glanced at his watch — barely seven-forty. The wait staff was just serving the first course.

Guests clapped and whistled when the musicians struck up their next number, a renowned torch song, led by a sultry-voiced siren with flame-colored hair and a clingy, sequined gown to match:

"I need your love so badly, I love you, oh, so madly ... but I don't stand a ghost of a chance with you ..."

Luca rubbed a hand over his face and wondered how much longer he should wait for Sarita. Had she changed her mind?

He glanced around the table. Douglas being the exception, they'd all left their drinks virtually untouched. If he were going to fall off the wagon, now would be the ideal time. But even with the ordeal the evening had been so far, he was pleased that the urge had passed for the time being. It wasn't alcohol he wanted.

Checking his watch again was unnecessary, but he did so anyway. He'd wait a few minutes more. He pivoted in his seat to get a better view of the stage. The lovely vocalist was truly hypnotic. Every note she sang of the old Bing Crosby standard evoked the poignant sensation of unrequited love:

"If you'd surrender just for a tender kiss or two..."

"Hi. Sorry I'm late. Where is everybody?"

Before she spoke, he sensed her behind him. What flowed through him when he heard her voice was more than just satisfaction that she'd opted to turn up. And when he saw her — impossibly beautiful, yet somehow ill at ease, in a dress that looked as though it were made out of dreams — his resolve to take things slowly between them melted away like candle wax.

As Luca gazed at her, Sarita was unnerved by the sudden, strange connection to him she felt. She had always been linked to him psychically, but psychic links were nothing unique for her. This was different. The way he looked in that tuxedo, the way he was looking at her, supplanted the clutch of nerves in her belly with pangs of another kind.

When he stood up, still wordless, they moved together to the dance floor, as though they'd planned it ahead of time. His touch felt right, exactly right, and everything within her untangled and eased. As they danced, he rested his cheek on the top of her head, and an absurd notion came to her that every fear, every worry she'd ever had, was just a foolish waste of time. This was what life was about — this feeling, whatever it was.

That he also felt no compulsion to speak told her much, perhaps more than she was ready to know. She gave a fleeting thought to the others. Wherever they'd gone, she was thankful they weren't here to see her ... capitulation. She'd never hear the end of it.

Simultaneously, they shut their eyes, inhaled each other's scent, rejoiced in the feel of one another. They swayed to the music, and it was a moment of pure, light joy, one single moment untouched by the onerous weight of heartbreak they each carried within them.

The ghosts in the room drifted closer to the bandstand to watch them as they danced. And because Sarita's eyes were closed, she didn't see the looks of terror on their faces.

CHAPTER SIX

"So, all that, huh? I was only half an hour late."

They'd taken the elevator up and walked to the starboard side of the Sun Deck for some fresh air. The day had been warm, but when the sun set, the temperature cooled down enough that Sarita accepted Luca's tuxedo jacket gratefully when he offered it. He was happy to be free of it. Telling Sarita what took place at the ball before she arrived also felt liberating. Although, he didn't divulge the inimical exchange he'd had with Cristiano.

Leaning against the rail, he sent her a quick smile as he loosened his bow tie and — hell, why not? — unfastened the top stud of his shirt. "You were forty-two minutes late. Not that I was counting."

She laughed at that easily, and he was elated that she was finally letting her guard down. "If I'd known you were ensnared in such melodrama, I'd have hurried to your rescue. But I got a call from Security. A timer on one of the lights went wonky, but they thought there was a break-in. They even sent Alan to double-check."

She still had residual creeps from that whole experience, but just as Luca had, she kept some segments of what had happened before they met in the ballroom to herself. She couldn't think of one reason he needed to know she'd practically passed out from jitters at the thought of going to a party.

"Yeah, Angela told us." Luca's brow knit. "Is that the new guy on the cleaning crew? I thought they came in on Mondays."

"They do, but he said he picked up an extra gig working Security because of the ball."

Luca chuckled. "I imagine he's one of the first bobbies with dreadlocks."

Sarita was impressed by how much he'd noticed about the practices on the ship in only a month. "Oh, he wasn't dressed as a bobby. They have him in plainclothes, in case he needs to blend in, he said." She rolled her eyes. "He sure snuck up on me. Second time he nearly scared me to death in my own office." She lifted her hands in a what-can-you-do manner. "Alan Rabinowitz is unique, that's for sure."

"Yeah, so I've heard. But Inez says he's a veteran. That can screw up anybody's head." A memory tried to surface, but didn't quite make it. "His last name is Rabinowitz?"

She arched a brow. "Please don't tell me you're going to say he doesn't look Jewish."

The comment surprised a laugh out of him. "I wasn't. And by the way, I just got a quick look at him, but he could be Jewish. Or Greek, or Italian, or any number of nationalities." He waved his hand in a gesture that she'd seen Angela and Vincenzo make. There was no question that they were related. "I only asked because … the name rings a bell." He thought about it. "But I guess it's probably not uncommon."

Keen to move on, he said, "Anyway, enough about him. I'd much prefer to talk about more … personal things."

Sarita was instantly wary. "Such as?"

He knew it would be a mood killer, but he needed to know. Still, he couldn't bring himself to ask right away. When he did, he could feel his throat muscles tighten up. "It was you, wasn't it? You were the girl I gave the roses to that night."

"Oh, damn." Her eyes scrunched shut. When she opened them, they were filled with distress. "I wondered if you knew. I wasn't sure … I didn't want to bring it up, in case you hadn't … in case you didn't want —" she stopped herself, tried and stopped again. "I'm sorry. I'm babbling."

"It's all right. I get it. I just … I guess I wanted to know if that's the reason … I mean, I feel that sometimes, you avoid talking to me. And I thought —" He sounded like a moron, and now he'd upset her. Way to go. How to fix it?

His mouth quirked up, and he repeated what she'd said, "I'm sorry. I'm babbling."

That made her laugh, as he'd hoped, although the sound was skittish. With a groan of mortification, she spun to look out at the harbor. "I'm such an idiot. Here I thought I was respecting your privacy." He should only know the half of it. "Instead, I made you feel unwelcome." She glanced back at him, too quickly for him to catch the look in her eyes, but he could hear the compunction in her voice. "I didn't mean to."

He waved a hand in dismissal. "It's okay. Forget it." He leaned his forearms on the rail. They were silent as they observed the colors that the lights reflected on the water: cool blue, smoky pink, tangerine. On the deck behind them, they could hear talking, laughter. The harbor was tranquil, but the ship bustled with activity. "Do the others know — that you were there, I mean?"

She kept her eyes on the skyline as though she'd never seen it before. She stared out for so long, he thought she might not answer. "Angela was the one who got us the tickets. I was there with my mother and stepfather." She paused again, loath to share the next part. "They surprised me with the trip for my birthday."

His head whipped around. "Your birthday?" he echoed. "Oh, hell. I don't know what to say." He stared at her, appalled. "That's some birthday present."

Sarita could do nothing but lift a shoulder feebly. "I suppose now you can see why I didn't mention it."

When he laughed, her mouth dropped open. "You think it's *funny*?"

"No, I don't," he responded at once. "It's just that I can't help but think of that old joke about Mrs. Lincoln and the play." He chuckled again, but this time, Sarita caught the undertone of hideous regret and even guilt on her behalf, as though he and his brother were culpable in her ruined birthday celebration.

Her heart lurched as she tried not to let him see how sad for him she felt. She'd been self-absorbed for keeping her distance from him, she realized. She told him she'd wanted to respect his privacy, but the truth was, it was herself she'd been protecting, wasn't it? For the first time, she got past his striking good looks to see how isolated and lonely he felt.

So what to do to make amends? She went with instinct. In a tone she hoped was casual, she responded, "Well, if you were to ask, I think Mrs. Lincoln would have to say that you were splendid together."

It felt nothing less than profound to see she'd managed to say just the right thing. She could tell by the arrested look on his face as she continued softly, "We were mesmerized — my mother, stepfather, and I. So was everyone else in the theater. Honestly, I don't think I've ever seen anything as marvelous as The Miceli Brothers performing their magic."

She watched his eyes fill. He blinked to clear them. "Thank you." Pressing his fingers to his eyes, he cleared his throat. "Thank you, Sarita. Santi would have loved to hear you say that." To give himself time to recover, he faced the harbor again, but he didn't see the ripples dappled with moonlight, the lightning quick changes of the water that might have been a fish or a night bird skimming the surface. To him, the harbor was a gaping, black void. After a while, he added, "It was all Santi, you know. He was the genius behind it."

Once more, she was at a loss. "I'm sure that's not true."

"It is, absolutely. I was there solely as window dressing. I just wanted to help my brother. I never wanted to be a magician."

That intrigued her. "What did you want to be?"

"It's not important," he said. Why was he talking about this? They'd been making such good progress. With an effort to get things back on a lighter footing, he gestured to the water, then circled back to the deck. "This is all so different from the Strip. It feels good to be away from the parched air of the desert, all the noise and neon lights."

She understood that he needed a new topic, so she obliged him. They had their backs to the harbor now. Resting against the rail, she tipped her head in agreement. "I get what you mean. But there's a lot more to it than that. I used to love going to Lake Mead, hiking in Red Rock Canyon …"

"Red Rock? You're kidding." That surprised him. "You weren't afraid? You know — rattlesnakes, scorpions? What about camel spiders?" He shuddered. "Those things give me the creeps. You know they can eat your face?"

She elbowed him in the side and teased, "No, they can't, Brooklyn kid."

"Go ahead, make fun of me. I know I'm right." He pulled out his phone. "I can find a dozen videos right now —"

"Oh, please. Those are fake. Trust me, they don't bother you unless you threaten them."

He was astonished by the casual attitude. "And how, pray tell, does anything threaten a giant spider?"

She laughed.

Studying her, he put his phone away. "No offense, but you don't strike me as the outdoorsy type."

If only he'd known her before her run-in with Naag. She tucked the tuxedo jacket more tightly around her as a cool breeze drifted past. Now it was her turn to change the subject. "You and my mom would have a lot to talk about. She worked as a cocktail waitress at some of the casinos."

"Yeah, Angela mentioned it." He reached over and pushed back a strand of her hair that the wind had tousled, needing the physical contact. "There's a lot to appreciate about the Strip. The ingenuity, the talent, the fun. But —" he grimaced — "there's a lot of tragic stuff going on there, too. The homeless population is massive."

"I remember," she chimed in. "My mom told me that they'd all hang out at the edges of the poker rooms. And when winning players came out, they'd beg for five dollars and —"

"Use it to gamble," Luca finished for her. "We'd see that a lot. Security chases them out of Caesar's too. Not all of them are gambling addicts, though. Some are veterans." He shook his head. "It makes me sick how a vet in this country can end up. That's why Santi started feeding them."

"He volunteered at a shelter?"

"No." He chuckled at the image of his urbane brother slinging hash at a soup kitchen. "No, more like he'd send a crew member out for bag-loads of sandwiches, and then hand them over to the homeless who waited in the back lot. Every day, they'd pick up the bags and hurry away. They knew they could get in real trouble with the casino if they hung around, spoiling the façade." His face mirrored the righteous frustration in his words. "We like to pretend being homeless is a choice, a circumstance that stems from degenerate laziness. But that's a load of crap. Nobody with a sound mind chooses to live like an animal. Nobody wants to be hungry and cold, filthy and feculent."

When she wrinkled her nose, he stopped at once, his look repentant. "Sorry for grossing you out. Quite the spiel, eh?"

"Not at all. I agree completely." She went silent, thinking about Santi and his sacks of food. What a tragic loss, she thought again.

He sensed the change in her. To lift the mood, he shifted sideways, picked up her hand and toyed with her fingers. "You know what? I'm pretty sure I've managed to make this the most depressing first date, ever."

"Um ... I wasn't aware this was a date," she felt compelled to correct him.

The smile that curved his lips was the first that felt real to him in a long, long while. "Weren't you?" he asked gently.

Damn. Why had she said that? Technically, she'd told the truth — they weren't on a date. But she was lying by pretending she hadn't wanted something to happen between them tonight. And he knew it.

Even so, his response irked her. He sounded damn sure of himself. In an attempt to come across as confident as he, she gave him a haughty look. "That's slightly conceited, wouldn't you say?"

And just like that, his gladness in the moment faded. He let go of her hand. "Come on, Sarita. You know that's not true. I'm not conceited, any more than you are." He tried to hide the letdown he felt, but then decided to be blunt. "I didn't think you were a game player, either. But maybe I was wrong."

The remark put her on the defensive at once. Her voice stiffened primly. "And what do you mean by *that*?"

"Don't you know?" It was rash of him to take up the dare, but he didn't stop himself. "Okay, fine — I'll spell it out." He leaned one elbow on the rail again, but his words belied the casualness of the pose. "Until I said it out loud, you wanted to be here with me. I know you did, and you know you did. You've changed your mind, fine." He shrugged. "Your prerogative, certainly. But don't pretend that you didn't want to kiss me, because that's childish, and insulting to us both."

Sarita stared at him speechlessly, bowled over by his arrogance. "Wow, dude. Really?" she finally managed. "And you don't think you're conceited?"

"I'm not finished," he said, his tone clipped. Was it anger that made his eyes smolder? She wasn't sure. When he stood up straight, her hand jerked on the rail at the sudden movement, then stilled. Luca caught the reaction and it baffled him. Was she afraid of him? His voice softened. "You wanted to kiss me, and I wanted you to kiss me. I've wanted it from the first day, when you laughed at me for being such a clumsy dork and handed me that mop." His gaze grew more intense. "I still want it, very much, Sarita, more than you can possibly imagine."

Her eyes stayed locked on his as he spoke, and her pulse quickened. She was alarmed by her reaction to him. It felt too primitive, too uncontrollable. Nonetheless, she heard herself whisper, as though she were somehow compelled to ask, "If that's true, then why don't you kiss me? Why do I have to go first?"

His physical response to that question was immediate. If he thought she'd uttered it to provoke an action on his part, she'd be in his arms right now. But she hadn't. She'd asked because she truly wasn't sure that he wanted her. Her lack of sexual sophistication both puzzled and aroused him.

He slid his hands into his pockets, balled them into fists, to restrain himself from lunging for her. When he answered, nothing in his voice or face betrayed his clawing need. "I want to, but I can't. I'm bigger and stronger than you are. That's ... that's how my mother died. She resisted a bigger, stronger man — my father — and he broke her neck." He heard her intake of breath, but he kept his look and his voice steady as he continued, "You seem like you want to be here with me. At least, I sure hope so. But you're also afraid of me — of *this* — for some reason.

I'm not going to vanquish your maidenly qualms by forcing myself on you. I won't touch you if you're not sure it's what you want."

Sarita looked down at her hand. She'd been gripping the rail so tightly, her fingers ached and her knuckles had turned white. His father had killed his mother. Now she understood even more of what she'd seen in her vision. Would she have the whole picture before Luca left the *Mary*? And if so, what then? In more ways than one, she felt suspended in murky waters, not sure which way to swim next.

She needed to pull herself together before she could speak. When she did, Luca had to stoop to catch her words. "I'm not afraid of you."

That wasn't completely true, Luca knew, but maybe it was true enough. Maybe.

Christ. He was out of his depth here. Up until now, every woman he'd been involved with just took what she wanted. He'd been on first dates where some had their hands down his pants before they'd even finished dinner. Now here was this girl — lovely, inside and out — who was more flustered than seemed rational at the thought of a simple kiss. And why, he wondered, was that?

"Then, if you're not afraid of me, would you look at me?" The light amusement in his voice was deliberate. "You're staring down at your hand."

Her head shot up and she narrowed her eyes. "Are you laughing at me?"

"Nope." But his eyes gleamed with humor. And something else she wasn't able to identify. Though she couldn't tell what he was thinking, she for damn sure didn't want him to feel sorry for her.

She pulled in a deep, settling breath. "I'm not afraid of you," she repeated, firmly this time.

"No?" His expression changed. "Then, kiss me. Kiss me, Sarita. *Please*?"

The yearning on his face was her undoing. It mirrored her own. He looked so enticing standing there, tall and elegant against the rail, his tuxedo shirt open at the neck, the lights of the *Mary* reflected in his thick, dark hair. She never felt herself move. It was as if by magic that their lips were suddenly a hair's breadth apart, so close she could see his pupils dilate with desire, making his dark eyes appear luminous. And yet, he waited, patient and still, until she leaned in and pressed her mouth to his.

At her touch, he closed his eyes to revel in the sensation of her lips against his, the flavor of her, the clean, lush scent of her skin and hair, the greedy ache of hunger she spawned in him. He wanted to gorge himself on her, but he steeled himself to do no more than nibble, to give her the option of stepping back.

But she didn't. She couldn't. Despite the warning bell that sounded somewhere in her brain, she plunged forward, besieged by sudden, electrifying want. Her arms snaked around his neck like a drowning woman desperate to be saved. It had only taken that one touch of his lips, and it was as though her body had recognized him, a cherished lover who'd been lost to her for centuries, and then miraculously found again.

He met her with equal fervor, immersed in her every texture and taste, her every quickened breath and soft moan. A kiss that had begun with such constraint and artlessness was now untamed and reckless, as both their minds were stripped of everything that had come before the veracity of being in each other's arms. They were cognizant of nothing but each other. They didn't think about where they were, that there were others outside on the deck who could see them.

Being so swept away, they were likewise unmindful when the lightbulbs in all the lanterns on the deck flamed eerily, brighter and hotter the longer they embraced. Until one of those bulbs burst, and the sound of glass shattering and a passerby's yelp of fright at the noise made them jolt apart in a daze.

Panting, they stared at each other.

Sarita pressed her palms to her cheeks, staggered by what she'd felt, mortified by the fact that she'd all but devoured him whole. How could she have been so unbridled in her response? God help her — pulling away from him had been like pulling away from a life source.

Her only consolation was that he'd been as consumed by the kiss as she, as equally stunned by their … loss of reason. That was evident on his face right now, along with a lingering desire. His hair was rumpled from her hands, his lips were swollen from her love bites. She wondered if she looked as disheveled as he.

It was when her eyes moved down to the lipstick she'd left on his collarbone that she saw it: the red birthmark in the perfect shape of a star. She'd only seen one other like it. It was identical to her own.

She sucked in a gasp and stumbled back from him. "What is this?" she whispered. "Who *are* you?"

Luca was still reeling from what they'd just experienced. He could barely speak. All he knew was that she'd gone from shy and skittish to dynamite in his arms, and now, this. He had no idea what had frightened her, but there was nothing less than terror on her face. Startled by that, he reached for her. "Sarita —"

"No, don't touch me. Please." If he touched her again, she'd fall apart. Even now, the craving for contact still tore at her. To feel this much for him — so urgent, so unexpected — and then to see his mark, it scared her right down to her bones. She became aware, gradually, of sounds, of voices. Her head swiveled to her left to see two men from the Security team sweeping up glass. For the first time she noticed that there were others on the deck, some of whom were staring baldly. She blushed at the thought that they might recognize her from the Spice.

She hated herself for her licentious behavior, but at the same time, she hated herself for blushing over it. And for being afraid of Luca, when it was becoming apparent that he was just as shaken by what had happened between them as she was. Most of all, she hated herself for her cowardly impulse to flee. But just as she was about to do so —

"Cintia? … Cintia de Azevedo? Can that possibly be you?"

A frail-looking, older woman was sitting on one of the nearby benches, drinking wine with several others. She'd called out to Sarita in Portuguese, mistaking her for her mother.

Oh, perfect, Sarita thought. This is just what she needed right now — one of her mother's cronies from the old country to have seen her and Luca groping at each other. And if she went back to Cynthia and gossiped, knowing Cynthia — Brazil's version of Edina Monsoon — she'd be on Skype the next day, hounding her only daughter for every detail.

Her breath skipped as she steeled herself to put on a veneer of composed courtesy, responding, also in Portuguese, "I'm sorry. I'm not Cynthia. I'm her daughter, Sarita."

The woman stood up, wine glass in hand, and came forward to peer at her. "Yes. Now I see. You are not Cintia. It wouldn't be possible for her to still be so young. But you look so much like her."

Sarita was sure she'd never seen the woman before, yet something on her face made her step back toward Luca. Of the two, he seemed the safer bet. "Are you a friend of my mother's from *Brasil?*"

"Not exactly." The woman was close enough now for Sarita to cringe at the hate in her eyes. Luca picked up on it as well, and in reflex, he curled his fingers around Sarita's wrist. "I met your mother once when she still lived with your grandfather there," the woman continued in Portuguese. "Luis Mendes de Azevedo," she spat out the name. "A monster. A thief who stole everything from us — our land, our livelihood. His lies and his treachery destroyed my husband and my son."

Even in the dim lighting, Luca could see the blood drain from Sarita's face. He was blown away by what he'd just heard, but he didn't dare let on that he could understand the language. Discreetly, he signaled to one of the bobbies who were running flashlights over the wooden planks of the deck, searching for any remaining fragments of glass.

"I'm sorry," Sarita said to the woman again, and this time, she meant it. Her voice caught on the apology, for it wasn't only hatred she could feel coming from the woman, but pain. "I'm sorry for whatever he did to you and your family. But please understand — I don't know my grandfather. My mother would never allow us to meet. She left home when she was eighteen, and hasn't seen him or spoken to him since."

"*Quão conveniente,*" the woman sneered. Her animosity toward a powerful and evil man had, by happenstance, found a target in his granddaughter. Whether that granddaughter was innocent or guilty was irrelevant. Years before, Luis Mendes de Azevedo had driven her husband to suicide. They'd been financially devastated as a result, and her son, now grown, spent his entire life seeking retribution. There was no way she was going to relinquish the opportunity to publicly air the injustices that had been done. She gestured to Sarita's dress with resentment. "How convenient for you to distance yourself and your mother from his crimes, when I can see that you've both benefitted lavishly from them."

Sarita shook her head, compassion in her eyes. "That's not true. That's not at all true."

"That's enough." Luca's command was soft, but his eyes were cold. Discretion be damned. Whoever Sarita's grandfather was, whatever he'd done, she wasn't to blame. To Sarita he said, "Don't listen to her. Don't let her hurt you. None of this is your fault." He confronted the woman himself, doing his best to keep a check on his temper. "Lady, you're picking on someone who's never harmed you." He nodded to the security guard who'd been alerted at his signal, then turned to the woman again. "I think it's best if you go back to your friends over there, and enjoy the rest of your night. *Now.*"

Undaunted, and possibly more intoxicated than she'd first appeared, the woman shouted at Sarita, "You're a liar, just like your grandfather. I curse you, and the demon seed you come from — both your mother and you. Blood will out!"

At her shouts, the security guard stepped in, his statement impassive, but final. "Ma'am, I'm going to have to ask you to leave."

When the woman refused to budge, the guard gave a long-suffering sigh and took firm hold of her arm. First popping lightbulbs, now this. He was in for a long night.

As he led her away, the woman's last shot was to fling the contents of her glass at Sarita. She'd have been drenched with chardonnay had Luca not caught the motion in time. He flicked his fingers. For one infinitesimal blink, the liquid halted in midair, inches from Sarita's face, then slid straight down to the deck, as though blocked from her by a glass pane.

Sarita saw the wine come at her, and took a hasty side step. Luckily for Luca, she hadn't discerned his part in averting another calamity. The evening had already had its fair share.

The woman and, guilty by association, her unfortunate companions, were escorted off the ship. Sarita watched them go, her fist clutched to her stomach. Like it or not, she'd have to tell her mother. Cynthia would want to know that Luis was still as greedy and grasping as ever, irrespective of his advanced age.

Blood will out. She prayed every day that wasn't true. Depravity on one side, Vodou on the other — the gene pool from which she sprung was too unconventional for her taste. Why couldn't she have been born into a family of librarians? It was as though she drew occurrences like this to her. If only she'd stayed in, as usual. When would she learn?

The only bright spot was that she'd evaded having a panic attack. It had been close, but all things considered, she'd kept her composure. Apart from when she and Luca had kissed, that is. Then she behaved as though she were possessed. And that would not do. Not if she was sincere in her desire for the conventional. That kiss, coupled with the birthmark she'd gotten a glimpse of, didn't point Luca in the direction of the commonplace.

Luca has no idea what she was thinking, but he felt terrible on her behalf. What an unpleasant thing for her to have shouldered. Yet, he got the impression that she believed the woman's story, although now was certainly not the time to ask. He watched her struggle for equanimity, and fumbled for something to say. "Sarita, don't let this bother you. We can't be responsible for the things people in our family do —"

"Luca, I'm sorry." She sounded brusque, even to her own ears, when she cut off his words. "I'm very tired. This whole evening was a mistake."

He wouldn't pretend that he didn't know what she meant. Or that it didn't hurt to hear it. "That's a shame," he whispered. "Because it didn't feel like one to me. It felt like a miracle."

There was too much to see in his eyes. She couldn't bear it. "That's just it." She willed herself not to cry, and in the hopes that it would make him take a step back, she told him the truth. "I'm just not ready for it. And frankly, I … I don't trust you."

He raised his eyebrows. Well. She'd thrown him a curveball with that last part. It was forthright, at least. And it stung like hell. He gave a short, bitter laugh. "Funny, you're the second person to say something like that to me tonight." He folded his arms across his chest, not in challenge, but as a shield. "Okay — hit me with it. What's so shady about me?"

Just by his turn of phrase, she knew she'd offended him, and she braced for fallout. "All right. I'll give you one example. But then I'm going in, and I don't want you to follow me."

"*One* example? You mean there's more than one?"

"Yes, and here it is: For the last five minutes since that woman came over, your entire conversation has been in Portuguese. We're still speaking it, in case you haven't noticed, and your command of the language is better than mine. So, tell me — how did you learn to be so fluent?"

That jolted him. How had he not been conscious of it? He opened his mouth, then closed it, looking at her helplessly.

Nodding once, she handed him back his tuxedo jacket. "Thought so. Good night, Luca."

He didn't try to stop her. For one thing, the view of her from behind as she walked away was outstanding. For another, she was right. He was lying to her. If he wanted to build an authentic rapport with her, he was going to have to rectify that.

But first he needed to have a heart-to-heart with Angela. He glanced at his watch. Still early enough to go knock on her door. He debated. Would she want to be left alone after what he'd observed at the ball, or would she welcome the company? He slung his tuxedo jacket over his shoulder. He supposed he'd go find out.

As Luca headed inside, he walked directly past the bench where the man who called himself Alan was sitting. Alan had been hiding in plain sight, right where he was now, unobserved the entire time, privy to everything, from their passionate interlude to their altercation with the Brazilian woman. And now that they'd left, he sat alone, gloating, pervaded with hatred.

Despite all the sermons to the contrary the priests from his childhood had spewed, even as a boy, he'd experienced the savage inequities of this world, and they'd taught him that existence was nothing more than randomness, luck, and timing. Only the weak and gullible assigned to it a higher purpose or meaning. But now he considered he might have been wrong. Perhaps there was some sort of a supreme entity that oversaw the mortals it had conceived, manipulating their lives for its own gratification. If so, then tonight that entity had decided to play this game on Alan's side.

With a new addition to the plan formulating, he stood up, wandered over to the darkest corner of the rail to wait until the crowd thinned before he slipped away. When a rat ran over his shoe, he nearly blew the low profile with his quick shout. He watched the small, dark shape as it scurried across the deck to disappear over the side of the ship.

The beady-eyed little bastards were following him.

CHAPTER SEVEN

The next day was Sunday, and everyone at The Secret Spice fell back into their regular routine. Perhaps because the restaurant was closed the night of the ball, they were slammed with reservations that next evening. Every table was occupied right up until they locked the doors for the night. Which meant that everyone was run off their feet until then, giving them little time to discuss the event that had been cataclysmic for them all.

But there was much unspoken.

While Angela and Luca worked in tandem over pounds of pastry, bowls of fresh fruit and berries, batches of custards, mousses, and jams, along with every variety of chocolate from dark to white, they were thinking about the eye-opening conversation they'd had in her stateroom. And when not thinking about that, Angela was thinking about Vincenzo, and Luca was thinking about Sarita.

As for Cristiano and Rohini, having never been so far apart on any issue in the whole of their lives together, both were concerned about the same thing: whether they'd lost their ability to connect forever. Imagining such a thing was unbearable to both. And yet, they'd each borne far worse. Which was why, even in the face of their unhappiness, they were still able to work together. Their Winston Beef Wellington, their Majesty Mushroom Pasta in Pink Gorgonzola Sauce, their Shrimp Rohini, and every other dish that the restaurant was now famous for, turned out as beautifully as always. But if a chef's heartache can be tasted, as some storytellers say, every patron that Sunday would have collapsed into tears with the first delicious bite.

On the other hand, Sarita was doing her utmost to avoid thinking about the event at all. The packed dining room helped her in that effort, but even so, there were occasional lulls in her duties that made time for her thoughts to wander. When she remembered the taste of Luca's lips, she blocked it by treating the pleased but perplexed diners at table three to complimentary desserts, along with her personal dissertation of the *Mary's* history. When the pained, angry face of the woman on the Sun Deck swam into her consciousness, she battled that by entrapping her somewhat exasperated sommelier into a debate on the virtues of cabernet versus pinot noir. Sarita had this technique down to a science. Avoidance had been her modus operandi for years now, and nothing that proved its failure — persistent nightmares, chronic panic attacks, medications that helped only marginally — had put her off the practice thus far.

And then there was the wait staff, who didn't know what to think. They'd noted Sarita's unnatural conduct and verbosity, as well as the charged, yet lugubrious environment of the kitchen. For them, the latter was the main concern. Having seen and heard all manner of go-ings-on in that galley, their only clear consideration was that, despite the great tips they'd gotten as a result of the unexpectedly high volume of patrons, they couldn't wait for the night to be over. They wanted to get themselves home, away from the café and its latest peculiarities.

If they knew just how peculiar things would soon get, some might not have come back ever again.

———●

"I wish it had been me there instead of you. I never expected my past to catch up with my daughter."

"It's not your fault."

It was eleven p.m. The Secret Spice was quiet and empty, at last. Sarita was alone in the office, with the door closed and locked. As far as she knew, everyone else had either gone off to bed or home for the evening, but in case that weren't so, she wanted no interruptions while she talked with her mother.

Cynthia and Raul were currently at Raul's townhouse in London, where the local time was seven o'clock Monday morning. Raul had already left for a business meeting. Cynthia had poured a second cup of coffee, and settled in for a private chat with her daughter. There were things Sarita needed to know, that Cynthia had avoided telling her.

"I'm not sure if there's anything we can do," she cautioned. "Luis has vast political control, not only in *Brasil,* but elsewhere. Think the Koch brothers, Sheldon Adelson, George Soros. Those sons-of-bitches are influential enough to start a world war just by making a phone call."

Sarita could feel her mother's shudder right through her laptop screen. "Even Raul's considerable clout is no match for theirs. To Luis, the woman you came across is nothing —" she snapped her fingers to emphasize her point — "a bug. Make no mistake, whatever she told you about him is likely true. If she had something he wanted, he had his team of lawyers and the politicians in his pocket find a way to squash her to get it. And now, he wouldn't remember her if he stepped on her all over again."

Sarita watched her mother's grim-faced image. "I'm so sorry to have had to tell you this, *Mãe.* I'm sorry it makes you feel bad."

"How could it not, Sarita? He's my father."

This was a keen wound in Cynthia's psyche, one she'd never revealed to her daughter. "There was a time when I believed with all my heart that he was a hero." She hugged her coffee mug with both hands. She needed to feel its warmth. "It was an encounter very similar to what you just experienced that stirred my suspicions about him. Except that I was only eighteen when it happened."

Now her articulation of disgust was for herself. "I was so naïve. My trips, my wardrobe, my horses, my education — all justified, or so I thought, by my role as the benevolent socialite. I didn't know that every charity event my mother and I hosted gave back less than pennies on the dollars my father stole. You can't imagine how I felt when I learned the breadth of his depravity, Sarita."

Her throat felt dry. She drank some coffee to wet it. "He … he laughed at me when I confronted him. He told me how clever I was to have uncovered his —" she made a face of loathing as she recalled his phrase —"business dealings." When she stopped speaking briefly to collect herself, Sarita wasn't sure if their audio connection had been severed. "Clever, because I was *his* daughter. Can you believe the hubris? I thought for sure he'd show some remorse. Instead, he told me that it was none of my concern. I was to go on with my life as it was, continue to utilize what he provided for me, and eventually marry into another powerful family and give him grandchildren."

The memory still stung. A parent's betrayal was impossible to forget. "I understood then that he'd never loved me. I was nothing more to him than a … a tool to carry on the family line after he was gone. But if there were a way for his riches to buy him eternal life, he'd have had no need for me at all."

"Oh, *Mamãe*. I'm so sorry." She wished they were in the same room, so she could give her mother a hug. This was the first time Cynthia had opened up to her to this extent about those years. She understood more about her mother now than she ever had before — her entrenched sense of right and wrong, her willingness to help those less fortunate — every righteous, and even foolhardy thing Cynthia had ever said and done played back through Sarita's head. "Well, this certainly explains a lot."

Cynthia peered at her charily. "Does it, now?"

"It certainly does." Her love for her mother was in her smile as she teased, "Your distrust of Raul when you first met, for one. And let's not forget your bossiness."

That coaxed a chuckle out of Cynthia. But the matter was too important for her to be cajoled. She went back to it without missing a beat. "Find out the woman's name, if you can. The guard who intervened might have it. Perhaps Raul and I can contact her and try to make amends in some small way." She lifted her shoulders unhappily. "I can't think of anything else to do. I can't give her back whatever he stole from her. I gave up any rights I had to an inheritance when I renounced him. After he dies, his blood money will go to his other children."

"Excuse me?" That last statement took Sarita aback. "*Other* children?"

Cynthia's tone was sardonic. "You didn't think a man like him would be faithful to my mother, did you? I might have been his only progeny from his marriage, but along with every other disappointment, I learned he had a number of mistresses."

Sarita couldn't believe the offhand way her mother had imparted the information. "You waited twenty-five years to tell me you have siblings, *Mamãe*? And you've never met them?"

"No, Sarita, no." Cynthia held up her hand like a traffic cop. "I don't have 'siblings.' My father has other children. Believe me when I say they don't consider me a sister, either. If they did, they'd have had me murdered by now."

"*Mãe*! Why would you say such thing?"

This time, when Cynthia chuckled, it was rich and full. "You honestly have no idea how much the old bastard is worth, do you?" She arched a brow, gave Sarita a smug look. "Just to clarify, one of the reasons Raul trusted me before I trusted him, *filha*, was because once he found out who I was, he knew I couldn't possibly be a gold digger. If it were only money that was important to me, I'd have stayed with my father."

Sarita regarded her mother silently, picturing the luxury she gave up. She thought of her own childhood — Cynthia coming home drained from a long shift on her feet, but still preparing them both a hot meal. She'd helped with homework, taken her to the park, organized birthday parties. She put money aside in a jar all summer long so that she, Sarita, could have new clothes for school in the fall. She thought back to her mother's daring, reckless plan to use Raul Sr.'s gift to launch The Secret Spice, and her determination to return every penny, plus interest, to his son. And then she thought of how far they'd both come since that one-bedroom apartment in Las Vegas, how everything they had, everything they were, was all because Cynthia had wanted them both to earn it honestly, because she was brave, and strong, and true.

When Sarita spoke, there were tears in her voice. She suddenly missed her mother, although she'd never dare say so. "You know, *Mãe*, I've always been proud of you. But I don't think I fully appreciated who you are until right now."

———

When Luca got to the office, he could hear Sarita crying behind the closed door. He didn't stop to think. When the knob wouldn't turn, he placed his hand on it. The lock disengaged.

Sarita jumped at the clicking sound. The next thing she knew, the door opened, and Luca was striding in. Her mouth dropped open. "How did you —?"

"Magician. Lock." He held up his fingers and waggled them before she could finish. When she just stared at him, red-eyed and pink-cheeked, but clearly annoyed by his intrusion, he started to feel foolish. "Ah … I heard you crying."

Her hackles went up immediately. "Just because you can do something, doesn't mean you should, Luca. I locked the door because I wanted privacy."

"I'm sorry." Abashed, he hugged his arms to his chest. "I've never heard you cry before. Not even last night, when you almost got a face full of someone's drink. I thought there was something seriously wrong. I thought —" he stuffed his hands in his pockets — "Damn me. I don't know what I thought."

At his look of chagrin, she relented. He shouldn't have barged in, but she couldn't fault his motives. "Forget it." She grabbed a tissue to dab at her eyes, her mind still replaying her talk with Cynthia. "You startled me, that's all. Let's start over. I assume you weren't outside my office door this late at night just so you could practice magic tricks."

He winced. "Ouch, Sarita. That stings." He was only half-joking. "The preferred term to a magician is 'illusion,' not 'trick.' You're right, though — that's not why I'm here. Angela said this is where you were, and I wanted to talk." His kept his hands in his pockets and watched her crumple up the tissue. "Looks like this isn't the best time."

"No. It's fine. I was just —" she gestured to the laptop — "that was my mother." Now she was more annoyed with herself than him. She'd been on edge since last night. It wasn't his fault that she lost her composure around him.

"Uh huh." He folded his long legs into one of the empty chairs, and sat back, still wary of the tears. "Does she make you cry every time you two talk?"

She smirked. "Not usually, no. It was something she said that got me thinking about … other stuff." She debated whether or not she wanted to bring it up. "We were talking about my grandfather."

"Oh, right — *that* guy. And the woman from last night." With remarkable grace, he picked up the discussion, making her feel as though the distressing way their evening had ended wasn't an issue for him. "Grandpop sounds like a prize."

"Yes. Although, I've never met him, so I've only got the hearsay from my mother. And," she added ruefully, "from screaming strangers."

"Hey, if you can't believe the things a stranger screams in your face, what can you believe?"

Now she laughed outright. He was getting good at putting her at ease, even with the fact that when they were together she still felt so … aware of him.

Seeing that she had relaxed with him again, he dove right in. "Coincidentally, that's what I wanted to discuss. And a number of other things if … if you're up for it. But, mostly that. That conversation. In Portuguese."

"Oh."

She honestly had no idea what else to say besides that. He'd knocked her for six. She thought she'd put him off with what pretty much amounted to a suspicious-minded, semi-accusation. After all, people learned to speak other languages for all kinds of reasons. She never thought he'd be back to offer an explanation, and most certainly not so soon.

Unbeknownst to her, she'd asked just the right question. Luca's answer to it would open a door for her that opened only to a select few. Time would tell if she'd dare to step over its threshold.

"Sarita," he began, "I like you. I like you a lot. I want us to be friends."

She blinked. "Friends?"

A slow smile curved his lips, a smile that made her feel like he'd reached over to trail his fingers lightly down her spine. "Friends, to start," he clarified. He brought his chair in closer, and reached across the desk to take her hand. "Friends have to be able to trust each other, as you said yesterday. Friends don't lie to one another. And I have been lying. By omission."

He cleared his throat. "My brother was the only other person I trusted with this. It'll probably make you think I'm insane. But I swear I'm not. And I need your promise — whether you end up believing me or you don't — that you'll keep it to yourself." He waited for her to mull that over. "Will you promise?"

"Okay. I guess." She might be sorry, but she'd soon find out.

At her word, he inclined his head. "All right, then." He started with what he supposed would be the easiest to believe. "You asked me why I'm able to speak Portuguese. The fact is ... I can speak every language known to man."

"Every language?" She kept her skepticism out of her tone. "You mean, like even ... Zulu?"

"Yeah."

"How did you learn them all?"

He answered her as honestly as he could. "I don't know."

A tiny line marred her forehead as she frowned at him. "You ... don't know?"

"No, I don't. That's the truth." He was watching her face, trying to gauge her reaction. "It started when my mother was still alive. She died when I was about six and a half, so figure a year or so before that, when it came to me that I could understand it all — the priests at church when they spoke Latin during Mass, the Vietnamese grocer telling his wife to make sure I hadn't stuck any of the candy I was eyeing in my pocket — everybody. At first, I didn't put it together that I wasn't ... wasn't supposed to understand. I remember telling that grocer that I hadn't stolen any candy. I even showed him my pockets. You should have seen how he looked at me. When we left the market, my mother scolded me. She said it wasn't nice to make fun of other people who were different than we were."

"I don't get it. Why would she say that?"

"Because that's what she thought. She thought I'd been mocking him." He smiled because now, as an adult, he appreciated the irony. "How would she know I'd spoken to him in authentic Vietnamese?"

When Sarita said nothing, Luca let go of her hand and leaned back again, not once taking his eyes off her. "You think I'm nuts? Or that I'm making this up?"

"No." She swallowed, remembering the star birthmark. "No, I don't." She paused. "How did you feel when you realized you ... were different from everyone else?"

The tension in his shoulders eased. She might not be comfortable with what she was hearing, but by some miracle, she believed it. Or at least was open to it. Still, the rest of what he told her could change everything. Having never revealed these things about himself to anyone since he was a child, he had no clue how to go about it. He decided the unvarnished truth might be best.

He put his elbows on the desk and leaned his cheek on one hand. "As a kid, it was the one part of myself I liked. I felt like a superhero. Kind of a weird power for a superhero to have, but still."

Though she still looked disconcerted, her next comment was encouraging. "So, in your mind, you were ... Polyglot Man?"

"I like it. I should get that on a t-shirt." He beamed at her. She was listening, she was making jokes. Bolstered by that, he went on with his story. "We lived in Brooklyn. After I came to understand that I had this —"

"Superpower." She couldn't resist.

He winked. "You got it. After I realized I had this superpower, I looked forward to the times we'd use the subway. There's no place like the New York subway for hearing a wide variety of languages. Greek, Spanish, Cantonese, Russian — you name it. I'd just sit there quietly and absorb it all."

124

"Oh —" She held her hand over her mouth. "I'm sorry for interrupting, but I just have to ask. I've always wanted to know — are they saying more interesting things? Because in languages I don't understand the conversations certainly seem more interesting."

Luca was delighted by the question, delighted with her. Those opinions showed in his smile, and made her blush. "Nope. Same old, boring stuff." He thought for a minute. "Everybody talks about fruit, for example. The price of it. Stuff like that. Rice is also a big topic."

"Fruit and rice, huh? I'd have never guessed." She was leaning on her elbows too, enthralled.

"By the time I was ten, I wanted to use my ability in a helpful way. I thought maybe I could be an interpreter, or a teacher of languages overseas. You know, a profession that helped people communicate with one another."

Oh, my gosh, she thought. He's so sweet and sincere. You are in so much trouble, Sarita.

He stopped speaking, self-conscious suddenly. She was looking at him in the most intent way.

After a while, she asked, "Why didn't you do it, then? Why did you become a magician, instead?"

Tightness came and went in his chest. "Well. You might say I had a life-changing experience. Rather, we did. Santi and me."

She went very still. She knew what that experience was, quite intimately. She wanted to kick herself for asking, but she wouldn't stop him from talking about it now, if that's what he needed.

"Santi was there when my father killed my mother. He saw the whole thing happen. She knew my father was coming, and she … she hid Santi in the cupboard under the kitchen sink."

The dark, cramped place, Sarita thought. That's what it was, then. A cupboard. That's what she'd seen in the vision.

"It was two days before Easter," Luca was saying, "I wasn't there with them. I was with my grandfather, at a special Mass."

On a bridge, holding a candle. She hadn't forgotten. How could she possibly?

"My brother was never the same after that. I couldn't leave him, not ever again." Luca spoke softly. "After we finished high school, he came up with the idea for us to form the act. That's what he wanted, what he seemed to need. So, I agreed." She heard the pride in his voice when he told her, "He started working toward his goal by time he was ten. At sixteen, he was already so good, he was teaching magic courses at the local college."

"Impressive." If she thought his devotion to helping his brother fulfill his dream was on the extreme side, she didn't voice that opinion. Having no brothers or sisters, she had no idea how she would feel.

"I wonder why he wanted to be a magician," she mused.

"I think I know." But when he hesitated, Sarita hazarded a guess.

"Was it because he didn't have the same multilingual abilities?"

So much sorrow came into his face at her conjecture, that she automatically took his hand again. "He felt … since we were identical twins, that he'd been cheated. Not only of that ability, but the others."

She had no experience with sibling rivalry either. But his weighty sense of obligation to his brother made more sense now. As she was digesting that, the last part of what he'd said registered. "Wait. 'Others?' You mean, you have more?"

And here was his chance to reveal all. He examined her face. She didn't look repulsed or afraid, so far. She just looked interested. But did that mean she could handle it?

"Are you sure you're ready for this? I was planning on telling you everything, but in smaller doses. The abilities I have … they're … unusual. I wouldn't want you to be afraid of me. Or worse, avoid me."

"Oh, Luca." She'd had no idea he carried that much vulnerability inside him. "I'd never do that." But she had done just that, hadn't she? "Well, I mean, we're past that. Besides, how much more unusual than speaking every language can these abilities be?"

She should only know. "A lot more unusual, Sarita." He reiterated to be certain she got it. "A hell of a lot more. I'd love to show you. If I do, you'd be the only person — the only living person — besides me who knows."

That sounded like a huge level of trust to be granted, and Sarita wondered at the commitment it entailed. But she had to admit she was intrigued. "You have me very curious."

"Being curious is one thing. What I want to know is, are you brave enough — the girl who's not afraid of spiders?"

That remark made her think twice. She bit her lip. "You mean it's dangerous?"

"No, no. It's very safe," he assured her, his mood brightening considerably, perhaps even too much so. He didn't take into consideration that she had no inkling of what he could do, while he, on the other hand, was used to it all. But in his excitement, he'd convinced himself that even with her question about any possible dangers, she didn't appear to be frightened. And it would be exhilarating to share this secret with her. If his mother were watching, she'd have seen that his eyes brimmed with the same flirtatious fun his father's once had. And just like his father, Luca's impulsiveness was going to get him in trouble.

"Sarita," he whispered, "You'll *love* it."

The devil in that promise was too enticing to resist. Like the dress she'd bought with Rohini, like the kiss she and Luca had shared, she got caught up in the newness and the thrill. It surprised him just as much as it surprised her when she jumped from her chair like a child.

"Okay, I give. What is it? What is it? I want to know. I won't tell anyone. I'm not afraid."

He couldn't have been happier. "Okay, then. Come around the desk." He stood behind her, his arms encircling her, her shoulders pressed against his chest. He planted a quick kiss on the top of her head. "Ready?" When she nodded, he told her, "Close your eyes, and keep them closed until I tell you to open them."

With no clue what she was in for, she obeyed. He kept hold of her, and she heard some brief bursts of sound, like the noise bubble wrap makes when one steps on it. There was a quick gust of wind, and she felt a dip in her stomach, as though she were on an elevator that had just headed down. She shivered with sudden chill.

"Damn," she heard Luca say, "I should have thought of this. It looks like it might rain. Okay, Sarita — you can open your eyes."

As soon as she did, she stiffened in disbelief, and grabbed onto his arms with both hands. "Oh, *God*. Omigod, omigod — what *is* this?"

"We're in Italy. Rome, to be exact."

Still clutching his arms, her eyes, frantic and crazed, darted everywhere. "You're full of crap! I don't believe you. That's impossible. This is some kind of hypnosis."

He'd never heard her swear before. Unaware of the implications, he was tickled by her reaction, even though he knew this was an overwhelming experience for her.

That was an underestimation of what she was feeling, by far. With no idea how close she was to one of her panic attacks, while she was still clamped to him like a vise, he turned, ninety degrees, and she sucked in such a deep lungful of air that she started to wheeze.

The Colosseum was right in front of her. She'd never seen it before, and it was glorious. She looked down at the cobblestone street she felt under her shoes. Frantically, she swiveled her head, left and right. People were everywhere — tourists of every stripe and size, fashionably-dressed natives chattering in Italian on their phones, a group of nuns, some very attractive men in black uniforms with red striped trousers, the word 'Carabinieri' printed in white lettering on a pocket-sized car they stood near.

By the time she'd taken this all in, her heart was galloping like a race horse and she was faint from hyperventilation. She whirled back around to face Luca, and his stomach sank when he got a good look at her. "Get me out." She could barely manage to speak. "I want to go home. Get me the hell back to the ship. *Now.*"

"Okay, okay. That's it. Slow, deep, complete breaths. Easy. Relax your body. That should reverse some of the adrenaline."

They were in her stateroom, on her couch. Luca was holding her in his lap, stroking her hair, rubbing his hands up and down her arms, doing whatever he could think of to soothe her. Apart from that, he was mentally kicking himself. What an asinine thing to do. For him, teleporting was so every-day, it never occurred to him that it would scare the crap out of her. He thought she'd think it was fun. How typical of him. He was such a moron. He'd spoiled everything, for sure.

When the blood made its way back into her brain, she looked up at him, nauseated, pale-faced, and still mad as hell. "You asshat. Do you think that *maybe* it might have been a good idea to warn me that you were about to break down my atomic structure and transport me intercontinentally?"

Luca thought that he would have cut off his left nut, willingly, if he could just go back fifteen minutes and make a different decision. "Well, that's not what happened. You stayed whole." When she slit her eyes at him, he held his hands up in surrender. "But you're right. You're so right. I'm an asshat. I have no impulse control. I don't know what I was thinking, that's the truth. I'm so used to doing it. I got caught up in your enthusiasm during our conversation. It was wrong of me to not warn you first. I'm sorry. I scared you and … I'm sorry." He smacked himself on the forehead. "Damn. That's all I seem to be saying to you today." He took a long breath. "I'm glad to hear the sarcasm, though. It's a good sign. It means you're feeling better."

After listening to all this self-admonition, she climbed off him, checking to see if she could stand. When she was sure that her legs would hold her, she wobbled over to the armchair opposite and sat down to face him. "Is this the last of it, or is there more?"

Luca skimmed his eyes over her, decided she'd do better with the truth. "There's more. But I think you've had enough for now. This whole weekend has been pretty traumatic. For both of us."

"You think?" A stray thought wandered into her head. "This is irrelevant, but I just want to know. That white horse — did you zap it somewhere for real, or was that a trick?" She corrected herself. "I mean, an illusion?"

White horse? It took him a minute to catch up. And, since she was still asking questions, could he take that to mean she wasn't going to bail on him? "It was illusion. Santi would never have allowed any … anything else."

"Huh." She disregarded the information about Santi as she focused in on a hunch. "Wait a minute — the desserts, the foods. Angela and Rohini have been raving about you, and Cris has been gnashing his teeth."

He ran a hand over his face. It had to be after midnight. The hour, all the disclosures and ramifications thereof, had sapped his energy. "Look — it's not sorcery. It's science."

She snorted. "How do you figure that?"

"Because it *is*," he insisted, with a faint hint of impatience. "I use my eyes to focus on whatever I need to focus on, I concentrate on what I want to happen, and … it happens. Sometimes it's easy, sometimes it's hard." Just like Angela, he gestured the whole time he talked.

"Do we understand the full potential of the human brain? Do we know all the physics and biology there is to know? Hell, do we even know for sure how we got here, Sarita? No, we don't. Has it ever occurred to you that we might be stopping ourselves from doing all that we're capable of doing because we've been told — *convinced* — that it's not possible? Or not acceptable?"

He got up, frustrated suddenly, although not with her. But he felt compelled to point out the meritocracy of the mediocre. "Ever notice that it's only the unexceptional and banal that makes people feel safe? Why is that?" He hit his fist against his palm. "I hate this, you know that? I hate having to hide what I am, having to worry that I'll lose someone I care about if I don't. This is what it's been like for me my whole life. Why do I have to feel, every minute of every day, that there's something shameful about me?"

He stopped speaking when she shot up out of her chair. Her face was colorless and she was trembling. He closed his eyes momentarily, feeling even more remorse. "Now I've upset you. Again."

"No," she whispered. "You haven't upset me. Quite the opposite." In contradiction to that statement, she covered her face with her hands, and to his absolute shock, she started to cry. Not the soft tears he'd walked in on earlier, but unrestrained sobs, as though a dam of them inside her had burst and she had no way now to hold back the outpouring of anguish. "You're right. Oh, God, you're so right. I'm such a coward. And a liar."

In an instant, he was beside her, pulling her to him. "What are you talking about? Sarita —"

"No, you have to believe me." Curling her fists against his t-shirt, she wept as though her life were ending. "You just made me see it. I'm not brave, like you. Or like my mother. Oh, Luca, there's so much about me you don't know. You've told me everything, and I've told you nothing."

"Hey." He cradled her, pressed her head to his shoulder. "Hey, come on. Don't cry. It's all right. What is it? What is it you haven't told me?"

She let go of him and stepped back. "I want to tell you. I'm so scared to tell you, but I want to tell you." Scrubbing at her tears, she began to pace. "I need to think. How … how do I tell you?" Though she fought to steady her voice, it wouldn't stop trembling. "Will you give me some time? To go over it in my head?"

"Time?" he repeated the word with dread. That could only mean one thing. "You mean you want me to go away … to leave the ship?"

"No. No. Oh, please don't look at me like that — like I've crushed you. I'm not saying this to send you away, or keep you away. I just — oh, dammit!" She pulled at her own hair in frustration. "I'm not doing this right. I'd never planned to tell *anyone*. And now, you've made me see how wrong that is. But I … I just need to figure out how to do it." She walked back to him and put her palm against his chest. "Please, Luca."

He couldn't move. He hadn't registered anything she said after he heard her say she needed time. As vulnerable as she was feeling, so was he. There was only one other person in his life he'd told about his powers, and that person had resented him because of them. Santi had died trying to prove he was as good as Luca. He'd lost his brother because of what he was, and now it looked as though he would lose what had just begun to bloom between him and Sarita.

In the perilous state of being that he was currently experiencing — that of a man falling in love for the first time — he could conceive of no other reason for her to have gone to pieces like this, other than delayed reaction to what she'd experienced. His thoughtless showing off had terrified her. And with his focus on that, the only logical conclusion for her tears he could draw was that she was saying good bye.

"All right." It was painful to step back when they'd made it this far, but it was his fault that she was so distraught, so he'd be a gentleman about it. "All right, I'll give you some time."

He took in every feature of her face, wanting to memorize them, so he wouldn't forget how alive he'd started to feel again when he was with her. Leaning down, he kissed her cheek, sure that it would be the last time he touched her. "Good night, Sarita."

The door didn't click shut behind him when he left. He didn't see that it stayed open, just a sliver.

The night wasn't over for either of them.

After he left her, he walked outside and went up to the Sun Deck, back to the spot at the rail where they'd shared such a promising kiss. He would have been gone right then, but he couldn't. Not after what had happened the night of the ball. Especially now that he knew that Angela had received a visitation from his mother too. Sarita might be in danger, and whether she approved of his powers or not, he'd use them to protect her, if necessary.

She wasn't the first to push him away because of what he was. The first who lingered in his mind was old Mrs. Zarcone. She'd been so nice to him once. But from that day on the bridge until the day she died, she crossed herself whenever she saw him, like he was some kind of a malignant being. There were the kids at school who somehow sensed he was different, even though he'd kept a low profile. He wasn't joking when he told Sarita that he'd pretended to be a superhero. He would think of Clark Kent, Peter Parker — all the good guys who kept their true identities a secret. But even so, there were still so many who treated him like he had the three sixes of Satan tattooed to the top of his head. And how could he ever forget his brother's last words to him, only hours before he died?

For whatever reasons he'd been rejected — superstition, jealousy, insecurity, fear — his brain told him that the problem was theirs, not his, but his heart wasn't nearly as rational. The wounds to it from the loss of his twin had only just begun to scab over, but he hadn't been cautious, and tonight they'd ripped open anew.

Consequently, he decided to blow off more than two months of sobriety and get thoroughly plastered. Not on the ship, though, where people now knew him. Wasn't he lucky, wasn't it 'fun,' as he'd told Sarita today, that he could go anywhere else he wanted, and be back before he was missed?

Yeah. He was one lucky bastard, as Santi had never tired of telling him.

And so, while Luca was in Equador, where the Zhamir was cheap and potent, and his chances of being recognized were slim, Sarita was in her bed, having another nightmare. A new one. One that she was seeing though the eyes of a young man.

He was on a beach. Other young men were with him. She knew they were some type of infantry — American, she believed. They looked so pitiful, barely more than children, as they lay in dog-tired sleep on sandy, threadbare blankets, stealing a few hours before the sun came up and the bombing started again.

But there were rats out at night. To the rats, the young men weren't the brave, foreign liberators they'd been told they were. They were just a fresh, warm meal. And while they slept on, unaware of the small, creeping shapes that blended in with other murky shadows on the beach — the rocks, their helmets, and knapsacks — he was awake, and could see those rodent eyes gleaming in the moonlight, slinking closer. There were dozens. Hundreds. He tried to move, to pull out his KA-BAR, but somehow, he couldn't. He lay paralyzed, as all those long, orange teeth came nearer and nearer; he could feel their breath on his face, and the smell —

The man, whoever he was, woke up with a shout, and Sarita knew that this nightmare was *his* nightmare. She'd been seeing it in her sleep along with him, and she was still in her trance. Though his face was obscured, she could make out his thrashing form. Not on a beach this time, but in a small, dim room, on a narrow cot. The light in the room changed, and someone else was with him. A woman, soothing him, in a voice Sarita thought she might have heard before:

It's all right. I'm here with you, my love. I'll never leave you.

When the vision went black, Sarita lay in the dark, her skin damp with sweat, her hands fisted in the tangled sheets.

This time she would be braver. This time, she wouldn't run for a sleeping pill to try to obliterate what she'd seen. She sat up, switched on the bedside lamp, picked up the pen and notepad she kept on her nightstand, and wrote it all down.

Her mother and Luca had inspired her. She was going to deal with this one. This time, she wouldn't let herself forget what she saw.

CHAPTER EIGHT

The sea change that had started with Luca's arrival and escalated during the Art Deco Ball had not nearly reached its peak, and by Monday it was thrumming not only at the Secret Spice, but throughout the ship and beyond.

At six a.m. that morning, Angela was already working. She'd made pastry dough and set it to chill, and now she was brandying cherries. Due to the early hour, she was alone. Alone, apart from the spirit who had chosen their kitchen as her preferred dwelling place, that is. It had taken Angela longer than it had for Rohini and Cris to become cognizant of that presence, but once she had, she wasn't averse to sharing the space with a ghost. No, she relished their remarkable acquaintance, even though their conversations were generally one-sided.

"I'm so glad I tested these out on Douglas. Without at least one outside endorsement, I'm not sure I'd have had the guts to add them to the menu. They're becoming as popular as our Raspberry Chocolate Truffle Tarts. Goes to show, doesn't it?"

She sampled the spices, sugar, lemon and brandy mixture that would be poured over the freshly-pitted cherries. More ground cardamom, she decided. Just a smidge. "I wish you could try some," she continued to the kitchen. "I'd especially love to hear your opinion. None of us would be here without you." She took another taste, added a dash of lemon zest. "Did they have Brandied Sour Cherry Tartlets when you were alive?"

If the spirit had intentions of replying this time, she was forestalled by Rohini's arrival. "Good morning, Your Majesty. Good morning, Angela."

No one who worked at The Secret Spice was certain that the spirit in their kitchen was of royal blood, but Rohini, being an empath, had started calling her 'Your Majesty' upon first engagement, and the others decided to follow suit. Whether the estimation of their active and sassy ghost's peerage was accurate or not, it was best to err on the side of caution. They'd all experienced what she was capable of when her nose was out of joint. Rohini took the matter of address even further than that. Her feeling was, if her favorite spirit was indeed the former Queen of England, then as the highest ranking person, it was only proper she be greeted before anyone else in the room.

"Good morning to you too," Angela replied. "You're up early."

"As are you." Rohini went straight for the kettle and set it to boil. She needed tea — chamomile to calm her nerves. "Couldn't you sleep?"

Angela had her back to Rohini as she swirled the syrupy mixture. "Nope. Not a wink. Vincenzo sent me a text last night. It wasn't a nice one." She tried not to sound as despondent about it as she was. "He and Douglas broke up. He says they fought because of me."

"Oh, what nonsense." Rohini pulled out a chair. "I'm surprised at him for saying such a thing. You might have been the catalyst, but the issues between them have been there. Am I right?"

"Maybe. But I do feel responsible, Ro. It seems to me everyone was a lot happier when I just fell in line."

"Well, you certainly weren't."

"Nope. I wasn't," Angela agreed, thinking about what Harry had said before he left Saturday night. "At least Luca stopped by for a while." She glanced back at Rohini, gave her an 'I've-got-big-news' look. "He knows about Gina."

"Ah." Rohini folded her hands in her lap, sagely. "That doesn't surprise me."

"Considering how easily he agreed to come here, I guess it shouldn't have surprised me, either. Being so Catholic, we never talked about this kind of thing in my family. Apart from the occasional mention of exorcism. Oops. Sorry." The pots had rattled against the wall at the word.

Checking that the sugar had melted, she switched off the flame, and went back to the subject of her late night chat with Luca. "I'll have to fill you in on the details of that conversation. It kept my mind off my son's complaints, for sure." She leaned back against the stove as she waited for the mixture to settle and cool. "It's like déjà vu listening to the kid, honestly. My mother, my husband — I hear them the minute he opens his mouth. Geez. I hate to say it, but Douglas has all my sympathy."

Seeing the slump of Angela's shoulders, Rohini recognized that she'd taken on a fresh burden of guilt. In her opinion, Vincenzo had some soul-searching to do. She so wished that she didn't have to be the bearer of more troubling news. But it couldn't be helped. It concerned two of Angela's business partners, so she needed to know. How to tell her, though, to lessen the blow?

"This year's ball sure didn't turn out as we'd hoped, huh?" Angela went back to work, placing a strainer over the bowl of cherries and pouring brandy mixture into it.

"Isn't that the truth?" Seeing a small opening there, Rohini decided that, like pulling off a bandage, it was best done quickly. "Actually … Douglas and Vincenzo aren't the only ones, I'm afraid. Cristiano has been sleeping on the couch since the ball."

Angela's hand slipped, spilling some of the liquid. She spun to face Rohini. "Oh, Ro. That's terrible."

"Yes." Rohini's voice quavered. "I don't know how things got so far off track between us."

"Oh, my God." Angela clasped her hands. "Please tell me this isn't about that stupid argument you two had over Luca."

"I knew you would think that." Angela's eyebrows flew up when Rohini stamped her foot in frustration. "I knew you'd take this on yourself, just as you do everything else. That's why I hated having to tell you."

The tea kettle began to whistle as she wiped at eyes that had gone moist. "Again, we're talking about *catalysts*. If it hadn't been Luca, it would have been something else. Although, if you were to ask my husband, it's just my irregular menstrual cycle that's causing the problem." She stomped over to the kettle and switched it off with a snap. "That man is so thickheaded." Pulling a cup off the shelf and a spoon from the drawer, she slapped them down on the counter. "And so overbearing." She poured hot water into the cup recklessly, and it sloshed over the rim.

A petulant Rohini was a rare sight, and the reason for it struck Angela as humorous. "Let me get this straight — you're mad at Cris because he's thickheaded and overbearing?" Her tone was playful as she repeated Rohini's assessments. "You're just noticing now, Ro? I'm not married to him, but I might as well be. I'm in this kitchen with him every day. He's been the same man for the past ten years."

Rohini looked down at her steeping tea. "Well, perhaps I'm not the same woman, Angela."

The quiet conviction in that statement stopped Angela cold. She'd tried to cajole Rohini out of her marriage woes, but now she saw there was more going on than she'd let on. No one knew better than Angela how challenging it was to pretend that you were happy when you weren't, to have resentments trapped inside that you didn't dare unleash.

She chose her next words with more care. "Of course you're not. You're stronger and braver." She paused, then pressed gently, "But sweetie, don't you think those changes are, at least in part, due to him?"

"Yes." Rohini lifted her teacup and blew on it as she thought back. "At first, I only dared challenge myself because he encouraged it. And then I learned to do so on my own. But he ... he prompted my journey."

With a small smile, Angela tipped her head. "Exactly." She kept her face as neutral as she could manage. "Whatever your answer is to my next question, you need to know — I'm your friend, and I'll support you." Braced for what she might hear, she asked, "Do you still love him?"

Rohini could feel herself getting weepy again. "I do, yes. I love him very much. I just ... I suppose ... there are some things I need to sort out."

Sighing, Angela took off her apron, shook it out and hung it on its hook. "You know what? I have an idea. I'm going to let Luca finish these tarts. Since you and I are up, let's go to the market now. We'll get our orders in early, then have ourselves a nice breakfast somewhere. Maybe even do some window shopping, if we're up to it." She took Rohini by the arm and steered her out of the kitchen. "I think we could use a day out, don't you?"

They were off the ship by seven, an hour earlier than usual for them on marketing day. Had they left fifteen minutes later, they'd have seen Sarita drag herself into the office and make a beeline for her coffee maker. She hadn't slept much better than they had.

As her favorite French roast perked and the invigorating scent filled the room, the same questions that kept her up for half the night were still spinning in her head: Who were the man and woman in her vision? Did she honestly want to know, or had she been bolstered into bravado by the things Luca had told her about his own abilities and struggles?

Luca. She admired the fact that he was straightforward, that he'd had the mettle to tell her who he was. He could make her laugh. And he'd shared his magic with her — not 'magic,' but genuine 'magick' that any other human being would have been thrilled to experience. Honest, brave, fun, and smoking hot. She pursed her lips as she acknowledged that last thing. All in all, a great combination. If any man would be able to deal with her unique qualities, it would be him. So what was she waiting for?

Even though she promised him that she would tell him more about herself, in the bright light of day, she was vacillating again. For the first time, she asked herself why she, whose lineage boasted such fierce and fiery women, was such a scaredy-cat.

Yes, she'd suffered a major trauma. But so had Luca. He'd suffered more than one, hadn't he? He had powers that made hers seem negligible in comparison. And yet, he didn't let either his bad experiences or his abilities get in the way of his having a life.

She poured steaming coffee into one of the lovely Deruta mugs Jane had sent her for her birthday. Until yesterday's unimaginable sojourn, she thought the treasured ceramic set would be the closest she'd ever come to experiencing Italy. Jane and Antoni extended her invite after invite to visit them there, to go sailing with them on the *Gabriella*. She always found an excuse to turn them down. The possibility that she'd have an otherworldly episode at an inconvenient time, like the one she'd had when she was in Vegas with her mother and Raul, was her deciding factor for every adventure she didn't embark upon, every opportunity she didn't take.

She swallowed some coffee. Might as well admit she was one step away from being a recluse. And while she was at it, she should also admit that, as much as she loved living and working on the *Mary*, in every other aspect of her existence, she was … unfulfilled. But, if she told Luca everything — even about Naag — could he be trusted?

The popping noise that came from behind her almost made her drop Jane's very expensive mug. But recognizing the sound for what it was, she was prepared before she turned.

The ghost of the pretty young woman she'd twice encountered in Vegas sat perched on the edge of Angela's desk, looking just as solemn as she had previously. And she still couldn't retain a consistent opacity. Her arms and legs were already going transparent.

Don't freak. Speak to her. Ask her why she's here, Sarita, damn you, she prodded herself.

"Hello." She was pleased that her voice sounded even. "I remember you. What's your name? Is there something you want? Do you want to tell me why you're so sad?"

"He needs you." The spirit sounded just as muffled and remote as she had in the ladies' room at the Guy Savoy, but her desperation was palpable. "And you need him." She opened her mouth to say more, but was interrupted by a blast of icy air that whooshed through the room and aimed straight for her. It hit her in the face, disheveled her hair and pulled at her neat, white cardigan. Papers from all four desks blew everywhere, pen and pencil holders tipped and rolled. The lack of welcome was unquestionable. With another quick pop, she was gone.

"Nice, very nice." Sarita chastised aloud. "The first time I purposely communicate with an unfamiliar presence, and you chase her away." With a huff, she perused the room. "If you'd have waited a minute, you might have noticed that the poor thing was trying to tell me something. Don't you think it might be important, considering that she's tried twice already?"

The only response she got to her scold was another flutter of air. And a brisk knock at the door.

"Sarita?"

"Yes." She ordered her body to relax. "It's not locked, Inez."

Inez zeroed in on the disarray as soon as she stepped in. "*Ay.* What happened?"

Sarita waved away the question and bent to pick up the things closest to her. "A show of pique by one of our residents. Nothing unusual." A thought occurred. "You haven't bumped into any new ones recently, have you?"

"New ones?" Inez repeated with a dark look. "*Dios,* I hope not. I've come across every one of them that's in this place, and always when I'm trying to get work done." She gestured to the shamble that had been made of the office. "As you can see, they keep me plenty busy. We don't need any more, that's for damn sure."

Sarita lifted her head at the tone and the language. "Is something wrong?"

"Have you seen Alan recently?"

"Um ... just briefly, on Saturday night. But not this morning. Why?"

"Damn him!" More than upset, Inez was on the verge of a hissy fit. "I was counting on him today, and he's already over an hour late. He wasn't here yesterday, either. I thought there was some confusion with the schedule, but he's not answering my texts. He's gone and quit without telling me." Sarita stared when Inez yanked out Rohini's desk chair, dropped herself into it, and proceeded to turn the air blue with Spanish swear words. This was not like her at all.

She further surprised Sarita when she counted on her fingers, making her day's tasks sound like the Labors of Hercules. "The Royal Salon, The Tea Room, The Victoria Room — all need to be prepared for events that are taking place *today.* How is my crew supposed to get them all done, plus everything else, without his help? How could he do this? I trusted him, even when everyone else warned me I shouldn't."

"Hold on, hold on, Inez." Putting the fallen papers aside, Sarita attempted to smooth feathers. "This isn't the first time something like this has happened, and it won't be the last. You know you'll figure this out, just as you have dozens of times before."

"No, I will not. I need to quit this job — that's what I need to do. It's the only thing that will help."

It was the fact that she sounded so defeated that had Sarita closing the office door, but she did so with an inward groan. On top of all else, now this. She glanced wistfully at her coffee. "Inez, I know you can handle this. We've all dealt with unreliable staff. This isn't about work. Something's been going on with you for a while. What is it?"

"You want to know what it is?" Inez jumped up and started pacing. "I'll tell you — my daughter is driving me crazy. And my husband is not helping the situation."

Having lived with the three drama queens, Cynthia, Angela, and Cristiano — not to mention the spectral one that reigned over her restaurant — fits of temper were nothing new to Sarita. But as theatrical as it had seemed at first, Inez's distress sounded more genuine, more critical. Grabbing her mug of cooling coffee, Sarita put her own needs aside, and settled in to listen.

"When Michael and I got married, I chose to keep working." Inez continued to parade across the floor and back. "It was hard to trust at first, you know? I wasn't about to give up my position here, my seniority, and depend on my new husband for money, no matter how good he was to me and my daughter. Just in case, Sarita, I was wrong again, like I was with Marisol's father. I needed that security. When they promoted me, I knew that if anything happened — if Marisol and I should ever be alone again — we would be okay." She stopped pacing, and looked at Sarita as though she expected her to argue the point.

"Well, naturally. My mother felt the same way." Sarita gave her a thumbs up. "Good for you."

But instead of being comforted by that, Inez's eyes filled. "Except that I think by putting those needs first, I destroyed Marisol. I have not taken care of her nearly as well as your mother did you."

"Oh, come on, Inez. First of all, every mother makes mistakes. And second of all, that's not true. You've been devoted to Marisol for as long as I've known you."

Hugging her arms to her chest, Inez sniffled back tears. "Then why has she become a criminal?"

"I ... um ... what?"

Inez went back to pacing. "I got a call from her school. She has been cutting classes. She and that new friend of hers. That ... that *Lizzie*." She pronounced the name like an invective. "It's the only friend she has. I don't know why." She threw her arms up, helplessly. "She says she doesn't like the other girls at school. But this Lizzie is a troublemaker. I *said* it to Michael that she was going to be a bad influence, but he told me I was worried about nothing. I hate it when he does that. He thinks he's showing her love, but he's spoiling her." She made the same face she made when a guest left a stateroom particularly untidy. "Now he'll be sorry he didn't listen to me. And do you know what else she did? The school sent home a letter about this for me to sign, and she forged my signature."

Sarita had lost the thread. "Wait — Lizzie did that?"

"No." Inez made a sound of frustration. Was she listening? "I'm talking about my Marisol. This is serious, Sarita."

Sarita didn't know what to say. She wouldn't have dreamed of cutting classes and forging signatures, although sometimes she got the impression that her own mother had expected her to, and might have even been disappointed when it never happened. She played hooky only once, on her sixteenth birthday, and what happened that day as a result was one of the reasons she never skipped school again. Like everything else she never did again, or never would do. It was the story of her life.

What to say to Inez, though, who clearly preferred that Marisol be much more tractable? "I understand why this worries you. But for most teenagers, this is so normal." She held up a hand when Inez grumbled at the assertion. "I'm not saying that it's right, and I'm not saying she wasn't influenced by this new friend. But she's not a juvenile delinquent, for heaven's sake. I think you have a right to be upset, but I don't think it's the end of the world, either."

Sarita bit back a smile. Inez would never know the irony of this conversation. She admired Sarita, whose behavior had been circumspect as a teen. Or so she thought. How drastically her opinion would change if she knew who the true criminal was. And that the woman Inez viewed as Mother of the Century was her accomplice in the cover-up of a homicide.

Tapped out from her rant and her worry, Inez propped herself against a desk. "I'm very concerned, Sarita. She ... she seems depressed, she stays in her room all the time. She never wants to talk to us anymore, and when we do talk, she argues about everything. The only time I can get through to her is if I tell her she cannot bake with Angela unless she obeys."

Sarita winced in sympathy as Inez unconsciously twisted and tugged at the apron of her staff uniform. "I never did things like this when I was her age. My father was a good man, but the way we were raised, we wouldn't have dared to lie to my parents or disobey them." She thought it over. "Then again, it wasn't many years later that I had a baby by a man who used me. Perhaps if I'd been more like Marisol

—not so afraid of my parents—I would have had more experience, not been so gullible to fall for his lies."

Sarita felt her stomach grumble. Not only hadn't she been able to drink her coffee in peace, she hadn't eaten breakfast yet. Even so, her heart went out to Inez. It was a worrisome situation. She floundered for something positive to say. "Well, there you go — she's more independent. That's good. … Right?"

"I suppose so." Inez gave Sarita a beseeching look. "Will you talk to her?"

"Me? Oh, Inez, I … I don't think that's a good idea," Sarita stammered. "I wouldn't know what to say."

"Please? I can't think what else to do." Inez was pulling out all the stops. "You know Marisol looks up to you. She has a … a … special bond with you."

They both knew what that meant. And maybe that was at the root of Marisol's rebellion. Marisol was only four when her particular abilities had helped Angela. It was very possible that she was acting out because she was trying to fit in, trying to feel 'normal.' Sarita knew all about that, for sure.

With a reluctant sigh, she gave in. "All right. I'll try. I'm not promising it'll make any difference, but … I'll try."

"Thank you. *Thank you*, Sarita."

Her gratitude was worrisome. It felt excessive. Sarita was already regretting she'd agreed, when Inez glanced at her watch.

"I'd better get back to my crew." Her mouth pinched in such a way that all the pretty softness of it vanished. "With any luck, *el pesado* is here too." She was almost to the door when she stopped short. "Did you say you saw him on Saturday?"

With barely any caffeine in her system, '*el pesado*' was too ambiguous. Sarita needed clarification. "If by 'the pain in the ass' you mean Alan, then yes. He was working Security for the ball."

"That's not possible. He'd have to clear it with me first. An extra assignment like that would be considered overtime."

Sarita's stomach growled again, louder this time. "I don't know what to tell you. He was on the ship Saturday night, for sure. Security thought there'd been a break-in here, and Alan showed up —" she pointed to the closed office door — "a few minutes later. I just about jumped out of my skin from fright too. He never announces himself." She circled her finger around the rim of her cup, her smile apologetic. "Appears to be his behavior pattern."

"Yes, so I've heard several times." Inez was sounding vexed all over again. "But working Security? That's very strange." Her brow furrowed as she mulled it over. "Well, I suppose I'll learn more when he contacts me for his final paycheck." She rolled her eyes. "Even when they leave me in the lurch like this, they're never too ashamed to ask for their money."

Inez left in a slightly better frame of mind than when she'd walked in, Sarita was relieved to note. She was even more relieved to have her office to herself again. Her mind was a cauldron of deliberations, and now there was her impending talk with Marisol to add to the brew. The ping of the microwave was the sweetest sound she'd heard all morning. Reheated coffee was better than none, and she needed the pick-me-up badly.

The timing couldn't have been more inconvenient when, no sooner did that tiny bell ding, than the next sounds she heard came from the kitchen: men shouting, and glassware crashing to the floor.

Luca was so hungover even the ends of his hair hurt. When he walked into the galley, the scent of the lemony *magdalenas* Cristiano was making for breakfast didn't have their usual effect. Instead of making him hungry, they made his insides churn. As did the venomous look the chef threw his way. He'd gotten friendlier looks from bouncers who'd thrown him out of bars.

Jesus Christ. Not today — he did not need any shit today. He would have slept in, but there was a text from Angela about cherry tarts. Considering all the alcohol he'd consumed, he wasn't sure he could bake with his usual ... finesse. Especially not with the chef glaring at him.

Following Luca's progress to the coffee urn, Cristiano squinted at the sluggishness of the younger man's movements as he poured one cup, downed it, then poured another.

His lip curled with disdain. "You've been drinking."

Luca had the cup halfway to his mouth when Cristiano made the accusation. Deliberately, he set it back down, deciding whether or not to respond. Excluding the fall off the wagon and the foolhardy whim to show off his powers to Sarita, he'd been working hard to improve his self-control. This included keeping his volatile disposition in check. Those who knew him appreciated that he had a temper that simmered on a constant low flame. If he didn't keep careful watch, it could explode like the lid off a pressure cooker.

Cristiano did not know him. At all. He didn't see the vulnerability, the perpetual sadness Luca carried with him, nor the bottomless love and loyalty of which he was capable. In short, Luca was very much like Cristiano himself, but Cristiano was blind to it. To his mind, Luca had the world by its tail, setting aside some purported life tragedies. He'd chosen a frivolous profession, he led a rich, pampered life, and he might have inherited his father's murderous compulsions.

The irony of that last indictment wasn't lost on Rohini. It was why she'd relegated him to their couch two nights before. They'd argued, and Cristiano had revealed his thoughts about Luca. Impulsiveness was another commonality he shared with the younger man. Rohini knew his judgements were unfounded, and that was one reason for her sudden lack of desire. And there were others reasons too, that she couldn't put into words. Being outspoken would always be a challenge for her, a woman raised to be subservient. But she was able to communicate that she didn't want to sleep with him, and her husband was heartbroken that she was rejecting him with no explanation, when she'd always met him with a passion that rivaled his own.

In summary, Cristiano was suspicious, angry, hurt, and above all, sexually deprived. He threw that list of gripes at Luca's feet. And now, here they were. Alone.

In the silence, the kitchen waited and watched.

Without a word, Luca opened the fridge near Angela's workstation and stuck his face in. The pastry dough and bowl of cherries in brandied syrup were right where she said they'd be. Was he supposed to make the tart shells first, or cook the cherries? Damned if he could remember. He needed more coffee. He needed to be left in peace. It looked like he was going to get neither. Still silent, he placed the bowl of cherries on the work station and ran his hand across his forehead. He couldn't remember a single one of the umpteen goddamn steps it took to make Brandied Sour Cherry Tartlets, and if he couldn't remember them, he couldn't use his magicks to make it happen.

"I asked you a question." Cristiano spoke with soft and deadly precision behind him. "You heard me, so don't ignore me. If you've been drinking, get the hell out. No drunks in my kitchen."

That did it. Luca pivoted to face him, his eyes just as sinister as Cristiano's voice. "Back the fuck up." He enunciated each word, and sneered at the chef's surprised look. "Now, did *you* hear *me*?"

All right, then — gloves were off. Luca was at least thirty years younger and four inches taller, but it wouldn't have deterred Cristiano if those gaps were twice as wide. He strode up to Luca and pointed a finger in his face. "Do you think you're going to talk to me like that and get away with it?"

"Why not?" Luca shot back. "You've been talking to me like that since the minute I walked in here." He leaned in. They were nose to nose. "I don't know what your deal is with me, but I'm sick of it."

"I heard her last night." Cristiano spoke through gritted teeth. "I couldn't sleep, so I went out. I saw you leave her room. I walked past, and I heard her crying." He poked Luca in the chest. "What did you do, eh? What did you do to make her cry?"

He was taken aback by the raw pain he saw flare in Luca's eyes. Fleeting but unmistakable, it caused Cristiano to falter momentarily. Until Luca knocked his hand away.

"Get your hands off me. Worry about your own life, old man."

"My *own* life?" Cristiano lost all sense of reason. He had a grip on the neck of Luca's t-shirt and was shaking him before he could even think about the consequences. "Sarita is part of my life, you *hijo de puta*." Livid with insult, he shook Luca again. "Let's see how much of an *old man* you think I am when I kick your ass!"

Luca was getting the sense he could do it. The guy was ripped. Apart from that, a fistfight was the last thing he wanted. The previous night's binge served to prove that his body couldn't handle any more abuse. His brain felt like it was swelled with alcohol and was now pressing against his eye sockets. Not to mention his stomach. If the chef shook him one more time, he'd probably get a face full of vomit. Luca averted a physical confrontation by fixing his attention briefly on the oven where the *magdalenas* were baking. When he slid his eyes back to Cristiano, he made sure to look bored rather than queasy. "Uh huh. Sure you will. But check on your little Spanish cupcakes first. They seem to be on fire."

"My —?" It took a second for Cristiano to interpret the wisecrack. The smell of scorched sugar was the tipoff. "My *magdalenas*!" He released Luca at once and ran to the ovens. As soon as he opened the one containing his breakfast, smoke billowed out. Grabbing a mitt, he pulled out the muffin pan. It was in flames. Cursing, he threw it into a sink and doused it with water, singeing his hand in the process.

"Why?" He held his blistered palm up to the kitchen. "Why would you do this? I had them on a timer. Those *magdalenas* should not have burned!"

Luca watched with unholy glee as the great chef screamed at the ceiling. It was just about the funniest thing he'd ever seen. That he'd been the real culprit made it all the more gratifying. He sniggered.

That was his mistake.

A metal spatula whipped toward him and slapped him across the face. The surprise was so great, it rendered him speechless. He gawked as it hovered, upright in front of him, as though warning him to watch his step. Cristiano was smirking even before it darted back to its place on the hanger with the other utensils.

"Ha, ha, *ha*," he taunted, as Luca rubbed his stinging cheek. "You see? Not so funny when it happens to you. I —"

His harangue was interrupted by the bowl that sailed straight for him, upending its contents over his head. Both men sucked in a breath of shock as cherries and syrup dripped down Cristiano's hair and face. They had no time to recoup before it was Luca's turn. A glass jumped off a shelf and hurled itself at him. He ducked just before it hit him, and it smashed against the wall behind him.

This started a free-for-all. Kamikaze glasses soared left and right across the kitchen, trying to hit the men, trying to hit each other. A stack of plates joined in. Like helicopter blades they spun through the air, one after the other. Crockery and glassware crashed like cymbals as they shattered.

Luca's eyes darted everywhere as he hopped and scooted out of their way. "What the hell's happening?"

Cristiano wiped frantically at the syrup trickling into his eyes. "I don't know, I don't know. She's never done this before." He didn't see the paring knife jump off the butcher block to fling itself at him.

"Cris — get down!" Luca yelled. He leapt at Cristiano and shoved them both to the floor. The knife barely missed before it plunged head-long into a wooden table leg.

"*Holy shit!*" they said, as one. That was the limit. Lucy looked at Ethel, Ethel looked at Lucy, and together they scrambled and crawled out the swinging double doors, dodging flying objects the whole way. They made it out into the dining room, and Luca pressed his back against the doorjamb as he sank to the floor. He felt sick as six dogs.

Cristiano pushed against the doors an inch and dared to poke his nose in, just as one of the refrigerators crashed open. The vegetables and meats stayed where they were, not taking sides, but the dairy products wanted in. Milk containers tipped themselves sideways, their contents spilling a white lake onto the tile. Blocks of butter vaulted off their shelves and splashed into the liquid, like sailors jumping ship.

"*Ay Dios mio.* This is a fiasco." Cristiano's face was as pale as the milk that was spreading across the kitchen floor. "If it goes on much longer, there's no way we'll be able to prepare for tomorrow. We'll have to cancel all our reservations."

Luca had to know. "How often does this happen?"

"Never. Not like this, anyway." Cristiano sank to the floor next to Luca, setting his animosity aside, for the time being. They had bigger problems. And there was the fact that the boy had just saved him from being stabbed by a flying knife.

"What's going on?" Sarita hurried in. She stopped short when she got a look at Cristiano. "That's not blood, is it?"

"Cherries," he said succinctly. He tilted his head, prompting her to look, and she peered into the kitchen through the diamond-shaped windows of the double doors. "Wow! What set this off?"

She didn't see the men exchange guilty glances. Whatever explanation Cristiano was about to come up with was forestalled by Sarita's interjection. "Wait a minute — there are two of them in there."

"Two? You mean, two ghosts? How is that possible?" Cris sprang up from the floor to peer in through the window next to her. "I don't see them. You can see them?"

"Not … exactly, no. But there are definitely two entities." She pressed her nose to the glass, trying to get a wider view of the kitchen. "I think they're both female." Cristiano knew better than to question her. "Omigosh — they're throwing the things at each other. That's what this is — it's a *fight*."

From the degree of astonishment in their voices, Luca could tell that this was an unprecedented event. Curiosity won out over biliousness. "A cat fight? With invisible cats?" He got up and stood on the other side of Sarita, who'd *tch*-ed in annoyance at his pejorative, and now all three watched as the galley was torn apart. Mid-skirmish, one of the combatants became visible. For mere seconds, she showed herself, and then — just like that — receded from view again.

"Did you see —?" Cristiano glanced at Sarita.

"Yes. I saw her." Sarita didn't take her eyes off the goings-on in the kitchen. "And you know what? I've seen her before."

"I saw her too." Of the three, Luca was the one who sounded the most affected by the sight. He angled his head to Sarita. "You've seen her? When?"

"She was in my office this morning. And she's appeared to me twice before that. I can't think who she might be, or why she's here." She winced as another crash resounded. "But whatever the reason, it would seem Her Highness isn't happy about it."

Luca held his gaze on Sarita, but said nothing. She frowned as she watched his Adam's apple bob up and down, saw his look of wondrous desperation. And when she thought back to the previous times she'd seen the woman and where, it came to her. "Oh, Luca." She rested her palm on his cheek. "Oh, Luca."

When Cristiano saw Luca's eyes fill, he put it together as well.

Luca tried to smile, but it was bittersweet. "I can't believe you've seen her three times. I haven't seen her in over twenty years. She looks just like she did then." A tear fell. He couldn't prevent it. Hastily, he brushed it away. "She's even wearing the same clothes."

He rested his forehead against the window and scanned the kitchen, longing for another glimpse. It flustered Cristiano that the image brought to mind stories from his childhood about orphans out in the cold, peeking in at families celebrating Christmas.

The three remained at the door, harboring separate feelings and questions upon the discovery of their visitant's identity, and waiting for what would happen next.

But it was over. The fighting had stopped and the kitchen was still.

CHAPTER NINE

When they could be reasonably certain that all numinous discords had ceased, they made their way back into the galley, cautiously treading around broken glass and spilled food.

"Oh, this is awful." Sarita put her hands to her cheeks as she looked around. "It'll take hours to clean. We can't even call Housekeeping. Inez was just complaining about being swamped and short-staffed." She sidestepped over the milk, which by now had trickled its way along the tile until it was halted by a damn of spilled cherries. "What could have caused them to fight like this?"

When she was met by a very loud silence, her attention veered from the mess to the men, who were looking at her like children who got caught stealing bubble gum. "Oh, no — what did you two do?"

They knew they'd have to explain themselves, but when Angela and Rohini walked in just then, they got a reprieve —

"Oh, my God!"

"Oh, good heavens!"

"What *happened*?"

A very short reprieve. Both women had exclaimed over the other. When Sarita gave them the rundown, now all three were talking at once, posing questions that fell fast and furious.

"Oh, my God — Gina was here again?"

"You've seen her too? Why is she here?"

"Why were they fighting?"

That last was from Rohini. It wasn't that she was ignoring the fact that Luca's mother had appeared to him for the first time in decades, or that Gina was still hovering about the ship. Being who she was, Rohini had already put a lot of this together, although she'd kept her speculations to herself. What she wanted to know was whether a certain chef had insinuated himself into something that was bigger than all of them.

She repeated her question, and this time when she asked, it sounded more like an interrogation than a simple query. "I *said,* why were they fighting?"

For the second time that morning, Luca threw himself in front of a knife. "It was my fault. I did something the kitchen didn't like, and she ... reprimanded me for it. I guess my mother didn't like that." Still dazed by the situation, he added, with a small smile, "She always was a little protective. And hot-tempered."

Rohini wasn't buying it. She was watching Cristiano while Luca gave his testimony and she didn't like the hunch she was getting. With her fists on her hips, she went on with her cross examination. "What was it you did, Luca — precisely — that offended Her Majesty?"

Luca found himself looking down at his boots. It was impressive that she managed to intimidate him when she was barely five feet tall. She had him in her sights, though, so he might as well come clean. "I burned the muffins Cris was baking. On purpose."

"No, you did not," Cristiano countered. "*She* did it." Enough was enough. He might not like the boy, but he wasn't going to let him take the fall by himself.

"Cris, it was me." Luca's tone was soft, but adamant.

He swiveled to look at Luca. "How could it have been you? You were nowhere near the oven."

At the question, Sarita sent Luca a glance that told him everything — that she'd connected the dots and knew he was about to out himself, and that the shit would categorically hit the fan if he did.

What Luca didn't know was that he wasn't to be the sole player in the spotlight during this apex of truth. His big reveal was interrupted by Rohini. Still playing Miss Marple, she was singularly unimpressed with the 'how.' What she was intent on was the 'why.' Before Luca had a chance to continue, she fixed a razor-sharp gaze on her husband. "And he burned your breakfast on purpose because …?"

When Cristiano hesitated, that was when the world turned red for Rohini Mehta de la Cueva.

"I knew it. I *knew* this was your fault. I asked you to leave him in peace, but no — you couldn't listen to me. Not even just this *once*."

She was shouting, something no one in the room had ever, ever heard her do. Her voice sounded high-pitched and dissonant, so unlike her usual mellifluous tones. "There are forces at work here that even you can't control. But you had to try, didn't you? You just couldn't leave it alone." Her body shook as it was purged of pent-up frustration. "And now, look what's happened as a result of it. *Look* what you've done to my kitchen, you — you stubborn, bossy, horse's ass!"

At that, even the grinding noise of the ancient freezer ebbed, as if it had stopped chatting with the other appliances in order to eavesdrop. But there was nothing else for it to hear. Every other being in the kitchen — human and otherwise — was stupefied, unable to fathom what they'd just heard. It was as unparalleled as two spirits brawling in their galley.

In a decade of working and living aboard the ship with her, none of them knew that the Rohini they loved throbbed with hurts and dissatisfactions she'd never exposed. Cristiano, in particular, was gawking at his wife as though she were a stranger — a stranger who had just shrieked profanities at him with no provocation.

The hush continued. And it was several heartbeats into that hush before Luca spoke. "I can fix it."

Sarita, the only one who understood what he meant, gave him the same look of apprehension that she had before. "Luca, are you sure you should do this?"

He lifted his shoulders in a gesture that was pure Italian. "Sarita, would it really be all that traumatic for them? They work on a haunted ship. This place is like Grand Central Station for Casper and all his friends."

"What are you two talking about?"

It was Angela who posed the question. Rohini and Cris were still processing the fact that their relationship had just shifted by seismic magnitudes. Everyone in the room knew that, but spirits and sorcery were safer to address than elephants. They would ignore Rohini's outburst. It was not for them to discuss.

"I'll explain by showing you, *cugina*," Luca replied. "I need everybody to stand by your work stations, please. Sarita, if you could stand wherever you might usually stand when you come into the kitchen to talk with everyone else, that would help too."

They followed his directive, three of the four quite puzzled while doing so. "That's great. Thank you. I know it seems like a weird request, but play along with me." Taut with nerves, he observed their different expressions in turn — Angela and Rohini looking curious, Cris suspicious, and Sarita supportive.

Damn, this was going to be a tough one to pull off. He still felt like crap. If it failed, he'd make a fool of himself. "Uh … Sarita, would you mind — since you're the closest to it — can I get some of the coffee in that urn?"

"Sure. Did you want me to put in the microwave?"

He almost laughed. If he couldn't manage to heat up a few ounces of coffee, he was screwed when it came to the rest. "No, I got it. Thanks."

There was no steam rising from the cup when Sarita handed it to him, but as soon as Luca touched it, it rose in gentle spirals. Angela and Rohini didn't notice, but Cristiano did, and his mind was like a steel trap. In a matter of seconds, it went from Luca's mastery of recipes to the burned muffins. Now his attention was no longer on his wife, but fixed on Luca. If the boy wasn't doing magic tricks, what the hell was he doing?

Luca took a few quick gulps, then put the cup down. The coffee washed away some of the pastiness in his mouth, but it still felt dry. Running his tongue over his teeth, he spread out his arms to embrace the room just as he did when he was on stage.

His eyes changed, Sarita noticed. They looked potent and hungry, like a panther on the scent of prey. The background reverberations of the galley — the singular sounds of a haunting they'd all grown accustomed to — had been subdued in resonance ever since Rohini's explosion of temper. Now those sounds returned, but with a new denseness, as though every type of energy from the potential to the kinetic was being called upon to sing together in a chorus of power. For everyone in the room except Luca, there was a pressure in the ears that felt just the same as being on an airplane.

He concentrated first on the area where Sarita was standing — to the left of the refrigerator nearest to Angela's pastry station. He'd have the least resistance there because Sarita believed in what he could do. He wasn't seeing into their minds — he was piggy-backing off their auras, their own individual wishes for their kitchen to be restored. When his eyes turned her way, Sarita knew he was no longer aware of her, of any of them. She flushed when she imagined what it might feel like to have him focus on her the way he was focused on this task.

The broken glass and crockery in her corner were his concentration points. He started with the plates. They would be easiest, as they were in fewer pieces. They all watched as though hypnotized when the fragments pulled together like magnets with opposite polarity. As the plates reassembled, they made the cracking sounds they made when they'd broken, but backwards, as though a recording were being played in reverse. When the sounds stopped, the plates were whole. Rohini and Cris were awestruck. Angela, on the other hand, laughed and clapped as if it were indeed a magic show.

"Oh, my God, Luca, that's amazing." She shook a finger at him. "You stinker, you. This explains so much of the monkey-business you got up to when you were a kid." In her head, she ran through a list of relatives, both dead and alive. "Huh. I wonder which side of the family you got this from?"

He smiled at her and looked at the rest, enormously relieved that they were handling this so well. For the most part. The look on the chef's face was impossible to read, so what was going through his mind was anybody's guess.

By the time he got through Angela's station, he was feeling it. His brow was moist, the back of his neck was stiff, and his eyes were dry and scratchy, as though he'd been driving too long with the sun in his face. The glassware was the main cause of the eye strain. There were so many shards that each one was a real task to put back together. Doing it while hungover was a real bitch. It would have helped if he'd eaten first, at least.

"I can put the milk and the rest of the perishables back where they were, but I can't guarantee they revert to their original condition in a situation like this."

Angela wrinkled her nose. "Eww. I think we should discard the food items that were involved. Right, everybody? We've gone this long with no citations from the CDPH. It would be nice to keep it that way."

The others were astonished at how she was taking this, as though she hadn't just witnessed the singular, most profound, most inconceivable event. They were still processing it, yet here she was, thinking about the health department.

After everything was set to rights, Luca was thoroughly depleted. Although he didn't want to exhibit his fatigue, he pressed the heel of his hands against his eyes in an unconscious gesture.

"Hey." Sarita touched his shoulder as she assessed him. "Your eyes are red. And you've gone pale. Are you feeling okay?"

"Yeah, yeah. Just … it wore me out a little, that's all." His head felt like it had cement blocks strapped on top of it, and he was so hungry, he would have wolfed down the blackened *magdalenas* if he hadn't already teleported them to the trash bin. But it was worth it. Everyone looked much less stressed, and Sarita was beaming at him.

He should only know how sexy she'd found the whole experience. There were quivers in her belly.

"This looks fantastic. You did a great job, Luca." Angela sounded like a proud family member who'd watched him hit his first homer in Little League.

"In another minute, he's going to fall flat on his ass."

That was from the chef, naturally, but though the statement was gruff, he wasn't regarding Luca with his usual severity. There was a different emotion on his face, another one that Luca couldn't decipher. "Go lie down," Cris told him. "You need rest. One of us will bring you some food."

"That's a good idea," Angela put in. To Luca she said, "What would you like, sweetie? Carbs? Protein? I can make scrambled eggs if you want something quick. I noticed we still have a gallon of milk that must have been playing Switzerland."

"Toast would be terrific, *cugina*, thanks. Toast and some coffee." Luca was damned grateful for the offer. "I'll come down later and make something with more substance after I catch some sleep."

"Put some honey on the toast, Angela," Rohini advised, speaking for the first time since her meltdown. "The healing properties will help."

After Luca left, the women waited gingerly as Cristiano folded his arms across his chest and leaned against a counter to regard all three of them.

He spoke to Sarita first, his voice quiet. "I can assume, based on what I heard, that you knew about this?"

"Well ... sort of. But only since yesterday."

"I see." He digested that, then asked Angela next. "What about you? You are his cousin. Yet, you knew nothing?"

"Cris, I swear, I had no idea." Angela made a cross over her heart with her finger. She looked at him hopefully. "Kind of came in handy today, though, don't you think?"

"It did," he agreed with all sincerity. "It certainly did." He paused before he directed the question to his wife. He had a terrible, sinking feeling he knew what her answer would be. "And you, Rohini? Did you know?"

Rohini held in a breath. "I knew enough to surmise. Yes."

That news was mind-boggling to Sarita and Angela. They were staring at her the same way Cris had after she'd nearly screamed the walls down. First that, now this.

But this time when Cris studied his wife he looked bleak.

"I was afraid of that." He took off his apron, set it across the now scrupulously clean work table. And without another word, he left.

Sarita didn't know that her mouth was hanging open. "Oh, holy crap," she said to Rohini. "You knew? How on earth did you know?"

"How do you know the things you know, Sarita?" Rohini sounded composed, when in truth, she was anything but.

"Geez Loueez. You're like the Sphinx," Angela commented, with no little veneration. "Ro, why would you keep this to yourself?"

"I have my reasons." Her answer was more snappish than she intended.

"Fair enough." Angela held up her hands, not quite knowing how to handle this new version of Rohini. "But, frankly, you should go after him."

"She's right," Sarita put in. "He looked devastated."

Rohini's mouth trembled once before she managed to set it. "So, you're saying you're both on his side?"

"His *side*?" Angela was stunned. "Ro, are you kidding? There's only one side in this — your marriage's." Watching the emotions play over her friend's face at those candid words, Angela asked her gently, "Do you or don't you want to save it?"

CHAPTER TEN

It was more than two hours later when a soft scraping noise woke Luca. Disoriented by the darkened room, he sat up stiffly, having no idea how long he'd been out. There was another small sound. When he looked in its direction, he thought he might still be comatose with weariness, and what he was seeing was just a wishful fantasy. But the aromas of hot food and freshly perked coffee gave evidence to the contrary.

"I can't believe you're in here." His voice was husky with sleep. "You realize I'm in my boxers." He paused to underscore the fortuity. "And the only reason I'm wearing those is because I thought my cousin was on her way."

Sarita stood next to the tray she'd just set on the marble-topped table. She looked contrite, skittish, and, to Luca, delectable. "I'm sorry to barge in. She did come up, but she said you were already out for the count." She bit her thumbnail. "So … I ate your breakfast."

He tried not to chuckle. It was cute that she sounded so apologetic. "Oh, did you, now?"

"Well, I didn't get a chance to eat, either," she defended herself. "And it was a shame to let it go to waste. Anyway, Angela went back out to replace the cherries and the other things we had to throw away. And I have no idea where Rohini and Cris are. So —" she gestured to the tray — "I made you another."

"*You* made it?" Foolishly pleased, he stumbled over his words. "Well … thank you. That was … very nice of you."

"You're welcome. It was the least I could do. It's scrambled eggs and blueberry pancakes. They won't be nearly as good as what Angela made," she warned, "but at least you'll have something in your stomach." Her smile was self-conscious. "That's why I came up. You've been sleeping a long time. I got worried."

That admission was even more gratifying. "It smells great."

"The pancakes are from a mix." It amused him that she came out with that the way someone else might own up to a crime. "I use it sometimes when the others aren't around and I feel like making something quick. Don't you dare tell on me."

"Be careful, Sarita," he deadpanned. "Dark secrets like these can be used for extortion."

She knew he was teasing. But considering her true purpose for being in his room, the remark still made her jumpy.

Switching on the bedside lamp, he rested against the headboard. "But if you want me to eat those pancakes from a mix right away, you'll have to carry that tray over here, I'm afraid. I don't think it would be well-mannered of me to get up."

"Oh." She could feel the heat flare in her cheeks. "Oh, of course." She brought the tray to him and placed it on the bedcovers. He assumed she'd just leave it and go, but there she remained, so motionless and sober-faced. "You still look a little pale," she observed, "but your eyes are clear, at least. The food should help."

"It sure will. Thanks." The savory and sweet scents brought back how ravenous he was. He unrolled the napkin, picked up the fork, and dove right in. He was into his second scoop of eggs before he glanced back up. She hadn't moved. When his mouth was empty, he asked, "Did you want to share this with me, or was there something else?"

"Yes. No. I mean, yes." Why did she always feel so clumsy around him? She tried again. "No, I don't want to share, but yes, there's something else. Would you mind if I stuck around while you eat? I was hoping I could talk to you."

After watching her struggle through that, he put the fork down. "Okay. How about this?" Pointing to the curtain-covered porthole, he said, "How about if you go look out at the excellent view, so I can put on some pants? This seems important enough that I should be wearing more than underwear when I hear it."

She nearly changed her mind, then. "Are you sure?"

"That I should be wearing pants? Yes."

"No, I mean, I can come back. You've had a tough morning. And you must be starving." She closed her eyes in a palpable effort to gather her composure. "I should go —"

"Sarita," he said softly, patiently. Her eyes were so enormous they looked like they would take over her face. "Let me put on a pair of pants. Okay?"

Afterward, she thought he might eat at the table, but he chose to sit on the bed, on top of the covers this time. He'd opted for the jeans he'd been wearing earlier that morning, and though he threw on a shirt as well, he left the buttons undone.

That might become a problem. Though she was a bundle of nerves when she walked in, it didn't prevent her from noticing his naked upper body. It was quite the impressive sight. But his bare chest peeking out from behind the open shirt was even more distracting. Instead of the all-you-can-eat buffet she'd been treated to earlier, now she was being fed only a morsel or two of firm, sculpted male pecs and abs, with a just-right dusting of torso hair. As appetizers are meant to do, it made her hungrier for the full meal. How would she manage to slog through what she'd decided to tell him with all that splendor on view? And there was that pertinent birthmark. It was visible whenever he moved and the sides of his shirt gaped. Sooner or later, he was bound to notice that she avoided — scrupulously avoided — aiming her eyes in its direction.

"So I don't pass out from hunger, I'll eat while you talk. Sit down. Tell me what's on your mind."

Playing for time, she dragged an armchair closer to the bed, angled it first one way then another, sat, leaned forward to adjust the accent pillow so that it felt comfortable at the base of her spine, and sat back again.

The whole while she fussed and fidgeted, he could see the pulse in one vein at her neck pounding like a hammer against an anvil. He wanted to spring up off the bed and pull her to him, assure her that whatever it was that was causing her such angst, he'd do everything he could to make it right. Instead, he waited silently, went right on eating eggs and toast, pouring syrup on the pancakes, well aware that she would want him to pretend he was oblivious.

At last she began, but kept her eyes down and her hands clenched together in her lap while she spoke. "When I was a little girl, my grandmother sent my mother and me a package. In it was a little red candle and a leather pouch. The pouch contained a nickel — an old, tarnished Buffalo nickel — and this smooth, light blue agate stone with pretty, delicate white striping. There was a … a gnarled-looking root of some kind too." She paused, mentally recalling each object to be sure she didn't leave anything out, although she'd never in all this time forgotten. "And a chicken feather. It was pure white. And one sprig each of basil and rosemary. Their leaves were sticking out of rubber-sealed tubes of water to keep them fresh. That was why, even though they'd been shipped to us from halfway across the country, they were still so fragrant."

She lifted her eyes to his, expecting to see distaste perhaps, or at the least, derision. But he showed nothing more than polite interest as he sampled his coffee and watched her.

"That's a Vodou charm," he said evenly. "Your grandmother was a practitioner?"

Considering that he was a magician, his knowledge of the art shouldn't have impressed her, but it did. Undoubtedly, the open shirt was working in his favor. "A priestess. The most well-known priestess in New Orleans, as a matter of fact. And make that 'is,' not was. She's still alive. At one time she was as famous for her beauty as she is for her power."

"No surprise there." He smiled lazily as his eyes skimmed over her face. An unpleasant thought occurred. "She's not married to that guy, I hope — the Daniel Plainview of Brazil?" When she looked at him blankly, he clarified, "You know — *There Will Be Blood*. You didn't see that movie?"

"God, no." She shuddered. "I hate violent movies."

"You're missing out. It's a great movie." He polished off the toast, and poured more coffee, offering some to her.

"No, thank you." She got back on point, explaining the familial connections. "No, she's not married to my Brazilian grandfather. This is my father's mother. I call her, '*Granmè* Taylor.' She's Creole."

Ah. That explained the intrinsic glamour, he thought, as he dug into pancakes. "You hit the gene pool jackpot, didn't you?"

She managed to smile and look pained at the same time. "Let's see if you feel the same way by the time I finish this." With a deep breath, she forged on. "The box from my grandmother also came with a handwritten note of instructions. After my mother read them, she clipped a bit of my fingernail and put it in the pouch along with all the other things that had been in there before, and tied it closed. She lit the red candle, and we just stood there until it melted and the flame flickered out. And then, she did something she rarely did: she bowed her head and crossed herself."

Wanting to be certain that he understood, she emphasized, "I mean, she crossed herself for real, not just the way she does sometimes when she's being dramatic. She ... she meant it. After that, she handed the charm to me and told me to put it under my pillow."

At this point, she paused again, to bolster herself for what might come. She couldn't begin to guess what his reaction would be. If he rejected her on the grounds of what she was by way of nature, could she come back from it, or would it break her?

He'd finished eating, so he stretched over to put the tray on the opposite bedside table. Shifting sideways, he sat on the edge facing her, his forearms resting on his thighs. "Go on," he prompted gently. "You've gotten this far. Tell me why your mother and your grandmother wanted you to have the charm."

The tears came straight away. She knew they would, that they had to, so she didn't even try to stop them. "I was having a vision. It was my first one ever. We didn't know that's what it was. My mother thought it was just a bad nightmare, but it went on every night for at least a week, and I was terrified to close my eyes. I didn't want to see it. It was so awful." Wiping at the tears, she gulped, "The charm blocked it, and I didn't see it again, or even understand what it meant, until recently, when it came back. And now ... I know."

Steadily, he opened the nightstand drawer, pulled out a plastic packet of tissues and handed it to her. "And what was it? What did you see that scared you so much?"

For the rest of his life, he would remember the look on her face when she replied.

"I saw you. I saw you and Santi. On the day your mother died."

The confession burst open floodgates. It all came rushing out — she couldn't stop it once it started — one segment tumbling into the next — a little boy shrieking on a bridge, the appearance of the spirit she now knew to be his mother, the roses he handed her that prompted another vision, the hazy forewarning of fire. And when she finished there, although one part of her psyche screamed for her to silence herself for her own preservation, she plunged on and told him about Naag.

He felt his body grow colder, his muscles more rigid with each atrocious experience she divulged. It was only when she stopped that she took in his appearance, the change that had come over him while she spoke. His face looked grey, almost cadaverously so, his expression so tightly drawn and strained that he looked like a different man altogether.

Seeing that transformation, she thought that this was when she would lose him, when he would begin to hate her for not having told him what she knew about him. The fear of that loss wrapped tightly around her, constricting her lungs. And yet, she had enough pride not to show him that. She sat stiffly, nobly, waiting like a condemned warrior about to receive the killing blow.

"Oh, my God," he whispered.

She flinched when he reached over and brushed his knuckles against her cheek. "Oh, my God. Sarita — I was six when she was killed. That means you were weren't even four. You were just a baby. You shouldn't have had to see that. You shouldn't have had to go through that. Oh, my poor darling, my poor, poor girl."

And, as he'd wanted to from the moment she sat down, he pulled her out of her chair and into his lap, where he cradled her head against his shoulder protectively, his arms wrapped tightly around her as she cried.

But they were tears of relief now. "I was so scared to tell you," she murmured against his shoulder.

"Of course." He stroked her hair. "Of course you were."

Everything about her made more sense now. How torn up she must have felt when she took in who the Miceli Brothers were that night at the theater, how conflicted she must have been when she learned he was coming aboard the ship. He thought with disgust of his idiotic, egoistic assumption that she was brushing him off when she'd told him she needed time to think, when the reality was that she was in torment. His abilities had brought him some ostracism, some sibling rivalry, but mostly they'd brought him opportunity and a hell of a lot of fun. Hers had brought her fear, sorrow, and death.

Now that she quieted, he eased her along with him as he rested back against the headboard again. Emptied of tears and buried truths, she lay against him, limp and hollow, settling her cheek against his bare chest, which felt even better to her touch than she'd imagined.

It had been terrifying to speak of it, but she was so glad of the aftermath. Whatever happened between them going forward, he was the first person outside of her immediate circle to whom she'd risked giving her trust, and today, he hadn't failed her. Could she hope that would always be true?

When he felt her relax against him, he lowered his head and brushed his lips over her temple. "You're the bravest person I know."

Her head shot up so fast it nearly smacked him in the chin. "Me? No. I'm the biggest coward, ever."

"Beg to differ." The timbre of his voice soothed her. "There are a couple of things you need to hear. Let's talk about the most important thing, first. In everything you told me — and believe me, Sarita, all of it was —" there was a wry twist to his mouth — "pretty fucking mind-blowing, if you'll excuse me for expressing my feelings that way — there was one thing you said that stuck out more than the rest. You said that you killed a man."

She stiffened up so fast that he thought she might already regret having told him. Ignoring that, he went on. "No, you didn't. You killed a monster. If you expect me to condemn you for it, then you told the wrong guy."

"It's not something to be proud of." The tears came back into her voice at once. "It's not. How can you even think that, let alone say it?"

"I didn't say it was something to be proud of. You're not a hero, but you're not a villain." The statement was unexpected. The statement was unexpected enough to stop her from crying again. "He would have killed you. All of you."

Pulling away from him, she sat up, crossed-legged on the bed. "You don't know for sure that he would have," she insisted. "Or even that he could have. He only had a knife. He couldn't have killed six people with just a knife."

Luca's snort was mirthless. "Just a knife? Good thing he dropped dead before he could show you how wrong you are about that." Before she could argue, he added, "You're not the only one who has visions."

That got her attention. "What do you mean?"

"I mean that I saw it. I've had two visions about you, and that was one of them. I saw a man who had a knife at your throat. It was a very clear image."

Her pupils went glassy with shock when he traced across her neck exactly where Naag's knife had been. "There — that's your carotid. The son-of-a-bitch had the sharp edge of that knife angled right at your ca-rotid. One tiny twist of his hand, and you'd have been finished — dead before you hit the floor." Tamping down his outrage, he emphasized, "His plan was to kill you, every last one of you. It was a lucky fluke — *not* a sixteen-year-old's sinister plan — that you killed him first."

Now he took her chin between his thumb and forefinger, gave it a tiny pinch. "It was an accident. He's dead. You're not. End of story." He released her. "I have to tell you, it's a hell of a relief to learn this was something that happened already."

Her brows snapped together. "Did you think it wasn't?" Her look had him shrinking back. "Is that why you're here? Are you on some … some rescue mission?"

Now he'd done it. Damn, she was quick. Stalling, he pushed himself up, mirroring her cross-legged position. Not exactly."

"Luca."

He winced at the tone, at the way she slit her eyes. He was a ten-year-old boy all over again. It was creepy how much she reminded him of his grandmother right then.

"What do you mean, 'not exactly'?"

"Look, Sarita." Reaching for her hand, he spoke plainly. "I've always had every intention of telling you the real reason I came aboard, but now's not the time for it." She opened her mouth to argue, but he touched his finger to her lips, forestalling her. "No, I mean it. It's complicated, and when we talk about it, I'd like us both to be … in a less emotional frame of mind. It's been a hell of a day so far, and —" he glanced at the bedside clock — "it's not even noon yet." He gave her hand a reassuring squeeze. "You've given me so much today. Can I ask you to give me a little more — to trust me on this, for a while? I'll tell you everything, I promise. Just not today."

When he put it that way, it was hard to say no. "Fine." Reluctantly, she yielded, but not before she asked, "Would you at least tell me what your second vision of me was?"

He had to hand it to her — she was quick and crafty. She slid that the added proviso in just at the right time. "It was my first vision of you, actually. And it was years ago, long before I knew who you were." His eyes glinted mischievously. "At nineteen, pretty girls were probably what I spent most of my time envisioning."

"Nineteen?" She scrunched up her nose. "You were nineteen? That means I was sixteen."

"Uh huh. And thinking back, I'm pretty sure you were on some part of this ship when I saw you. The room was dark, and had all these old, bare wooden beams. And there were candles."

She froze. Oh, Holy Mother of God in Heaven, *please* don't let him be talking about where and when she thought he was talking about. She would die, instantly.

Wetting her lips, she asked, "Was I ... was there anyone with me?"

"No, you were alone." Unlike earlier, this time he truly hadn't picked up on her discomfiture. "And you were crying."

It was only then that it occurred to him this sojourn down memory lane might shake her up all over again. But it was too late now. He had to finish it. For some reason, her eyes were welded to his, like she needed to memorize every word he said for some big exam.

"That's it?" she snapped out the question. That's all you saw?"

"Uh... yeah." Why did it feel like he was being cross-examined by Johnnie Cochran? On his guard now, he went on. "I didn't know why you were crying, but I remember getting the feeling ... the idea ... that there was something you wanted to do, or had to do, and you were afraid. I tried to reassure you. In my vision, I spoke to you." He lifted his shoulders uncertainly. "I can't remember what I said."

All at once, her face cleared. "Omigosh. That was *you*?" She lifted herself to her knees on the bed and put her hands to her cheeks. "Omigosh." He could see she was thinking back to whatever the incident was. "I thought that, on top of everything else, I was starting to hear voices." When she took her hands from her face, she was glowing and a bit teary-eyed again, which was worrisome.

"I remember *exactly* what you said. You said, 'Embrace it. Don't be afraid.'"

Despite the near reverence of her tone, the feeling that he needed to be judicious remained. The vision was vague in his own mind, but whatever it had revealed was clearly a momentous occasion to her. "So … what I said was a … good thing?"

"It was a fantastic thing." He nearly fell backward when she threw her arms around his neck and hugged him with such exuberance that she surprised a laugh out of him. "Wow. Just wow. I can't believe that was you. You spurred me into doing something that made a tremendous difference to … someone. To several people, really."

He waited for her to tell him more, but she drew away, and sank back onto her haunches again with a sigh. "It's a long story." She yawned. "I'll tell you about it, but let's leave that one for another time too, okay? Like you said, it's been a hell of a day. I'm exhausted." She could only imagine what she must look like from all the crying.

"Yeah, no kidding." He studied her pensively. "I guess it's fair to say we're connected, linked, whatever you want to call it."

She was deliberating over whether or not she should show him. Decision made, she pushed her hair out of her face, shoved down the neck of her t-shirt and wriggled her left shoulder free of its sleeve. The look on his face was priceless.

"Sarita, what are you doing?"

"Not what you think. I want you to see something." His eyes moved to the hand she had covering a portion of her clavicle. "Look." Watching his face, she moved her hand to reveal the little angioma star that had defined her since puberty.

It took a few seconds for him to absorb it. "It's the same. Identical to mine." His voice was hushed and awed, like a child sitting in a church for the first time.

"Yes."

"I thought I was the only one."

"Me, too. I thought I was the only one, too."

"What does it mean?" As unnerved by her mark as she'd been by his, he didn't know whether to feel fear or elation.

. "I don't know." She shook her head, her shoulder, the birthmark, still exposed to him. "I don't know, Luca. It scared me when I first saw that you had it. It was at the ball. You'd undone the top studs of your tuxedo shirt. Remember?"

He did. He remembered how she'd pushed away from him so abruptly after that amazing kiss.

His mind jumped back to the day he was sitting on his kitchen floor, drenched, confused, and even more hungover than he was this morning. "I touched my birthmark," he murmured, then broke off as he ruminated, and Sarita angled her head as she waited for him to continue. "I did it unconsciously, and that's when I saw you in my mind. That's when —"

He didn't finish the sentence. Sarita remained still as stone when he edged closer, until he was near enough to trace her collarbone lightly, his eyes searching for elucidation as he focused on that little red star. Delicately, he slid his finger back and across the mysterious mark they shared, and at that simple touch — his touch — she felt her body loosen and unravel. A languor filled her, as though her blood had turned to honey and her muscles to warm, soft water. Her hands fell to her sides and she swayed a little before he caught her. The look in his eyes was clear and powerful, and she felt the whole core of her clench and swell with undiluted desire.

The next thing she knew they were at each other, their mouths locked together, feasting themselves on another deep and drugging kiss. It was just as miraculous as the first. She felt his hands on her everywhere — her hair, her face, her body, while hers were frantic and eager on him. The only lamp he'd lit blazed wildly, and the air smoked with sorcery and sex.

"Wait, Sarita, wait." She didn't hear him at first, didn't understand, until he drew her back from him. "We have to stop."

"What? No." Dazed, she held onto him, as though he'd pulled her out of sleep, out of a wonderful dream, and all she wanted was to go back. "Why? Why, Luca?"

They were kneeling on the bed. The sight of her — tousled, slumberous, willing, ready — waged a war inside him. There was nothing more he wanted in this moment than to take her, take this to its culmination. Breathing deeply, heart pounding, he marshaled every ounce of willpower he had to put on the brakes. Clasping her upper arms, he lay his forehead against hers. "Give me a minute. Please, give me just a minute."

"But why did you stop?"

There was a tremor in her voice. Tilting her face up to his, he saw it, mixed in with the lingering desire: Uncertainty. And, dammit, he knew he'd been right to call a halt. The very last thing he wanted was for her to have regrets. She might be into it right now, but she'd had an emotionally charged day. Still, it wasn't easy.

Frustration threaded through his words. "If you think for one minute that I stopped because I don't want you like hell, you can get that out of your head right now."

The statement, the tone, hung in the air, out of place with the leftover yearning and magick. She was new to this. If it wasn't that he didn't want her, then what was it?

He let go of her and got up off the bed. She watched him as he ran his hands though his hair. Seeing her dismay, he knew he didn't have much time to think about what he wanted to tell her, and how to tell it.

So he just said it. "I'm more than halfway in love with you."

That wasn't what she'd expected to hear at all. Surprised into silence, she did nothing but suck in a breath.

To Luca, that was a marginally better reaction than an out-and-out rebuff, so he persevered. "I'm not going to lie — I've never been in this situation before." Sticking his hands in his front pockets, he hung his head. "I've dated." Uncomfortable with the topic, he lifted a shoulder. "You know … they were nice girls. But I never felt like this — the way I feel about you — with any of them." Looking back up, he saw that she was still just sitting on the bed, not moving, watching him gravely, as he rocked nervously back and forth on his heels.

"I don't want to screw this up. And believe me, that's one thing I'm good at." He was embarrassed hearing the words come out of his mouth. He wondered how they sounded to her. "I feel that, even with all our big reveals, we still don't know each other."

Though his voice remained steady, his hands were clenched in his pockets. "You don't know, for example, that, even though I've got plenty of money to get by, I don't feel like I earned it, I feel like my brother did. Technically, I'm unemployed, and I have no damn idea what I want to do with myself now that he's gone."

When she didn't look troubled by that admission, he risked declaring a darker one. "I drink too much. I spent months after Santi's death stinking drunk. I only cleaned myself up a little before I got here, but last night —" he sneered at himself — "I got drunk again for the first time in over two months, because I thought you were giving me the brush off when you said you needed time."

That he would lay himself open like this astonished her, more than the drinking. She'd had no idea that's what he thought, or that he'd gotten drunk the night before. Then again, she wasn't much of a drinker, and with everything that had been on her mind, she'd totally missed the signs. She might ask him about that later, but for now, she just listened.

"That's how much of a self-absorbed jackass I can be, Sarita. I had no clue you were going through all of this, all of what you told me today." Clearing his throat, he went on. "And I want to know more. About *you*, not just about your … extra abilities. Case in point — what in hell kind of movie do you like, if you don't like a Daniel Day-Lewis movie? He's one of my favorite actors. And by the way, the violence in that film is germane to the plot."

If he weren't so serious, she'd have laughed. Her mood was definitely lifting. This was all very interesting, and she was going to let him finish it out without interruption.

"We don't know each other," he said again, "but we're being —" he made a motion with his hands — "pushed together by forces beyond our control. Visions, and … and weird birthmarks, and I kind of think — God help me — even my dead mom is matchmaking."

Now she had to laugh a little — a nervous laugh. She heard the humor in his voice too.

"But what we do, or don't do as far as a … a relationship, I want it to be our decision. Yours and mine."

Kneeling down in front of the bed, he linked his fingers with hers, and gazed into her eyes, already certain that he would always be captivated by them. "And when we make love for the first time — you know what? I think it would be much better for both of us if it happens on a day that maybe isn't … oh, I don't know … as psychologically harrowing as this one has been."

When the quip made her giggle, the tightness in his chest loosened. And when she said, "All right, Luca," her smile soft and easy, it told him that they were going to be okay.

Just like that, he felt lighter, younger. "So, here's my suggestion. Can we just do some normal things, like maybe go out on a date? Do you know we've never been off this ship together?"

The word 'normal' would always have its appeal to her. "That's true, we haven't. Although, we did go to Italy," she teased.

"How about we go someplace a little closer to home, like downtown? Have you ever been to BO-beau's? Great atmosphere, and they have the best burgers."

He didn't know much about her, it was true. She wondered how surprised he'd be to know that she hardly ever left the ship, that it had been her solace for the past ten years.

Well, maybe it was time. She smiled. "I'd love a burger. Cristiano only makes them if Angela and I threaten or beg."

At that answer, his grinned and kissed the back of her hand. "Let's go early, so we can walk around while it's still light. Meet you by Reception at six?"

—•—

While Sarita rifled through clothes and put on makeup with a lightness she hadn't felt in forever, Alan paid the admission to get back on the ship.

No one recognized him. The dreads had been genius. He congratulated himself. When a man wore dreadlocks, most didn't notice the face that went with them. No one checked his backpack either, which was a good thing, considering what was in it.

Casually, he walked past the valet, went up the elevator along with a carload of excited tourists, and headed straight for the Observation Bar.

He'd stay for Happy Hour. If the opportunity arose, in order to blend in, he'd make conversation with some of the regulars. And since it was Monday and the Secret Spice was closed, after dark, when the staff had gone, he'd use the master keys he'd stolen from his 'boss.'

When he thought of Sarita, it was with derision. At the ball, he'd heard her tell her new boyfriend that she wasn't afraid of spiders. Let's see if that were true.

CHAPTER ELEVEN

The strangeness of that Monday continued, but the unusual occurrences were now taking a positive turn. While Sarita was in Luca's stateroom pouring out her heart, Angela was at the market for the second time that day, fretting over the remaining selection of fruits.

Savvy shoppers of the farmers' market knew to be there as soon as they opened in the morning or risk having to pick through leftovers. Luckily, Angela had clout. Several weeks back, she'd complimented the berry vendor on how well the new dessert was selling, and that it was all thanks to the quality of his cherries. That praise coming from a pastry chef who was by now renowned in the area, felt as good as being named World Food Prize laureate.

Consequently, when he spotted her at his stand for the second time that day, and she told him about the accident in the kitchen — leaving out the salient points about hauntings, of course — he pulled out a hidden sack of exquisite cherries that he'd been saving for another customer. Whoever they might be, they were in for a disappointment, but Angela was too thankful to worry about it.

As she was leaving, she ran into Harry, there to buy his favorite artisanal cheese. They stopped to chat. He made a joke about cherries that was not too saucy, just enough to make her laugh, which he'd always managed to do so easily.

That's when she thought, What am I doing? What am I doing to myself, all over again?

When he risked rejection a third time and invited her to lunch, her answer was 'yes.'

And while they sat by the marina, eating Hawaiian barbecue — Angela in guilty pleasure over both the food and the company, and

Harry with no remorse whatsoever over either — Cristiano was down by the shoreline near the *Mary*, contemplating whether his life with Rohini was over.

When he sensed her approach behind him, felt her tentative touch on the back of his shoulder, he closed his eyes. She'd come.

"I got your note," she said.

He took her arm, and they walked silently along the sand. The weather was in the high seventies, the sky was a particular shade of blue — a regal blue, he'd always thought, fancifully — reserved solely for a certain stretch of miles surrounding the *Queen*. They watched the sailing vessels, the people, and one lone cloud floating by that looked just like a fluffy toy poodle.

After a while, he asked, quietly, "How long have you been unhappy with me?"

She gazed at him, genuinely surprised by the question. "I'm not. I'm not unhappy with you."

He stopped short, more bewildered than ever by that response. "And then, what, Rohini? You knew about Luca and you didn't tell me. And you called me a horse's ass."

"I didn't tell you about Luca because …" she faltered, pushing at her hair, and in the gesture, he caught a glimpse of her turmoil. "I can't explain it, except to say that I find it difficult to tell you certain things. You have a tendency to take charge, to dismiss what I say, to ride right over me." Feeling herself getting worked up all over again, she pressed her lips together and gave herself a moment, as she watched two seagulls land simultaneously, one next to the other, by the edge of the water. "That's why I called you what I did. I'm sorry I spoke to you in such a ghastly way. I just … it just came out after all this time. But sometimes, Cristiano, it frustrates me that we have to do things only as you want them done."

"Who said that?" He was stunned. His mind raced as he tried to figure out why she held the misconception. How was he supposed to soothe feelings, heal hurts he didn't know existed?

"It's just the way it is." Weary, forlorn, she shrugged.

"No, it is not." Shaken, he reached for her, turned her gently to face him. Clearly she felt subjugated, and he had no idea why. "All you have to do is tell me what you want, tell me what you need, and it's yours."

"I can't!" She pulled away from him, her tone, her look, annihilating him. She held her hand out to him, palm up, as if to beg. "I just *can't*. Don't you see that? I wasn't raised that way. This is the best and the strongest I can be. I would rather do it all your way, say nothing about my feelings on any matter, than lose you."

"You would never lose me. Never." The pair of seagulls strutted and squawked behind him as he gaped at her. Was he such a self-absorbed man then, that he hadn't seen this? But how could he not have, with everything she'd told him about her background? She was right — he was a horse's ass.

"Cristiano," she began again, "You saved me in so many ways —"

"*Ay!*" He whirled away from her. "*Por favor* — please don't tell me it's gratitude you feel." Flinging his arm out, he pointed it toward the water. "I will drown myself in this ocean right now!"

An elderly couple ambled by just as he shouted those words. They glanced at him in alarm and picked up their pace. Observing that, Cristiano restrained his natural flair for the dramatic. "If anything, I am the one who should be thanking you," he said, his voice lowered.

"I don't want your thanks."

"Nor I yours."

They stared at each other, as much in love as ever, but with a chasm of conventions and customs between them. Yet it appeared that the love would win, that they would continue to accept each other in their 'as is' condition, just as they always had.

Even so, Cristiano thought about their life over the past ten years — six days a week at a stove together, he issuing orders, she quietly obeying them. It was only now he understood that, all this time, she believed he was acting as a domineering husband, not as a meticulous chef. He'd separated the two roles in his mind. She hadn't. That wasn't at all what he wanted in their relationship, and that made his decision for him.

"I'm going back to the ship. To pack."

Her eyes went wide with anguish. "You're leaving me?"

The laugh rolled out of him, even with such heaviness in his heart. Another miscommunication. It was almost comical. When he pulled her to him, lifted her in the air and spun her around, he startled the seagulls as well as her.

Setting her on her feet, he kissed her forehead, her cheeks, her lips, her nose. "You wish." He kissed her again, but underneath the love and affection, there was unease. "You can't get rid of me that easily, *mi vida*. The only way I leave you is when they carry me away from you, horizontally, a sheet over my face."

She still looked unsure, so he tried once more. "When I said I was packing, I meant we should both pack." It occurred to him that he was being high-handed yet again, not giving her a choice. "That is ... will you? I mean, do you want to?"

"Do I want to *what*, Cristiano?" She lifted her shoulders, held up her hands. "I'm sorry. You're just not being clear."

"Go to Italy with me, of course. Didn't we say we wanted to go?"

Her expression didn't change. She heard the words, but she didn't believe them. At least, she thought that he couldn't have meant them, or that she'd misunderstood him again.

When she didn't move, didn't say a word, his palms grew damp. Had he waited too long? Was it too late?

"Rohini." Her name sounded like a plea. "Don't you want to go?"

Now she got it. He was truly asking. But she still found it impossible. "Are you joking? How can we do that — just like that? What about the restaurant?"

"The hell with it."

"I beg your pardon?" Her head was reeling.

"I said, the hell with it. We've saved plenty of money. We'll be fine."

"That's not at all what I meant, Cristiano. I meant, don't you care about the restaurant, about being a chef?"

With one shrug, he dismissed a lifetime of work, a lifetime of passion. "Frankly, no."

He stopped with those two words, and just stared at her. She never imagined that after a decade of marriage, he would still look at her the way he was looking at her now. By the time he spoke again, her heart was drumming like a young girl's at her first crush. "What I care about is right in front of me."

"But …" Her breath shuddered out. "Sarita? What about Sarita?"

"Pah. After what I saw this morning, she's in good hands." He remembered the flash of pain he'd glimpsed in Luca's eyes. "He's in love with her, you know." He didn't have to say who he meant. "I think Sarita has strong feelings for him too, but either way, she's safe with him. And the three of them can handle things without us. That has been made plain to me." He allowed himself a brief pout. "Our clientele will not even notice we're gone."

Eyeing him keenly, she ventured to ask, "Does that still bother you — that he can duplicate your recipes?"

"A little." He mulled it over. "Okay, yes. It does. But to be truthful, I'm torn. There's one part of me that feels replaced. But there's an even bigger part of me that feels a weight off my shoulders, knowing that we won't destroy what we love and worked so hard for by leaving. Knowing that we're not trapped here forever."

Putting aside that former comment for now, she focused on the latter. "What do you mean, 'trapped'?"

Weighing the pros and cons of total candor, he decided that if he wanted a more authentic relationship with his wife, he was going to have to reveal certain things that he'd kept to himself also. "She never left the ship after she killed him. It was like she was punishing herself." He watched Rohini's face. "I've always felt that … even if we wanted to, we couldn't leave until she did …" He wasn't sure he could finish it.

But Rohini said it for him. "Because if it weren't for me, Naag would never have come here." When he didn't reply, she exhaled a long, slow breath, but whether it was a sigh of regret for the past, he didn't know. Then she said, "I felt that way too," and he had his answer. It was relief. Relief that they might finally be unshackled from a guilt that was in some ways as much of a prison as the cell to which he'd once been confined.

They stood where they were a moment longer, taking in the view. The sky had changed color with the lowering sun, and there were fewer people about. The elderly couple who'd passed by earlier were gathering up their things. The two seagulls were now further down the shore, still walking together and splashing in the water.

He held out his hand, tipped his head. "Shall we go back and tell them?"

"Yes. Let's see what they say." As they locked fingers, she had a lovely thought. "We'll get to see Jane and Antoni." Two lovely thoughts. "Ooh — and I'll get to go shopping for new clothes."

He chuckled.

They walked back the way they came, and in the distance ahead, they could see three massive, orange-red smokestacks with their distinctive black trim, beckoning them home.

Angela still liked stealing time alone on the top deck of the ship. After so many years, she knew when she was most likely to find it deserted. It seemed a lifetime ago that she'd met the enigmatic Lee Branson, and that meeting had changed everything for her. She still missed seeing him. That was why, when she climbed the staircase to that secret refuge, her heart gave a little leap when she smelled cigarette smoke.

But it wasn't Lee she saw when she reached the top of the stairs. "Luca."

"You caught me." The look on his face could only be described as sheepish. "I know I shouldn't be smoking, but up here feels like the perfect place for it."

"It does, doesn't it?" Her chuckle sounded wistful to him.

"Yeah. Trying to quit, though. I'm down to two."

"It's a tough habit to break. I stopped years ago and I still miss it."

They both leaned against the rail toward the harbor. The rays of the late afternoon sun swept a top coat of translucent gold across the water and the deck, making for a deceptive appearance of warmth. These days, Angela knew to bring a sweater up with her, and she draped it about her shoulders when the coolness of the air hit her skin. Since he was up here, they might as well talk about it, she thought. "That was something else this morning."

When he didn't say anything, just continued to smoke, she asked, "Could Santi do it too? Was that why you become magicians?"

"No." He studied the lit end of the cigarette. "No, Santi was the true talent there. Me — I'm just a freak of nature."

"Don't say that." She poked his side. "It takes talent to do what you did today."

"It doesn't, *cugina*." He didn't sound self-deprecating when he said that; he was merely stating a fact. "What I can do is like … I don't know." He searched for a comparison. "Having brown eyes, or being six feet tall. It's just part of the package. Random luck of the draw."

"Huh," was all she said. "How does it work — do you know?"

He exhaled smoke, gave a careless shrug. "I'm not sure. But I do have to use my eyes. It's like —" he gestured with the cigarette — "anything I want to do, I have to have something to focus on. If I want to make something move, I have to look at it. If I want to make something disappear, make myself disappear —"

"Hold it, hold it." She had to interrupt, she was so floored. "You can make yourself *disappear*?" When he nodded, she gaped. "Wow. Geez, would I have loved to be able to do that when I was growing up." She grinned like the devil. "On my honeymoon would also have been an excellent time."

He snorted out a laugh. "Yeah, well, you don't actually disappear. You just move. But if I can't see, I'm the same as the average person. That's why Santi was always the one who wore the blindfolds in the act. He was the better magician. I wasn't much more than his … top assistant." He took another drag. "My abilities rarely came into play during our act, believe me." It hurtled into him, how much he still missed his brother.

She let out a long, loud sigh. "I wish there was something magical about me. I'm so conventional."

"What are you talking about?" He gave her an elbow jab. "You're best buds with British royalty."

"Oh, yeah." It warmed her to think about it. "You're right. How could I forget that? The things we start to take for granted, huh? Ten years ago, I would never have believed anything that happens on this ship was possible, and now it's become almost ordinary."

They enjoyed the view in silence, and Luca worked up his nerve to broach a subject he'd wanted to discuss with Angela since Sarita told him about her visions.

"There's something I've been meaning to ask you too." He flicked an ash into the ashtray he'd picked up off the rickety old table behind them. Angela gazed down on it, and he had the thought again that she was not sad, exactly, but something like it. Maybe she was thinking about Vincenzo. Maybe she'd come up here to be by herself. "Do you have a few more minutes, or would you rather be up here alone?"

The way he hesitated made it sound important. "Nope. I've got some time. Shoot."

Here goes nothing, he thought. "Do you know where they buried my father?"

Her eyes shot up to his. She'd hadn't been expecting that. "I don't." And there was no mistaking that what he saw on her face was sadness. "I'm sorry, Luca, sweetie, I don't. There was no service, no funeral for either of them. That was the way your mother's family wanted it. Rocco's parents were dead, Gina was his next of kin, so the Miceli side just let your grandparents handle it." She moved her head slowly back and forth with pity for him, for all of them. "Considering … well, the way the media ate that story up, they were afraid there'd be gawkers, press …" she trailed off. "You were all already so traumatized. How could we not go along with their wishes? The military took his body. That I know. I'm sure you could contact them."

Guilt overwhelmed her as she remembered the things that had been said and thought about Rocco Miceli. She knew better now, but not then. "I hate to say this, but at the time, even our side of the family had more sympathy for your mother than for him."

He hadn't taken his eyes off her face. Truth be told, he was working up his nerve to ask the more important thing — the thing he'd been too young to remember and desperately wanted to know.

"Did they love each other?" He had to stop for a few seconds. "Were they happy together when you knew them ... before?"

"Yes. Absolutely yes." She said it with such conviction that he had to believe her, and something inside him loosened a little.

They could have passed for mother and son right then. Their eyes — the color, the shape, the grief in them — were so alike. She touched his forearm, then removed her hand hastily when she saw his jaw work as he turned his face away and struggled not to cry. But she had to risk telling him, because she wanted him to know.

"He was sick, Luca. The war, the drugs they gave him after, made his mind go bad." She touched his arm again, squeezed it, so that he would look at her. When he did, as she expected, his eyes were red-rimmed and lost. "I didn't believe it at first, and I know I wasn't the only one. But then I met someone. Another soldier. Right here, by the way —" she tipped her chin to the spot where Lee's deck chair once was — "and he opened my eyes, made me see the terrible things war does."

Her tears fell freely now. She let them. "Your father loved your mother. I promise you — I *swear* to you — he loved her. And when he was in his right head, he made her very happy."

As was his habit when he was emotional, Luca cleared his throat. "Sarita said he was crying."

"Who?" He'd lost her.

Luca had to turn away from her, to walk a bit. It took a few minutes. When he came back, his emotions were under control. "She can see things. I know you're aware of it."

"Oh." Angela wiped at her cheeks. "She told you that? You two must be getting pretty close."

Ignoring the gentle probe, he filled her in on Sarita's childhood vision. By the time he'd finished, Angela's eyes were as round as the moon. "Oh, my God. That poor kid."

"Yeah." Luca leaned his back against the rail. "That sums it up, all right."

Apparently it did, as that was all Angela managed to say at first. "You know, Ro keeps telling her she has a gift. I wonder if she'd think that if she heard this."

"That's why I didn't ask her any questions after she told me." He had to light another cigarette. He was over his quota, but he needed it for this. "Uh … she would prefer that no one else knew, but she told me it was okay to talk to you. Because she said something I didn't know."

Angela held her breath.

"She said …" Luca stopped, cleared his throat a second time, and started again. "She said that when she saw my father, he was crying." Even though he hated the way the words felt on his tongue, he said them, to be sure she understood. "The day he killed her, I mean. He was crying then."

"He was?" This was news to Angela too. "I thought … I mean, I heard —"

"I know what you heard." He was looking straight ahead. He couldn't look at her. Not yet. "That he broke her neck on purpose. That's what my grandparents told me too." Now he managed to face her. "Do you think … could it have been an accident?"

She didn't answer right away. She needed to tread carefully. "Santi was there, right? Did you two ever discuss it?"

"He hated to talk about it." He studied the smoke as it curled off the end of the fresh cigarette. "But I couldn't help asking. And he never told me that our father was crying."

"He was so young. Maybe he blocked it out. Maybe he doesn't … didn't … remember." She prevaricated. "Could Sarita have made a mistake?"

"Funny thing about that." Luca pushed himself off the rail, crushed out the cigarette after only two puffs, and put the ashtray back on the old table. "She didn't see this part at first. Don't forget — she was doing everything she could to block it. But this morning she told me that ever since I got here, she keeps getting more pieces of it, a few at a time."

Angela pointed her finger. "There you go. All you have to do is be patient." She gave him a smug look. "She told you all this today, huh? Did she bring you breakfast after I left?"

"*Cugina*, I didn't know you were so nosy." He kissed the top of her head, grateful for the change of topic. "But since you are, I'll tell you that I have a date tonight."

Her jaw dropped. "You talked her into going off this ship? I'm very impressed." She decided to tell him. "Since we're sharing — you're not the only Miceli who has a date tonight."

"Is that right?" His eyebrows lifted. "Harry?"

"Yep." She bit her pinky finger. "Vincenzo's going to hate it."

"Nah." He slung his arm around her shoulder. "He'll get used to it."

CHAPTER TWELVE

The sun set on a proliferant Monday that had begat a face-off between a chef and a sorcerer, a battle between a mother and a queen, revelations of dreams and professions of love, a tempestuous embrace, a new question about an old murder, a marriage repaired by a stroll at the shore, a couple reunited over slow-cooked Kalua pork, and the acquisition of some truly magnificent, purloined cherries.

That evening, Sarita and Luca's outing went splendidly well. BObeau burgers were as tasty as purported, and even though the bar was crowded, Sarita was too busy having fun to feel any anxiety. Over a glass of chardonnay for her and an iced tea for him, he told her about life as a Vegas magician. She joined in with her own stories of the city, including Cynthia's rescue of Raul Sr.

But the best part of the night for Sarita came just as they were leaving, as she would tell Angela and Rohini with a liveliness that surprised them, when asked the next day. Luca's attention was caught by the harassment of a waitress at the hands of a customer — literal, lecherous hands. Said customer's bad toupee made a sudden leap off his head into his bowl of cheese onion soup. Luca swore innocence all the way back to the ship. When he walked her to her stateroom and gave her a chaste goodnight kiss, he left her longing for more.

And when Cristiano and Rohini heard that the others had plans to go out, they decided to keep their big news to themselves until the next day. They spent their Monday night composing an email to Jane and Antoni, searching online travels sites, and, at long last, making love.

Not only did Sarita find them in the kitchen the next morning, giggling together as they chopped vegetables, she also saw Angela and Harry having breakfast in the dining room, his presence on the ship at the early hour saying all. The new work week was off to a marvelous start for everyone.

Until Sarita tried to open the office door and it was stuck fast.

She turned the knob both ways, then set her hip against it and pushed. It didn't budge.

She tried the key again. Maybe she'd left it unlocked last night, and now she'd locked it inadvertently. But, no, the knob had turned. The door was simply jammed.

Angela and Harry heard her struggles and came around the corner. "It's stuck like glue," she told them.

Harry tried next, and put his back into it. Nothing. He scratched his head. "Looks like you're going to have to call Maintenance."

But Angela gave Sarita a bug-eyed look, and mouthed Luca's name.

Oh, yes — they already had a 'maintenance' guy, didn't they? And he was the best.

"Okay, you do that, sweetie. You call Maintenance," Angela said, for Harry's benefit. "I was just going to walk Harry down to his car."

Sarita went back to the kitchen, hoping to find that Luca had come down in the meanwhile. If not, she would call Maintenance, for sure. A jammed door was their job, not his, and she'd hate to wake him up for such a silly reason. But since he'd stopped the partying, he was becoming an early riser too, and so, there he was — drinking coffee and looking endearingly mussed from sleep.

"Hey. You're up."

That was all she said. Cristiano was looking at the golden egg zucchini he was slicing when she said it, not at her. But at the sound of those three words, at their undertone, his eyes shot to her face.

Her face was telling a story, as she stood, smiling at Luca. "I'm glad you're awake. I won't have to call anyone. The office door is stuck. Like, sealed shut. Would you come help?"

When they left the kitchen, Rohini looked at her husband and raised her eyebrows. "Oh, my. Did you see that?"

"Yes," he said, gruffly, and kept slicing.

Two minutes later, they both dropped what they were doing and hurried into the dining room when they heard Luca scream.

———●

"Don't scream. You'll scare them. And that would not be good."

"Holy crap — they can hear? How? Where the hell are their ears?"

"They don't have ears. They have sensory nerves — like tiny little hairs on the ends of their legs that can pick up sounds from across a room."

"Eww. Eww. Oh my God, this is gross." In his squeamish panic, he sounded more like a relative of Angela's than ever. He could almost be mistaken for her, at present.

Not that Sarita wasn't equally unnerved. But while Luca yelped, she managed a whisper. "Let's try to stay calm. Getting upset will only agitate them."

"They're everywhere!"

When they got to the office door, Luca didn't have to apply any of his special talents for it to come unstuck on its own. It remained just slightly ajar, as though someone had released it and then stepped back, so as not to disturb anyone within. Sarita, being what she was, understood right then: It was the *Queen*. Something was wrong, and she'd sealed the door herself, waiting for Luca's magickal help.

Luca couldn't have guessed that. Assuming the problem was solved, he'd already turned to go back to the kitchen when Sarita said, "Wait," and cautiously pushed the door all the way open. When she could see in, her stomach dropped.

They looked like sea creatures that had gotten lost. But they were camel spiders — huge, beige spiders with enormous, dark brown heads, each one almost the size of a pack of cigarettes. And they were, as Luca had pointed out, everywhere. She saw ten, at least, huddled together near the ceiling in the darkest corner of the far wall. One of the largest had positioned itself in the center of the leather blotter on Angela's desk, as though it had an appointment and was annoyed that she'd kept it waiting. Three more made a sanctuary of the peace lily on Rohini's desk. Jane's old desk, which was now being used by Cristiano, had one creeping up its side, another nestled next to his coffee mug, and a third seemed captivated by the photograph of his deceased sister, the young and pretty Isabel. On Sarita's desk, which used to be Cynthia's, there were six — three on top of a pile of manila folders, two on top of her calculator, and one balanced elegantly at the edge of her stapler. Others were scattered across the floor and curtains.

The spiders had been still and quiet until Luca shouted. Then they started moving and stridulating — a strange little sound that was like a click and a hiss at the same time. Sarita knew that meant they were just as terrified as he was. And some might even be angry.

"Oh, my God — why are they making that noise?"

"Will you please stop yelling? Right now, they don't know if they're safer where they are, or if they should try to hide. If they run, we'll never find them all. And trust me — they can run pretty fast." A thought occurred that made her blanch, and when she stated it out loud, it did nothing to calm Luca down. "Omigosh. They're female. I can tell by their size. The females are twice the size of the males. If they lay eggs, we might as well close the restaurant."

Rohini and Cris came up behind them. "What is it?" Rohini peered in and slapped her hand over her mouth.

Cris looked over Sarita's shoulder. "What the hell ...?" He knew enough to keep his voice down, but he was just as repelled as Luca was. "How ... how did they get in here?"

"I don't know, but we have to get them out." With a tinge of disparagement, Sarita looked at Luca. "Can you help us, or are you going to pass out?"

"I'm not going to pass out." He was annoyed, embarrassed, and scared shitless all at the same time.

"What's everybody doing here?" Angela was back. "Luca, did you fix the d — oh, my God! Eww. Oh, this is terrible. How did they get in here?"

More spiders started to move restlessly.

Sarita shushed her. "Angela, *please*. We have to keep them still. No offense, but we already have one panicked Italian, and that's more than enough right now."

"I'm not. I am not panicked, dammit." But there were beads of sweat forming on Luca's forehead.

"Should I call Pest Control?" Angela had lowered her voice. She'd gotten ahold of herself much faster than her cousin had managed to thus far.

"Sure. That's all we need eight hours before we're supposed to open for dinner — a visit from Pest Control. The tourists on board will find that sight very appetizing." Cristiano was counting spiders in his head. "I see thirty-four. No — there's two over there I missed. Thirty-six. Thirty-six spiders the size of rodents."

"Let's let them simmer down a bit." Rohini reached over and closed the door. "We've agitated them. We need to think about what to do."

But nothing came readily to mind.

"If we go in there — all of us — and try to pick them up a few at a time ..."

"The others will panic and start to run, Rohini. That's why Luca can't do it, either. He won't be able to focus on all of them at once." Sarita blew out a breath. "Hell. I just don't know. We might have to call Pest Control whether we want to or not."

"I'm trying to figure out where the heck they came from." Angela rubbed her arms and shivered. "I've got goosebumps. Could there have been a nest?"

Just then, something registered for Luca. "Hold on a minute." He looked at Cris. "You said thirty-six? An even three dozen?" He sounded less agitated and more like the wheels in his brain had started turning again after fright had ground them to a halt.

"Yeah, pretty sure." Cris frowned at the look on Luca's face. "Why?"

"That's not a random number. That's … that's how you buy live things — you order them by the dozen. That's how we would order doves for the act." He put it together after that, and his manner switched rapidly from Angela to Al Pacino.

"These fuckers were brought in. Somebody did this on purpose. Somebody wanted to hurt Sarita."

———•

"I'm not very bothered by big spiders. We had plenty in India. You get used to them."

The latest crisis had been averted, at least temporarily. They'd phoned the police, and within an hour, a team from the L.B.P.D. were on site, led by their old acquaintance, Detective Betty Montalbano.

She greeted Angela warmly. "Long time, Mrs. Perotta. It's been quiet around here, lately, hasn't it? Keeping track of all your earrings?" she teased.

All business after that, she and the others got to work. They had an entomologist with them. All thirty-six spiders were captured and contained, and the office dusted for fingerprints. Betty told them it might not be possible to trace where the spiders had been purchased, since the nastiness of the deed indicated that they'd been illegally obtained. She took down Sarita and Luca's statements about their confrontation with the Brazilian woman. The incident would now be part and parcel of the investigation.

After Betty and her team left, the five sat down in the kitchen for a spider symposium.

"I don't know how you'd get used to them." Luca amused Sarita by channeling Angela again, shuddering just as she had at Rohini's comment. It was even more entertaining to see Cristiano do the same.

Sarita scoffed at all three of them. "Honestly, it's sad how misunderstood they are. Spiders are remarkable creatures. If it weren't for them, the earth would be overrun with disease-carrying insects. And did you know the silk they weave has a number of medical applications?"

"As a matter of fact, I, for one, was not aware of that, sweetie. It's good to know." Angela gave Sarita a placating pat before getting down to business. "Spiders aside, how bad do we think this situation is, and what should we do about it?"

"I don't know." Sarita thought back to the night of the ball. As usual when she was feeling anxious, she bit her thumbnail, and gave them all a pleading look. "But can we not say anything to my mother? We have no information yet. There's not a thing she can do except worry."

"I think that's reasonable. For the time being, at least. But ..." Rohini looked at Cristiano to see if he concurred. "It's probably best if we cancel our trip."

Three faces perked with interest. Angela posed the question for them all. "What trip?"

After they were filled in, Sarita made her thoughts adamantly clear to Cristiano and Rohini. "You're not going to cancel. I won't allow it."

When she saw their hesitance, she decided it was time to be candid. "I don't need a babysitter. I know that's what you've been doing for the last ten years. And I know why."

They said nothing, but when they dared not look at one another, she had to smile. She knew she'd startled them with her observation. "I love you both so much. But I'm fine. Angela is here." She paused, bit her lower lip, then decided to admit it. "Luca is here too. And I feel safe with him."

All attention switched to Luca, whose eyes went soft at her testimonial. He reached across and took her hand.

Sarita went on. "For gosh sakes, there's a former queen of England looking out for me, not to mention a battalion of other spirits aboard at her beck and call. How much more protection do I need? I think you can go on a two-week trip without worry."

"All right, *menina*. We will go."

If Rohini was surprised at Cristiano's ready acquiescence, she hid it well. Later, when they were alone, she'd make sure he was as comfortable with the idea of leaving Sarita as he had made it sound.

Looking down at his phone, Luca spoke up next. "Well, if that's settled and I'm not needed down here for a while, I should find out why my accountant texted me three times in the past hour."

As he got up, Cristiano caught his eye, motioning discreetly that he'd like to have a private word. With a point of his finger, Luca signaled back that he would wait for him in his stateroom.

Cris's knock on his door came shortly after. The two men stood, feeling awkward, one inside the doorway, one out. Braced for more recriminations, Luca motioned him inside.

He was caught off guard when the chef got right to his purpose. "I owe you an apology."

Luca's response surprised Cristiano as well. "No, you don't. You definitely don't." He sat on the edge of his bed. "She told me everything." He pinched the bridge of his nose, shook his head, still astounded by what Sarita had endured. "Every hideous thing. I understand you now. I know you were trying to protect her. Who can blame you?"

For the first time, with just those few words, the depth and breadth of Luca's feelings were evident to Cristiano. He couldn't help but chuckle. "Holy shit — you're in deep, aren't you?"

"Yeah, I am." Luca saw the masculine humor in his predicament too. "But believe me, not knowing what her thoughts are on the subject, I sure feel like … I don't know. The word 'clown' comes to mind."

"Oh, don't I know it." Cristiano sniggered again. "I have been there myself." He decided to be magnanimous. "I think you've got a good shot, though."

Hope flew into Luca's face. "You do?"

It was then, observing how much the offhand commendation had meant to him, that Cristiano joined Team Luca. He'd been wrong about the boy. It was that simple. And it appeared that Luca wasn't holding any grudges. "Yes, I do."

He sat in the armchair where Sarita had been sitting when she bared her soul. "Will you tell me —" He stopped, considered what Rohini had said about his imperiousness, and decided to ease his way into it. Friendly conversation first might help. But what to say? What did he have in common with a … not a magician, but a sorcerer? He ran through a few topics in his head, and then grasped at one. "So … your mother. Tiny, eh?"

"Yeah, she was. I get my height from my … my father."

Oh, hell, thought Cris. He didn't want to get on that subject. "My mother was tiny too," he threw in hastily, "and … and Rohini." His smile was nervous, unsure. "They pack a punch, those tiny women, don't they?"

Luca knew what the chef was trying to do and he appreciated it. "Yeah, they sure do." With a supportive grin, he added, "Any time somebody made a crack about her height, my mother would say, 'the most expensive gifts come in the smallest boxes.'"

Cris laughed. "That's a good one. I'll have to remember it, to say it to Rohini." Although he'd heard it dozens of times and they both knew it.

He waited one more beat before posing a question with much more diplomacy than Luca would have expected. "So. Do you feel comfortable enough to tell me what brought you here? I don't believe that making pastry holds a deep appeal for you."

Luca rubbed the side of his neck. "Okay. But I'd like your word on something first, if you'll give it."

"What is it?"

He was as fervent and grave as a preacher when he said, "Promise me that you'll trust me to take care of it — to take care of her. And I'll give you my solemn oath that, whether she loves me or not, I won't leave here until I know she's safe."

Cristiano didn't answer at first. He truly had to think about whether or not he was ready to put that much faith in someone else when it came to Sarita's welfare. In his mind, it felt like ten months, not ten years, that he held her while she cried after Naag's death.

I never wanted to be a killer.

He could still hear her.

But then he thought about how much she'd changed in just these past weeks since Luca's arrival. And finally, he thought about his own life, his own marriage.

It was tricky, all right. Even so, it was time to pass the baton.

"I think I can give you my trust on that."

Luca sagged with relief. "Good." He studied Cristiano. He had something else he wanted to say, but wasn't sure if it would be well-received. "I mean no disrespect by this. I'm glad you said that, not only for me, but —" he looked at Cristiano somberly — "I really think you need to go on that trip with your wife."

Cristiano acknowledged that with a tip of his head. "I think you're right." He waited. "So, are you going to tell me?"

Luca told him. When he finished, Cristiano leaned back in his chair and just stared. "Your *mother* sent you?"

"Yeah."

In his well-established reaction to anxiety, Cristiano got to his feet, ran his fingers through his hair, mumbled to himself as he walked up and down the carpet. "It's bizarre." He frowned down at Luca. "Forgive me, but it is bizarre. Why Sarita? What's the connection to her?"

Luca hesitated. "There is a connection. I can't tell you what it is, though, because Sarita asked me not to. She ... she gave me the okay to tell Angela, though. Angela knows." He cleared his throat. "And while we're on the subject, I haven't told Sarita yet. About my mother sending me here, I mean."

"Why not?"

"She's been so different. So much lighter." Cris heard the yearning, the worry. "I just want her to have a little more time before I put more anxious thoughts into that ... that overburdened brain of hers."

Cris snorted. "You think thirty-six spiders didn't give her a clue that she has an enemy?"

Before Luca could respond, his phone buzzed. It was Desiree again. "Ach. I'm sorry, Cris. I have to take this. It's my accountant, and something must be up. She's been trying to get in touch with me all morning."

When Cristiano left Luca, he wished he could tell himself that everything was fine. On the one hand, he now felt reasonably certain that the boy could be trusted. On the other, there was still something nagging at him, and he would be damned if he could figure out what it was.

CHAPTER 13

Two weeks later

The dead no longer have options. Some accepted that and moved on. Some clung to this side of the veil because they were angered or confused by their changed circumstance. Others had an important message or were fearful about the welfare of someone they'd had to leave behind. And still others knew that departing this plane was the one choice they had left to make, so they simply delayed making it.

It was for this reason that the spirits who inhabited the *Queen* — those among them who cared for the living, that is — felt secondhand satisfaction, and perhaps a touch of envy, when they observed how much happier the five principal crew members of The Secret Spice were due to their having made different decisions, at last.

The de la Cuevas were leaving in two days for Rome and their excitement over this first-ever trip together was contagious. The entire staff marveled at the change in Cristiano. He laughed more often than he shouted orders. When he went out into the dining room to visit tables, his demeanor was playful rather than solely courteous. When a busboy dropped a tray of dirty plates, he didn't admonish, he consoled. And once, in the middle of a dinner rush, he flustered his wife by pulling her to him and kissing her soundly.

It was Rohini who loved him more than her own life, but when it came to his work, it was Cynthia who had understood him best. A *cordon bleu* chef was like any other artist — emotional, moody, impulsive, and relentlessly compelled to create. The bits and pieces of running a restaurant — pricing, promotion, profits, regulations — were exhaustive. And running one aboard a historic and weathered ship that was sometimes leaky or having repair work done, added another layer of complexity. That it was a haunted ship was another consideration that most outsiders dismissed as a publicity stunt, but that those who worked aboard knew to be a fact.

All Cristiano wanted to do was make beautiful food. He wanted his beef dishes to be unique, succulent, perfectly seasoned, and pleasing to the eye. He didn't want to think about how much the beef cost him, or how much their clientele would be willing to pay for his creation. This was his perspective on everything from the lowliest potato to the type of peppercorns he used. He was meticulous in his choices, and the concept of 'margins' was exasperating to him.

Knowing this, Cynthia had left him out of that end of things, and he'd been glad of it. If she could purchase what he wanted for a price that made sense, she did so. If she couldn't, she cajoled or browbeat him into compromise. But when she left, Sarita took over, and she was more diffident with him than her mother had been. He was forced to be involved, and the strain had taken its toll. He was only now coming to see how glad he was to be free of it for two weeks.

He'd been to Italy before. For a chef such as himself, it was almost mandatory. He'd studied there, cooked there, had his first great romance there — although he'd never tell that last nugget to Rohini. He was so looking forward to going back. He'd be happy to see his old friend, the prickly yet big-hearted Jane, who, suspicious of him at first, had later become his champion. And how could he not like Antoni? Within an hour of their meeting, he'd helped them get rid of a corpse.

Cristiano's anticipation was eclipsed by his wife's, however, and no one but she knew by what measure. Since these arrangements had been made, Rohini had her moments when she truly thought it couldn't be real, that she'd wake up and find herself back in Kolhapur, holding Zahir's head as he vomited, with Vanu standing guard, watching them anxiously from the closed sickroom door.

Years had passed, but the trauma of her early life experiences remained. Her daring escape, the friendships she'd formed with her business partners, her experiences aboard the *Queen Mary*, Cristiano's love, had all scrubbed patiently at the bloodstains on her soul. But those stains would never completely fade.

She had the bad luck of being born in a time and a location where female children were not human beings, but commodities. That she was born beautiful was more bad luck. Her beauty made her bartering value that much higher. Her natural intelligence, her deep and loving heart, her dreams and desires, were of no significance. What she looked like — how her body was curved, how her nose was shaped — were the primary focal points during the bidding process for her. Those, and the fact that she had been raised with the proper malleability. But even if she hadn't, compliance could be beaten into her by her new in-laws and the husband who was selected for her.

Rohini's fate was never in her own hands, but in the hands of the men who'd governed her — her father, her brothers, her husband. Her life choices were limited to how much ginger she might put in the rice she cooked, which tomatoes she picked from the bin at the market, what kind of herbal tea she drank. Even the clothing she wore was supervised by someone else.

Now, no matter what she did, whether she worked in the kitchen at The Secret Spice, or chatted with her friends, or made passionate, life-affirming love with the beautiful, Spanish husband she adored, one thought — one very chilling thought — was always, *always* at the back of her mind: If Zahir had not realized the depth of his brother's depravity, she might, at this very moment, be under Naag, his hot, evil breath at her neck as he plowed her, not with care or desire, but with malice.

Or, she could be dead. Poisoned at his hand, as he'd poisoned his brother, his parents, and his fifteen-year-old wife.

These possibilities from the past stayed with her as tangibles. They'd been presented to her parents and brothers when she'd first fled. But their standing in the community was more important to them than her life. They would have preferred that she died with honor as Naag's wife. When she'd been given the choice to live instead, by her own dying husband, they disavowed her. They were her family, but it were as if she never existed for them.

For women like Cynthia and Jane, a trip to Italy was a possibility, perhaps even a whim. For women like Angela and Sarita, it was a daring adventure. But for women like Rohini, such an opportunity was nothing less than a miracle.

And so, as she shopped for the things she wanted to wear on her trip, as she made suggestions to her husband on restaurants they might try or side tours they might take, in the eyes of their friends, she did so with simple pleasure. She kept it a secret that what she felt in truth was more in line with what someone who'd been liberated from an internment camp might feel — exhilaration that it was happening, and terror that her freedom would be taken away as capriciously as it had been bestowed.

Angela's thoughts about her decision to see Harry again were less complicated than the ones running through Rohini's mind, but they were no less vital to her. She loved Vincenzo, and would almost certainly never get past the guilt that she'd abandoned him for two years. But, not only was she back with Harry because it gave her happiness, she was back with Harry to set a precedent, to be an example to her son.

Without a doubt, it was an example she should have set years before. She hadn't had the self-assurance then to live as she wanted to live, but she did now. It might be too late for Vincenzo to learn any more life lessons, but she was ten years older than he was currently when she'd had her defining moment, so she would hold onto the hope.

That issue aside, she and Harry were having a blast. Harry's worldliness, his live-and-let-live attitude, were a refreshing change of pace and two qualities she strived to emulate. Unlike Jack, he didn't care if someone was or wasn't gay. He'd only comment about it if it were brought up to him in a derogatory way. In that situation, he had no problem flaying the detractor, generally doing so with such satirical humor that even the person he mocked had to chuckle. Unlike Marco, Harry didn't make a reproving face if she wore a dress that showed a little cleavage or some knee. With Harry, it was okay for her to be sexy, to feel sexy. He liked it. He liked *her,* in general.

Angela's appeal to Harry was her youthful enthusiasm for everything from a so-so film to a new acquaintance. She never assumed the attitude of ennui that some of the women his own age did, thinking it made them appear more sophisticated. She embraced life and didn't mind that her gratification was so apparent. She was revitalizing. When they were together, she approached whatever they did as if it were new and unique. Harry was learning that in her case, sometimes that was true. That she was fourteen years older gave him hope for his future. There might be better things ahead than growing bitter, jaded, and paunchy.

It probably wasn't love in the traditional sense. But if it wasn't, it was something equally gratifying — a 'my-coolest-buddy' friendship that was comprised of mutual respect, shared escapades, lots of laughter, and the added bonus of great sex. It was a lovely and liberating association for them both. And if there was an ache in Angela's heart that she still hadn't heard from Vincenzo, she did her best not to let it bother her too much.

But the spirits knew that of all of their favored humans, the one who'd transformed most over the recent weeks was the youngest one. The others had been flowering toward their fullest, most beautiful blossoms for some time now, but it took Luca coming aboard for Sarita to even begin to unfurl.

As Luca had suggested, he and Sarita spent time together being 'normal.' They went to the aquarium at Rainbow Harbor, and were the only two adults willing to pet a shark in the kid-friendly touch tank. They shared a tender kiss in front of a glass wall of tropical fish, a kiss beheld by a group of third graders, who giggled and made gagging sounds.

On the Monday after their first date, Sarita put aside her paperwork to give him a tour through every corner of the ship, with the exception, needless to say, of the cargo hold where the prisoners had been kept. Her passion for the *Mary*'s history ignited his own. When they stood by the empty swimming pool, he listened with profound emotion as she told him about Jane, Gabriella, and Jackie.

For the first time in ten years, Sarita was happy and relatively carefree. Relatively. People didn't change that drastically in such a short period of time, but she was making a promising start. It wasn't for a reason as inane and shallow as having a 'boyfriend.' It was that she'd finally met another being like herself, someone with qualities not shared by the average human, someone her own age who had experienced unfathomable loss and made it through, if not completely whole, then nearly so.

But the thing about Luca that she valued above all was his capacity for seeing humor where she too often saw only tragedy. Just as when he joked about the woman who had screamed at them the night of the ball, if there was even a grain of farcicality to be found in any situation, he'd find it and, most of the time, help her see it too. Humor was his way of thumbing his nose at the sound and fury of life. He'd lost that knack after Santi's death, but with Sarita, he was regaining it. He probably hadn't put it together yet that a tendency for fatalism was a trait Sarita and his late brother shared.

Cristiano found out for sure that he'd been right to put his trust in Luca three days before he and Rohini left. After Sarita dragged the young man all over the ship, subjecting him to what they were all certain was one of her comprehensive history lessons, the couple joined the others in the kitchen for some lunch. As Sarita was pulling out plates, Luca winked at her and murmured something in her ear. Whatever he'd said, she threw back her head and laughed — a loose, free laugh no one had ever heard from her before. Three surprised, pleased people whipped their heads in her direction, and a brightness flashed through the kitchen like a sunbeam peeking in through the walls.

It was that light, as well as the laugh, that put Cristiano's mind at ease. He recognized that burst of radiance for what it was — a proclamation, a seal of approval by the presence in the galley.

He was correct. Her Majesty was pleased. Luca and Sarita were both noble forces. And when these two extraordinary young people became lovers, their power would be unsurpassed.

It was thanks to the 'uninvited one' that Luca was here, the *Queen* knew. Every other spirit aboard the ship was in some way connected to it, but perhaps it was time to make an exception, to declare a sovereign truce with the presence that had been known in life as Gina Castelletti Miceli. Like the four women who had come together to create The Secret Spice, Gina and Mary's experiences in life had been markedly different. But their commonalities were in their tragedies: Both had sons that, one way or another, they'd lost.

Now, they would join forces in an alliance to be formed within the spirit world, an alliance helmed by two strong, feminine entities — one who had died as a young mother, one who had lived as a bold queen. For, even with Luca and Sarita's combined magicks, it would take all the help the spirit world could give them to stop what was already lurking aboard.

CHAPTER FOURTEEN

Wednesday, September 17, 2014 - 5:30 a.m.

On his last morning before leaving, the instant Cristiano opened the doors to The Secret Spice, the delicious, exotic aroma coming from the galley stopped him in his tracks. He sniffed the air. Garlic and tomato. When it came to food, his nose was like a bloodhound's. With another sniff, he picked up the scents of pepper, bay leaves, and oregano — an especially piquant oregano.

Who was cooking in his kitchen?

When he went in, he was met by the unexpected sight of Luca at the stove, stirring something in a stock pot kept heated on low flame.

"You're cooking something for real? Not just ... photocopy cooking?"

Luca chuckled, taking the jibe in the amiable spirit it was meant. "To be honest, this is the only thing I enjoying cooking the old-fashioned way."

Cristiano couldn't resist a peek. The smell was mouthwatering. "What is it?"

"My grandmother's tomato sauce." With a separate teaspoon, Luca sampled it, put the used spoon in the sink behind them, and then ground two twists of black pepper into the pot. "You guys are leaving tomorrow. I thought ... I don't know ..." Feeling foolish, he shrugged. "After all the great food I've had in this place, I figured I should at least make you one meal before you go."

"Oh. That's ... very nice," Cris stammered. "It smells very good." More touched by the gesture than he was comfortable with, he quickly changed the subject, pointing to the dewy, fragrant, jade-green herb Luca had on a cutting board. "Where did you get that fantastic oregano?"

"My grandmother's old place. She's not there anymore, but the lady who lives there now kept her garden going." When Cris looked at him blankly, he elaborated. "I had to get there while it was still early, before she lets her dog out. Last time, he snuck up on me and almost bit me in the ass."

"You're telling me you went to Brooklyn, New York. This morning?"

"Uh huh." Luca added a pinch of salt and stirred again. "I got bread too. I figured, while I was there. Satellite Bakery has the best. We're lucky — they were just taking it out of the oven. Ever have braided semolina bread with the sesame seeds?" He pressed the tips of his fingers to his mouth, kissed them, and then flicked them open. "Oh, my God. *The* most incredible bread. I used to eat it every day when I was kid. *Nannuzza* — my grandmother — she would put her homemade ricotta cheese on it, heirloom tomatoes, a little fresh basil, and boom — you had an open sandwich fit for kings." His eyes sparkled like a naughty puppy's as Cristiano frowned dubiously. "It's over there —" he tilted his chin toward Angela's station. "Go ahead — try some."

Still skeptical, Cristiano squinted at the white bakery bag packed with braided loaves. The side of the bag had the logo: Satellite Bakery, Brooklyn's Best Italian Breads. When he touched the bag, it was warm.

"Unbelievable," he muttered.

"Yeah, I know. That's why I keep it a secret, for the most part." Luca went back to his sauce. "But I did say I could take you and Rohini to Italy, if you wanted. That's a long trip. Seems like a waste of time when it's not necessary."

"No, no, no. No, thank you." Cristiano's tone was resolute more than it was appreciative. "We will go — as you called it — the old-fashioned way."

"Up to you." With a teasing half-smile, Luca lifted a shoulder. "It's just as safe as a plane, you know. Maybe even safer." He covered the pot, but left the lid slightly askew so that steam could escape. When he turned, Cris was observing him thoughtfully. He wanted to say something, but wasn't sure if he could. "What's up?" Luca prompted.

"I have a confession." But he put on a clean apron first, went to the sink to wash his hands with the thoroughness of a surgeon. Whatever it was he wanted to say, he was taking his sweet time. After he picked up a hand towel, he came out with it. "I'm envious of you."

Luca kept his face impassive. "How so?"

"Not of all your skills. Just of one. That … you could duplicate my recipes. Recipes that took me years to perfect." In hindsight, he disliked himself for it, which was why he was owning up to it. "I see now that your ability to do so with such ease added to my distrust of you." He draped the towel by the sink. "But that part wasn't distrust. It was jealousy. I'm not proud of it."

"I get it." Luca cleared his throat and, even though the sauce didn't need to be checked just yet, he checked it to give himself something to do. "My brother felt the same way. He was a true magician. The best. And that took work — way more work, skill and talent than people on the outside would ever guess. And yet, he never gave himself the credit he deserved. He always focused on what I could do that he couldn't." He thought of their last performance again, Santi's words before they got on stage. He would always think of them. "I can't help but wonder how bad things would have gotten between us if he'd lived."

Cris could see both the pride Luca felt in his brother and the burden he carried over the emotional distance between them. How he ever could have imagined that this boy might have been behind the accident was beyond him. Jealousy has sharp teeth, he thought. Once it bit into you, you were focused on nothing else but the torture of it. "I'm sorry, *amigo*." He meant about Santi, but he was sorry for much when it came to Luca.

"Well. You know how it is. Sibling rivalry. Sometimes, I let myself think that if it weren't for that, maybe he wouldn't have risen as high in his field as he did. He'll always be known as one of the greats." He added a cup of Sangiovese wine to the pot, swirled it into the thick, bubbling blend of tomatoes and herbs. "But that's only on a day when I'm feeling good about myself."

"I had no brothers, so it's hard for me to imagine the situation." Cristiano leaned against the sink behind Luca. "I had a sister, and she was much younger, so she adored me."

"Huh." Luca got another teaspoon, took another taste. "Lucky you."

Cristiano wasn't sure he could share his past with the ease that Luca had. "Not so lucky." He stopped. Every now and then, the scars still oozed like fresh cuts. "I let her down. Big time."

Luca's short, brutal laugh was meant to be ironic, but came out too much like a sob. "Join the club, man. I let my brother down too."

They exchanged a look that spoke volumes. In the brief silence, Cristiano understood that not only did Luca know about his felony, but like so many others, he'd judged him for it. So, it had been a mutual dislike, then. That evened things up between them somewhat, to Cristiano's mind.

"Luciano Paolo Miceli — is that my *Zia*'s tomato sauce?"

Angela and Rohini had made their way into the kitchen, Angela leading with her nose. Her smile couldn't have been any brighter if Luca had handed her a diamond bracelet.

"Oh, my God, it smells like Brooklyn in this kitchen! I haven't had this sauce in years." She saw what was on her work station, and Luca beamed when she made a sound that was halfway between a gasp and a squeal. "You got the bread too? I *love* this bread. I've tried to duplicate it here and it just never tastes the same." So ecstatic was she over food from back home that she grabbed him by both sides of his face and kissed his cheek soundly.

Rohini and Cristiano stood by, getting a kick out of the family scene. "Hey," Cris joked, pointing to himself and his wife. "The two of us have been cooking for you for ten years. How come we never got any kisses?"

By the time Sarita walked in, Angela was perking coffee and Rohini was brewing tea.

"Good morning." She was greeted by four happy faces, the smell of toasted sesame seeds, and another zesty scent that got her thinking about ordering pizza for lunch. Making the natural assumption, she turned to Cristiano. "Whatever you're cooking smells incredible."

"No, no, no." Cris held up his hands, delighted that everyone was in such a good mood. "Don't blame me for this stench." He pointed to Luca, who was still by the stove, now scraping out the sauté pan he'd used for the onions and garlic. "It's your Sicilian friend over there. He's the one who made it. By himself."

"Luca did? Really?" Sarita was another woman who preferred to be presented with great food over good jewelry.

Rohini's eyes smiled from over her cup of tea when Cristiano added, "From scratch, by the way. It's his grandmother's recipe."

Sarita peeked into the pot. "Oooh. Tomato sauce. I love it." She looked so pleased by it and by him, that Luca stood there basking in that, before he remembered to reply.

"Uh … it has to simmer for at least five hours." He checked with Cris. "Will it be in your way?"

"Put it on one of the back burners and it will be fine." Cristiano glanced around at everyone. "I assume we will all eat together tonight?"

"Definitely," Angela declared. "In fact —" she draped her apron over her head as she asked Luca — "I see you bought pasta, but how about if I make homemade to do that sauce justice? I'm happy to."

They all chorused their enthusiasm on that.

"Okay, but remember." Sarita got some coffee. "Tomorrow Scotland votes on their independence."

Angela tied her apron strings twice around her waist. "I wish them a lot of luck, but what does that have to do with me making pasta?"

"I'm talking about the airport. The referendum is a big deal. I don't know if there'll be more people at LAX as a result — don't forget the flight's international — but it might be better to get there a little early." She added milk to her mug. "And then there's the *Mary*'s anniversary celebration next week. There's already lots of people here for that, so we have reservations until nine tonight."

When they all still looked clueless, she huffed with exasperation. "All I meant is that we'll be eating late, but Ro and Cris have to get up early. That's all."

"Thank you for your concern, Mom," Cris said, dryly, "but I think you can let us stay up for one night."

"I'm just saying." Sarita's tone was a tad touchy. "You have to get up so early and it's such a long flight. You could have let Luca take you."

Rohini smiled. So that's what this was about. The girl was so in love and still had no idea. No hint of how right she and Luca looked together, or what a lightness of heart it gave them all to see it.

"Next time." Rohini nudged her husband discreetly before he could object. "Next time we will, darling." She ran a hand over Sarita's hair to mollify her. "We've never been on an airplane together. We're looking forward to it. It's like a honeymoon for us."

"I guess." Sarita looked down at her mug. "But ... just call us as soon as you land. You know Angela worries."

Angela nearly laughed out loud at being thrown under the bus. "That's right." She looked over Sarita's bowed head to Ro and Cris with humor. "I'll be a nervous wreck until I hear from you, so call us — me — the minute that plane rolls to a stop, okay?"

"Of course we will, Angela," Cris affirmed with a grin. "Of course."

"Indeed we will, Angela," added Rohini. "No need to fret."

They both went over to hug Sarita.

———————

As Sarita had anticipated, the restaurant was packed that evening. People were already aboard for the next day's event that would honor surviving veterans, war brides, and refugees of World War II who had sailed aboard the *Queen Mary*. These outstanding representatives of 'The Greatest Generation' were to be feted by the ship's management team. They, along with some of the original crew members, would be interviewed about their experiences aboard, their stories filmed to be later viewed by tourists in the *Mary*'s Heritage Room.

This was all part of the upcoming celebration the following Friday for the 80th anniversary of the ship's launch on September 26, 1934. The celebration would be ship-wide, with the *Queen Mary* opening her gangways and ballrooms, decks and salons, attractions and eateries to the public all day. The highlight of the event would be a grand birthday cake fit for a *Queen*. Celebrity baker Jose Barajas had been commissioned to create the cake, and Angela was thrilled to be assisting him. The cake would weigh approximately a quarter of a ton and measure over fifteen feet long. Angela had been interviewed by the local news station, and she'd promised that the cake would be as "exact a replica of the ship as flour, eggs and frosting would allow."

Sarita was pleased as punch that the date was exactly one day before her twenty-sixth birthday. If truth be told, she was a little disappointed that Rohini and Cristiano wouldn't be aboard for the two occasions, but she understood that they'd made their plans on impulse and that it was huge for them. But Angela had already asked if she would like her usual vanilla mousse cake, or if she'd prefer something new. Sarita chose the usual, naturally. It was their tradition by now, and nothing could top Angela's vanilla mousse cake.

Luca was taking her out for her birthday also. A special surprise, he said. She hadn't expected him to, since it was also so close to that other anniversary — the dreadful one of the fire. But he insisted that he preferred to think of Santi as he'd been when he was alive, not focus on how he'd died, and if that's what Luca preferred, then that's what they'd do.

Now that she'd gotten used to the idea, she'd worked up the nerve to give traveling 'Luca style' a second try. She wanted to go back to Rome, to sit by the Trevi Fountain, and have a gelato. Maybe his plan was to pop in on Jane and Antoni while Rohini and Cris were there. She grinned to herself as she tried to imagine what their reaction might be.

But for now she had a restaurant to run, and her job included going over to tables to greet her guests. She enjoyed that duty for the most part, and tonight it had been an exceptional pleasure. The guests of honor for tomorrow's event were all dining together at a dais table reserved especially for them. Sarita had met two of those honorees only once before, and she was excited to be seeing them again.

One was June Boots Allen. In 1946, June was one of eighteen hundred young women who were the first war brides to sail on the *Queen Mary* from England to the United States, to be reunited with their American soldier husbands. Though June's husband had passed on, her children and grandchildren were with her to celebrate her joy at being aboard the *Mary* for the first time in over six decades, and they surrounded her, proudly and happily, at the table. Sitting nearest June and her family was the charming Ralph Rushton, who was a crew member until 1962, starting as a bellboy and eventually working his way up to waiter in first class. Ralph's tales of the sea were enthralling and often humorous.

But at the other end of the table were George Schneider and Elliot Abramson, the two war veterans whom Sarita had not yet met. Her deep love for the history of the ship, her knowledge of how compelling and vital it was, made the opportunity to meet the two men an unparalleled experience for her. George and Elliot had served in the 30th Infantry Division, a division that had sustained over nine months of intense combat during the war, and the *Mary* had been their troopship. During the war, she'd been nicknamed 'The Grey Ghost,' for the cloak her wartime grey paint afforded her during nighttime runs, and her ability to sail faster than Hitler's U-boats. How did it feel to George and Elliot, Sarita so wanted to know, to be back on the *Queen* after so many years, and under such changed circumstances? The last time they were aboard was when she pulled into New York in August of 1945, with thousands by the harbor welcoming the soldiers and the ship that had come back victorious from war. George and Elliot, along with fifteen thousand other soldiers, had endured being packed together aboard the ship for months on end. They ate bland food that was slapped together quickly so that all could be fed in the same day.

And at night, they traveled through the ocean, undercover in the dark, not knowing if they might be hit by a bomb from above or a torpedo from below. They feared for their lives, relentlessly, until the last day, that August, when the cheers, and the flags, and the banners of those who were waiting told them they'd finally made it home. Now, sixty-nine years later, the two hailed heroes were aboard once again, this time eating an elegant dinner at The Secret Spice Café, surrounded by thankful family, friends, and strangers.

Sarita had already gone over once to say hello, but she waited until the table ordered their desserts before she went back again, bringing Luca along with her.

It was when they were both talking with June that Luca got quite the surprise. A few seats down the table, Elliot, who was sitting next to George, fixed his gaze on Luca.

"Hold on, everybody, hold on." Elliot's voice was deep and booming.

As instructed, everyone stopped talking and 'held on,' as he reached around George and tapped Sarita's arm. "Young lady, your boyfriend over there —" he pointed to Luca — "did you say his name was Luca Miceli?"

Right then, Luca wished a sinkhole would open up and suck him down into the water beneath the ship. This had to be about the act. It was not uncommon for groups of senior citizens to take a bus to Vegas. Now everyone in the restaurant would look his way, and some would remember the fire.

Before Sarita or Luca could respond, Elliot stood up. "It *is* you, isn't it? Do you remember me? The last time you saw me, you were only six years old."

It took Luca another minute. More than twenty years had passed, after all, and though the man looked familiar ...

He slapped his palms to his mouth. "Oh, my God. Mr. Abramson? I can't believe it." He hurried around to Elliot's side of the table to shake his hand, but Elliot brushed that off to grip him in a bear hug that was surprisingly strong.

Overcome with emotion, Luca explained the connection. "Sarita, everyone — Mr. Abramson is my old neighbor. He used to live downstairs from my mother and brother and me. Can you believe it? Small world, huh?"

Swamped by memories, one terrible one in particular, Luca and Elliot stood staring at one another, taking in the changes the years had wrought on both of them.

Finally Luca said, "It was a lifetime ago."

"Oy. It sure was." Elliot couldn't resist the impulse to reach up and ruffle Luca's hair just as he used to. "It's good to see you again."

They had a lot to share when they finally sat down in the kitchen to eat with the others.

"I remember Mr. and Mrs. Abramson. Nice people." Angela twirled linguini around her fork. "He was a little deaf. Always forgot which ear I was supposed to talk into."

Luca helped himself to some bread. "He remembers you too. He couldn't believe it when I told him you were the pastry chef here. He says his wife used to buy biscotti at your bakery."

Angela pointed at him. "That's right. She liked the ones with the chocolate on them, God rest her soul. When did she pass, did he say?"

"No, but you should come with me when I meet him for coffee. I'm sure he'd like that."

"I'll try, sweetie, but it's going to be crazy busy until the end of next week. I've got a lot of extra baking to do. And there's the anniversary cake. We're starting on that tomorrow. But he'll be at the celebration on Friday, so I'll see him then, for sure."

"It was fascinating to talk with all of them. Can you imagine doing what June did — being eighteen years old, with a baby, and sailing away from your family and friends to go to a strange, new place? Or being part of a daring mission at sea, like Elliot and George? Or meeting all those glamorous people, like Ralph?" In deference to their *cordon bleu*'s sensibilities, Sarita picked delicately at the small portion of pasta she put in her plate, but the truth was she wanted to scarf it all down. It was heavenly. As she told Luca when they went out for a burger on their first date, sometimes there was nothing better than simple comfort food, although she'd loved Cristiano too much to ever say so and risk hurting his feelings.

That thought was running through her head when he smiled at her.

"I agree with you, *menina*. I only spoke with them briefly, but it made me feel good, at my age, to meet four people, so much older than I, who are still living such fulfilling lives. These people were, and are brave adventurers." Cristiano's tone became reflective. "I wonder what kind of a man I would be, what sort of a life I would be living, were I to live as long as they?" There was an undertone in the question, as though he already knew he wouldn't have the chance to find out. When he felt four pairs of eyes on him, he swiftly lightened the mood. Tapping his now empty plate with his fork, he addressed Angela and Luca. "So. Are you planning to turn this place into an Italian restaurant while I'm gone?"

Luca winked. "A pizzeria, actually. Right, *cugina*?"

"Yep," she teased. "Ooh, Luca — let's get Cousin Luigi. That pizza he makes? Oh, my God." Angela pressed her hands to her heart. "Out of this world. The line at his place is out the door. Maybe we could talk him into coming out to the west coast. "

Rohini chimed in. "I think it's an excellent idea." At the look on her husband's face, she snickered. "We could change the name to The Secret Spicy Meatball."

They all found the quip that much funnier because it was unexpected coming from her. It was only a few minutes later, however, that she yawned behind her hand. "Well, I hate to break up this lovely party, but I'm quite tired. Sarita is right that we have to be at the airport early. What do you say, Cristiano? Shall we go up?"

Angela got to her feet. "I'm coming up with you. Tomorrow's a big day for me too."

But when they went to clear their dishes, Sarita stopped them. "Leave this. Luca and I will do it."

"Are you sure, darling?" Rohini fretted. "That doesn't seem fair after he made the meal."

Sarita put her hands on her hips. "It's five plates. And it's Luca, remember? We'll be done with them before you can even get to the stairs."

After the three had thanked Luca again for the lovely meal, said their good nights and left the kitchen, Sarita turned to him. "Good, they're gone." She said it as though she were about to commit a dastardly act of betrayal. "Now I can have seconds, without worrying that it'll hurt Cris's feelings."

Luca raised his eyebrows. "You wanted seconds?"

"Omigosh — are you kidding? This is *delicious*." She sat back down and scooped pasta into her plate. "Is there any more of that bread?"

"Yeah." She liked the food. No, she loved the food. He was thrilled. And when she broke off a chunk of semolina bread to dip into the sauce, he was aroused. From the beginning, it had turned him on to watch her eat because she did so wholeheartedly. The girls he dated in Vegas — everything was about the calories. No way would they have eaten with such gusto.

"Yum. I love it," she said.

Luca's heart beat like a tom-tom as he watched her swirl pasta on her fork and push it past those luscious lips. She dipped in another morsel of bread, and as she brought it up, a tiny drop of tomato clung to the side of her mouth.

He touched his own face. "You have … just a little …"

"Here?" she asked, as she tried to flick it off with her tongue. "Did I get it?"

No. But it was too late now, anyway. "Let me get it for you," he said, his eyes so deep and dark on hers, that she felt herself immediately go limp.

And when he leaned down to lick off that bit of sauce and then covered her mouth with his own, the pasta was forgotten, and she lapped up the richer, muskier taste of a kiss that made her mind go soft and her insides go as liquid and heady as smooth, red wine.

She dropped the fork. It clacked to the floor as she surged against him and clutched him to her. Their mouths locked together and clung. Even with the urgency he felt, he found himself gliding his palms and fingers over her slowly, smoothly, everywhere they could reach — arms, shoulders, back, buttocks, breasts— he didn't want to miss one spot, he wanted to memorize the feel, the taste, the scent of her. But Sarita was much more frenzied in her exploration of him. She was trembling as she yanked his shirttails out of his pants, ran her hands frantically up and under to touch his bare skin, that hard, muscular chest she'd been fantasizing about ever since she'd brought him breakfast in his room.

Through all this, their mouths were still cleaved together, they hadn't let go for a moment. She forced herself to tear away just an inch. "You're not going to stop this time. Are you?"

"No, no," he murmured, now as fevered as she. "Just tell me where — your room or mine."

"Mine," she said. When she threw herself back into the kiss, he dragged her to him, as close as they could get.

Cristiano heard what sounded like bubble wrap crackling when he came back down to retrieve his phone. He opened the swinging double doors just as Sarita and Luca disappeared — one second here, the next gone, clenched together in a passionate embrace. He glanced about the kitchen and took in the dishes that hadn't been tidied as promised, the second helping of pasta on the plate in front of the chair where Sarita had been sitting, and the overhead lights surging wildly bright.

With a long, deep sigh, he cleared the table himself. He understood she was an adult. He understood they were in love.

But still.

His little Sarita. Seduced by Sicilian spaghetti sauce.

He got his phone, switched on the dishwasher, switched off the madly glinting lights.

Thank God he was leaving tomorrow.

CHAPTER FIFTEEN

"Wow. So that's what it's like. No wonder people are so obsessed with it."

They were lying on her bed, naked, molded together like melted wax. She had her cheek resting against his pectoral and one leg stretched across his hips. She could feel his chest moving up and down as his breathing slowed, the dampness of his skin, and the hair below his belly button tickling her inner thigh.

"Be more specific. I need the feedback. What was it like?" She couldn't see him smiling, but she could hear the lazy contentment in his voice.

"Hmm. Let's see ..." She glided her hand back and forth across his rib cage as she gave it some thought. He had muscles like iron despite his long, lanky build. "Oh, I know — like speeding down a long, steep water slide, and then when you hit the bottom — splash!"

When he chuckled, she felt it vibrate. "That's got to be the most unique description of an orgasm I've ever heard." Then he got serious. Shifting them both so that they were facing each other, he levered up on one elbow to look down at her. "Why didn't you tell me before we started?"

She didn't know what he was referring to. Then she got it. "Oh." She rolled her eyes.

"Yeah." He cupped her cheek, studied her, his expression filled with regret. "Yeah, Sarita. I hurt you. If I had known —"

"If you'd known, it still would have hurt, but you just would have been all weird and nervous about it beforehand. How would that have improved things? Besides, it only hurt the first time." The curve of her lips was smooth as cream, her eyes smiled sensuously into his. "The second time was amazing."

"I ... really?"

"Mm hmm. Couldn't you tell?" She traced his mouth with her finger. "I'm curious — is this a skill you developed with practice, or did it come as part of the magic kit?"

He snorted and felt some of his apprehension fade. She seemed relaxed. And ... pleased. "No. When it comes to this, I'm just an ordinary guy who wants to make the woman he's with happy." He ran his fingers through her hair as he gazed at her, awash with tenderness and love. "I think you're the one who brought the magic to it." He tipped his head toward the bedside lamp with its shattered bulb. "We need to figure something out with the lights, though. Can't be worried about starting a fire every time we want to do this."

Now she was the one who needed reassurance. "Does that mean ..." She wet her lips, tried not to sound as uncertain as she felt. "The lights ... that's never happened before?"

"Are you serious?" He stared down at her, astonished by her self-doubt. "Do you honestly think I've ever had an experience like this? As a matter of fact ..." He grinned. "If I didn't know better, Ms. Taylor, I'd say you were an old hand at it." And that gave him the opportunity to put forth the question. He was dying to know. "Speaking of, I just have to ask — how is it you've never —"

Sarita groaned. "Oh, here we go."

"I'm curious."

"Okay, fine." She tossed back her hair, lay flat on her back again. "I'll tell you, but then I get to ask you questions too."

He rubbed his chin, wondering if this would be a bargain he'd live to regret. He fluffed up his pillow and laid back, his hands behind his head. "All right. Deal."

They opened one of the portholes after they'd made love, and the night air wafted against the curtains, the crickets and cicadas outside chirped merrily along as she told him about the day of her sixteenth birthday, Emilio, the soldiers, and Lee.

When she finished, the first thing he said was, "Huh. Well, that explains why you were interrogating me like General Zod when I told you about my vision. You thought I saw the whole thing." He burst out laughing.

She sat up, flabbergasted. "What's so funny?"

"It's not funny, it's not funny at all. I'm sorry." He was doubled over, he was laughing so hard. "It's just —" he couldn't get his breath.

"You moron." She shoved him so hard, he almost fell off the bed. "You laugh at the most inappropriate things. This is the last time I tell you anything."

He held his hands up in front of him, signaling for peace. "Okay, okay. I'm sorry. I know I shouldn't be laughing, but I can't help it." He was still trying to get ahold of himself. He even had to blink away tears. "Ah." Calmer now, he shook his head. "Jesus Christ, Sarita. That poor guy."

"Who? Lee?" She was still indignant.

"No. Well, yeah, him too. But at least he was already dead. I'm talking about your buddy — the guy you went down there with. What was his name, again?"

"Emilio." She frowned, not getting it. "Why do you feel sorry for him?"

That took him aback. "You're telling me that never once, in ten years, did it occur to you what a psyche-shattering experience that must have been for him — a seventeen-year-old kid?"

When she just stared at him, he shook his head again, in disbelief. "How is it that women don't get this — that we're just as vulnerable as you are?" He laid it all out for her. "There he is, with the girl of his dreams, naked in his arms."

"I was only half naked," she corrected him, hotly. "I just … had my top off."

"Oh good, that must have made a big difference to him." She gaped at the sarcasm. Like the magician he'd been, he waved his hands up and down in front of her, from her hair tumbling over her shoulders, to her skin glowing and flushed, and just a portion of the bed sheet to cover her delicious nakedness. "Look at you. Look at all this … this beauty. To you, it's just … you, I'm sure. But to us — us men, I mean — it's heart stopping, is what it is." He waited as she digested that. "And from the story you just told me, didn't sound like he was just looking to get laid. Sounds like he really cared about you."

She hung her head. "He did. He did care about me."

"Hey." He took her chin, tilted her face back up. "I'm not telling you this to make you feel bad. You did nothing wrong, and you have nothing to be ashamed of. I'm just saying, as bad as that experience was for you, it was bad for him too. Maybe worse." His eyes glinted with humor again. "And then Cris goes for him? Holy toledo, Sarita. I've gone a round with the dude myself, and let me tell you, he's scary. And I'm not seventeen anymore. The rejection, the ghosts, the chef —" he held his thumb and forefinger a half an inch apart — "this is what size your friend Emilio's balls were at the end of all that."

"Stop it." She shoved him again. "Don't be so crude." But he'd certainly given her a different take on the incident. "I never thought about what happened from his perspective. I don't know why. I guess I was so overwhelmed by it …" She was truly distressed now. "Maybe I should try to contact him."

"After ten years? I don't think so." He hadn't meant to fluster her, so he tried to cajole her out of it. "He's probably locked away somewhere, anyway. In a strait jacket. Like you, he could never bring himself to have sex again. That's what drove him insane. But now, he's finally worked up the courage to try to love again, and he's making eyes at the orderly who changes his sheets."

"Stop it," she said again. But the wicked humor had done the trick. She loosened up enough to give him a half smile. "He went to Berkeley, you idiot. I'm sure he's fine."

"I'm sure he is too." He reached for her, rolled her back down on the bed and covered her with his body. "My point was …" He kissed her lightly on the nose. "You tend to get stuck in your own head about things. But if you let those things out, or even just think about them from a different angle, they might not consume you so much."

She watched him steadily as he went on. "It was a bad experience for you, for him, but if it hadn't happened, the bones of a very good man would still be disintegrating at the bottom of this ship, with his family never knowing what happened to him."

"You're right," she said, and sighed. "You're right." She wiggled around a bit, adjusted herself more comfortably. He thought she meant for him to move, but when he tried to do so, she held him in place, her hips against his, her hands on his buttocks. "Now it's your turn."

"My turn for what?" Her hands were distracting. She was squeezing and cupping back there and enjoying the hell out of it, he could tell.

"Did you have a girlfriend before I met you?"

"Uh … yeah."

"What was her name?"

"Desiree." He cleared his throat. "I think it was Desiree. It's a little hard to concentrate on your questions, Sarita." God, she felt so good under him. He moved his hips against her, wanting her again. He wondered if that would be too much for her, considering she was still a newbie.

"Mm. That's a pretty name." She squeezed again, gave him a beguiling look that told him she knew perfectly well the effect she was having. "Why did you break up?"

"She broke up with me, actually."

Sarita's hands stopped moving. "Oh."

"'Oh,' what?" He raised a brow. "She was right to do it."

That comment set alarm bells ringing. "Was she? Why?"

"Because I was a drunk and an asshole."

She didn't know what to say to that, so she went very still and quiet.

"Huh." He narrowed his eyes. "Something tells me there's information in there that's upset you. It wasn't her name. You liked that. So, what was it?"

"I'm not upset."

"Oh, come on." He made a face as though he'd been hit by a muscle cramp. "I hate that. Every guy in the world hates that. It's a trope for standup comics. Yes, you are upset. Just say it."

"Okay, fine. But I feel silly."

"Spit it out, Sarita."

"I don't know how this works, because I haven't done much dating —" she scowled at him — "as you found out this evening, so don't you dare make fun of me for this. But it just occurs to me that if she broke up with you, and you're admitting it was your fault, then maybe that means you ..." She hated the way she sounded, but she had to know. "You still ... like her."

Well, now. The only way to take that was that she was jealous. Which meant — at least, he thought it meant — that she was invested. And that was very good.

"Yeah, I still like her." It was low of him to throw that at her, but he couldn't resist. For what felt like eons now, he'd been pining after Sarita Taylor, while she, for the most part, seemed to have a much more 'take-it-or-leave-it' attitude toward him. It gave his ego a boost to see that her interest in him might go a little deeper than he'd thought. However, as they were naked on her sheets, their torsos melded together like peanut butter on bread, it would be ungentlemanly to drag this out. "But not in the way you think. She's a nice girl, that's all."

"How nice is she, Luca?" There was that slit-eyed look again. Damn, she was good at that. "Is she still in your life?"

Oh, shit. He'd better fix this.

He measured out his answer. "Hmm. This is probably a good time to tell you she's my accountant." When her bottom lip stuck out, he corrected that assumption. "Or maybe it's not. But I hope it won't be a problem for you, since she's been doing it for years. In fact, she just called the other day because she's tracing a string of illegal withdrawals from Santi's estate. I didn't even know there was any money missing, and I guess he didn't know either, but she's on the scent." He gave her an 'I-hope-we-can-be-sensible-about-this' look.

Sarita wasn't sure she could be sensible. "So, she's smart."

"Yeah, she's smart. She's also funny and kind."

As he talked about Desiree, he thought that Sarita couldn't possibly know how much her eyes were giving away. Those eyes were not only gorgeous, they were expressive. He wondered what he'd see swirling in them when he said what he was about to say. "But she and I are in the past. She wasn't in love with me, and I wasn't in love with her." His throat closed up a little, yet he managed to make his next words sound light, almost teasing. "You, on the other hand, have slayed me. I'm in love with you, not her. Not halfway in love, like I told you. That was a lie. I'm all the way there, Sarita. Kind of silly of you not to notice."

Her breath caught. "Luca —"

He stopped her with a quick kiss. "I know, darling. I know you're not ready." Even so, he felt good. What she hadn't been able to say in words, he saw in those eyes. She just needed time, and he was more than willing to wait. For now, he was going to see if they could make love again without it hurting her. If not, he'd wait for that too.

So he winked at her, deliberately lightening the mood. "Besides which, I'm not sure if this can work between us anyway." He leaned down to nuzzle her throat.

"Oh?" She arched her neck to give him better access. "Why not?"

"Mmm. Well, first of all, you like spiders." He gave a mock shudder even as he continued to trail kisses from her throat down to the center of her chest. "And then there's all this history stuff. Not sure that's my cup of tea either, you know?" He went left to kiss one breast, and then right to kiss the other. When he closed his mouth over her nipple, she moaned. He trailed his tongue down her stomach, swirled it around her belly button, and her thighs clenched tight with need. "But ... you did like my sauce, so that's something to take into consideration."

She fisted her hand in his hair to pull his head up. She wanted to see his face when she hit him with this. He'd knotted her up with lust, and she was determined not to be alone in that.

"Do you know what else I read about, besides spiders and history when I was alone in this room, Luca?" Her voice was languid, her expression both dreamy and carnal at once. "Sex. I read all about sex." She pulled herself up to a sitting position. "And there's something I'm curious about — something we haven't tried yet." She leaned forward and whispered in his ear. Her suggestion got his immediate ... attention.

"On the other hand, I could be wrong." His voice sounded like the purr of lion. "Maybe we do have some common interests, after all."

It was after one in the morning when they fell asleep in each other's arms, a deeper and more restful sleep than either had experienced in too long a while, and it was a shame that it didn't last long enough.

The sound of Sarita's heart — the sudden, mad pounding of it — was what woke Luca.

He sat up, watching her whimper in her sleep, no way of telling whether she was having a vision or just a nightmare. He didn't know if he should wake her or let that happen naturally.

The decision was taken out of his hands when her eyes shot open and she bolted upright. Her breath came in deep gulps like someone who'd been running wildly, and she scanned the room, as though she were searching. It was terrifying, yet compelling to see her in the throes of it. He knew she wasn't in the room anymore, but somewhere else, seeing something else.

He went with instinct. "Where are you, Sarita?" He kept his voice low and his tone soothing.

"I'm on a beach. It's too dark. The moon isn't bright enough." She responded to him right away, but she never once looked in his direction. Her eyes darted back and forth. "The others don't see them coming. The rats. But he does. He's the only one awake. There are so many. It's the smell of blood that attracts them, did you know that? From the wounds."

The hair on the back of Luca's neck rose. "Who?" he whispered. "Who sees the rats, darling? Who is he?"

"I can't see his face. But he's so young. And he's so afraid. They're all so young. They're all so afraid. So many of them are going to die." She sucked in a breath that ended on a cry. "Oh, he's trying to wake up, but he can't. He can't pull himself out of it."

His heart broke for her as he watched her take it in, take it all on herself. There was a peaceful breeze coming in from the open porthole.

It kept the room comfortably cool, and yet, with the faint light coming in from the harbor, he could see the perspiration on her face. The night sounds were soft and lulling, but she was in turmoil, her breath ragged, her mind gripped by an unknown tragedy that she was compelled to witness. He lifted his hand, then thought that perhaps he'd frighten her if he touched her.

"She's with him." Relief crossed her face. "She heard him. She knew he needed her. She … I can't see their faces. I don't know why it's not clear. But I know her, I know her. Oh, why can't I see them?"

All at once, her shoulders slumped, her head tilted to one side as though something — an actual entity — had left her body, leaving it exhausted. "It's gone," she said.

When her eyes shifted to him, saw him, alert, watching her, she stiffened all over again. Oh, God. She should have told him to go, right after they'd made love. "I'm sorry. I'm sorry I woke you. It's probably best if you sleep in your own cabin —"

"Don't."

The way he'd bitten off the word, the harshness in it, jolted her. Still shaken from the vision, she thought she might be misreading it. But she wasn't wrong. He was angry. Fumbling to switch on the lamp, he cursed when he remembered the bulb was broken, flung out his hand toward the shards, and the glass snapped back together so quickly, it sparked. Both she and he blinked like owls from the sudden brightness, but it wasn't the abrupt light that made his eyes blaze. She'd never seen him so furious. And yet, his voice was low and calm. Somehow, that jumbled her nerves even more.

"Did you actually expect that I would leave you — after what I've just seen you go through? What kind of a man do you think I am?"

"I …" She couldn't speak.

But it didn't matter, he wasn't going to give her a chance to say much, anyway. "A few hours ago, I told you I love you. That doesn't mean sometimes, Sarita." He leaned back against his pillow. "I'm not going anywhere. If you want to talk about what you saw, we can do that. Otherwise —" he held out his arms — "come here and let me hold you. Let me hold you, until you can go back to sleep."

She gazed at him, at his open, waiting arms, at the ferocious love on his face. And it hit her then that, beneath the twisted sensations lingering from the vision, she felt something else. Something that she only now realized had been missing from her life for years. And that was a sense of faith.

She could believe in him. She could be certain that, although he might hurt her someday, it would never be his intention, he would never do so purposely.

It was only a moment more before she gave in to it, and flung herself into his arms. "I thought you would hate it. It's why I was afraid to get close to you. I never know when this is going to happen."

He bent to kiss the top of her head, thankful, so thankful, that she was beginning to trust him. He loved her so much, but if he couldn't win her trust, they had nothing. "Do you want to tell me what you saw?"

"I don't know exactly. It was similar to a vision I had a few weeks ago." She kept her face burrowed against his chest. "I ... it was because of you that I wrote it down."

He rubbed his chin across the top of her head and smiled. "Did you? Good for you."

"It's a warning." Now she looked up at him, and he could the shadows of it, see how troubled she was by it. "I know that, but that's all I know."

"Well, whatever it is, you're not dealing with it alone anymore. Remember that."

She examined his face as though she'd never seen it before. Patiently, steadily, he looked back at her. "I never expected you." She blurted that out, and once she did, she rushed through the rest. "I never expected to have feelings like this for you, for anyone. Now that I do, I don't know what to do with them."

Gently, he cupped her cheek, gave her a sleepy smile. Despite everything — her fears and doubts, the reality that he'd been drawn here because there was indeed a danger to her — this was the good news. Him and her. "Go to sleep now. Shut that mind off for a while and sleep."

Surprisingly, she did drift off.

But he didn't. He lay awake, holding her, wondering what was coming, and when.

Miles away, in the dingy darkness of his room, Alan was also awake, drenched with sweat, his hands clenched to his ears, as the same vision of rats on a faraway beach echoed in his head.

And he was crying.

CHAPTER SIXTEEN

Monday, September 22, 8:00 a.m., four days before the Queen's 80th Anniversary

Cristiano had told his wife that he doubted they'd be missed, but he was wrong. Not having the de la Cuevas in the kitchen was a tremendous adjustment. Luca took over the bulk of Cristiano's work, but it was a challenge to do so without arousing the suspicions of the rest of the kitchen staff who were not in the loop about his powers. Angela was assisting him, which helped minimize that difficulty, but her added duties on top of the preparations for the *Queen*'s anniversary were taking their toll.

She'd even commandeered Marisol, with Inez's permission and with the teen's promise that she would keep up with her schoolwork. Marisol was sticking with her pastry-making obsession thus far, and was getting good enough to be a genuine asset during this exceptionally hectic time.

Marisol also had a crush on Luca. Try as she might, she wasn't very successful at hiding it, especially when they were all in the kitchen together. Luca was very kind about it, recalling himself at that age, and the unrequited love he'd felt for a thirty-five-year-old neighbor whom he was sure would leave her husband for him, once he was old enough to drive. Sarita planned to take Marisol along to the salon on Tuesday after school so they could have their chat and also enjoy a girls' day. The anniversary was Friday, Sarita's birthday was Saturday, and she was treating herself to a manicure and pedicure this week no matter how busy things were.

They were juggling a lot, but they were getting by, even if that meant relaxing a few of their meticulous standards. That's where Angela was having trouble.

"But how will you know which berries to pick?"

"Angela, by now I think I can be a pretty good judge, but if I have to, I'll text you." She lost her patience when Angela still looked unconvinced. "Look, you can't be in two places at once. You either help Mr. Barajas with the anniversary cake, or you go to the market for fruit. Your choice."

And that was how Angela came to be alone in the restaurant for the first time ever on a Monday morning. She was meeting Jose at nine a.m. sharp, and she didn't know what to do with herself until then. It felt strange not to be at the market, and since she only had an hour, there wasn't enough time for any baking.

But she soon got a diversion when a call came from Reception. They were holding a certified letter for Rohini, delivered by special courier, from India.

Luca had taken the opportunity on the one day he had free to meet Mr. Abramson. He invited him for breakfast at The Secret Spice, but Elliot preferred to sit at one of the small bistro tables that had been set up outside the takeaway coffee shop on Promenade Deck. Though the tables faced the parking lot, not the harbor, Elliot had eaten breakfast there every morning since his arrival, preferring to feel his feet on the teak deck rather than on the carpeting in the restaurant.

"Lot of memories on this ship, Luca, my boy." He slurped his coffee and pecked at one of the scones they bought. Luca left his untouched. It was worrisome how spoiled he'd become by Angela's baking and Cristiano's cooking.

"Must feel strange being on the *Mary* again after so long. Especially since she looks so different than she did during the war."

"Eh." Elliot picked out a raisin, and bits of the scone crumpled under his fingers. "Things change. People seem to have a problem with that. I don't. The minute something is over, it becomes part of the past, anyway. The trick is to know what to do with all the experiences, both good and bad."

He watched the tourists who milled about, some with destinations in mind, others just in the mood to meander. A small boy, about six years old, was with his mother. She held his hand as he took in the vastness of the ship with awe. Elliot smiled at them as they walked by. He shifted his attention back to Luca. "I'm very sorry about your brother. How are you coping?"

"It was hard at first." Luca knew this would come up. He spared Elliot the details of his less than ideal survival mechanism during his bereavement. "I'm much better now."

"I'm glad to hear it. Wouldn't have anything to do with that beautiful girl from the restaurant, would it?"

Happy to change the subject, Luca smiled. "You might be right."

"Love helps. It's the only thing that does." He thought of his own wife. He'd missed her every day of the five years she'd been gone. Waking up in the mornings, in those seconds between sleep and full awareness, he still stretched his hand out to her side of the bed, expecting her to be lying there next to him.

With an inward sigh, he finished his coffee. He didn't want this to be a maudlin conversation, and it was none of his business, but for the sake of a fellow veteran, he decided to throw it out there, just to see what he got back. "I saw your father recently. I'm not sure how much he comprehends, or retains. But he knows about Santi."

Luca was sure he'd misunderstood. "I'm sorry — what, Mr. Abramson? What did you say?"

Elliot reached across and put his hand on Luca's wrist. "I'm not family and I shouldn't interfere. But Luca, he's sick. He's been sick for almost thirty years, and he's even sicker now. If you could bring yourself to go see him, even just once, I know it would mean the world to him."

Luca's whole body went cold. He looked down at Elliot's hand — at the gnarled, swollen knuckles, the weathered skin and liver spots, the worn, too-tight gold band around his ring finger. And in that moment, he became fully aware of just how old the man was.

"Mr. Abramson." How to handle this? There was such a constriction in his chest. "My father is dead. He died the day he … the same day my mother died."

Elliot released Luca and sat back, his bushy white brows beetled into a frown as he assessed Luca through eyes that looked too sharp and keen for dementia. "No, my boy. He's not dead."

"Mr. Abramson —"

"They didn't tell you, did they? They didn't tell you or Santi." He was looking at Luca as comprehension dawned. "This is terrible. This is just terrible."

It was terrible. That was one thing the man was right about. Luca glanced around, looking for what, he didn't know. He needed help here. What the hell was he supposed to do? Or say?

Elliot observed Luca's tension. "You think I'm senile?" he said, with a touch of dry humor. "Think I've lost my marbles?"

Luca fidgeted, cleared his throat. When his phone signaled, he pounced on it. "Hello. Yeah, this is he."

The voice sounded familiar, but with Mr. Abramson foremost on his mind, he didn't place it until the caller identified herself. "Oh, hello, Inez."

People continued to walk by, taking little note of the younger man and older one sitting together. But Elliot was alarmed by the panic that splashed across Luca's face as he listened to his caller and surged to his feet. "How bad? Where is she? I'll be right there."

However much he'd been shaken by his conversation with Elliot, it didn't compare to what he was feeling now. "Mr. Abramson, I'm very sorry I … I have to leave. My cousin — she's at the hospital. She … she fell." He stuck his phone in his pocket. "I have to go."

"Wait, Luca." Elliot's voice was calm in the face of Luca's impatience to be away. "Look at me."

Luca absolutely did not want to look at him, but he felt trapped.

Elliot waited until he thought that Luca might truly be seeing him, not some demented, feeble old man. "You go and take care of your cousin. But know this — I'm not crazy. And … your father's not dead."

Half an hour before Luca and Elliot ordered coffee, Angela had placed Rohini's letter on the counter in the galley and looked at it as though their religiously-hygienic work space had been invaded, unaccountably, by a deadly snake. After some internal debate about ethics versus precaution, she found herself boiling water in a pot, running the letter through the steam until the glue loosened sufficiently and she could pull the folded papers out of the envelope with unsteady hands.

"Oh, my God," she whispered after she'd read. Now what to do?

After a few moments of thought, accompanied by the urge to bite off all her nails, she went into the office and sat in front of her laptop. One of these days, like it or not, she'd have to get a smartphone. She was the only one she knew who didn't have one, and she was teased about it mercilessly by Harry. Call her a dinosaur, she just hated the idea of carrying a mini-computer with her wherever she went, so she planned to hold off as long as possible.

She brought up Skype, and checked for the little green dot next to Jane's photo. Thank God it was there. It didn't take long for the call to connect and Jane's face to come into focus.

"Angela, hello." Jane sounded happy to hear from her.

"Where are you, Jane?" From the brightness behind her, the ambient sounds, Angela could see she was out.

"We're in the piazza, having drinks, all four of us. Say hello." She turned her phone, and a chorus of hellos and waves came back from Cristiano, Rohini, and Antoni. They looked like they were having a wonderful time, an observation that Jane shortly confirmed.

"We're having such a lovely time! It's been so much fun having them here. Can you believe Cristiano actually has a sense of humor? Who'd have guessed?"

In the background, Angela heard a bright, feminine laugh in response to Jane's banter, and realized with pleasure that it was Rohini. "That's great news. Listen, Jane —"

"Oh. And wait until you hear this. He's quite famous, apparently. We've been treated like royalty at every restaurant we've been to. Last night, they wouldn't even let us pay for our meal."

"That's terrific. Listen, I need to talk to you about something."

"Oh, I beg your pardon. Here I am, babbling on. Go ahead." Jane waited, but when Angela said nothing, she got it. "Oh. Hang on, then." Angela saw her get up, heard her mumble something. "All right. I'm by myself. What's happening?"

"Jane. Oh, my God. I'm dying here. A letter came for Rohini from India. And I ... I opened it, Jane. I feel terrible."

"Well, bloody hell, Angela. I would have done exactly the same."

"I mean, because … you know."

"Yes, Angela. I certainly haven't forgotten. Who's it from? I mean, could you read it? Was it in English?"

The mildly hysterical, rapid fire questions were doing nothing to calm Angela's own case of nerves, but then again, there was definitely something to be nervous about. "Well, first of all, there were two copies — one in English and one in —" she raised her hands — "whatever other language she speaks. I forgot." She couldn't help it — she did bite a nail now. "Oh, but Jane — it's from her dead husband's family. She … they want to send her money. It's an inheritance. Can you believe that?"

Jane's shocked face looked slightly distorted in the camera lens.

"What do we do?" Angela picked at the uneven tip of her torn nail. "Should we tell them?"

"No." Jane's response was swift. "No, not now. To hell with that. They're having too much fun. I've never seen either of them look so happy. I'll be damned if we're going to spoil it. They're coming back there next week. Whatever's going to happen — if we're all going to hell, or jail, one more week won't change it."

"You're right." She was less panicked now that they'd talked it through. "You're absolutely right. I'll put it in the safe for now." With yearning she added, "I wish I were there too. It's been crazy here."

"How's Harry, then?"

The thought of him prompted a smile. "He's great. Really great."

"Good. And is Vincenzo still being a git?"

She chuckled wryly. "I'm afraid so. Although, to be honest, I've never been sure, even after all these years, what exactly a 'git' is." She heard Antoni call out to Jane.

"I'm coming." Jane looked at Angela fondly. "I'm proud of you for standing your ground. You've grown up, my girl. I miss you. Keep me on top of things, will you?"

"I miss you too. And I will."

They signed off, and Angela stood up to put the letter in the safe. No sooner had she done so when she sensed someone behind her. Before she could even move a shoulder to turn, her eyes were swiftly covered by one of their own aprons. She managed a short burst of sound before her head was jerked back with an uppercut punch to the jaw. It knocked her out instantly. Down she went, her face slapping against the right angle edge of the desk. She lay flat out on the floor, face down. Blood pooled around her nose and chin from the deep gash on her cheek, and seeped into the fibers of the carpet.

Alan hesitated for mere seconds when he saw the wound. Then he picked up Rohini's letter and hurried out.

CHAPTER SEVENTEEN

"Oh, for petessakes, everybody's making such a fuss. This is silly. I'll be fine."

"I like the positive attitude, Mrs. Perotta, but you're not fine. Not just yet. You need rest and you need to stay here, at least overnight."

"But Dr. Niehaus, I have to go back to work. We're short-staffed until next week, and I'm supposed to help frost a fifteen-foot cake. Can't you just give me an aspirin and a couple of Band-Aids?"

Angela was at Saint Mary's Medical Center, feeling trapped there by a doctor who was, in her opinion, overzealous.

However, there was cause for concern, as she was about to be told by the neurologist who, at nine-thirty in the morning, had already put in eight hours with no end in sight, and was in no mood for arguments. "Look, Mrs. Perotta, let me put it this way — ever watch cartoons when you were a kid?"

"Well, sure."

"Remember how Daffy Duck would get hit in the head and then see those little yellow stars? That, in essence, is what happened to you." The doctor tapped the chart she was holding. "You have a concussion. Your brain has been rattled around but good, and brains do not like that. You need to be observed for the next twenty-four hours at least. In addition to that, your cheek was cracked open like an egg. We cleaned and bandaged it to slow the bleeding, but you'll need a plastic surgeon to stitch it so it doesn't scar. Now, we have one on staff, but I've just examined you, and it looks to me like you already know one." She pulled her pen out from behind her ear. "So, who's it going to be — yours or ours?"

Well, this doctor was certainly sassy, wasn't she? And the way she was standing — the whole 'power pose' thing — Angela could tell she had no intention of giving in. With a defeated sigh, she rested back against the pillows. "Mine, I guess."

"Good. We'll set that up." Now that she'd established herself as the one in charge, Dr. Niehaus was much more amenable. "Looks to me like he does a good job." As she was leaving, Angela heard her mumble to herself, "Maybe I'll keep his number."

Not long after the doctor left, Luca came in, and with him was Detective Betty, who looked almost as torn up as he did.

Typical of Angela, she was more concerned about their feelings than the concussion. "Oh, geez, you guys — look at you two. Come on. Don't worry. I'll be okay."

Luca rested his hip on the edge of her bed and took her hand. "Are you in pain, *cugina*?"

"Not too bad. I can feel my jaw and my cheek, you know? And my head feels a little … muzzy."

Betty sat in the one chair the room offered. "Mrs. Perotta, do you feel well enough to take me through it? As much as you can remember?"

And there was Angela's quandary. There were three things she remembered: the feel of the apron, a particular odor, and the certified letter for Rohini. That letter was the main reason she was so desperate to get back. She knew she'd left it out in the open, on her desk, when whatever son of a gun it was snuck up and sucker-punched her. She had to get the detective out of here as soon as possible, before her team descended on that office again. If she could let Luca know, he could pop there in a jiffy.

"Well … he came up behind me and dropped one of our own aprons over my eyes —"

"He?" Betty seized on that. "Did you see him?"

"No." Angela lifted her arms, let them fall. I guess … I just assumed it was a he." She was having some trouble thinking clearly, but she tried her best. "You know … maybe because of the height. The way the apron was dropped down over my eyes. From … above, it felt."

"So, you think it was someone taller than you?" Betty stood up, and motioned Luca to do the same. "I'm five foot seven. Would you say your attacker was closer to my height, or Mr. Miceli's here?"

Angela looked from one to the other. "It's hard to tell from this position. And if I get out of bed, Nurse Ratched is going to give me grief about it."

Knowing that Angela was concussed, Betty didn't press the issue. "All right. Is there anything else? Anything at all you can remember?"

"Yes." Angela closed her eyes. As much as she hated to admit it, the doctor was right. She was feeling the effects of the attack now. "There is, but I don't know how it will help." Opening her eyes again, she focused on Betty. "I have a very sensitive nose. And … I think that whoever attacked me … smelled like someone I've met before. But I can't remember who right now."

Betty blinked. This was a new one. She repeated it, to be sure Angela meant what she said. "'Smelled' like someone you've met, did you say?"

"Yep. Their clothes, I mean."

"Okay. What was the smell?"

"A little bit like fried fish."

———●

Angela told Luca about the letter the minute the detective left. He pointed out that there would be no reason for the police to see anything suspicious about a letter from India. But to make her feel better, he popped back there so he could check things out.

Her surgeon, Dr. Menville, came by, and stitched up her cheek. Between the discomfort of that, and the trauma to her body, she fell into an exhausted sleep.

And was woken up again in what seemed like only moments.

"Dr. Neihaus." Angela's eyelids opened groggily. "What time is it?"

"It's noon. I'm sorry, Mrs. Perotta, I can't let you sleep more than two hours for now." The doctor was sitting on Angela's bed, leaning over her. "Open your eyes wide for me, and let me have a look? Wide, I said. That's not wide. I need to see those pupils. There you go." The doctor shined a little flashlight into her eyes. "Good," she pronounced, and straightened up. "You're doing great. And you have a visitor who seems anxious to see you. Are you up for it?"

When Angela angled her head to see behind the doctor, there in the doorway stood Vincenzo. Even with the spots dancing in front of her from having a flashlight shined in her face, she could tell he'd been crying.

"Yes," she said. "Yes, I'm up for it." When the doctor left, she held out her hand. "Sweetie. I'm so glad to see you."

"Ma." He hurried over and clasped her fingers. "Luca called me. Oh, my God. Are you all right? Do you hurt?"

"I feel better now that you're here."

They did nothing but silently take each other in, two people who had a bond that could never be broken, but who'd each had a turn in tripping foolishly over the other.

Vincenzo brought it up first. "I'm a horse's ass."

She puffed out a short laugh that made her cheek throb. "That's not the first time I've heard mention of that malady recently. Must be going around."

"I mean it. I was so wrong. I didn't have the guts to come to you and say it." His voice was thick with regret, and he cupped the uninjured side of her face. "God forbid if something worse had happened to you today. You never would have known that."

"Yes, I would. I know you. I know who you are." Her smile was wan with fatigue, but it was one of the happiest smiles of her life. She had her baby back. She pulled herself up against the pillows, wincing with the effort. "Talk to me. Tell me what you were feeling."

"I don't know if I can explain it." He reached over and helped her with the pillows.

"Try."

He studied her. Her face was pale, but patient. Her eyes looked different than he remembered from his teenage years. He was about twelve the first time he noticed how defeated-looking those pretty brown eyes were. Now, more than twenty years later, they looked younger somehow, despite her injuries, despite that she'd aged. She looked happier, he realized. Happier with herself.

He shifted to sit sideways on the bed. "You were right when you said I sounded like Pop. I think I was trying to ... be like him." It was hard to tell her this, but he would. Dammit, he would. "I knew you loved me. I knew it. But you were embarrassed by me. You tried to cover for me all the time. With him. With others. You would make up phony excuses for ... who I was." He paused to see if she would contradict that, or defend herself, but she didn't. She just watched him and listened.

"And Pop. I know he didn't approve of me. I'm not even sure if he loved me. Sometimes I think he did. But most of the time ... I think he didn't."

Noises came from the corridor. Vincenzo turned his head toward the open door. Through it they could see a nurse pushing an elderly woman in a wheelchair. The woman had to be hard of hearing, as the nurse was speaking to her in a markedly elevated, but reassuring voice. Vincenzo waited until they made their way further down the hall. When he continued, he kept his head turned toward the door.

"I tried everything to win him over. When I was in elementary school, I wanted to join the choir. He said choir was for sissies, so I joined the math team instead. When I was in high school, I wanted to play baseball, but he said real Italian men —" his laugh was short and bitter as he made the gesture in the air for quotation marks — "played soccer, so I quit the baseball team to play soccer, and I still regret that to this day. You know why?"

Now he faced his mother. "Because it didn't make a damn bit of difference. I did what he wanted me to, I wore what he wanted me to, I even went into accounting because that's what he suggested, and none of it earned me his respect." He took in air past the lump in his throat. "Isn't that the way it was? Or am I wrong?"

Angela looked him straight in the eye. "No," she said. "You're not wrong. Every terrible thing you said is true. With one or two corrections."

He struggled not to cry. He hadn't expected her, of all people, to be so forthright. He felt vindicated by her affirmation, a vindication that was long overdue. When he could trust himself to speak, he asked, "What corrections?"

Her mouth felt so dry. There was a plastic pitcher filled with water and two plastic glasses within Vincenzo's reach. "Could you pour me some of that, sweetie? Thank you." After he handed her a glass, she continued. "First of all, Pop did love you. I know that for sure. You don't, and that's because the love he was capable of wasn't good enough. But it was the best he had, the best he could do. It was the same with me and him. He loved me in his —" she grimaced "— repressed and miserly way. It was what he'd been taught a man was, and it was all he knew."

She drank some water before she could continue. "Marco and I were raised —" she gave a swift, vicious laugh — "the same stupid way we raised you. I was barely twenty when my parents and his talked us into getting married. He was twenty-three. Less than a year later, we had you. A decade after that, we were still clueless. We were surrounded by people — extended family, neighbors, the members of our church — who were just like our parents, just like us. We knew nothing else but what was around us. Neither of us was happy — with ourselves, with our marriage, with … anything, truthfully. But we had no idea why we weren't. I mean, I had an inkling that I didn't want to be where I was, doing what I was doing. But Vincenzo, honestly? The two of us were like the blind leading the blind through the mountains after a plane crash. We had no clue what the fuck was what."

Vincenzo audibly gasped. Never, in thirty-four years, had he heard his mother use the word. He stared at the bruised and bandaged woman on the bed and wondered if he knew her at all.

Wrapped up in her story, she was unaware of the impact her uncharacteristic language had made. "I was twenty-one when I had you." This time her laugh seemed more genuine. "You poor kid, to have had a mother as dumb and helpless as me. I might as well have been twelve." She pointed at him. "But I knew you were gay by the time you were six. I suspected it by the time you were four. By six, I knew for sure."

"You didn't!" He'd been looking at her in amazement since her use of a swear word. With this new revelation, he thought his eyes might fall out of their sockets.

"I did. There were many clues. But of course, I couldn't talk about it with you. Yet I knew it was going to change everything." She stopped talking to touch her bandage. It felt like there was fresh bleeding underneath. She should probably text the surgeon, but this conversation was too important to interrupt. If worse came to worse, and she'd torn a stitch in her sleep, she'd live with the scars.

Nonetheless, she ruminated before she told him the rest. "You being gay saved my life."

He didn't respond at first. The declaration had hit him too hard. As long as he could remember, he believed his sexual orientation was a burden on his parents — two provincial people who were raised militantly Catholic. To hear her say something like this instead, it was as though he'd entered an alternate universe. He wasn't sure how to handle it — her — *this* — this entire, world-shattering conversation.

So he did what many do when something becomes too tricky to handle. He joked about it. Playfully, he tilted his head and hit his ear. "I must have heard you wrong, Ma. What was that?"

"I know it's hard to believe. You probably have no idea what I mean."

To give himself time to come to grips with his feelings, Vincenzo got off the bed, dragged over the chair that Betty had been sitting in earlier, and made a comic show of settling himself into it. "This is better than Sharon Osbourne on *The Talk*. Do tell."

"Okay. Here it is." She took another gulp of water. "The only reason I had the courage to open the bakery was because I was going to divorce your father. And I knew I would need the income." She saw his surprise and anticipated what his next question would be, so she answered it before he asked. "It took me way too long to work up the nerve to even think about divorce. I know I didn't protect you as I should. I know I failed you. I was terrified to break rules, terrified to leave him. My parents would have been horrified by it. I mean, so horrified, it might have killed at least one of them. But I couldn't stand it anymore, the way he was treating you."

There were tears now. She'd held them off as long as she could. She tried blinking them away, but one fell, soaking into the bandage on her cheek. "I don't know if he would have been as dictatorial if you were straight, but I saw that it was killing you, just like it was killing me. So, as scared as I was of my parents' disapproval, of my husband's, I opened that damn bakery." She paused to let him think about that. "Aunt Jane and Uncle Tony helped me."

"Of course they did."

"Yep. It took me three years to pay them back. Your father never knew. He would never have forgiven them. And then, before I could start proceedings, he had the heart attack."

"Oh, my God. I had no idea."

"How could you? But you see it now, don't you? I defied everyone and got a life, and it only happened because of you." Her mind was way in the past. "I wouldn't have the restaurant here, either. That started with you too."

Even with the bandage and bruises, her face showed all she felt for him. It was more than love. He was astonished to see pride too. "Don't say you don't have guts. You do. It took guts for you to say it out loud — in that neighborhood, in that family. Heck, it took more than guts, Vincenzo." Her mouth quirked as she held her cupped hand in the air. "It took a pair of *cahones* like this."

He burst out laughing. Why had he tried to be like his father and suppress this spirited side of her? What was the threat? She was wonderful, he realized. Wonderful and brave.

She wasn't finished. "When you came out, in my own mousy way, I came out too. But I was already forty-three years old. And all I'd been told about being a wife, a mother, a good daughter, a good religious person, was a lie — a lie to keep me under the control of everybody but myself. It took time to accept that. Once I did … I don't think I'll ever be able to explain what that felt like. I had to negate everything I'd been taught. So when I told you I had to think, I swear to you — it wasn't a rejection of you. I *did* need the time in order to ... to come to grips with what a waste my life had been until then, and to try to discover who I really was."

She still got a sick feeling whenever she let herself think about that time period. That was why, when people said they had no regrets, she never believed them.

The same nurse passed by Angela's room again, and they saw that she hadn't been speaking loudly because her patient was deaf. She was just a bubbly, boisterous talker. Now they could hear her saying something to someone about flowers. And the next thing they knew, she was back their way, her head in the door.

"Mrs. Perotta, you have another visitor. We made him wait by the reception desk. We weren't sure if you were up for more company."

"Who is it, please?"

The nurse called down the hall. "What's your name, honey?" She held a hand to her ear. "What was that? I can't hear you, honey. Speak up."

Faintly, they could hear a male voice respond.

The nurse poked her head back in. "Says his name's Harry. Got some pretty flowers with him too. Should I tell him to come on back?"

"Wait. Don't go yet," Angela told Vincenzo when he got to his feet. To the nurse she said, "Can you ask him to give us five more minutes, please?"

Angela ran her hand through her hair, but quickly gave up the attempt at vanity. No one was expecting her to win any beauty contests right now. "It's none of my business, but ... you and Douglas?"

With a sigh that made her want to clutch him to her as protectively as she used to when he was a child, Vincenzo sat back down. "He's ... I heard he's seeing a stockbroker."

She winced. "Darn it. Those people make a lot of money."

"Hey." He poked his own chest. "What about me, the CPA? I do all right."

The affronted retort made her giggle. "I'm teasing you, silly." She sobered. "He never struck me as someone who was only interested in your wallet. If that's who he is, forget him. But if he's as sweet as he seems, then use some of that Miceli charm and win him back."

Vincenzo smiled. "You think I have charm?"

"From the Miceli side. Yes."

—●

As Vincenzo was leaving, he closed the door to his mother's room. It was an unintentional reflex, but a fortunate one, since Harry was coming down the hall, an enormous bouquet of red roses in his arms.

When Harry spotted Vincenzo, he thought, *Crap*. But for Angela's sake, he was polite. "Vin."

"Hey, Harry." Vincenzo still had his hand on the doorknob.

What was the best thing to do here? Harry didn't know. But he did know that Angela was on the other side of that door, banged up from an attack that could have killed her. That took precedence over anything he might have said to Vincenzo had they met head on and alone under other circumstances.

Therefore, with a civility he wasn't really feeling, he held out the flowers to Vincenzo. "I got these for your mother. Would you give them to her for me, please, and tell her I hope she's up and about soon?" He hoped like hell he wouldn't be left standing like a fool, with his hand out.

He was pleasantly surprised when Vincenzo did him one better. "You know what, Harry? I bet she'd love it if you gave those to her yourself. Why don't you go in and sit with her for a while?" When he turned the knob and pushed open the door, Harry took it for the olive branch it was. With a nod of thanks, he stepped in.

Any thoughts he had about Vincenzo fled his mind when he took in Angela's appearance. Her face was mottled with bruises and her bandaged cheek was swelled up like an acorn-storing squirrel's.

Before he stepped away, Vincenzo caught the quickly masked fury and concern that came into Harry's eyes.

"Angela. So this is where you're been hiding." For her benefit, Harry commandeered joviality. Indifferent to whether or not Vincenzo might still be standing behind the partially closed door at his back, he stepped further into the room, and put his finger to his chin. "Hmm. You've done something different with yourself. Wait … don't tell me. New haircut, right?"

Vincenzo heard her laugh. He knew he shouldn't be eavesdropping, but he needed to, for just a few minutes. He needed to know what she would say. He couldn't see that Harry had dropped the roses on the vacated chair, or that he sat next to her on the bed and gave her a gentle peck on the lips. But he could hear their conversation.

"I saw Vin outside."

"Yep." She tapped the side of her head and grinned. "Brain rattled or not, I was able to figure that out when I heard you two talking out there."

He knew she wanted him to smile at that, so he did. Still, he asked, "Is everything all right between you?" The exchange at the door had been positive, but he could see she'd been crying. If Vincenzo was the cause — on the day she'd been injured — that's where Harry would draw the line, and Vincenzo might find himself with a few bruises of his own.

Angela reached for his hand, to feel his warmth and strength. "You know what? I owe the person who attacked me a big thank you. It was worth stitches and a concussion to get my son back."

"Is that right?" Harry felt some of the tension in his neck ease. "So, you didn't even get a glimpse of who it was?"

"Nope. Not a peek."

"Ah. Well, then, since you owe him a big thanks, I might as well tell you, Angela." With his thumb, he massaged her palm. "It was me."

When Vincenzo heard his mother laugh for the second time since Harry's arrival, just like that, his perception shifted. He nodded to the nurses as he passed the desk, left the hospital, and stepped out into the bright sun.

He took a few cleansing breaths. Then he pulled out his phone to call Douglas.

CHAPTER EIGHTEEN

"They haven't been able to trace where the spiders were bought. And there are so many fingerprints in the restaurant that it's like looking for a needle in a haystack."

"So we've got nothing?"

"Well, I wouldn't say that. Betty's working hard on this. They're sorting through all the prints. It's just going to take a while."

"Great. Just great." Angela tipped her head back on the pillows. It was the second day of her confinement, and all she wanted to do was go home. "There's a lunatic on the loose, we had to close the restaurant, I didn't get to help with the *Queen*'s anniversary cake, my face looks like a moldy, lumpy, cheese strudel, and I'm stuck here for another night because that darn doctor won't discharge me today like she promised."

Seeing how glum she was, Sarita felt terrible. "Oh, Angela. I'm so sorry. All this is my fault."

Angela picked her head back up. "That's ridiculous. Stop that, Sarita." But she could have kicked herself. She and Luca had discussed this. Sarita fretting that she might be the target would do nothing to help the situation.

"It's not ridiculous. All this goes back to the woman at the ball. What else could it be?" But expressing guilt probably wasn't the way to make Angela feel better. She tried thinking of something more positive to say. "On the other hand, closing the restaurant for a few days won't kill us. I'm glad of the break. And I don't want you to go back before you're healed."

"Oh, come on. It's not that bad." The inactivity was making her testy.

"You had a dizzy spell last night, Angela. Brain injuries are nothing to take lightly. I think the doctor's right — a CT scan is wise."

Angela fiddled with the bed controls, sending the top part of the mattress forward so she could sit up. "I want to get back. I'm worried sick about that letter. I was sure I left it on top of my desk. But if it's not there and it's not already in the safe, then where is it?"

"Once you're healed, you'll remember, I'm sure. Besides, Luca and I talked about this. We just don't think that letter is ominous." If she could press home this point, Angela might relax a little. She needed to rest in order to heal, and as far as Sarita could tell, she'd done anything but since she got here. "Think about it — Zahir died over twenty years ago." She lowered her voice. "And you know when the other one died. They must have divvied up that estate to every relative under the sun before they concerned themselves with Rohini. My guess is whatever's left is a pittance, and they just sent the letter for form's sake."

Angela was thinking. "How'd they find her? She never used her real family name, and then she took Cris's."

"It's not like she's been hiding for the past decade." Sarita lifted a dismissive shoulder. "We've been in so many food and travel magazines. And Vanu's family has known her whereabouts from the beginning."

By the easier set of Angela's jaw, Sarita saw her words were sinking in. She put one last thing out to her, hoping it would do the trick. "Apart from all that, Luca said that when Rohini gets back, he'll ... pop over there and check things out. He can get in and out as fast as he needs to ... just in case. And he speaks Hindi."

"Luca does?" For someone whose brain was bruised, she put it together readily. "Oh — is that to do with ...?"

"Yes." Sarita sounded almost like she was boasting when she added, "He can speak any language he wants. Isn't that incredible?"

"It is. Too bad he can't abracadabra my concussion away."

"He says he tried to do stuff like that a couple of times, like on cuts and things. It doesn't work on living tissue, unfortunately. He's got a wide scope of abilities, but they have their limits."

Angela sighed, and wondered what time they'd do her CT scan. Her attention was nudged back to their present dilemma when another thought popped into her head. "You know, I hate asking this, but do you think Alan's involved?"

"Alan?" Sarita shifted uncomfortably. "Um ... well ... he's been gone for ages. Inez said he never even came back to pick up his last check."

"That's strange too, isn't it? He certainly looked like he could use the money." She regretted the words as soon as they were out. "I shouldn't make assumptions. It's not nice to pick on somebody just because they come across as peculiar."

Sarita said nothing. She didn't have the nerve to say it out loud, but she'd mulled over the same possibility. Alan was strange in ways that had put them all on edge. But it was their sense of fairness, their own experience with being unkindly judged, that would close their minds off to the possibility that he was their culprit.

Angela studied Sarita with interest. "I have to say, you're taking this whole situation a lot better than I would have expected."

"Am I?" Sarita steeled her expression.

"You just said you think this is all to do with your grandfather." She hastened to emphasize, "Not that I agree, but if true, you seem pretty calm about it."

When Sarita didn't reply to that, either, the light dawned.

"Wait a minute, wait a minute." With a bawdy smirk, Angela pointed at Sarita. "Now I get it. You've been ... 'Miceli-ed,' haven't you?"

Sarita could feel the blush start at her chest and rise all the way up to her hairline. "I don't know what you mean."

"You do so, you little stinker." Her mind did such a rapid U-turn from missing letters and oddball janitors to sex, that she should have been issued a traffic violation. "Oh, my God, how did I not catch on to this out sooner? You, of all people, even more of a Nervous Nelly than I ever was —" she spread her arms out wide and slow — "so, relaxed, even in the face of everything that's happened, acting like you haven't got a care in the world." She wanted to throw her head back and crow with laughter, but with her injuries, that might be risky.

"Be quiet, Angela." It was the best retort she could come up with, squirming with embarrassment as she was.

"He's that good, huh?" She was enjoying herself immensely. "Good enough to make you forget all your troubles?"

"Yes." Sarita gave in. "Yes, he is, damn you, Angela."

Angela did laugh then — so loud and hard that she held onto her head with both hands, to be sure she didn't jiggle things around in there too much. When she caught her breath, she said, "Good for you. Life is so much more fun when there's good sex in it, don't you think?"

It was hard for Sarita to hold out against her good-natured ribaldry. Besides, if she were honest, she did want to talk about it with someone who'd be happy for her. "Well ... I guess so."

"Yep. That's what recent experience has taught me." Like a teenage girl at a sleepover, she picked up one of the pillows and hugged it to her chest "So, tell me — when did this all start?"

"Um ..." Sarita looked down at her shoes and fiddled with her necklace. "The night he cooked for us all."

"Ah. ...The sauce. Of course." Angela nodded shrewdly. "And?" she prompted.

"And ... what?"

"How was it? If I'm not mistaken, this is a new activity for you." It was with concern and caring rather than nosiness that Angela asked.

Jokes aside, there wasn't anything she wanted more than for Sarita to be happy. The kid had been through hell, and it looked like she might finally be crawling out of it.

Sarita played with the little charm around her neck, sliding it back and forth on its chain. "Well, at first … I mean, the first time, it wasn't … very comfortable. I knew that was normal, but he felt terrible about it. Because I —" she gnawed on her lip — "I hadn't told him beforehand." She wasn't sure what Angela would think regarding that choice. "I just didn't want to."

"I get it. If that's what you're both focused on, takes all the romance and spontaneity out of it." The insightful commentary put Sarita more at ease. "But I also understand that he would feel bad about it. He's a very good boy, our Luca."

"Yes." Sarita looked down at her shoes again. "Yes." The rest came out in a rush. "But the second time —" she put both palms to her cheeks and blew out a breath — "It was like he was determined to make up for it. Oh, Angela, it was wonderful. I can't even tell you. And … that's how it's been since." Her face got even warmer the more she thought about it. "Each day, I look forward to when we can be alone together. I just … he makes me so happy."

They exchanged a long look of knowledge — a woman's secret knowledge. And as Angela gazed at the flushed and blissful young woman in front of her, for the first time in weeks, she felt a sense of rightness. There was so much going on in her little circle that was troubling — more than troubling — downright disturbing. But this was something positive. Even with the danger that Gina had warned them of, now so evident, she hoped that this was the silver lining to that cloud. Angela would never do what her family had done to her — dump her expectations on the young couple, but she could hold certain, secret wishes in her heart.

When she came up with just the right thing to say to put Sarita at ease, she knew her brain was working just fine.

"Huh. Sounds like you found a guy who knows how to get the job done right. As for me, as soon as I get better, I'm making Harry some of that sauce."

They were giggling over that when the familiar, yet still otherworldly sound of distant, cracking bubble wrap surrounded them. "Hey, you two," greeted the materializing Luca, "Lot more laughing going on in here than I expected."

He eyed them quizzically when they stopped laughing at once, and looked at him like he'd caught them trying to steal his wallet.

Sarita and Angela were saved from themselves when Dr. Neihaus knocked briskly. She gave Luca a look too. Hers was suspicious rather than guilty. "Where did you come from? I didn't see you go past the desk."

Angela jumped in. "Of course not. You're exhausted. I've been here for more than twenty-four hours, and I've seen you for almost every one of them. Don't you ever go home?"

The observation took the doctor by surprise. Nobody but her husband ever noticed how many hours she worked. "I'm working a double shift. One of the other doctors has flu, unfortunately."

"Well, that's not good at all. You need to take care of your own self too, you know." Angela squinted at the name tag on the doctor's coat. "What does the 'M' stand for?"

"Marietta. My name is Marietta."

Angela's eyebrows raised. "No kidding? That's an Italian name. You know, we have two Mariettas in our family." She looked at Luca for verification. "Don't we?"

"We do," he confirmed, enjoying Angela's misdirect. She would have made a good magician.

Angela continued. "Well, Dr. Marietta, tomorrow, when these two come to pick me up, I'm going to have them bring you some of my Italian Seven-Layer Cookies." She put her fists to her hips and looked at her balefully. "I *am* going home tomorrow, correct?"

Marietta had to smile. That was neatly done. "Let's see what your scan says, shall we? That's why I came by — we'll be taking you downstairs in an hour. That gives your surgeon enough time to check those stitches. He's coming up." She stopped by the door on her way out. "I love those cookies, so I hope you keep your promise, Mrs. Perotta."

Angela's smirk was crafty. "You do your part. I'll do mine."

The two doctors must have crossed paths in the hallway. Soon after the neurologist left, Angela's cosmetic surgeon, or, as she got a kick out of calling him — her 'booby doctor' — stepped in. He stopped short when he spotted Luca, and just stood, staring at him.

Okay, what the hell was going on? Luca hated being the focus of attention, but he had been from the second he arrived. He could disregard Dr. Niehaus's fish eye because the woman was sharp — she was damn sure he hadn't come past the desk. But first Sarita and Angela giving him weird looks, and now this guy. He glanced down at his t-shirt. Did he drop his breakfast on it and not notice?

"Sarita, Luca, this is Dr. Menville." Focused on the surgeon's purpose for being there, Angela didn't pick up on the effect Luca was having on him, but Sarita hid a smile. She'd caught the doctor's walloped reaction — he was still staring — and could only empathize.

Dr. Menville shook himself out of his trancelike absorption, gave them both a brisk nod, then turned his back and set to work on Angela's face. He said nothing while he removed bandages, until, keeping his eyes on his patient, he asked, "Where are you from, Luca?"

"Uh … Brooklyn." For Angela's sake, he resigned himself to the man's unprovoked interest. He wasn't homophobic by any means, but geez, was this really the time or place? Sarita was enjoying the scene. Her eyes danced and she smothered a laugh. He'd get her back for that later.

"How long have you been on the west coast?" the surgeon asked, as he put antiseptic on Angela's stitches.

Clearing his throat, Luca responded, "I'm a recent transplant to Long Beach. My brother and I moved to Las Vegas about nine years ago."

"Ow!" Angela said, before she could stop herself.

"I'm so sorry. My hand slipped." Menville was visibly shaken by the mishap.

"Sarita, what are your plans today?" Luca thought a shift in focus was in order.

"I'm meeting Marisol. We're having our nails done. Since the restaurant's closed, we'll have lunch out too. There's a teachers' meeting, and she's off from school, so it works out great." She gnawed on her lip. "I'm still not sure I'm the right one for this talk. She seems to have a lot on her mind. But I promised, so I'll do my best." Slanting a glance toward Menville, she posed her question to Luca carefully. "Isn't today when you said you were going to … pop in on your accountant?"

"Yeah." Luca winked at her for the smooth phrasing. He was leaving for the penthouse as soon as they were done here. "I shouldn't be there for more than a few hours."

He kept the possibility that he might also stop in New York to himself. He'd already decided to wait until Angela was home before he said anything to either woman about what Mr. Abramson had told him. He was sure the old guy didn't know what he was saying, but he couldn't stop thinking about it. For now, he just spoke about his plans with Desiree.

"She's hoping I might be able to shed some light on those withdrawals. She can't execute Santi's estate until she finds out where all that money went."

"Ow!" Angela said again. "Darn it, Dr. Menville. A little warning, please." This time the surgeon mumbled his apology, and Angela took note of the unusual inelegance of his movements. "Have you eaten this morning?" she asked him. What was wrong with these doctors that they didn't look after their health? Lack of sleep, lack of food — they should know better. It made her wonder if it was a good idea for her to put her brain and her face into their care.

That Dr. Menville was mortified by his ham-fistedness was clear by his rush to be away. He hastened through the rest of his work and through Angela's questions when he was through, and with once last glance at Luca, he dashed off.

"Well." Luca said. "That was interesting."

Sarita got back to the *Mary* at noon and headed to her stateroom. She had an hour to kill before she was to meet Marisol at Michael's shop. It was such an oddity on a Tuesday not to be preparing for the restaurant to open in the evening, that she couldn't think what to do with herself.

It crossed her mind that she could call São Paulo. Raul and her mother were back there now. On the other hand, better not — the contact at the irregular time would prompt a million questions, and so far they'd managed to keep Cynthia in the dark about the messier goings-on. She decided she might as well read. She hadn't done much of that since she and Luca started dating.

And didn't it sound strange to say that? She had a boyfriend. No — a lover. A lover who was also a true friend.

She was scrolling through her e-reader library when there was a knock on her door. A familiar staff member was waiting when she opened it.

"Hey, Avi." He was holding a food service tray that held two stainless steel covered dishes, a pot of coffee, and one red rose. "Is this for me? I didn't order anything."

Avi was sweet, handsome, and had a megawatt smile. Sarita knew that half the entire ship's crew had a crush on him. "Hi, Sarita. This was called in for you, from —" he handed her the order ticket — "Luca. He said to surprise you since The Spice is closed today."

"Oh, how nice. Thank you, Avi. I'll take it. You don't have to bring it in."

"Nah, I got it." He came in and set the tray down on the table. "How's Angela doing?"

"Getting better. Thanks for asking, Avi." There was that smile again.

"You tell her everybody's thinking about her, and we hope they catch the guy soon."

After he left, Sarita sniffed at the rose. There was a sealed envelope too, with a note inside:

Since no one's there to feed you, thought you might like breakfast from one of your competitors. Don't tell Cristiano. See you tonight. XXX, Luca

Charmed, she uncovered the smaller dish first. Fresh sourdough rolls and butter. Lovely, they were still warm. And under the larger cover there was a plate of scrambled eggs and bacon.

She chuckled. She never had a heavy breakfast, but Luca was as bad as Cristiano and Angela. If she ate half of what they tried to feed her, she'd be the size of a barn. The roll and coffee would be more than enough, since she was having lunch out. Luca need never know.

She was sitting on her bed, halfway through her second cup of coffee, a partially-eaten roll on a plate beside her. Her e-reader was on her knees, and she was engrossed in *The God of Small Things*. The novel made her think about both Rohini and Luca — what it might be like to grow up in India, what it might be like to have a twin — when out of the blue, she felt remarkably sleepy, almost impossibly so.

She tried to place her cup on the nightstand, but it slipped out of her fingers, its contents spilling on the bed. Her knees seemed boneless all at once, and when they gave out, her e-reader slid down the coverlet to the floor. She couldn't feel her arms, but if she could have, she would have slapped herself for being so gullible.

That was her last thought before she passed out.

Luca popped back in to his stateroom straight from Vegas. He hadn't stopped in New York. Going over books with Desiree in his penthouse, a theory had crossed his mind that was so outlandish, he'd already discarded and revisited it half a dozen times. He needed to run it by Sarita. With her abilities, a conversation might spark a few clues. But she hadn't answered his text.

He changed into a fresh t-shirt — his method of travel when combined with warm weather always made him perspire — and then walked down the corridor to Sarita's.

She didn't answer his knock, but he thought he heard some noise from within.

"Sarita? Are you in there, darling?" He rapped on the door again.

No response. He could have sworn he heard something. Then again, his imagination was taking him lots of places today. The sense of doom it had spawned was tempting him to disengage the lock. But the one time he'd used his powers to do that, she hadn't appreciated it in the least. He dithered for a minute longer, his ear angled, listening for any small sound, when it occurred to him that what he was doing was dangerously close to an invasion of privacy. Maybe she was down at The Spice.

The restaurant was empty. He was in the kitchen when he remembered she was supposed to meet Marisol. They were probably off the ship somewhere, or if not, she might have her phone on silent mode so they could have their talk without interruption. It was with a sense of relief that he wrote out another text, telling her to disregard his previous one.

He was typing that he'd see her later, that he loved her, when Alan snuck up behind him. It was a hell of a lot easier to knock out a woman than it was to take down a man his same size, but his training would help. Twelve seconds was what he'd need.

He had another apron. Swiftly, he dropped it over Luca's head. Luca let go of his phone and made a grab for the cloth covering his face. Alan kicked the back of his knee out from under him, and down Luca went, shouting, flailing for balance. With a twist on the apron, Alan jerked Luca's neck back, exposing his carotids. All in four seconds. He reached around, knowing just where to press. In three seconds, Luca's head started to swim, and in five more seconds, everything went black.

When he regained consciousness, disoriented and nauseated from the loss of oxygen, he was already blindfolded, legs and ankles tethered to a chair, arms behind the chair back, wrists tied together with rope. He had no idea where he was, but it was cold.

When the sluggishness lifted to some degree, it occurred to him that he couldn't have been out for long. He was familiar with the method used by his attacker. He and Santi had both studied martial arts — it helped with the act — and if he'd been as good at it as his twin had been, he might have been able to get himself out of trouble, even with the apron over his face. But he'd been a mediocre martial arts student just as he'd been a mediocre magician. Nonetheless, he remembered that a squeeze on the carotids, unless you planned to kill, rendered a victim unconscious for no more than five or six minutes.

He did some fast thinking — if there was only one assailant, no way the dude could haul him very far and tie him up in that amount of time. He might still be at the restaurant. Which would mean he was in the office. He stayed still, listening for familiar sounds, even a familiar scent. The office would be the only place he wasn't likely to be discovered.

Which meant he was screwed. The cleaning crew didn't come in on Tuesdays. Shouting wouldn't help him in here. If he could somehow get himself to the door, he might be able to open it. But when he made the attempt, the voice he heard stilled him at once.

"Don't move, Luca *mia*."

"Mama." His body went weak again. "You're here. You're really here."

"Yes, my baby, my lovely boy."

"Oh, Mama. I'm so happy to hear your voice. I ... I heard you in my head. And then I saw you in the kitchen, just for a minute, and ... I've missed you. I've missed you so, so much."

He wished he could see her. Even if she was the last thing he saw in this life. He felt his eyes go wet behind the blindfold. Hearing her like this, so close, so real, it flooded into him how much he loved her. There were so many things he wanted to ask her, so much he wanted to tell her.

"I know, I know, my baby. But listen to me. We don't have much time. You need to try and loosen the rope."

"Can you help me, Mama?"

"I'm sorry. I cannot touch you, *figgiu mio*. It would give you frostbite."

Her voice sounded woeful when she said that. She wasn't real, not in the same sense he was, no matter that she sounded the same as he remembered.

"He's coming back, and you need to listen to him. We'll all help you as much as we can, but you need to be brave. Don't remove your blindfold, even if you get your hands loose. He might harm you if he thinks you can hurt him."

By some phenomenon granted to him by Providence, the loving mother he thought he'd lost forever was here – a manifestation of her, at least. But in a cruel twist to the miracle, he wasn't permitted to savor her presence, to absorb the moment, to take in her every word. He could only recoil at one.

"Blindfold? ... Does that mean he knows?"

She didn't answer right away. She knew it would tear him apart.

"Mama – does he know about my eyes?"

"Yes, Luca, *mia*. He does."

After that, he knew she'd left, as the room was no longer cold.

A key turned in the lock.

Sarita came to five minutes before Luca did. Her eyes felt heavy-lidded from whatever had been in the coffee. In took a while for it to sink in that she was in the deep clawfoot tub in her bathroom. Her arms still wouldn't move. Now she could feel them bound to her sides, her elbows straight, her palms against her thighs. The chemically-induced lethargy didn't prevent the panic. It washed over her like a tide when she realized that her knees, her ankles and toes, were also bound with duct tape, with her legs folded behind her, so that she couldn't stretch out. She was wrapped up like a twisted mummy, the tub as her sarcophagus. Duct tape was pressed against her closed lips too, as though they'd been sewn shut.

Someone was in the bathroom, moving behind her, by her head. Alan came into view and sat on the edge of the tub. Alan without dreadlocks. "I'm sorry," he said. "I thought I would be glad to do this, but I'm not. Unfortunately it can't be helped."

It would almost be funny if it weren't so terrifying. She'd suspected him just as Angela had, and now she was going to die because she'd felt her assumption was discourteous.

"This won't take long, I hope. I hope it won't be painful, either." His tone was almost soothing, as though he were talking about pulling her tooth. The fake dialect was gone, and there was something chillingly familiar about his voice. "It would be faster for you if I sliced your throat. But I can't bring myself to do that. I've never killed anyone before, and I'm more of a coward than I thought, Sarita. This way I won't have to see it."

When he put the rubber stopper in the drain, and used more duct tape to secure it, she moaned behind her gag. She didn't want to die. Her reflexes were dulled, but the drug had done nothing to dull the fear, the sadness that she would lose her life just when she'd started to live it. Her eyes filled. He frowned when he saw her tears. Why was he doing this? She wondered if he would tell her, but she was so sleepy.

She studied Alan's face, tried to see something in him of the woman who'd confronted her. Was this the son she'd spoken of, the one hell-bent on revenge?

Her thoughts were black and syrupy-sluggish, like thick, bitter molasses. She'd always loved this tub. So pretty, so old-fashioned, so deep. And there was no way she'd be able to worm her way out of such a tub the way he'd taped her up.

Luca. I love you so.

Her poor mother. This would kill her. Not even Raul would be able to help her get past this, get past the reason for it.

Perversely, he lifted her head to place a pillow behind it. "At least you'll be comfortable. And the drug should keep you calm. Try to let the sound of the water lull you back to sleep. I'll make sure it's not too cold. It should be over soon."

At his touch, her eyes went wild with a searing terror, a terror that brought on an adrenaline surge and dispelled some of the listlessness.

No, no. Please, no.

Nothing to do with the woman at the ball. As soon as he touched her, she knew who he was, and what her latest visions had been about. It wasn't her he was after, not her at all. Her death was merely one vehicle by which he would harm someone else.

CHAPTER NINETEEN

It would take exactly fifteen minutes and thirty-nine seconds for the creaky old pipes to pump out enough water to fill the deep vintage tub and swallow over Sarita. One minute after Alan had turned on the taps and left, Marisol McKenna voiced her impatience. She'd been sitting in The Queen Mary Memorabilia and Postcard Shop for forty-five minutes, and she was bored.

"Dad, how much longer do I have to wait?"

"Did you try texting her again?" Michael was preoccupied with rearranging displays to make room for new inventory. He cosseted and fussed over his shop almost as much as he cosseted and fussed over his wife and daughter.

"Yes. She's not answering."

He decided it was best to ignore the sulky notes in Marisol's voice. "Did you try the restaurant?"

"*Yes.* Where did you think I went? I told you, everything is locked."

"I meant the phone number, Marisol."

"There's no one there to answer. All the lights are off too."

Michael shifted a new book in its holder to a jaunty angle so it would be clearly visible on the shelf. "Just trying to help, sweetheart." He stepped back to appraise his handiwork, then arched a brow at Marisol. "Here's an idea — instead of Sarita, why not talk to your old dad, and tell him what's bothering you, hmm?"

Bad mood aside, she couldn't resist a smirk at the face he was making. At one point during his bachelor years, some girl he dated had given him the idea that his infamous 'eyebrow maneuver' was adorable and persuasive. She just thought he looked silly. Although she had seen it work on her mother.

He meant well. He always meant well, because he loved her. Sometimes she thought he was the only one who loved her just as she was. She knew her mother loved her too, but Inez had expectations, and Marisol wasn't sure she could live up to them. Or if she even wanted to. Though it made her sad to think about it, talking to her mother these days about anything always ended in an argument. As for Michael, who'd treated her like a daughter even before he'd married her mother, she couldn't talk to him either. How could you tell someone who believed you were perfect that nearly everyone you went to school with thought you were weird?

So, she didn't. She told him something else entirely, with a peevishness she'd perfected to get her parents to retreat. "I wish you both would leave me alone. There's nothing bothering me. I don't know why you and Mom think that."

"Marisol." Rather than get angry, he detected another quality in her tone and made his all the milder in contrast. When had she become so unsure of herself, so despondent? "Your parents aren't perfect. We make mistakes. But the important thing to remember is that we all love each other, and we're here to support ..." his voice trailed off. She was no longer listening, but looking past him, little flecks of panic in her eyes.

He knew the look. The first time he'd seen it had been ten years ago, right in this shop, when she was hardly more than a baby.

He clenched his teeth, kept his eyes locked on hers, as though he'd noticed nothing unusual, as though her entire demeanor hadn't transformed in seconds. That was harder than pretending he wasn't just as creeped out as she was whenever she asked him to squash a bug. He didn't dare turn around. Not out of fear for what she saw behind him, but out of fear for her. If he turned, he would see nothing, and she would only feel unmasked again. The battle against her intuitive ability was forever at the root of her unhappiness. He knew that all too well, which was why he was prepared for moments like these, but also why he found it so hard to rein her in when he should.

And so, as the sun shone in from the wide windows of the pretty little shop, reflecting in his hair like a halo, he stood, silently bleeding for his cherished little girl. Inez had told him years ago that Sarita also had the gift, and that was why she wanted Marisol and Sarita to talk. He and his wife hadn't seen eye to eye on how to handle their daughter as of late, but on this they did agree. She needed someone to talk with, someone who could tell her it was okay to be different, when that was the last thing any fourteen-year-old believed to be true.

Michael was right in his assessment. Marisol's gifts rivaled Sarita's, but just the way Sarita had, up until the recent past, she actively suppressed them. She didn't want to see the woman shimmering in the light behind Michael, near the boxes of books he was unpacking and the display of guide maps. She didn't want to know why the woman was looking at her so solemnly. She didn't know who Gina was, or that she was there in the hopes that Marisol — the one person on board today besides Luca and Sarita who could see her — would save her son and the woman he loved.

Gina wanted Marisol to connect with her. If she did, she could stop it. At that very moment, the water in Sarita's tub was up to her hips, and the man who'd done that had rendered Luca helpless and was now confronting him.

But Marisol turned away from Gina with deliberation, and interrupted Michael. "Dad, can I at least go up to the Sun Deck to wait for her? Do I have to stay here?"

Michael stared at his daughter just as gravely as Gina was doing. He knew why Marisol wanted to leave, and he just didn't know what the right thing was to do. "All right, sweetheart. I'll send Sarita up when she gets here."

He watched her as she fled the shop, and then tried calling Sarita himself. She was never late, so where the hell was she?

Behind him, Gina faded away.

Alan stepped into the office at The Secret Spice and quietly closed the door behind him. He was used to making a big, splashy entrance, but in this case, the soft click of the lock was much more dramatic. Especially when he saw Luca tense. It was empowering to see him so defenseless. The best magicians in the world turned the ordinary into the extraordinary. Alan had done the reverse — he'd turned the extraordinary into the ordinary.

"So — did you figure it out? I sure as hell left you enough clues. I practically painted you a damn sign with the name Alan Rabinowitz."

Luca felt no anger. Not yet. There was only a deep, black pit of misery, as he listened to Alan's voice.

"He was the greatest escape artist in the world, Luca." Though Luca couldn't see him, Alan bent in front of him and spoke directly into his face. "Didn't even register, huh? Christ — he only died a few months ago. The man was credited with devising the most daring 'Burning-Rope Straitjacket Escape.' I bet every magician on the Strip was talking about it. Of course, they don't know *my* burning strait jacket illusion was even better. But you didn't put it together. How come? Oh, right — you were still trying to dry out."

Luca was truly confounded by the tone of glee. The first loss of Santi had at least been pure. But this ... this was the loss of an entire lifetime. Every memory he had of his brother — every laugh and embrace they'd shared, every plan they'd made and goal they'd accomplished

— everything he believed they were together, was as much of an illusion as any ingenious sleight of hand Santino Miceli had performed on stage.

"Look at you, sitting there, all trussed up like a turkey. Not so powerful now without your sight, are you?" He hooted. "The man behind the curtain. Some fuckin' magician you are. You can't even get your hands untied. I knew you couldn't. That's why I did it that way — for the irony."

The office was tight and airless. With Santi this close, Luca picked up the faintly perceptible smell of old fish that had seeped into all his clothing after months of being holed up in the dive by the Seventh Street Bridge. But the stench of malevolence was much stronger, and it came at Luca in waves.

The brother Luca loved, to whom he'd devoted himself for more than twenty years, had given up his penthouse, his fame, the face he'd preened over, the opulent life he relished, a woman who loved him enough to commit perjury for him, and most of his hard-earned money.

That was an unfathomable amount of hate.

He couldn't be completely sane, Luca knew. And yet, he had to ask, had to hear it from Santi's perspective. He kept his words even, his focus in the direction of his brother's voice.

"Why? Why would you do all this? Desiree said money's been siphoned off for five years. That's you — you took your own money. Which means, you've been planning this for a long time."

Each new fraction of the whole Luca uncovered was another jagged piece of deceit that sliced at his heart. Five years ago, they'd bought the penthouse, one more thing he did because he thought it would make his brother happy.

Santi whistled low. "I have to say, I'm impressed with you two. But then, Dez always was sharp. That's why I kept her far away from my personal account. She might've just picked up on annoying little details like that. How's she doing, by the way?" Man, he was enjoying himself. He'd waited years for this moment, and he was going to savor it.

Luca's next remarks put the brakes on the crowing. "She's doing a lot better than Joanie. I saw her today. She was hysterical. I didn't get it at first, but she thought I was you, didn't she? You gave her a key to the penthouse. You were that sure I wasn't going back." He let that sink in. "What did you say to get her on board for all this? I'm guessing that's why she pulled me away from the stage that night — so I wouldn't be there to stop the fire, right? Guess that's why she kept in touch with me too, after the accident — not to see how I was, but to spy for you. She doesn't know you're not going back, or about your face, does she? The new look — is that a recent addition to this master plan? Was it a co-incidence you used our cousin's doctor, or was that another goddamn 'clue' to mess with me?"

Santi's jaw tightened with annoyance. "What I do with Joanie is my business, asshole. As far as the surgeon goes … turns out halfway de-cent ones are in short supply. At least when it comes to valuing discre-tion. Menville did, for enough cash in hand. People with tax problems can be pretty reasonable."

"And cutting up our cousin's face? 'Your business,' too? Or did you promise Menville a return client as a bonus?"

He couldn't see the punch coming, so he wasn't braced for it. It slammed into his jaw, snapping his head back and splitting open his lip.

"Shut the fuck up, Luca." Santi watched as Luca spit out blood. He'd always wanted to punch him, but he shouldn't have done it, not while his eyes were covered, at least. He was going to kill his twin, but he didn't want him to die thinking he was a coward. It was Luca's own fault though, for making accusations. And now Santi had to explain himself.

"It was an accident, damn you." One he felt bad about, truth be told. "She came in when I was … I didn't expect her, all right? I was in the closet — I needed to hide the stuff to tie your dumb ass up with — next thing I know she barges in, gets on the computer talking to Jane forever about some letter. She was supposed to be gone that day, and now I'm suddenly hiding like some … common thief. Me — after I tracked everyone's movements for months."

Luca was so familiar with the tone of outraged insult, as was everyone who'd worked on crew for the Miceli brothers. If things didn't go unerringly the way Santi wanted them to go during a show, the beauty of everything that went right was lost on him. He'd find the person responsible and verbally and publicly rip them to shreds. "Why did that stupid letter have to show up? Why the hell did she have to come in the office? It was her fault. I needed to get away without her seeing me. I only meant to knock her out. I didn't mean for her to hit her face."

The haze of melancholy enveloping Luca had dispelled with that punch. He felt the first beats of anger throb along with the ache in his jaw.

"She used to give you cookies. Remember, Santi? Remember going to her bakery with *Nannuzza*, and she'd let us come behind the counter and pick out as many different kinds of cookies as we wanted? The ones you liked best were the ones with the rainbow sprinkles." He expected another punch when he brought up the childhood memory.

But he couldn't see Santi's startled look that his brother still knew, after all these years, what kind of cookies he'd liked.

"Shut up, Luca," he said again. This time he sounded just the way he did when they were kids, and he'd say it for lack of any other comeback. "You don't know anything about it."

"Then tell me!" The shout was so unexpected and loud that Santi jumped. "Tell me how you could possibly hate me that much — enough to do all this."

Luca's roar got Santi back on task. He was thankful Luca didn't see he'd scared him, glad he'd gotten that punch in, after all.

"Of course I hated you. I've hated you all our lives. Every fucking day. You had everything, and I had *nothing*!"

They were screaming so loudly they might have been heard, vaguely, by anyone walking past the restaurant or on the deck. But the *Mary*'s whistle blew at the same time, and the loud, deep timbre of her echoing blasts drowned out the brothers' shouts.

"What did I have, Santi, that you wanted so much? What did I have, except my brother? I thought I had … my brother."

He broke down and wept.

'All our lives. Every fucking day.' He cried as those words echoed in his brain, his arms locked behind him, his head hanging forward, and everything inside him — the hopelessness, the disgust, the guilt, the love — was in his tears. They dripped down his face, mixed with the blood on his chin and soaked his blindfold — the blindfold the brother he was crying over had secured over his eyes to cripple him.

Santi stepped back. This had been his goal. He felt gratified when Joanie told him that Luca had been slowly poisoning himself in the months after his supposed death. But seeing the depth of his grief, the desperate flood of emotion up close felt different than he thought it would. "Stop it."

Luca couldn't stop. He kept crying.

"I said, stop it." He turned his face away. "Stop pretending you care about me. If you cared about me, you wouldn't have left me."

"Left you? I never left you." Luca knew he was talking to a madman, but his pain was too genuine and urgent to be left unsaid. "You were all I thought about after Mama died. Everything I did after that — *every* decision I made — was with you foremost on my mind. I never wanted to be a magician. Didn't you ever wonder why I wasn't very good at it?"

He couldn't see Santi's gaze pivot back to him and hold, or that he was listening, assessing, that he might have felt a flicker of doubt over what he was doing. It vanished with Luca's next words. "But you used me as your flunky — my love for you was your weapon to manipulate me, just like it was with Joanie."

Luca stopped. It was unwise to have spoken his truth. Not now, not to this man. This man was not his brother. This man was 'Alan,' a man who had committed any number of crimes, everything from embezzlement to — shortly — murder.

The darkness beyond his blindfold became more menacing all at once. He could hear Santi's breathing, and in the harshness of the sound, his body clenched, sensing the coming explosion.

"Bullshit!" Santi yelled. "You filthy liar. I *said* — you left me. You left me alone when he came to kill her!"

And there it was. The seed of it all. Santi's jealousy of his twin stemmed not from the powers Luca had that he'd been denied. In Santi's mind, Luca was the true escape artist — he'd escaped, unbroken, from their childhood trauma. That was Luca's true gift — his ability to be whole.

"Santi — I was a *kid*. We were kids. I didn't know what was going to happen —"

"You did so. You came back, crying, from the bridge. *Nannuzzo* said you were screaming. You knew." Panic. Horror. Betrayal. The child inside the madman remembered it all, remembered how he was trapped inside that small, dark space alone — a womb of death — abandoned by the twin who should have been sharing it with him.

"No, I *didn't*." Luca's denial was vehement, his voice hoarse with tears and the battle to get through to his brother. "God, no. Listen. Santi, please listen — it was *after*. After she was already dead that I saw it." He leaned forward as far as he could manage and spoke desperately into the dark. "Do you think I would have stayed at the bridge if I knew? Do you think I would have even left the apartment?" More than Luca wanted to live, he wanted his brother to believe him. It could change everything, if he could make him believe the truth.

But Santi was beyond Luca's reach. He was back in his own world, to a life in which he had his own face and no doppelgänger to taunt him. Like Dr. Frankenstein, he'd broken laws of nature to bring forth that existence, and all he needed now to rejoice in his miscreation was a reason to deny its repugnance.

"You did leave, Luca. And you laughed at me." He was no longer shouting, his voice was soft, almost hypnotic. "And I've heard him ever since. It's your fault he never stops talking to me. He's in my head, and he won't stop."

"Who? Who talks to you?"

Santi didn't respond, and that brought the reality home for Luca that his brother was ill. For the first time since this monstrosity began, he felt pity.

It floated into his consciousness then, something he'd overlooked. "Santi? That night — whose body was it?"

At the question, Santi snapped back to himself. He started chuckling, and Luca felt the hair on his forearms rise. "Just a guy about my height. Charred flesh makes everyone look the same. And I gave up some teeth."

"Who, Santi?" he demanded, dreading the answer.

"One of the homeless guys who used to come to the backstage door for sandwiches."

That's why he'd been so magnanimous. Luca remembered how proudly he'd told Sarita about it the night of the ball. He tasted bile. "You killed him?"

"No. I didn't have to." Luca didn't need to see the careless shrug. "They were all sick with something. Sooner or later one was bound to go." He recounted the heinous deception as though bragging about a friendly game of cards in which he'd cleverly managed to switch in an ace. "We made the deal ahead of time — I'd feed them, and first one of the bunch who croaked was my corpse to keep."

Even with the macabre recitation, some of Luca's tension eased. "Well ... I guess I should be glad you never killed anyone else, then. Except me."

In more ways than one, Luca still couldn't see Santi. He'd have never guessed at the guilt curdled with satisfaction on his brother's face.

But there was a certain quality hanging in the silence. Ice formed in the pit of Luca's belly.

"Santi? You haven't hurt anyone else. Have you?"

The water in the tub had reached her neck. She could feel it there, warm and silky against her exposed skin. The legs he'd bound so tightly behind her were cramping, the pins and needles in them as piercing as the screams in her head. It hadn't seemed real that she would die this way. When the water started to pool, she believed there was time — that someone would come in time. And now, she was simply astonished that she would soon be dead.

She tried bucking her hips, in the hopes she could dispel some of the water, spill it over the sides. But in the bent position it was impossible, and he'd known that. The tape was slippery, and she was afraid she'd slide down further than she was. Her head was already danger-ously close to the water line.

Who'd find her first? Probably one of the cleaning crew. Poor Inez. They'd call her, and she would just freak.

How long could a body stay underwater before it got all bloated and gross? Would she end up haunting the *Mary* too?

Why hadn't she lived a full life while she'd had it? Did Luca know she loved him? When he'd said it to her, *why* hadn't she said it back? Where was he? Did Santi have him? God, she hoped not.

The pain in her legs was agonizing. And he'd thought this was more humane than simply killing her while she was out? She heard voices in the hallway, in the stateroom next door. Behind her gag she made sounds in the hopes they'd hear, but just then the *Mary*'s whistle blew, and foolishly, she felt betrayed by the ship she'd always thought would keep her safe. She was down to what were essentially the last few minutes of her life, right here in the room that had been her sanc-tuary for the past ten years.

What the hell — where were all her dead friends when she needed them? With all she'd seen them do, surely they could turn the taps. Her eyes were on the iron grey spigot. Had the flow of water slowed? She thought it might have, but she couldn't be sure. If the spirits had any plans to help, they'd better hurry.

———•

At eighty-four degrees, it was a flawless day by the harbor on the Sun Deck of the *Queen Mary*. But Marisol didn't see it. She didn't see the march of human history in the metals and woods of the majestic ship. She saw only its rust and wear. She didn't see the smile in the bright sun nor the pretty in the crayon blue sky. For her, today might just be the day that sent her over the edge.

She was shivering, leaning against one of the ship's giant telescopes that overlooked the harbor. Her world was dark and overcast. What was joyful for others held no pleasure for her, and she was so tired of pretending.

The only thing she liked was baking with Angela. In that, at least, she could forget how apart she was, how strange everyone knew her to be. When she and Lizzie were teased at school for anything and everything, Lizzie saw it as a challenge, but Marisol saw it as unbearable. Besides, Lizzie was the odd man out because she wanted to be, whereas Marisol saw herself as a freak with no choice in the matter.

Her mother didn't get it. Inez's advice came from such a different reality, and it was frustrating and alienating to try to explain herself. What could she say?

'Hey, Mom — guess what? I saw three ghosts already since we got here this morning. All of them were looking at me, like they wanted to strike up a conversation. There was a tall, blonde lady wearing a white evening gown when we got to the lobby, a young sailor with a beard standing right behind us when I was helping you stock cleaning supplies, and just now, there was a short one with dark hair, standing right behind Dad.'

No, she sure didn't want to say that. Even though she knew they'd believe it, she just didn't want to say it, any more than she wanted to see it.

She wondered if it would ever end, if she would ever be normal. If not, was it worth it to go on?

She stood up, walked to the rail to stare down at the shadowy water. What was it like to drown? Did it hurt?

Hearing people on the deck, she glanced behind her. Past the vintage life boats that were still suspended on the ship's side, the deck was empty, but on the other side, by the sparkling white gazebo, she could see a couple holding hands. Another wedding being planned, she supposed.

When she turned her attention back to the water, she barely stifled her scream. She knew what she was seeing was impossible — another apparition — but when she wanted to run, her feet felt nailed in place.

A creature dressed in women's clothing had emerged from the muck of the harbor, and with her bare hands, was clawing her way up the side of the ship. She was sodden with brackish, briny sea water, her skin turned greenish from it. The water had soaked so deeply through her dermis and subcutaneous tissue that it all flopped loose and heavy on her bones like wet, dirty towels. Her face was bloated, as was her tongue, which protruded from her mouth like a balloon. Her blouse and skirt were streaked with mud and plastered with seaweed, and barnacles were stuck in her matted hair. The skin and muscle of her fingers and palms that had slackened from her time in the depths appeared to be working for her like powerful tentacles. Marisol could hear the suction noises that her skin made against the side of the ship as she slunk her way up, the stumps of her legs dangling limply. Being dragged along behind her, tangled in a net of sinew emerging from her calf, was only one shoe.

As she inched her way closer to the level of the deck, she kept her eyes fixed on the teenager as though daring her to run.

Marisol couldn't twitch a muscle, so riveted was she by the horrific sight of the unlucky nanny who'd spent her last days sailing on the *Queen*, and ended up dumped overboard like sewage.

Dolores reached the rail, her decaying fingers clamped around the top, viselike, until with one more push, she heaved herself over and stood, dripping and putrid, next to Marisol, her eyes as dark and fathomless as the bottom of the ocean where she slept.

It was impossible for Marisol to believe that the couple still talked and laughed behind her, their voices floating across the deck, that the sun was still shining in its same spot in the sky, and all else was just as it had been five minutes before.

Except for her. Terror, icy cold as the air around the ghoulish vision in front of her, rendered her nearly catatonic — she couldn't scream, couldn't move, couldn't breathe.

And then the thing that had once been a woman spoke, in a gentle and pleasant voice, with a charming accent that reminded Marisol of Angela's sister-in-law, Jane. "What's wrong with you, lass — are you daft? We've been trying to get your attention all flippin' day." She had some difficulty speaking due to the bulbous tongue. "Your friend Sarita's in trouble. She's going to die if you don't hurry."

The skin of Marisol's neck and chest sucked inward as she dragged in air and then wheezed it back out again. "Wh-what? Where ... where is she?"

"She's trapped in her bathtub, drowning." She made a shooing motion, and a chunk of wet skin slipped off her arm and flopped onto the deck. "Go on, then. Run along."

Marisol's legs were working again. She took off like a shot without a backward glance.

Dolores *tch*-ed with irritation. Not even a thank you. "You're welcome!" she called out after Marisol. And satisfied with her work, she crept back into the deep.

———•

Luca asked again. "Santi, did you hurt anybody?"

He couldn't bring himself to say it, still clinging to the hope that his brother could be redeemed, that he could get help, that they could heal together as siblings.

Sometimes, love refuses to die as quickly as it should. What came to him next, out of the dark, in the voice so much like his own, would change that.

"I'm afraid so. You should never have come here, Luca. It was enough for me to live on — seeing you destroy your reputation and your health." Santi spoke casually at first, and then his voice turned dark and cold. "But she made you happy again, and I couldn't have that. You don't get to be happy when I'm not."

"Oh, my God." Luca whispered the words. "Oh, my God … Sarita? You killed her? She's … dead?"

Santi glanced at his watch: Sixteen minutes since he left her room. Should be over by now. "Yeah." There was enough humanity left in him to add, "I made it relatively painless and quick."

"Oh, no. Oh, no." This time when he cried, it was with great, racking sobs. "Sarita, Sarita. Not my baby … not my Sarita. Oh, God, please no. *Please*, God. No."

He couldn't know that he'd cried out the same words of anguish his father had, years before.

But the memory gripped Santi by the throat and squeezed, strangling him until he couldn't breathe. In his mind, Luca's cries reverberated, melded with Rocco's, until the two were the one. The office walls pushed in and the room became narrower. The ceiling pushed downward, lower and lower. The space was so tiny and dark now, he could barely fit. He was wedged in, huddled and terrified against the pipes. He could smell the musty, bare wood, the old bacon grease his mother kept stored in a coffee can, the lemon-fragranced dish detergent she preferred.

He could hear her voice:

Promise me you won't come out. Promise me, Santino!

He could see her hands. Her shaking hands.

And behind him, there were sounds — squeaks and scratching. He was afraid to move. From the corner of his eye, he saw it: A rat. They were coming in through the hole near the pipe, and the cupboard was filling with sand. He wanted to run, he needed to run, but he'd promised Mama. Where was she? She shouldn't have left him in here with the rats.

The wailing and crying went on and on.

"Shut up." He bent his head, covered his ears with his palms. "Shut up, Luca. Shut up, or I'll kill you right now too!"

"Not if I kill you first."

When Santi looked up, his brother was standing. His blindfold was off, and in the inferno of his eyes, Santi saw his own death.

"I was out of the rope before you came back in here. I guess I'm a better magician than we thought, huh, Santi?"

The air in the room spun and rumbled as Luca raised his palm up. Santi squealed as he rose off the floor to midair, his arms flailing, his legs grappling, trying to compel his body downward. But it was as easy as pushing a child on a swing — one gentle forward motion of that lifted hand was all Luca needed to send his murderous twin flying backward across the room and slamming into the far wall.

It was past her earlobes, just beginning to seep into her ear canals. It tickled at the bottom of her nose, with barely a centimeter of space between the line of the water and her nostrils. She had her head tilted back so far, her neck felt like it would snap off. And in that moment, she gave in. She took one last deep breath before the water covered her nasal air passages, closed her eyes, and said good bye to those she loved.

Good bye, *Mamãe*. I'm so glad I told you how wonderful you are the last time we talked. Good bye, Luca. Being with you was the best thing that ever happened to me.

By the time she got to Cristiano and Rohini, her head was under water. She'd held her breath for one minute as she was saying good bye to Angela and Jane.

Two and a half minutes and she started to feel lightheaded. Maybe she should have done less reading and more cardio. She knew she'd either lose consciousness soon or inhale by reflex and suck in water. Either way, she'd be dead. Dimly, she said good bye to Marisol next, wishing they'd had their talk. She knew the tough road the girl faced ahead. Been there, done that, was her final thought before she felt herself succumbing to the blackness.

And then someone yanked her head up by her hair. "Sarita!"

Sarita tried to suck in some air through her water-clogged nose. Blinking furiously, she saw Marisol, white-faced and wide-eyed, staring down at her, hand still clutching her hair.

Marisol wasn't alone. She'd had the foresight to call Inez's phone, in case Sarita's door was locked. Mother and daughter had run like hell from their respective locations on the ship to meet at Sarita's stateroom.

Inez twisted the faucets and shouted instructions to Marisol in hysterical Spanish. "She still can't breathe! Get that tape off her mouth — keep her head up — you get one shoulder, I'll get the other — pull her up — turn her over!"

Water was slopping everywhere, they had her slumped face down over the rim of the tub like a dead eel, with Inez steadily smacking between her shoulder blades with the base of her palm. There was no water in her lungs, but still Sarita coughed, sucked in air, coughed again, and croaked out one word: "Shit."

"*Ay, Dios mio.* Sarita — I can't believe it. Marisol … she …" Inez didn't quite know how to explain the rescue.

Sarita didn't need an explanation. Still panting and raspy, her face stinging from the duct tape being ripped off her mouth, she choked out the obvious. "My legs. I need to be untied. We need to call the police."

While Marisol and Inez cut and pulled at her bonds, all Sarita could think about through the excruciating process was finding Luca before Santi did.

"Hurry, Inez — please, hurry!"

"But I'll hurt you. This tape is so tight —"

"Pull it, cut it — I don't care. Just get me out, *please.* I have to find Luca before Alan does."

"It was Alan?" Inez stopped tearing at tape to clutch her hands in her hair. "*Ay,* my God, Sarita — this is all my fault."

"No, it's nothing to do with you. I'll explain later." The moment she was free, she called Luca's number. Cold fear trilled down her spine when it went to voicemail. Wobbling on legs that felt bloodless and rubbery, she ran to her safe and pulled out her mother's old Derringer. "Can you please call Betty at the L.B.P.D.? Her number's on the nightstand."

Inez wrung her hands. "Be careful. Do you know how to use that?"

"My mother taught me when I was twelve, but hopefully I won't have to. I have to find them. I … he could have knocked him out, like he did me. He could have dragged him anywhere. The *Mary*'s so big." Her thoughts were frantic, but her hands were a lot steadier than they might have been when she checked that the safety bar was set. Derringers had a tendency to go off if they were jarred, and she sure as hell intended to run.

"Um, Sarita?" Marisol's voice was trembling. "I think I know …" She stopped, took a deep breath. After everything that had happened, why was she still hiding? "I mean … they're in your office."

297

Again, Sarita didn't have to ask. But she took precious seconds to pull Marisol to her and hug her fiercely. "You're my hero. You saved my life." She grabbed her by the chin, squeezed. "Remember that."

Sopping wet, clothing still stuck with bits and pieces of duct tape, gun at the ready, Sarita ran barefoot out the door, her drenched hair flinging water droplets everywhere.

Marisol stared after her. It would take her weeks to process all of it. But maybe … maybe it wasn't such a bad thing to be weird, after all.

Her mother beamed at her. "My *chiquita*. I'm so proud of you. You're amazing. You're like that comic book you're always reading. You're like Saturn Girl."

Marisol felt a glimmer of fresh hope. "Do you really think so?"

"Certainly I do." Inez's response was unfaltering as she hastened to Sarita's nightstand.

———●

Santi's left eye was swollen shut, his mouth was full of blood, his new teeth implants were loose, and the nose Menville had given him was broken. He was barely conscious when Luca hauled him to his feet and propped him up against the wall.

"You succeeded, Santi. You managed to destroy me. I'll never be the same. But you'll be too dead to gloat about it."

His voice shook, as all around them a maelstrom thundered — the physical manifestation of Luca's anguish and fury — papers, pens, books, chairs, all blew, creating their own cyclone. Computers shattered, desks ruptured, the sharp bits of metal and splintered pieces of wood were sucked up by the vicious wind, whipping around dizzily, getting stuck in the walls like shrapnel, as Luca grabbed the front of Santi's shirt to steady his torso and plowed his fist into his jaw again.

"You know what the best part about killing you is? I won't even get in trouble. You're already dead. When I'm done, I'm going to weigh your piece-of-shit body down with bricks and dump it in the water. I give it an hour before the famous magician, Santino Miceli, is on the ocean floor with the rest of the bottom feeders. Just like *Cugina* Angela's Great-Uncle Nunzio."

His rage howled in his ears — hot, dark, oily, viscous as tar. He didn't hear the key turn in the lock, didn't hear the door swing open, didn't hear Sarita's sharp cry.

"No! No, Luca, stop. *Stop.*"

She couldn't get near him without the risk of being hit by an airborne object that was spinning in the storm. She shouted to him again, "Luca!"

Even in his eye line, he didn't hear her, didn't see her, his face so contorted by savagery and grief, she didn't recognize him. In his hold, Santi was blue and motionless, yet Luca kept hitting him with focused intent.

Swiftly, she scanned the room for the safest place to aim. Not the ceiling — there was a deck above. The wall that divided the office from the empty restaurant seemed best. She lifted the gun and fired.

The sound of the old weapon was deafening. It snapped Luca out of his trance, and the blaze in his eyes flickered. The whirlwind slowed, the objects floated to the floor.

"Luca," she called out again. "Luca, it's me! I'm here."

Her voice registered this time. He let go of Santi, who sank to the carpet. "Sarita! He … he told me …" He took in her appearance and stumbled, pulling her to him. "Sarita." He cried again, this time with a gratitude beyond imagining.

"It's all right." She choked out the words. "I'm here. We're here."

Luca didn't think he could stand up much longer. She was real. She wasn't dead.

She wiped away her own tears and held him tightly. Cynthia's Derringer still in her hand, she turned her head to where Santi lay bloodied and unconscious. "Oh, Luca. Santi. He's so sick."

"He tried to kill you."

"I know that, but listen." She put the gun down, gripped his arms, and watched his eyes. After all the shocks he'd had, there was still one more dreadful thing he needed to know. "You both thought he didn't have powers, but I think he's a clairaudient. And it ... it might have driven him mad."

She hesitated. Oh, God. She hated having to say it. He still looked so dazed.

"Luca, he hears your father's voice. Your father is alive."

CHAPTER TWENTY

On that Good Friday in Brooklyn, in 1991, shortly after Gina Miceli's death, the two police officers who'd been called to the scene stood outside on her front steps. Yellow tape cordoned off the area. Neighbors gathered outside as they would for a block party, and watched paramedics carry down the stretcher holding her covered body, and another holding her bleeding and insensate husband.

Rocco had taken a hit to his shoulder from a 9mm that shattered bone. The shoulder would heal, but his psyche would never recover.

"You did the right thing, Andy." Officer Snyder was observing her partner's agitated state.

Officer Davidson shook his head. "It wasn't the right thing, and we both know it. It was dangerous as hell, and I owe you one for this. If I'd missed, and he'd aimed that gun at us ..." He let his voice trail off. "But I had to try. I couldn't let him off himself, Nina. I went to Catholic school with him. You had to know him then. Before 'Nam."

"Good guy, huh?" Sorry for him, sorry for everyone involved, she coaxed him through it.

"The best. Not a mean bone in his body. Funny as hell. Used to drive the nuns crazy." He sidestepped to let an EMT pass. "And even back then, the whole school knew he was so in love with Gina Castelletti."

He rubbed at his face with both hands. Jesus, what a day. "Then he got drafted."

"Yes." Nina thought about all the tragedies involving veterans she'd dealt with as a police officer. "My husband had a number that scared the hell out of me. He narrowly missed being shipped over."

"I still sometimes wonder how I'd have ended up if I'd had to go." Andy kept his eyes on the ambulance as Rocco was loaded in.

Nina touched his shoulder. "You saved him. At least he's alive."

The ambulance doors slammed. Andy thought about Rocco's little boy, who was still screaming when they'd taken him off in the first vehicle. The image of that child, the image of his old friend crying as he cradled his dead wife's head from her broken neck would never leave him.

"I'm not so sure about that."

Twenty-three years later, Luca Miceli was in King's Park Psychiatric Hospital in New York City, following the nurse who was leading him to Rocco's room. Luca held Sarita Taylor's hand so tightly that her fingers ached. But she didn't say a word about it.

Everywhere the couple looked — down every corridor, by the medications counter, in the TV area — they saw another desolated man who was waiting for America to remember he was there. Some were as young as eighteen, others as old as ninety. Some were missing limbs and in wheelchairs, others stood, muttering to unseen fiends, their bodies whole, but their minds an abyss.

Tacked on the walls were posters on suicide prevention, help for drug addiction, government benefits, prayer groups, and a softball sign-up sheet with three hopeful names.

It smelled of strong antiseptic, fresh paint, yesterday's coffee, and decades of despair. But there were a few windows open. The temperature in New York was a brisk sixty-eight degrees, and the staff on duty knew that the residents benefited from the fresh air. It was clean in this particular hospital and the personnel was compassionate and dedicated. The families of the men confined here were thankful for it, knowing full well the same could not be said for every veterans' hospital in the country.

This is where my father's been for years, Luca thought. And soon, they'll be putting my brother somewhere like it.

After the police came aboard the *Mary* and the whole incredible story was dictated to a remarkably composed Detective Montalbano, Santi was taken away. The next day, Luca and Sarita met with Mr. Abramson at the coffee shop he favored on Promenade Deck. They listened as he told them all he knew about Rocco. With what Sarita had garnered from her visions and her physical contact with Santi, she and Luca pieced together the rest when they were alone.

In their anguish over her murder, Gina's parents never wanted the twins to see their father again. And so, when he was institutionalized, they told the family that Rocco was dead. But the trauma triggered Santi's clairaudience, and a corner of his brain became infiltrated by Rocco's thoughts and nightmares. Not knowing his father was alive, those noises in his head seemed like sinister delusions. Being on a foreign beach with rats sneaking up to attack an exhausted infantry was only one of Rocco's memories. While Sarita was seeing that nightmare, Santi was hearing it, and many others like it.

For Luca and Sarita, this shed a somewhat different light on his actions. What had begun to fester in Santi's mind as a child consumed him as an adult, but Luca tried to imagine the man he himself would have become if, instead of being able to pop off to Paris or speak fluent Japanese, his powers had made him hear, on an endless loop, the sufferings of a man who'd survived war.

On the other hand, Sarita had lived with horrific visions all her life, and yet even the unintended harm she'd done Naag had plagued her with guilt.

Why were some made more humane by tragedy, while others became depraved, and still others broke apart?

Luca didn't know what lay ahead for his brother, but he knew he couldn't abandon him as utterly as their father had been abandoned.

They arrived at Rocco's room. The nurse's smile was kind as she gestured them to a bench in the hall. "Wait here for a moment, won't you? Let me check on him, and see what kind of a day he's having."

Rocco was staring at Gina. She was sitting on his bed, looking beautiful, as always. When the nurse opened his door, Gina disappeared.

"Well, someone's popular today. You have two visitors, Rocco." The nurse thought he appeared well enough to see them, so she motioned them in.

He was sitting in an armchair by the open window, with the blinds up and the sun shining in. Sarita saw how much Luca resembled him. Except that Rocco's eyes were dulled — not by age, but by bleak thoughts and the medications that helped subdue them.

The room was small and bare, save for the narrow cot and a small metal nightstand that held a lamp and a Bible. The walls were an unrelieved beige, with not one photo of his boys or his wife. The albums had all gone to the Castellettis when Gina died.

And then, he saw his son. "Luca? Am I dreaming? Is it you?"

Luca wasn't sure what churned inside him, but his father knew which identical twin he was, and that was quite extraordinary.

Rocco's hand trembled as he reached out, and the eyes that were so much like his sons' seemed to brighten a little. "You finally came. I'd hoped …" When he saw that Luca made no move toward him, his hand dropped. "I know you hate me. I don't blame you." He braced himself. "You have things you want to say to me, I'm sure."

When Luca saw that posture, compassion won out. Here was the man who'd killed his mother. But Gina was the only one who hadn't discarded him.

"I didn't come here for that. I … I just came to see you." He knelt by Rocco's chair, and took his hand. "We didn't know, Papa. They didn't tell Santi and me — we didn't know you were here."

He swallowed hard, as it slammed through him — the terrible destruction of his family that had started more than twenty years before. No, further back than that — when a boy was dragged from a life of promise with the girl he loved, and sent away to kill or die.

"And Santi? Where is he?" Rocco covered Luca's hand with his own.

Luca bent his head, and Sarita thought he looked as though he were praying at his father's feet.

"Did he hurt you, Luca?"

Luca's eyes shot to his father's. "Who, Papa?"

"Santi. Did he hurt you?" Rocco's gaze grew feverish as it slid down to the cut on his son's lip. "He did, didn't he? I knew he would one day."

The room felt hot and crushing despite the open window. Luca and Sarita stared at Rocco in incredulous silence.

"I tried to tell her. She didn't believe me." Rocco's eyes welled. "I should have been there for you."

Luca touched his father's face. "I'm okay, Papa." It was so hard to speak. "I'm fine."

Sarita stepped over and kneeled at Rocco's feet. She wanted to give Luca some time to recover, but she also had something to say. "Mr. Miceli, I'm Sarita."

"Yes." Rocco pressed his fingers to his eyes to compose himself, and when he tried to smile, the effort almost broke her, as he looked so much like Luca. "I know who you are. Gina … she told me."

That news was welcome. "She did?" Sarita smiled back. "I'm so glad. I wasn't sure if you knew … that she's here. That she comes here, I mean."

This time when he smiled, the regret and sadness pressed down on them and left a heaviness that felt impossible to lift. "No, my dear. She's not here. She's dead. I killed her. And I can't wait for the day when this body of mine dies too."

Outside, the clear, crisp New York City afternoon was a balm to their senses. Still, it took a while for either of them to speak.

Finally Luca said, "If this were six months ago, I'd head straight for a bar."

Sarita could appreciate the sentiment. "Can I be your barfly?"

There was still a storm in his eyes, but he managed a short laugh. "Hell, no. We're not going to do that. I'm never doing that again." He spun her to face him, lowered his forehead to hers. "I've got better plans."

She slipped her arms around him. "Is that so? Let's hear them."

He gave her a light kiss on the lips, as light as he intended to turn the mood. "First, I'm taking you to Brooklyn, and we're going to Spumoni Gardens for the best Italian ice you ever tasted."

"Italian ice?" She angled her head. "Is that like a snow cone?"

"*What?*" He took a step back and looked at her as though she'd just compared chilled caviar to frozen fish sticks. "Are you serious, girl? You've never had Italian ice?" At her shrug, he shook his head tragically. "Oh, this is just so sad. We've got to fix this."

"What's sad is how New Yorkers are all the same — constantly talking about their food." She knew he was trying to pull them back up, and she would do her best to help. With a smirk, she poked him. "But you don't have Universal Studios, and we do."

"I love Universal Studios. You like Universal Studios?" He looked like a little boy when he asked.

Now he had her. "Um … well, truthfully, I've never been."

"Would you like to go?" His gloom was starting to lift, just a little.

"I think we should."

He studied her smile. The only way he could describe it was 'brave.' He wished they'd never have to talk about, but he knew they must, so he grew thoughtful again. "Sarita, I know it's horrible. All of it. But I refuse to let it destroy my life."

She let her smile fade. "Do you?"

"Yeah. I want to be happy. It's not going to be easy for a while, but I'm determined. I made that choice a long time ago, and I gave up on it for a time. Being unhappy is easier. There'll always be those who want others to be as miserable as they are, but there are enough who want happiness in the world too." He thought of his mother, who wanted that for him so much, that she'd come to him from the spirit world to help him achieve it. "I'm not going to let them down. Or myself. Or you."

He pulled her close again. "I have a lot to look forward to." She felt him lean on her, and was glad that he knew he could. "Want to hear what some of those things are?"

This time when she smiled, it felt more real. They were young to have had so much pain already, but he'd helped her through hers, and now she would help him through his.

"Yes, I do. Unless you're going to mention Italian ice again. Or — no, please, no — New York pizza."

"Heh. For the second time, darling, you are the uninitiated one." That sparkle, that delightful light she loved, was coming back. "And just like several other new things you've tried recently —" he wiggled his brows like Groucho — "once you've tasted that pizza, there's no going back."

"Oh, shut up, you obnoxious braggart." She gave him a shove, and grinned. "I hate you." She loved him. She loved him so much. "Tell me what you're looking forward to, before we get mowed down just standing here."

He did have things to say, but before he spoke, he needed to just look at her, just breathe her in. They were on the sidewalk of East Seventeenth Street between Park Avenue South and Broadway. The busyness and noise of Union Square were appealing and unique to Sarita. People dodged by them like players on a football field racing for the goal line with three seconds to spare. Bicyclists zipped past. Cars, taxis, buses, bumped and honked their way down the avenue.

But all he could see was Sarita's lovely face, her beautiful soul, her generous heart.

He took her hand, laced her fingers firmly with his. "Well, let's see. There are two birthday parties this weekend for two spectacular women — one is a queen and one is a princess."

She snorted. "Pu-lease. Is that a line from your magician's book of patter?"

That got a genuine laugh. "Good one. You're funny." He went on with his list. "And then, I guess there's that trip to India."

"We could get some spices for Rohini. She'd love that."

`Immediately, he picked up on the pronoun. "You mean ... you'd go?"

"I ... yes. I think so."

That sounded promising. At least, so far. He ventured another question. "And, say I wanted to travel to a few other places, get a chance — finally — to use some of my languages ... would you come with me?"

After almost drowning in her own bathtub, she was so ready to kick start her life. But there was one issue. "Well ... I'm not sure I can afford —"

"Oh, we've got plenty of money. There's no worry there. We probably have more than we need for a lifetime. Although to be honest, I feel like giving every last penny to Marisol McKenna. I'm going to buy her a Porsche, at least."

"A Porsche for a fourteen-year-old?" He was joking, but his eyes were so dark and serious on hers. There was something else under his invitation. Something big. She could hear it, and all at once, she felt shy.

"Never too early to own a Porsche. It'll definitely up her street cred." He was watching her carefully. She looked a little jittery. Was it just the thought of the travel, or did she guess where he hoped to go with this, down the road? "So, what do you say? Would you see the world with me, Ms. Taylor?"

Her breathing was unsteady, but she gave him the answer she wanted to give. "Yes. I think that would be lovely." Who was she kidding? It would be fantastic.

They stood there, in the middle of the sidewalk, just gazing at one another, the people, the traffic, the sounds, the smells of the city, all fading away.

What the hell, he thought, why not ask? He didn't have a heart left to be broken. It had been ripped out by his brother and his father. But maybe she could get it back for him again.

"Do you love me, Sarita?"

Hadn't she told him yet? No, she hadn't. She'd only said it to herself under gallons of water. She should say it, then, shouldn't she? He was looking at her like he very much wanted to hear it. Yet, with all her promises to herself to be braver and bolder, it was still a little scary.

That was the old Sarita's way of thinking. The stronger, more confident side of herself said, Take the jump. He'll catch you.

She sucked in a breath, held it, and let herself fall. "Yes, I love you. I love you, Luca."

His eyes closed on the words, as though they should be savored, as though their taste was even more delicious than his grandmother's tomato sauce. But for Luca, her love meant much more than that.

When he opened them, his look was so intense, so full of want, that it was a wonder she didn't melt into a puddle right there. "Well. You might be surprised to hear this, but that's the best news I've heard all week."

Her laugh was cut short when he pulled her close, held her tight. "Oh, my Sarita. My beautiful girl. How lucky I am."

He was one who would always find treasure buried beneath the rubble, simply for the reason that he always looked for it. This treasure was valuable beyond measure. They'd persevered and endured, until, under the heartache and loss, the terrible betrayals, they'd found each other.

His lip was still sore, but he needed the taste of her. Tilting her face up, he found her mouth, and they kissed for all they were worth, right there in the open, on the crazy-busy downtown street.

It was the kiss that hallmarked their love. As such, they forgot what they'd learned aboard the *Mary* about public displays of affection.

They didn't see the avenue spotlight glow a bright, brilliant green. They didn't see the shower of sparks. They only sprang apart when it burst like a firecracker on the Fourth of July, and several cars screeched to a halt.

"Uh oh. That's going to cause a traffic snarl for miles." Sarita was just too happy to feel guilty. "Can you fix it, and pop us out of here?"

"With all these people around? We'll be on YouTube tomorrow. We're going to have to cut our losses. And take the subway like everybody else." He had to shout. Horns were blaring like mad because of the broken light. And yet, the two of them were smiling like loons.

"Wow. The New York Subway." She winked at him. "Another new experience for me." Tossing back her hair, she held out her hand.

"Come on, Miceli. Let's go get your silly snow cone."

AUTHOR'S NOTE

(Warning: Just as in Book I, this author's note contains spoilers. So, if you want to go ahead and read it first, anyway, like I might do, you've been warned.)

Magic has enchanted me ever since I was a child. That's why, when I had the opportunity to speak with the man known as the world's greatest magician, it was all I could do to ask him the questions I needed to ask, and not act like some silly fan girl.

David Copperfield has sold more tickets to his performances than any other solo performer in history, including performers such as Madonna and Michael Jackson. He works tirelessly — as many as three shows in one day, seven days a week, forty-two weeks a year, in a theater that's exclusively for his performances. Not only is David Copperfield talented beyond measure, he is intelligent, gracious, and a longtime supporter of the magical and literary arts. Everything you've read in this novel about the creation and performance of magic, the hard labor behind it, is based upon my conversation with him, along with months of studying his work.

When Luca tells Cristiano that his brother Santi was teaching magic at a local college by the time he was sixteen, that's a biographical fact about David Copperfield. The "Fires of Pompeii" illusion performed by Santino Miceli is based on an actual illusion done by Mr. Copperfield, "The Magic of David Copperfield XV: Fires of Passion." You can watch this whole performance on YouTube and be just as awed by it as I was. And when I told David what Santino's dastardly plan was, he explained just what I needed to know in order to make it believable.

Truly talented magicians are like truly talented writers — they have a knack for giving their audience permission to suspend disbelief, to simply revel in the experience of what's being created by the artist for their — the audience's — gratification. There's so much more I could say about him in this note, but I'm limited by space. Suffice it to say that when David Copperfield puts his heart and soul into his work, he's giving us a gift, and I'm deeply grateful to him for being such an inspiration for this novel, and for taking the time out of his remarkably busy schedule to speak with me.

Here are some other things about this story you might like to know:

» Just as Santi tells Luca, Alan Rabinowitz was a real escape artist who died in July of 2014, the year this novel takes place, and the month that Luca steps aboard the *Queen Mary*. He was eighty-seven years old when he passed, and he too, was a remarkable magician, credited with, as Santino states in the novel, devising the Burning-Rope Straitjacket Escape. You can read more about him in the free Reader's Guide. The Reader's Guide is live-linked to this novel if you're reading this on an e-reader, and if you're reading a printed version, you can download the free guide at: www.spellsandoregano.com or by scanning the QR code at the end of this note.

» The 80th anniversary of the *Queen Mary*'s launch did take place on September 26, 2014, one day before the character Sarita Taylor's twenty-sixth birthday. Everything written about that event in the novel is true, including the creation of a fifteen-foot cake that was a replica of the ship. However, Angela Perotta did not help the real pastry chef, Mr. Jose Barajas, make his wonderful cake, and it wasn't because she was hit in the jaw in her office at The Secret Spice. It's because Jose is an actual person, and Angela isn't. Everything written about the Tenth Annual Art Deco Ball aboard the ship is also true, right down to the decorations and the name of the band.

» June Allen, George Schneider, and Ralph Rushton appear in this novel as themselves. Everything you read about them in the novel is true. You can see their stories on video in the Heritage Room aboard the *Queen Mary*. They are three extraordinary human beings whom I've gotten to know through social media, and they have inspired me and many others with the way they live their lives, even now in their eighties and nineties. They remember when Hitler was in power, so when they say something about the way things are going in politics today, I tend to pay attention. You can learn more about them and other characters in the Reader's Guide. On the other hand, Elliot Abramson, who is sitting at The Secret Spice Café in the novel with June, George, and Ralph, is a fictitious character.

» The plight of veterans in the United States is a national tragedy. What you read about them in the novel is true. Comments made by characters about the homeless population in Las Vegas is also true. The research I did on veterans, the discussions I had with a number of them about their war experiences, and about Post Traumatic Stress Disorder gave me many sleepless nights. The description of the hospital is not exaggerated, but I gave it the name of a hospital that no longer exists to protect the people who graciously spoke to me. Just like with Rocco Miceli in the novel, PTSD can worsen years after a veteran has seen combat. The vision Sarita has, which in the novel is one of Rocco's memories, as well as his memory of his men being blown up near a bridge, was told to me by a Vietnam veteran who actually experienced these events, as well as a number of other heart-stopping experiences that I didn't put in the story. What I've learned about war from reading George Schneider's book, what I learned from speaking to veterans, tells me we'd better find a different way of dealing with the world's problems. Sending people out to kill each other is not working out well for us, at all.

» Everything you read in the novel about the east coast Italian-American experience in the United States is true. The best Italian ices are made at Spumoni Gardens in Brooklyn, and Luca is right that they're nothing at all like snow cones. Luca is also right that you've never tasted bread as good as the braided semolina bread with sesame seeds that you can find at any Italian bakery in Brooklyn. But if you recall, in the novel he gets his at the Satellite Bakery, which was my Uncle Angelo's bakery many years ago. Just like Santi and Luca at Angela's bakery, when I was a little girl, I was allowed to go behind the counter and pick out whatever cookies I wanted. Angelo's younger brother, my Uncle Mario, left Brooklyn and started the Solunto Baking Company in San Diego, California. He was the founder of Little Italy on India Street there. His bakery not only had the best breads and Italian cookies, but he made them all by hand, just like his Sicilian pizza. Like Angela says in the novel when she talks about her cousin Luigi's pizzeria, the line for my uncle's pizza was "out the door." Angela and Luca have a cousin Luigi, and so do I. And while he doesn't make pizza, he did help me with the Sicilian dialect you read in the novel, a wonderful dialect that is quite different from the Italian I learned in school. Every man in my family can cook, including my own son, and there is simply nothing sexier to me than a man who can make a good Italian tomato sauce. This year, we lost my cousin Marietta Neihaus, Angelo's daughter. She was way too young to leave us, and we miss her, which is why I named a character after her. Though our Marietta wasn't a neurosurgeon, she was just as sassy as the doctor in the story. The real Marietta's favorite Italian cookies were the seven-layer ones, so I do hope Angela keeps her promise to send some to Dr. Neihaus.

I'm out of space here, but there's lots of fun stuff in the Reader's Guide and it's free, so I encourage you take a look at it. If you're reading this on an ereader, the guide will be right after the Author's Bio. If you're reading this in a print version, scan the QR code after this note, and it will take you to the guide, or you can visit my website, where you'll find the guide under the "Books" tab.

Once again, I'll ask that if you liked this novel, please leave a review of it on Amazon.com. Goodreads would be lovely too. You can't imagine how helpful those reviews are. If you have any comments or questions, you can find me on Facebook or Twitter, and like every other person on the planet with an internet connection I have a website: www.TheSecretSpice.com.

Thank you so much for reading! I hope you enjoyed *Spells and Oregano*.

AUTHOR'S BIO

Patricia V. Davis is the author of *Cooking for Ghosts: Book I* in The *Secret Spice Trilogy* and other works. Book III in the trilogy, "DEMONS, WELL SEASONED," will be released in early 2019. For a number of years, she was a high school English teacher, teaching in Athens, Greece, and Queens, New York. She's an advocate for human rights, and all her writing encourages female dynamism. To that end, she founded The Women's PowerStrategy™ Conference. Patricia lives with her poker player husband, and so divides her time between Southern Nevada and Northern California. For news on upcoming work, contests and giveaways, join The Secret Spice Book Series Page on Facebook, or visit www.TheSecretSpice.com

CPSIA information can be obtained
at www.ICGtesting.com
Printed in the USA
LVOW12s2207121217
559534LV00015B/2000/P